County Council

Libraries, books and more . . .

1-5-2015
28/7/15
L.A.D 11/1/19 I

WITHDRAWN

Please return/renew this item by the last due date.
Library items may be renewed by phone on
030 33 33 1234 (24 hours) or via our website
www.cumbria.gov.uk/libraries

Cumbria Libraries
CLIC
Interactive Catalogue

Ask for a CLIC password

THE END OF A
JOURNEY

By the same author

Time to Move On
The Runaway
Facing the World
Gull Island
Goodbye to Dreams
Paint on the Smiles
Nothing is Forever

THE END OF A
JOURNEY

GRACE THOMPSON

ROBERT HALE · LONDON

© Grace Thompson 2014
First published in Great Britain 2014

ISBN 978-0-7198-1323-8

Robert Hale Limited
Clerkenwell House
Clerkenwell Green
London EC1R 0HT

www.halebooks.com

2 4 6 8 10 9 7 5 3 1

Typeset in 11/14 Sabon
Printed in the UK by Berforts Information Press Ltd

Chapter One

ZENA MARTIN STEPPED off the local bus and turned to Maberly Avenue where, in the neat little flat left to her by her grandmother, she had lived for three years. Tonight she was going to start painting the walls of the kitchen. Jake was away for a couple of days, so she would use the opportunity to get on while she had no distractions.

He was in London visiting a friend, Stanley, who was to be best man at their wedding and they were probably making plans, even though the wedding was at least a year away.

She was preparing for their engagement party, arranged for the following Sunday. There were plenty of things to do and she was determined to get the kitchen painted before party-planning took over completely. As she reached the corner of the road she saw Jake just ahead of her. He was home sooner than she'd expected. She sighed when she saw he was carrying several shopping bags. Surely he hadn't been buying presents. They were saving for a deposit on the house which they planned to run as a bed and breakfast business. Their home near the sea in South Wales was an ideal place for such an undertaking, but it would need every penny they could save. The bags he carried were from expensive stores. She ran to catch him up and he looked startled.

'Zena, my lovely girl! What a surprise. I had some shopping to do and left London earlier than planned.'

'What's all this?' she asked, pointing to the bulging bags he carried. 'I thought we were saving?'

'Well, love, something's happened, see. I should have told you as soon as I'd talked to Stanley but I – anyway, we're so close to the flat that I might as well come and talk about it now.'

'What is it?' Zena stared at Jake in alarm, afraid he had changed his mind about marrying her. What else could it be to make him look so serious?

'I've got a marvellous new job, see, and, well, it's in London and I have to go in three days' time. That's what all this shopping is for. This new job, it's as a rep for a firm selling industrial clothing. Stanley arranged the interview and it sounded so wonderful I just had to give it a try.'

'Industrial clothing? But, Jake, what do you know about selling? You've always worked in a factory making copper and brass fittings.'

'You know I wouldn't be satisfied with that for ever. I've always wanted a job where I'd have clean hands.'

'But you've no experience.'

'None at all, love, but they'll train me, and, if I'm successful, I'll be earning a lot more than I do here in Cold Brook Vale.'

'Where will you stay? And what about me? Us?'

'You'll join me as soon as I get us a place to live. Imagine, Zena love: I might be travelling abroad selling and making contacts with firms who make the stuff. What d'you think of that, then? Marvellous? Such good luck to have heard of it. We'll be rich in a few years. The wages are unbelievable. And I've been offered a room in Stanley's flat, so you needn't worry about me, I'll be fine.'

'You are going to work in London? Leaving Cold Brook Vale? But how could this happen so suddenly? We spent the day together on Monday discussing our engagement party and today you tell me you have a new job and a room in Stanley's flat in London!'

'Sorry to spring it on you like this, love, but it happened so fast and I had to make a decision there and then after the interview. It's such a wonderful opportunity and I had no time to discuss it with you.'

'You had plenty of time! You went to London to see a friend and without any hesitation you were offered a job? Come on, Jake, I'm not stupid. You knew about the job before you went, didn't you?'

'Well, yes. But nothing was certain, and I thought it best to wait and tell you once it was all arranged.'

Zena felt physically sick. This wasn't the first time Jake had acted on impulse, careless of her opinion. 'The first thing I'll do is cancel our engagement party. How can I consider marrying someone who can make such life-changing decisions without discussing it with me?'

It took some time and the kitchen didn't get its coat of paint, but Zena eventually accepted his explanations, but the party was cancelled. Zena made him understand that a wedding would depend on what happened during the next few months. She felt the pain of doubt clouding her mind – not for the first time.

Marrying Jake had been her life plan since they were at school together and she just couldn't imagine a life without him. Unreliable he definitely was, but she believed that his love for her was the one believable fact amid his vague attitude towards the truth.

The plan to buy a house large enough to run as a bed and breakfast had long been their dream. Her parents' garage and one of the spare rooms were already filled with items they had bought or had been given.

They intended to attract summer visitors, then perhaps students during the winter. Jake was very capable at simple building maintenance and gardening. He would grow their own food, and keep chickens and she would do the cooking and the housekeeping and— She stopped the dream right there. If Jake settled in London it would never happen. They would grow apart, the simple certainty of his love and the plans for their life together would be gone.

The prospect of them separating, being alone facing an empty future was frightening. Everything had changed: she was no longer a young woman planning to marry the man she loved, and who loved her, a woman with a dream: she was on her own.

Zena said little as they went to his lodgings to deposit his shopping. She was thinking of how to tell her parents and her friends, but not yet. She had to accept it herself before she could allow the opinions of others to intrude. They went on to the house above the lake where her parents lived, but didn't go in. Zena needed to sort out what she would say to them first. A rough, steep path led down from the house, called Llyn Hir – long lake – and they walked down to stand on the narrow shore and look across the calm water. A raft moved gently, attached to a double loop of rope creating a pulley system by which the raft could be pulled across the lake. It had made a safe place for them to play as children and was still used occasionally for bringing shopping across. More difficult, as there was the path to climb, but used from a sense of nostalgia by her parents.

Lottie and Ronald Martin listened in silence as their daughter told them of Jake's new life. After Jake had gone, Ronald held Lottie's hand and said, 'It's painful, I can understand that, darling, but it's better for this to have happened now, while you have time to decide whether you want to share the life Jake's chosen so suddenly. Mam and I would hate it if you moved so far away from us, but London must be an exciting place to experience. Don't you think so, Kay?' Ronald said, using an affectionate nickname for Lottie. 'All those historical buildings to explore, so many places to see, theatres and exhibitions. I think it will be an adventure.' He hoped he was saying what his daughter wanted to hear, but wasn't sure.

Her brother Greg said much the same thing and it was when she spoke to Aunty Mabs that she had a more common-sense reaction. 'London's a place for you to go on holiday,' she said emphatically, her rosy cheeks surrounded by her unruly hair that defied a comb and made her look aggressive. 'Think about what you'll lose as well as what you would gain.' She was a short, slim lady and, as though to make up for her lack of stature, she always shouted and was emphatic in her comments. 'You know Jake well enough to realize he isn't the most reliable fish on the slab. To leave all you know and trust to him to look after you, well, it's your decision, but please, please, don't decide anything for a while. Right?'

On the following day, Zena received a phone call from her mother at the office where she worked and, to the disapproval of her boss, she ignored the customer she was advising and said. 'I have to go. My father's been taken to hospital!'

'It's only half an hour before we close for lunch, Miss Martin. You can go then, but don't be late back.' Zena ignored him, grabbed her bag and coat and ran out.

Through the ward doorway she saw Ronald in a bed with a

doctor and nurse attending to him. His face was almost as white as the three pillows that supported him. Zena's brother Greg came with a tearful Aunty Mabs and they waited until the doctor had left. Then Lottie came out and told them he had suffered a heart attack and would be in hospital for a while. Lottie waited until the nurse told her she must go and Greg and Mabs popped in for a few words with Ronald before they all left the hospital to sit and wait anxiously until the evening visiting hour. Mabs was worried. Ronald's brother, her husband, Frank, had died of a heart attack at forty-eight and it seemed that Ronald, who was fifty-four, had the same weakness.

The shock of her father's illness made Zena's decision about her future with Jake seem less important and life went on with regular visits to Ronald whose recovery was slow. Everything else settled back into an uneasy rhythm.

Zena had been threatened with dismissal if she ignored an instruction again and she almost wished she had been. Nothing was right in her life. She hated working in the boring office with the boring staff arranging flat and house rentals for boring people. She knew that was a temporary mood and that once her father had recovered and Jake had come to his senses, she would be back to enjoying helping people to make the right decision on where they would live.

During the weeks after Jake had gone to London, Zena's days were filled with concern about Ronald and frustration about Jake, who phoned occasionally, usually running out of coins in a matter of minutes. He had written only twice; letters almost as brief as his phone calls, asking her when she would join him, and notes about the places he'd visited and the plays he had seen. In the latest call he asked her to send letters to the office where he worked as the house where he now lived was multi-tenanted and letters were often lost. 'Madeleine will give them to me,' he'd said.

'Who is Madeleine?'

'The office secretary. She's been very kind, showing me around and recommending places to see.' Zena knew she wouldn't like Madeleine.

*

A few says later she was leaving the rental office, closing the door behind her with a sigh of relief. It was Friday lunchtime, only a few more hours before the weekend. She stood for a moment or two. She had a serious decision to make. With Jake working in London and spending so much time alone in her flat, she had to make a decision on how she wanted to live her life.

Marriage to Jake was still more or less a certainty, however unreliably he behaved. He'd come back home soon and things would settle down. She would not, could not accept that he would stay so far away from home. They had been together since school and his sudden move to London had unsettled her. She had considered moving to London, but leaving the small town where she was happy and the family and friends she loved was impossible. She needed to talk to Jake but that was impossible too. There was no one with whom she could discuss it. Her mother and father refused to utter a decisive comment either way; her brother Greg liked Jake and thought him great fun; Aunty Mabs had always been very outspoken and critical about her choice of husband and gave her opinion that if Zena married the unreliable Jake Williams, she would be making a big mistake.

She tried to push the problem out of her mind and picked up a daily paper, the *Radio Times* and some sweets, her weekly treat for Aunty Mabs. As she turned the corner to where her aunt lived in a small block of flats, she saw the twitch of the curtains revealing her aunt's regular watch for her to appear. She smiled, knowing her Aunty would then dash to the kitchen and turn on the kettle. Ever since her uncle Frank had died so suddenly, she went to her aunt's every Friday for lunch.

'It's only me,' she called, as she used her key and stepped inside. 'I've brought the papers and some chocolate eclairs.'

'Thank you, darling, I love bein' spoilt, I do.' Small, thin and with hair that refused to behave, she held out her arms and Zena went over and hugged her. Mabs then went to the oven and brought out two plates of cottage pie and vegetables.

'Come on, gel, eat it while it's hot. There's a wicked cold wind today and you need something to keep you from getting a chill.'

Fussing, making sure everything was in its place she sat opposite Zena and smiled. 'How's old misery today?' Zena laughed, knowing her aunt referred to her boss Graham Broughton, a man who strutted rather than walked and considered his role as manager was to criticize at every opportunity.

'I have to leave that place but I can't decide what I want to do next.'

'Going up to London to join Jake? That's what you're thinking about, is it?'

'I should be with him.'

'When you decided to marry him he was working here. Then he got a job that meant being away for weeks at a time. International rep he calls himself. Makes him sound more important, and him never before going further than Bristol! Did he discuss it with you before taking the job? No, he did not! And London! It isn't even in Wales!' she ended in disgust.

'All right, he should have discussed it, but he thought that if the decision had already been made then I'd have to agree.'

'Bullying, that's what that is, love. Making it impossible for you to disagree.'

Zena laughed. 'Jake, a bully?'

Mabs tightened her lips but only said, 'There's more cottage pie if you'd like some.'

'I'm thinking of staying with Mam and Greg until Dad's on the mend. He's been back in hospital, but the doctors think he'll be home in a few days and Mam would be glad of my help.'

'Keep a low heat on in your flat, darling, there's some bitter cold weather coming.'

'Thanks for the reminder; I will. The last thing I need is a burst pipe.' She glanced at the clock. 'Best I get back or I'll be in trouble.'

'Give your notice why don't you? A girl of your age shouldn't be unhappy.'

'And join Jake in London?'

'Perish the thought!'

Zena laughed at Mabs's outspoken comment but she was serious as she strolled slowly back to the office. She had only said what

Zena herself had been thinking for some time. Jake and London was one decision; the job where she was unhappy was another. She stood at the kerb and waited for the traffic to allow her to cross and saw a bus coming. She stood back and waited, in case her brother Greg was driving. A horn sounded and she saw his hand wave as he drove past slowly and stopped at the nearby bus stop.

'See you at the hospital at seven,' he called, before driving off.

She sighed. Why couldn't Jake have been content to stay in this small town where they had been born and had lived all their lives? Greg was a bus driver, like Uncle Frank, and he never seemed restless. Why did Jake want them to live so far away from everyone they loved?

Starting again among strangers didn't appeal, although, she admitted to herself, she should be grabbing an opportunity to see something of the world with both hands, and besides, shouldn't she be supporting Jake, not trying to hold him back?

Greg looked back as he waited for the bus to fill. He could see she was frowning and guessed it was Jake causing the worry. 'Jake would be a great brother-in-law,' he told his conductress. 'He's fun and quite unpredictable, like the time he gave a wonderful party to celebrate my twenty-first birthday then admitted he had spent money intended to buy a new bike for Zena after giving away hers to the new local nurse who needed one to get to her patients.'

Jake was always doing things for other people, often at the expense of someone else. He'd heard recently that he had sent a parcel of groceries to a mother who was unable to work because her daughter was ill. There was no insistence on a repayment. And he'd dug a back garden for someone called Roy Roberts when he couldn't manage it himself. Greg had given him a torch for use during the dark winter months but that was now in the pocket of the street cleaner who often started before the sun was up.

Now he cheerfully announced that he had a new job and they would be moving to London. Yes, Jake would be a great brother-in-law but, Greg realized, that didn't make him an ideal husband. Perhaps he should call on the way home from work, get Zena talking, try to help her to think out loud, as Aunty Mabs would put it. But perhaps he'd talk to Aunty Mabs first, she would know how best to approach the subject. As he finished his shift, the idea fizzled out like a dead firework and days passed.

He did call on Mabs but said nothing about his sister. Mabs glanced at the clock anxiously. Her bus was due at 9.45 and she didn't want to miss it. Greg began to reminisce about her husband, his Uncle Frank, who had given him the idea of becoming a bus driver like himself with his stories about life on the road, as he called it.

'My Frank would still be here, driving his bus, if it hadn't been for that big huge win on the football pools,' she said sadly. 'Biggest regret of my life that I didn't throw the coupon in the ash bin instead of posting it.'

'You don't really think that, do you?'

'It was too much. He spent ages thinking about how we'd spend it. Travel? A better flat? Fancy furniture and clothes? Such nonsense kept him awake at night. We didn't need any of it.'

'You could spend it on moving nearer to Mam and Dad, or closer to the shops?'

'I won't spend it; I'd feel wicked and uncaring to use the money that killed him. I did buy a fridge – we'd never had one of those, and I used some to do something your uncle would have approved of. But that's all. I won't touch the rest. I don't need it.'

Greg was curious about how the money had been spent, but didn't ask.

She ushered him out then, insisting she was ready for her bed. As soon as he was out of sight, she grabbed her old hat and coat and hurried to the bus stop.

Ronald was still in hospital, his improvement hadn't lasted and his planned return home had been delayed, then postponed until he showed a lasting improvement. Zena and Greg were at the hospital during evening visiting, when their mother Lottie arrived with Mabs. Two visitors at a time to a patient was the firm rule so Greg and Zena sat in the corridor while the sisters-in-law went to talk to Ronald.

'Heard from Jake?' Greg asked. It was always a difficult subject. He knew his sister rarely heard from Jake apart from a brief call from a phone box where he usually told her how wonderful his life was and asked when was she coming to join him, then ran out of pennies.

'He's hopeless at writing letters; you know what Jake's like. He means to and might even start to write one, but there's always something happening to distract him. I bet he already has a group of friends. I write often to tell him about life in Cold Brook Vale and hope to persuade him to give up and come home.'

'Will it work?'

She shrugged. 'I can only hope.' She frowned. 'He's stopped asking me to go there on a visit to see whether I can live in London. Are we both hoping for opposite things?'

'He'll be missing you and I bet he'll be home before Christmas.'

'Christmas 1953. Can you believe it's eight years since war ended? And food still rationed. Surely his enthusiasm for this new job and living so far away will have faded before then?'

'It isn't far off. But his enthusiasm for this job and living in London might last longer than that.'

Greg dreamed about Christmas. He imagined the house all decorated with the ancient trimmings they used year after year. He would invite his secret love, Rose, and introduce her to his parents. Dad would be out of hospital; Mam would fill the house with food; Aunty Mabs would be there, and Uncle Sam from the farm with his father, Neville. The house would be groaning at the seams as always. He knew Rose would like his sister and surely Jake would be there too. He wouldn't stay away for Christmas. It would be a perfect opportunity for Zena and Jake to talk and for Rose and himself to come to an understanding. A few visits and she would forget her shyness and her insistence on secrecy. Christmas was going to be perfect.

Jake was walking along a London street where many of the houses were derelict, doors and windows missing, holes where slates had fallen from the roofs into front gardens that were already filled with abandoned rubbish and remnants of earlier attempts to repair the once elegant properties. A few squatters found the place from time to time and were regularly chased out, often late at night. He could imagine Zena's reaction if she could see the awful place he called home.

There were many things he didn't tell Zena. It was a painful disappointment when he reached London to be told he would not be offered the job about which he had boasted to everyone. He had been exaggerating as he usually did. He'd been invited to attend an interview only, but had been sure that the job would be his. Instead, he had been offered a menial post as a caretaker and messenger for the firm, called Cover All. They bought and supplied industrial clothing – at least that part of his story had been true. He delivered local papers and sometimes collected payments.

He had given Zena the address of the friend Stanley, who had heard of the vacancy and persuaded him to apply, but there was no room for him to stay there. He lived in a decrepit multi-tenanted house and the post was often thrown away before the owner picked it up.

Madeleine, one of the secretaries at Cover All, had agreed that Zena should write care of the office when she heard about his difficulty, promising to pass them on to him. Not before I open them and read them, she thought with a smile. Finding out about other people's lives was a great interest to Madeleine Jones. She quickly learned that what he told his fiancé was totally untrue. That made her smile even wider.

She had befriended Jake; they had been on walks around the city and she pointed out places of interest which he stored in his memory for the time when he would be showing Zena her new home. He even made notes of things to tell her when they met at Christmas time.

Madeleine was amused by his small-town mentality, at the way he stopped and stared at everything, and admitted his ignorance of so much of what he was seeing. She couldn't resist having a little fun. Two of Zena's silly letters were read then thrown away. How stupid she sounded. Why didn't she realize what was so obvious to anyone with a brain, that Jake had outgrown her and was enjoying the freedom of a new exciting life far away from her? Given one of Jake's letters to Zena to post, she opened it intending to put it in a fresh envelope and post it on, but she was surprised at the contents.

Jake was asking Zena again to marry him and come to live with him in London. She threw that one away too. She had no interest in Jake herself; he was small fry from a small pool and she looked higher than that, but it was fun to interfere in other lives and be entertained by the results.

One night as Greg and a friend were leaving the cinema he thought he saw Aunty Mabs in the main road and, as it was late evening, he was surprised. He couldn't stop, if he missed the last bus it was a long walk. He'd probably been mistaken, Aunty Mabs didn't like going out at night, yet he was certain it was her. She was covered up with a long coat, a scarf and woolly hat, but she was recognizable by her walk, a sort of rolling gait, like a drunken sailor he always teased. She so rarely went out in the evening and tonight was cold with an icy wind blowing and she should be safe indoors. He decided to visit the following day and ask where she had been going and use the opportunity to talk about Zena, but, as before, he let the idea drift. Tomorrow he was meeting Rose Conelly and everything else faded from his mind.

He was very attracted to the quiet, secretive girl. She was older than himself and seemed self-contained, but he nevertheless felt protective towards her. Although they had been going out for a couple of months she had told him nothing about her family or about her past. He stopped asking questions, aware that she became upset. She would tell him in her own time, he thought. Once he had broken through the shell of her reserve she would talk to him. He tried not to ask awkward questions, but if he did she was adept at changing the subject or answering without giving anything away. She brushed away compliments as though they were insults. He hoped a day would come when she would accept him as a man she could trust.

Zena spent her lunch break doing some shopping and reluctantly stepped back into the rental agency where she had been unhappy for so long. The manager confronted her, looking at his watch, aware of the five minutes she was late so, before he could begin his lecture, she gave her notice. She typed it to confirm her decision.

He blustered and threatened, warning about the poor chances of getting a better job with her minimal skills, then, seeing she had made up her mind, insisted she needn't work out her notice but leave that day. 'Call on Monday for the monies owed to you,' was all he said.

There were several letters on her desk. He pointed to them and she typed them as he watched, and left them on his desk ready for signature, then, with a muttered goodbye to which he didn't reply, she left.

She wasn't ready to go home. She felt tearful, ashamed, as though she had been sacked for some misdemeanour. Graham Broughton was obviously glad of the chance to be rid of her. She had expected to be asked to at least wait until someone could be found to take her place, not dismissed with immediate effect.

She walked aimlessly along the main road, looking in windows and seeing nothing. Then began to wonder what she would do next and, for a brief moment, she wondered whether this was the moment to join Jake in London. She glanced at the phone box but instead, she went to the library and began idly searching the jobs vacant columns. With her father ill she was needed at home for a while. The excuse was a relief. There was still a chance that Jake would decide to come back home.

Browsing through the list of jobs on offer, a list of households needing a cleaner caught her eye and she wondered if doing house-work for strangers might be a convenient way of filling time while she considered her options. She didn't want anything permanent, just a way of earning some money while she decided what to do about London. She took out her notebook and wrote down names and numbers.

Picking up the post as she went into the flat, she searched through it for a letter from Jake but there wasn't one. Jake wasn't very good at keeping in touch. But in a few weeks' time he'd be home and seeing him, loving him like she did, that would be the time to decide about London; when he was close, telling her how much he needed her. She threw the rest of the post onto the kitchen table and went to her parents' house to begin making phone calls. Within a very short time she had arranged three interviews for the following day and two for that evening. A few hours later she had arranged another two interviews and had written to two others. The interviews went well and she had found two clients.

She rang her mother at the stationers where she worked, and then went to tell Aunty Mabs. Mabs almost screamed her approval. 'Good on you, gel. Some sense at last, just when I was beginning to give up on you.' Only then did she go to the phone box to leave a message for Jake.

She felt ridiculously excited. It was like being let out of a cage, she thought and wondered why it had taken her so long to make the move. The job had made her unhappy for a long time. The office phone of Cover All rang for a long time but no one answered. Then she realized that it was past 5.30 and the office would be closed. She tried the flat he shared but was told the number was incorrect. She was deflated at not being able to tell him. There was one more number to try. Jake often went out with his friend, Stanley, where he'd stayed when he first went to London and he might possibly be there.

'Hello, are you Stanley? It's Zena, Jake's fiancé. You don't know where Jake might be, by any chance, do you?'

'His fiancé?' the voice queried.

'Yes, Zena Martin, Jake's fiancé. You must have heard of me!'

'Oh, Zena, yes, I had someone else on my mind and—Sorry but I don't know where he is, he wasn't at the office today. Have you tried the house?'

'It doesn't matter, he's sure to phone me at Mam's as he's coming home in about a week, but if you see him, will you ask him to call me?'

Still sounding a bit bemused, Stanley promised to pass the message on if he saw Jake. Mildly puzzled by Stanley's vagueness Zena thanked him and rang off.

Packing a suitcase she prepared to go to her parents' house where she had arranged to stay the weekend. About to leave, she was dismayed when there was a loud, imperious banging on the door. At once she thought it was bad news about her father and, serious-faced, she opened it and, to her delight and relief it was Jake.

'Jake!' she gasped, dropping the suitcase, raising her arms to hold him.

'That's me.' he said, laughing. 'How's my girl?' He lifted her up in a bear hug. 'I was sitting alone in the flat, feeling so lonely and suddenly I had to see you, so I dashed to the station, caught a train, and here I am.' Then he saw the small suitcase standing near the door. 'What's this? Not going away, are you? Why didn't you tell me, love?'

'I was going to stay the weekend with Mam and Greg, but that was before I opened the door and saw you standing there.' She didn't tell him she had been trying to get in touch to tell him and Stanley hadn't known where he was. That was explained by his arrival although it was strange that Stanley seemed not to know of his whereabouts. She pushed the thought aside; this unexpected weekend was not going to include a moment of criticism. He was here because he couldn't wait to see her.

The weekend was wonderful, being so unexpected they had no plans made and everything they did was on impulse. They walked into the theatre without looking first to see what was playing; going into town and catching the next bus to arrive uncaring of where it would take them. Eating at expensive restaurants or at a market stall, everything was fun.

Seeing him leaving on the Sunday evening was emotional. They clung to each other as the train puffed importantly into the station.

'Please come to London, darling girl. Every weekend will be as good as this one's been,' he whispered, as his train stopped at the platform. She was tempted to say yes and go back to the flat and start packing. Her mind raced during those few minutes with the fact that she had no job to worry about, there was nothing to hold her, apart from letting a few prospective clients down. Then thoughts of her family intervened and she didn't say the words that Jake wanted to hear.

'I'll see you next weekend,' she said, but he shook his head.

'Sorry, love. I can't promise to get home for a while. I have to go to Belgium, not sure where after that, see. I've gone international remember! I'm visiting the factories where the garments are made to negotiate on price and delivery dates. It's wonderful and something I'm very good at. Zena, love, we'll be rich one day, just believe me. And London is the place to enjoy being rich.'

The first thing Zena had to do before starting work as a domestic cleaner was to buy a bicycle. It wasn't as smart or as road-worthy as the new Raleigh sports bike Jake had given away. Zena remembered she had asked why he had given her property away and he'd hugged her and said he knew she would understand. The bike was in the shed getting more and more in need of care and there was Jennie Morris needing one, desperate to be able to get to work visiting patients in their homes. Zena knew Jennie Morris, she was one of the team now helping her father. She had admitted she had rarely used it but now, because of Jake's generosity with her property, she had to buy another she thought with mild exasperation.

A few days later, with a second-hand bicycle, much more ancient that her previous machine, she began work in four of the five houses at which she'd had an interview. One she wasn't sure of; there was a hint at being treated like a servant and, cleaner she might be, she wasn't prepared to accept the woman's low opinion of her intelligence and abilities and being treated accordingly.

Roy Roberts was a retired delivery driver, in pain with arthritis and struggling to be independent, insisting he could cope with many of the tasks she offered to do for him He was considerate, and struggled to make her a cup of tea, apologizing for not having any cake to offer her. Zena warmed to him at once and decided to bring him a cake on subsequent visits. She found extra jobs that needed doing and left happy that she had helped.

She met his neighbour, who called him a 'cantankerous old devil.' 'He refuses all my offers of help. Perhaps, as he's paying you, he'll agree to accept help,' she said. 'I'm afraid he'll fall when he's trying to do things he shouldn't. On the shed roof he was last week, would you believe!'

Zena looked back to where Mr Roberts was stretching up to close a window. Zena was about to offer help but Doris shook her head and she smiled and went on her way.

Nelda Grey was divorced with two children and was the

manageress of a craft shop and café in part of the large property called Ilex House. Her home was full of beautiful things and, as they were muddled together with half-finished craft projects and boxes of materials for making them, three large dogs and two cats that came to her at once hoping for food, it was a household she thought of as completely scatty.

In the middle of the chaos, Nelda was knitting the handle of a child's bag decorated with glittering buttons and embroidery in a flower decoration. She put it down and spread her arms in a light hearted way. 'Can you do anything for us, Miss Martin?'

'I hope so, and please, call me Zena.'

'Then you'll consider working here?'

'I'd like to give it a try and, if you're satisfied, we'll make it a regular. What about twice a week for a few weeks then we can settle for a weekly call.'

'I doubt that,' Nelda said. 'But twice a week for a while sounds good to me.'

'You have two children?'

'I promised them a trip to the pictures if they stayed upstairs until you're gone. If you met them first you'd change your mind about coming!'

Zena thought she'd better get it over with and Nelda called, 'Bobbie? Georgie? Come on down and say hello to Miss ... Zena. Politely mind,' she warned.

Unexpectedly it was two girls who appeared. 'Hello, which one is Bobbie and which is Georgie?

'I'm Bobbie so you can work out who she is,' the nine-year-old said cheekily, pointing a thumb at her four-year-old sister. They solemnly shook her hand and sat on a pile of clutter on the floor and stared at her in silence. Zena decided it was time for a diplomatic retreat.

Her third call was on Mrs Janey Day. The comparison between this and the previous house made her smile. The house was large, the rooms expensively furnished and immaculate. Mrs Day also employed a gardener and a nanny for the children. Zena learned that she was a dedicated charity worker and her husband was very wealthy. Arrangements were swiftly made for a day and time and

Zena was on her way. She rode back to Llyn Hir thinking about the various people and their very different attitudes to life.

She hadn't told Jake about leaving the lettings agency, determined for there not to be even a slight disagreement during their wonderful weekend. She decided to phone him and tell him as soon as possible, but, as usual, he was difficult to reach. She had made another decision too. She moved back to live permanently with her parents and her brother. Aunty Mabs found her a short-let tenant for the flat and, when that was settled, she tried again to contact Jake to let him know.

Eventually a message reached him and he phoned her mother's house. She explained first about her change of occupation.

'Zena, lovely girl, that's marvellous! Give me time to find us somewhere decent to live then we can marry quickly and quietly, without any fuss and—'

'Stop, Jake,' she protested with a laugh. 'I haven't said I'm coming to join you! In fact, I've got a new job, cleaning for three families and I've moved back in with Mam and Greg. And Dad, when he comes home.'

'Cleaning? Don't you do enough housework, what with your flat and helping out at home? Surely you want something better, more interesting than cleaning?'

'I won't be earning much, but with the rent from the flat, there'll be enough to put something in the savings each week. Have you managed to put away the usual amount?'

'No, love, but I've bought a car.' He spoke quickly to cover her protests. 'It's because I enjoyed that last weekend so much, lovely girl. I love you and I want to see you more often, try to persuade you to come to London.'

'But we need every penny to buy a property, why waste money on a car?'

'Don't be upset, it isn't anything grand, I'll be down again soon and you can see for yourself that it didn't break the bank.'

'Living in London I wouldn't have thought you'd need a car; the buses and the underground trains are so efficient. Anyway, why didn't you discuss it with me? You make decisions with our money as though I don't exist.'

'You're never here. That's why. When I try to ring Llyn Hir you're never there. You haven't replied to the last two letters and, oh it's hopeless being so far apart. Darling, you make me feel so unimportant. Come to London. Sell the flat and come.'

'Sell the flat? You know I can't do that. Gran left the flat to me and the cottage to Greg with stipulations. We can't sell for a very long time.'

'There has to be a let-out clause. I spoke to a solicitor and—Not a proper consultation, just a friend,' he added quickly, as she began to protest.

She moved in to Llyn Hir with Greg's help and left the flat neat and tidy for her tenants. Jake phoned several times during the following weeks, but there was a strain in their conversations. Zena knew the edginess came from her. She and Jake had both made important decisions without discussing them and that was not how it should be.

It was pleasantly relaxing to be back home. She fitted into the routine with ease. The local farmer, Uncle Sam – honorary uncle – or his father Neville, called often, sometimes bringing eggs or a rabbit, or just to sit and talk about things. Mabs was a regular visitor. Neighbours sometimes called and the evenings were a great improvement on sitting in her flat on her own and she knew she had made the right decision. She'd decided not tell Aunty Mabs or her parents about Jake's car – more secrets. She'd wait until he came home and pretend she had shared the decision to buy one. She had been defending Jake for so long it was an automatic thing to do.

She *did* tell her brother about the car and that she hadn't known before the purchase. 'I can't really complain, Greg,' she admitted, 'I left my job without telling him and decided to rent the flat and move back here. But my excuse is that he never seems to get my letters and I can never reach him at the office.'

'Tell Mam and Dad,' he advised. 'Don't complicate things.'

At the hospital, her parents sat holding hands, reminiscing affectionately. She told her parents about the car as though it was the most exciting thing. They were not convinced that Zena had known beforehand of the purchase, but said nothing.

Mabs wasn't about to hold her tongue.

'So he's bought a car, then,' she said one Friday, as she set out sausages and mash for them both.

'Yes.' Zena concentrated on cutting a piece of sausage and didn't look at her aunt. 'Isn't it exciting? We can have some lovely days out once summer comes. We decided that coming home would be a lot easier for Jake with a car. The journey is so tedious, underground trains with two changes and all the rest.'

'Better sense if he'd bought it for you, gel. There's you going around on a bike with winter coming. Snow, ice and bitter winds ahead of you. You need a car, not him.'

'It'll be lovely to have transport when he's home.'

'So he'll be home every weekend, then?'

'He'd love to, but he often works at weekends and he travels abroad as well, remember.' The defensive lies came out, when would they ever stop?

Greg borrowed a car and took Rose out for the day. They drove through the pretty, beautifully cared-for Pembrokeshire villages, stood on a beach for a while but were driven back to the car by a cold strong wind with raindrops at its edge. After lunch at an hotel and a leisurely drive back, they were happy and relaxed as they approached the village of Cold Brook Vale.

'Come back and meet Mam and Zena,' he suggested, but she shook her head.

'Another day. I'm tired and I want to go home and sit and dream about the lovely day we've had.'

'One day soon?' he coaxed.

She kissed him lightly as she stepped out of the car and stood while he drove away. Then she walked to a house several streets away and let herself in, the smile gone, regret creating a sad frown.

Ronald's health had improved enough for him to be given a new date to leave hospital and although everything had been done, Zena and Lottie set to, dusting, rearranging things with unnecessary care. Greg helped move the furniture and clean the windows and with a fire laid ready to light, they were satisfied.

Her mother was at the hospital and Greg was out with friends and Zena was alone in the house. The day was ending early in a glowering darkness, the clouds were low and threatening and it was very still and cold. She placed the vegetables in the casserole and put it into the oven. She wasn't sure what time her mother and brother would be home, but guessed they wouldn't be very late. Mam was visiting the hospital after the stationers closed and visiting at the hospital ended at eight. It was only an hour's journey to get home.

She appreciated the warmth of the house, glad she had chosen to come back to Llyn Hir. It had been a retrograde step, she admitted that, but it would give her the chance to think about what she really wanted from life. Her greatest disappointment was the lost dream of running a bed and breakfast with Jake. His impulsive move to London had changed everything.

She looked around the room she had known all her life: the couches and chairs where they had flopped each evening, bringing friends and filling the place with their arguments and laughter; the rather battered table where they had eaten so many meals and shared so many secrets. Perhaps she simply hadn't grown up? Maybe she hadn't been ready to consider marrying Jake who wanted a life in the big city? A grown-up woman would have supported her future husband and followed him wherever he went, wouldn't she?

She had been so sure of what they both wanted but they were drifting apart, probably because they saw so little of each other. These last few weeks his travels had taken him further and further away. He rang sometimes to tell her he had been to Spain or Germany and other countries about which he seemed very reluctant to talk. He was out of contact for days at a time and the weekends had no importance in the decisions to send him. She decided that next week she would go to London and talk to Jake and see whether she could clarify her thoughts and maybe make him understand.

On impulse she phoned his office, crossing her fingers as she dialled the number, doubting he would be there, but very much hoping he would be. A young girl answered and told her, 'No, Miss

Martin, Jake isn't in the office, he's probably at the warehouse. Shall I tell him you called?'

'No need, I'll get him at the flat later.' She thanked the girl and replaced the receiver. That was another problem, the difficulty of reaching him when she needed to talk. Thank goodness her parents had a phone and she didn't have to go out in the cold to find a phone box.

She looked through the curtains as evening closed in and shivered at the thought of the winter months still to come. A fresh pile of logs stood near the gate where Sam Edwards had delivered them. The garden looked drab and neglected. Her mother usually made sure it was 'tidied away for its winter sleep', as she put it, but this year, with her father ill and Lottie spending so much time in hospital the grass and flowers had been left to slowly decay.

There was nothing to do until her mother and Greg were back from visiting her father, although, she thought with a smile, that might be only Mam; Greg would probably decide to stay in town and meet friends. At twenty-one, two years younger than Zena, his social life was very lively. She settled down to write to Jake.

She thought about Jake in London and wondered what he was doing; something more interesting than cooking a meal and an evening listening to the wireless with her mother. But London didn't tempt her. She had no intention of moving.

The truth was she was contented with her life here in the small Welsh village of Cold Brook Vale and couldn't imagine ever making such a move. London was a foreign country so far as she was concerned. Jake said he understood and was prepared to wait until she decided to join him but lately he was never willing to discuss it. 'Just tell me when you are ready to join me,' were the last words he had spoken to her on his brief visit.

Feeling guilty at the way she was neglecting him, she wrote a loving letter filled with enthusiasm with ideas of where they would live, and how she was looking forward to all the pleasure they would have discovering the joys and excitements of living in the capital city. She felt even more guilty when she finished it as none of it was true. She didn't want to move away, she was a small town girl at heart and didn't think she would ever change. She hoped that Jake would change *his* mind and come back to the village filled with friends. She tore up the letter and threw it on the fire. Adding lies and dishonest promises wasn't the answer.

She went to pull the curtains across and was surprised to see that it was snowing. It was only early December but large flakes were already settling on the garden and partly blocking the outside light. She hoped her mother was already on the way and would arrive safely. She pulled the curtains tight and, as she did so, the lights in the house went out and the oven fell silent.

'Oh, no!' she said aloud. The outside light had failed too and the darkness was almost complete, just the flakes softly falling catching the ambient light of the day's ending. She stared in the direction of the light for a few seconds. Surely it was just a blip and it would come on again? After a disbelieving few moments she felt her way through the house to the kitchen to where her mother kept emergency candles, torches and matches. She lit candles in the kitchen and the living room and carried the torch in her pocket.

The first thing to do was contact a neighbour. Although neighbour was a misnomer, the nearest houses were on the small estate at one end of the lane; in the other direction along the narrow lane shadowed by overgrown trees on both sides, was an empty property with a large overgrown garden, that everyone called the haunted house and beyond that, a bluebell wood and Uncle Sam's farm.

But first she'd ring the hospital to warn her mother to stay with Aunty Mabs instead of trying to drive up the lane. Then she'd ring her to make sure she was safe, but she was shocked to find that the telephone was dead.

Seriously alarmed, she opened the door to look out hoping to see or hear her mother's car but the silence was absolute. So far from another house and with that strange hush created by snow, she could have been the only person on the planet. She hoped her mother and Greg would have the sense to stay in town, but she stood a candle inside a jar on the shelf near the front door to help guide them if they managed to walk.

Greg came out of the cinema and was surprised at the suddenness of the snow storm. Seeing the thick covering of snow and aware of the rising wind that was threatening to build drifts, he wondered how he would get home. The possibility was that the lane would be blocked and he didn't fancy burrowing through snow drifts. He and Rose had been for a meal, but she had refused to go with him to the pictures and had gone home earlier, preferring, she told him, to have an early night.

If he could reach the hospital and meet his mother there, maybe they could work out the best way of getting back to the house. The only alternative was to stay with Aunty Mabs and perhaps, he decided, as he looked up at the large flakes, that might be the wisest decision.

Then his thoughts turned to Rose and her reluctance to progress to a different level with their friendship. He had never met her parents; she had been very reticent when he'd suggested it, but in an emergency like this she might be more easily persuaded. As he walked towards the hospital he wondered why Rose had been unwilling for their families to meet. Shyness was hardly an acceptable reason; after all they had known each other for a long time and had been dating steadily for six months, with neither his family nor hers aware of their growing attraction.

His mother was in the phone box outside the hospital and came out when she saw him. After discussions about Ronald's progress, Lottie said, 'Thank goodness you came here. We won't be able to get home in this. No buses, cars are slithering all over the place, and when I tried to phone Zena to tell her we'll be staying with Mabs, the phone is down too.'

'With Mabs? *If* she's in!'

'Don't be silly, of course she's in.'

'Mam, I saw her a few nights ago in the main street, dressed in about four layers of coats and that huge old hat of hers.'

'She'll be back home at this late hour for sure. She doesn't go far in the evenings.'

'I've seen her a few times late evening and I didn't know how to ask where she'd been going. She'd probably tell me to mind my own business!'

'Layers of clothes and a big hat? You were obviously mistaken. She doesn't go out at night, hasn't for years.'

'It was Aunty Mabs, Mam. There's no mistaking her swaying walk.'

His mother dismissed it with a 'Nonsense, dear', and Greg decided that tonight wasn't the time to argue. 'The flat is quite small, what if I stay with a friend of mine? Rose lives not far away, I could take you there, then go on to stay with Rose. I'm sure her family will take in a stray out of the storm.'

'Who is Rose?'

'Rose Conelly. She works in Davy's shoe shop. We've been seeing each other often these past weeks.'

'Someone special, is she? So when will we meet her?' Lottie turned her head to look at her son, preparing to tease but at that moment her foot slipped and they continued the journey laughing, with her hanging on to fences and being supported by Greg.

Mabs was in and welcomed them with a sigh of relief, thankful it wasn't one of her evenings for her night-time activities. 'Come in, I've put some blankets to warm in case you turned up. Kettle won't be long and I've got some soup ready to heat. You'll have to sleep on the couch, Greg.'

'It's all right, Aunty, I won't stay. I'm going to stay with a friend.' He darted off before the questions could begin. He had walked Rose home on many occasions so he didn't hesitate to push open the gate and knock on the door. When the door was opened an elderly woman stood there. He offered a hand. 'Hello. Mrs Conelly? Is Rose in, please? I'm Greg, Gregory Martin.'

'Who?' the woman questioned. 'Who's Rose? No one of that name here.' She closed the door and he heard bolts pushed home. Puzzled, he stood for a few moments staring at the door. He looked around. He hadn't made a mistake, this *was* the right house. There was the tree behind which they kissed goodnight. Slowly he walked back to Mabs's flat through swirling snow which had settled to an alarming depth and was almost obliterating abandoned cars. He had to think of an explanation that would be far from the truth. Then he had a better idea. Staying with a friend would avoid a lengthy list of questions to which he had no answer.

The wind was rising, the still falling snow finding ways to sneak around his collar and slide down his neck. He pulled his already wet coat tighter around him and walked on past Mabs's flat. A few people were walking purposefully along the road, under the street lights but unrecognizable, huddled as they were in thick coats and hats and scarves. His friend welcomed him and they made supper companionably then Greg settled on the couch and lay awake all night trying to fathom what Rose's true story might be.

Chapter Two

THE SNOW CONTINUED unabated and Zena settled in an armchair, somehow unable to undress and get into bed; the empty house and the silence outside was unnerving her. Unable to cook she had tried to sleep without eating, but that too was impossible. She foolishly waited for her mother and Greg to join her, three plates set out on the kitchen table. She sat up, pushing aside her attempts to sleep. She was hungry! And thirsty. Gathering a jumper and a dressing gown, she made herself a sandwich and wondered how long it would be before she could make a cup of tea.

An hour passed slowly and she emptied the last of the coal onto the fire. If she were to stay warm she needed to get more fuel. The flickering light from the fire was a comfort as well as warmth. With a torch to light the way she went to the barn to collect the two filled coal scuttles. A fox howled in the distance and she thought the poor animal would go hungry tonight.

The swirling snow, moved by the gusts of wind, disorientated her and she missed the door to the barn by a few feet. She found her destination with the aid of the torch and grabbed the filled scuttles, her heart racing. Something was disturbed by her moving them and there was the sound of something shifting behind her as she left the barn. With visibility so restricted, and imagining someone unseen standing close by watching her, she stumbled in an attempt to run the last few yards despite her burdens and hurried inside. The short walk in the darkness had unnerved her more and she picked up the poker for a false sense of protection, then laughed at her stupidity. She would never be able to use it on an intruder.

To reassure herself she held it aloft and went into every room, checking wardrobes and cupboards even glancing up at the loft door which was undisturbed. Slowly she relaxed, comforted by the thought that at least the fire wouldn't fail her.

She slept very little, just dozing and waking with the hope of someone arriving. She frequently tried the telephone, half believing she had been mistaken; its loss had been a bad dream. She also made up the fire: at least the house would be warm when her mother got home.

At nine o'clock in the morning she'd put bread to toast in front of the fire when the telephone rang and, with relief, she heard Greg telling her they were all right. 'Mam is with Aunty Mabs and I stayed with a friend. Grateful I am mind, but damn me that's the most uncomfortable night I've had in a long time.'

'Thank goodness you're safe.'

'Spoilt rotten I've been. Are you all right?'

'Cosy and warm.'

'Look, you won't see us for a while, Mam's car is at the hospital and she'll wait in the hope of being able to drive back. I'm off to work to see if any routes are clear yet. There won't be many even though workmen have been out all night. We'll see you as soon as we can, but with the lane certainly blocked I don't know when.'

Almost crying with relief, Zena stood for a moment staring at the phone then became aware of the smell of burning. She ran to the fire, threw the toast that was burned to a crisp out into the garden and put more slices on the fork in front of the red coals. Then she rang Aunty Mabs and burned those too.

After eating the third attempt she looked at the time. Jake should be in the office now. She dialled the number and the receptionist answered, but when she asked about Jake there was some hesitation. 'Don't tell me he's been cut off by snow too!' she said with a laugh. 'We're cut off and we've had no power for hours. Snow drifts have blocked the lane.'

'Jake isn't here,' the girl said hesitantly.

'Don't worry. When you see him, just tell him we're cut off but we're all safe, will you?'

'Yes I will – if I see him.'

Again she sounded hesitant, doubtful, but Zena put it down to the fact that the girl was new. She might not know who is who yet. The light and power was restored a hour later and, with a sigh of relief, she put the casserole on to cook.

At twelve o'clock she heard the sound of an engine and there at the gate was the tractor with Uncle Sam driving and her mother sitting beside him. Sam was grinning widely as he helped her mother down. 'More trouble than all my cows and sheep this one,' he teased. He stayed for coffee, handing Zena a box containing a quart of milk and some eggs. He wrote down their shopping needs which he would collect later then went off waving away their thanks.

Frost made the roads and pavement surfaces dangerous and Zena didn't attempt to visit her clients. It was three days before Greg could get home by crossing the fields. The main roads had been quickly cleared and he had been working, staying with his friend. 'It's like the end of a little war,' he said, as he hugged them. If only Jake would ring everything would be perfect, Zena thought. It was more than a week since they had spoken and, although she had tried the office again she'd had the same vague non-committal response when she asked to be at least told where he was. She had even asked to speak to Madeleine and was told that she too was unavailable. It wasn't that unusual for days to pass without contact, but his having been told she had been cut off by snow, she had expected a note of concern.

She wrote twice to his flat and for more than a week waited in vain for a reply. He rang eventually telling her he was in Belgium and wouldn't be back for a couple more days. 'It's a chance of some serious new business,' he explained. 'Too boring to explain now but it will mean some new lines and a pleasing number of new customers. I'll tell you when we meet, and that won't be long now, lovely girl. Meet me at Neath station two o'clock a week Friday and we'll have a wonderful weekend.'

'Neath station? The railway station? Aren't you coming by car?'

'Well, one of the other reps, Rick, was stuck for transport and, as I was off to Belgium for a week or so, I lent him ours. So far, he hasn't got back. If he gets his sorted in time I'll definitely drive down, give you a real weekend to remember.'

'He's lent our car that I haven't even seen yet, to someone else,' she told Lottie. 'If he has something needed by someone else he'll give it freely.'

'Very nice, dear,' Lottie said vaguely.

Zena stared at her, curious about the tone of her voice. 'I was angry at first, but really, he's just completely unselfish, isn't he?' And he makes sure you are too, Lottie thought, but she said nothing.

As usual, Mabs was more outspoken when she met her nephew. 'Lent the car to someone else, I hear. Kind of him, isn't it, Greg?' She looked at him, her eyebrow raised questioningly. 'It's Zena's car too and she doesn't have any say, does she? And Jake gets all the praise. She goes to work on a bike at this time of year with snow still on the fields and he lends their car to someone she doesn't even know. Very kind to anyone except Zena, if you ask me.'

'She doesn't seem to mind and after all wouldn't she do the same?'

'She never gets the chance!'

'He's a decent chap and I like him,' Greg defended.

'So would I if he was engaged to anyone other than your sister!'

More snow fell but the lane leading to the house and beyond wasn't seriously blocked and transport in the town ran without problems. Zena managed to get to her jobs easily, stopping one bright morning for a snowball fight with Nelda's daughters. Bobbie managed a few viciously accurate hits on Zena and Nelda, Georgie laughing too much to join in.

The worst danger was the ice. In places it was invisible to the eye and made pedestrians slide and stumble and the family all warned Mabs not to go out. Sam delivered shopping bringing what Lottie needed, warning her that carrying heavy baskets made it more likely she would fall. He also took whoever was visiting Ronald to the hospital, where the staff were no longer talking about his coming home.

Despite the inconveniences, the snow and frost were a beautiful sight. The gardens and the trees were so lovely people stopped to stare at them as they passed the parks and Greg and Zena struggled down to the lake to admire the winter wonderland of trees and bushes dressed in silver and white.

Nelda visited with the girls and they walked through the woods towards Sam's farm. The children played hide and seek among the trees and the scene was described by little Georgie as, 'trees painted by fairies'.

Greg laughed one morning when Zena brought in a shirt that had been on the line overnight and stood it to its full height on the kitchen table where it stayed for a while before slowly collapsing in the heat of the house. He laughed a lot but Zena guessed it was no more than defence against the misery of his love for the mysterious Rose.

The thaw came and the beauty was replaced by gloom and mud. Zena was busy getting to her regular jobs, Greg doing extra shifts as winter illnesses affected the drivers, Lottie visiting Ronald between working in the stationers.

Ronald still talked happily about when he would be home, and said there was something important he had to do in case he became ill again. He didn't explain and Lottie didn't pressure him; she was afraid of doing or saying anything that might upset him, his health was so fragile. She did mention a curious letter from the bank but he waved it away, promising that it would all be sorted when he got home. It referred to a debt on which payments were overdue. Ronald insisted cheerfully that it must be a mistake. A transfer of funds would put it right. Reluctantly she put it aside.

It was as the last of the snow melted away and the grass shone like new paint in the fields around that Zena began to be worried. Jake had not come for the weekend as promised. A hastily written note cancelled their meeting in Neath and since then there had been nothing.

Mabs didn't go out during the days, Zena or Greg or Lottie did her shopping, promising not to disturb her in the evenings as she liked to listen to the wireless and doze. They were unaware of the taxi that called for her four evenings a week and took her into town.

When Zena called for their usual lunch together, Mabs said nothing about Jake's silence, afraid a wrong comment would result in a disagreement. When Zena finally saw sense about the feckless

Jake, she would need her sympathy and support and a few wrong words now could spoil that.

Greg hadn't made further contact with Rose after she refused to explain her reason for lying about where she lived. He went out with friends and forced laughter, pretending they'd both made a terrible mistake and had parted. He put aside his curiosity and tried to forget her. Lottie, Zena and Mabs guessed there was something he wasn't telling them, but they were wise enough not to ask. Then, one day she was waiting at the bus garage and said she was sorry and would explain one day, tell him the truth, before hurrying away.

The weather became almost spring-like for a few days and Mabs went out with baskets and purse to fill her larder. It was Wednesday, half day closing and Lottie would be home. She wondered how Ronald was. She'd go with Lottie to see him this afternoon. She always dreaded the first sight of him, afraid he would have deteriorated and would not be coming home. Thank goodness Zena was living there and looking after Lottie. Such a sensible girl, apart from the aberration that caused her to fall for that useless Jake Williams.

The family had been kind and kept her supplied with essentials and the rest she managed from her store. Thank goodness for a fridge, she thought. That was one of the few things she had bought with Frank's money and one she didn't regret. She'd pretended it had been a Christmas present from him that he'd bought as a surprise. She hated using the money which she was convinced had caused his death. Winning all that money had been such a shock to the system, he'd had a heart attack and died within a month.

She closed the door and set off for the bus. Llyn Hir was still cut off with remnants of the drifts and the bus would take her only as far as the lake, and the steep path up to the house. Not for the first time since Frank had died she regretted not being able to drive. She smiled to herself as she waited for the bus. She could afford a taxi and many would call her stupid for not using one, but she was determined not to use more than a few hundred pounds of the fortune that had killed her Frank.

She began to shout as she reached the door. 'Zena? Lottie? Anybody home? I'm sinking for a cuppa. Damned stupid place to live this is, stuck up here at the end of nowhere.'

Zena came into the kitchen and hugged her. 'Aunty Mabs! So glad to see you. Mam's at the hospital, they phoned for her to go in, but she rang to tell us he's much better. He'd had what Mam called "a bit of a turn", but he's all right again.'

'I thought I'd go in with your Mam to see him.' She showed Zena the contents of her basket, producing sweets and a newspaper. 'Where's young Greg?'

'He's at work. Afternoons all this week.'

'I thought he was mornings?'

'Sickness has made them short of drivers.' They talked about Greg's shifts for a while, Zena amused by her interest in knowing where he'd be working and what time.

'Glad I am that he followed your Uncle Frank and became a bus driver,' Mabs said. Zena waited until Mabs was in front of a steaming cup of tea and a round of toast and said, 'I have a day off today.'

'Enjoy cleaning other people's houses, do you?'

'I wasn't sure, and it was only intended to be for a short time but yes, I enjoy it. I only take on work where the people are pleasant, so I'm happy doing it for a while. Living in the flat with Jake away, I had so many hours with no company. I see my clients and listen to them talk about their lives and it helps. My routine used to be the office and home with nothing much besides. My days in that office were repetitious, so rigid and, well, boring.'

'Of course it was boring. That's what they pay you for.'

'Without hope of running a bed and breakfast, as Jake and I had once planned, there must be better ways of earning money than cleaning up after others, but I'll do it while I think about what I want to do.'

'And Jake?'

'He wants me to go to London and start a new life there. Perhaps I should, at least I'd feel a part of this relationship. At present I'm no more than appendage, a hanger on. Even the girls in the London office treat me as though I'm a nuisance, calling and interrupting them. And I don't think the woman called Madeleine passes on my messages. Even Jake can't forget them all!'

'You haven't made up your mind, about London?'

'I can't imagine living so far away from this place, and Mam and Dad and Greg, and you of course. Stupid, isn't it?'

'Seems to me following your instincts is a sound way to plan your future.' She held up her plate. 'And now I'd love another cup of tea and more toast slithering with that illegal farm butter!'

Lottie and Greg arrived home an hour later and found the table set and Mabs busy peeling potatoes. 'Sausages and mash and onion gravy,' she announced before hugging her sister-in-law. 'Lovely chat we've been having. Now, tell me, how is that brother-in-law of mine? Anything I can take for him? I was hoping to go in with you but you'd gone. What's this about your shifts changing, young Greg?' Mabs chattered on throughout the meal and until Zena walked her to the bus stop.

'Now Zena love. Don't make any rash decisions. Think about the years ahead of you and how you'd like to live them. Right?' As the bus took her away she was still shouting, 'What about the flat? You've lost your tenants so when are you going to rent it again? Be careful about that, mind. And talk to that Jake!'

Zena had interviewed prospective tenants and two seemed suitable. They wanted to move in after Christmas, which was a few weeks away. She smiled as she walked back up the path, thinking of how involved Aunty Mabs was in the day-to-day happenings of the family; then she frowned. She hadn't told her the full story about her difficulties in contacting Jake. It was stupid to blame Madeleine and the others. Contacting her or not was Jake's choice. She hadn't mentioned her growing fear that they would soon be parted by his indifference and wished she had; telling it out loud might have helped her to face it.

She stopped at the gate of Llyn Hir and looked around her; at the bushes where they fed the fox, at the dilapidated platform in the oak tree that hadn't deserved to be called a tree house, but where she and Greg and their friends had played happily through long summer days.

'Mam,' she called, 'I wonder if that tree house could be mended?

We'll never use it again, but I love to see it there, a memory of lovely days.'

'I'll ask Uncle Sam if he knows anyone with the patience to try.'

Greg had expected little from life except a happy marriage and children, with a job that gave him enough to keep them comfortable. He had no desire to move away from the village where he had been born and that was filled with people he liked. He earned a reasonable wage as a bus driver, with occasional overtime and even more occasional extra money driving coach trips in the summer months.

The cottage left to him by his grandmother was added security, giving him extra money and a chance to learn new skills as he dealt with small repairs when they were needed. The tenants he had found had given little trouble and he was happy with the present arrangement with a couple now due to retire who used it as a holiday home while they decided whether to move to Cold Brook Vale to live out their later years.

Meeting Rose Conelly had promised to be the beginning of his dream of home, wife and children. She made him feel happy and he had imagined that it was the same for her, but her refusal to meet his family or introduce him to hers was a concern. He hadn't told her he'd discovered the fiction about where she lived. He had been hoping that she would tell him and explain her reason for lying, but although he had vaguely mentioned the house to which he had regularly taken her after their dates, no explanation was forthcoming. They could drift for a long time like this; a secretive love affair that offered no hope of anything more. It had to be sorted. But how?

He and Rose were meeting to go to the pictures that evening and he had suggested a meal afterwards. 'That was a hurdle too,' he told Zena. 'She doesn't like eating in restaurants. How can she be shy? She works in a shoe shop, dealing with customers; surely she couldn't do that if shyness was her problem?'

'Jake used to be uneasy when we ate in what he called a posh place,' Zena explained. 'It was something he wasn't used to. He was embarrassed, knowing the other diners would recognize him as a Joe's caff, pie and chips man. Perhaps it's the same for Rose. Why don't you bring her home? Or take her to a small insignificant café somewhere?'

Greg disagreed. 'I have to make her face whatever is troubling her, and tonight I plan to put a few of her demons to rest.' He didn't tell Zena he was going to propose. He was not that sure of Rose's acceptance and being turned down was not something he would enjoy admitting. He was tense during the evening, taking in nothing of the film they were watching.

He hardly said a word as they walked to where they were to eat supper, although Rose chatted away and seemed unaware of his mood. At the restaurant he had chosen she became quiet and was nervous as they went in and he coaxed her to hand her coat to the waiter who came forward. They were shown to a corner table and Greg offered her the menu. 'Anything you want, Rose. Tonight is a special occasion.'

'Not a birthday is it?'

'No,' he whispered smiling at her. 'I'll tell you later.'

She relaxed, tucked in their corner, and was soon laughing at his stories about some of his passengers, joining in with amusing observations about some of the diners. Greg looked at her with utter pleasure. Surely everyone they met must envy him? She was pretty and funny and tonight she seemed more relaxed, although she turned away when someone offered a polite 'Good evening'. He felt a great love and a need to protect her, keep her safe from anything that worried her. He could imagine a lifetime without an angry word between them. She relaxed him when he became irate – usually about something unimportant – and made him see the funny side of life.

There had been other girls, but Rose was the only one for him. The corner table had been a perfect choice as she could look around without a feeling of being on show.

They were walking home in the crisp December dark and Greg wondered anxiously if she would finally tell him where she lived. Taking a deep breath, he said, 'Rose, I want us to be married. Please, tell me you feel the same?'

She stood still and turned to stare at him. 'Why can't we leave things as they are? Why d'you have to spoil things? I'm happy with things as they are.'

'So am I, very happy and that's why I want us to marry, spend our lives together and make a home and have children and be a happy, loving family.'

In the strange light of a street lamp Greg was startled to see that she looked frightened. He held her close and felt her trembling. 'Rose, love, you must have expected this, we've been seeing each other for a while and I've never hidden the way I feel about you.'

'I don't feel ready to include others in our plans yet. I suppose I'm afraid of it falling apart once all the fuss and planning takes over. It won't be 'us' any more.'

'Our wedding can be as large or as small as you want it to be. A register office is fine by me if that's what you want. I have the cottage and all I need to do is give the tenants notice and it will be ours. It's that simple.'

She repeated her feelings and he listened and tried to understand. He didn't ask her where she lived, he felt he'd done enough damage for one evening. He left her at the same house as before although he knew that was not where she lived. He was tempted to follow but knew that was a risk he dare not take and went home to another sleepless night, glad of an early morning start.

A couple of days later he was waiting outside the shop when she finished work. He led her to a café, ordered tea and Welsh cakes determined to try again. He spoke to customers coming in and going out, waved to others, many he knew from being passengers on his bus, but was convinced he was boring her.

'How could I be bored with you, Greg? You're so observant, you like people and always find something nice to say about them.'

'And you'll marry me?'

'One day.'

'Then will you come and meet my parents and sister, and Aunty Mabs?'

Immediately she looked uneasy and her hands trembled. With reluctance, she agreed.

They caught the bus to the hospital to meet his father the following evening. Greg hoped his mother would be there too to get the biggest hurdle over. At the door to the ward, Greg looked in and pointed to where his father lay, his mother beside the bed holding Ronald's hand.

Ronald saw Greg and waved. 'Look, Kay,' he whispered 'our Greg is here and he has a young lady with him.'

'Come on, love, they're looking forward to meeting you,' Greg said, waving at his parents. He turned to usher her in but Rose had gone.

Rose ran home although it was a long way. She had to get as far from the Martin family as possible. She couldn't do this: a marriage, the intimacy of revealing all her life's secrets, she just couldn't. She squeezed in through the railings of the park and sat, shivering with the cold and despair and misery for almost an hour before setting off again to the gloomy place she called home. She walked slowly now, there was never any incentive to hurry. She doubted if she would ever have a place that felt like home; that was something she'd never had and never would.

Mr Roberts was one of Zena's favourite clients. He had seriously injured his back having fallen trying to rescue a kitten from a tree and was only able to walk by using two sticks. He employed her to help with housework, but after her first few visits, she had added shopping and the preparation his meals. The initial arrangements had been made by telephone and, when she had knocked his door, she was surprised to see a small, slim man with surprisingly powerful arms who stood with no apparent aid and who welcomed her inside. He had led her slowly and with some difficulty to a comfortable sitting room and then reached for a stick. He smiled and offered his hand, which was large, matching his muscular arm. 'I pretend not to need this, but my vanity doesn't last very long.'

'Being injured doesn't make you less of a man, Mr Roberts,' she said, smiling back. 'Now, shall we sit while you explain the best way I can help you?'

An hour later she was moving furniture and vacuuming the carpets, tidying clothes and newspapers. 'But,' she reassured him, 'I won't put away books or papers until you tell me I can. My father gets very frustrated when my mother tidies up and he can't find the book or magazine he's currently reading.'

During a few snatches of conversation between dealing with the clutter and deciding what he needed her to do, they discovered they had mutual friends and also, to Zena's delight, Mr Roberts knew Jake and had known him since childhood.

As she was putting on her coat to leave one day, the back door opened and a voice called, 'You there, Popeye?'

'In here, young Kevin.'

'Hi, Pops, I'm going into town, is there anything you need?' Zena was introduced to a smiling, attractive young man, slim, taller by a head than Mr Roberts. He was dressed in denim clothes and heavy boots and wore a donkey jacket over a thick home knitted jumper. With a brief discussion and a wave, Kevin left. They heard the sound of a motor bike starting and heading down the road.

'Always willing to help is Kevin. And his mother, Doris. Lucky with friends I am.'

'Do you get help with anything? Getting up and going to bed must be difficult?'

'A couple of ladies came every morning for a while, but I tried to be up and dressed before they arrived, so they gave up on me. I'm not in my dotage and I hate having young girls doing things I can do for myself. Young Kevin is a good neighbour. He was in the Navy, but he's home now and working in an engineering factory. He or his mam, Doris, calls every evening to make sure I'm in bed and there's nothing else I need. I've been blessed with good neighbours. Doris often pops in during the day, too. I'm so lucky.'

'I thought you must be a relation; didn't Kevin call you Pop or Popeye?'

Mr Roberts laughed. 'He teases me about my strong arms and skinny body and says I look like Popeye, so that's what he calls me.'

Zena had left the house that first time content with her oldest client, certain they would become friends. Sometimes on future visits, she made him a pan of stew or a cake, which she brought for him from home.

The second call was very different.

Janey Day, a pleasant if slightly eccentric lady, spent a lot of her time on charity work. She had two children, a couple of cats and an elderly dog, and was obviously very wealthy. The house was beautifully furnished but in serious need of attention. Furniture and silver needed polishing and once Mrs Day told her she would leave it to her to decide what had to be done, Zena set about bringing some shine to the place. She spent most of the first two hours tackling the sitting room and dining room, making a mental note of what she would do on future visits. Mrs Day was out so she stayed a while longer, and tidied bedrooms before starting on the kitchen. Another hour passed and, as she was leaving, Mrs Day returned, with her mother, whom she introduced as Trish. This was immediately corrected by the superior and suspicious Trish. 'The name is Mrs Francis. And before you leave here, Miss – er—?'

'My name is Zena Martin.' She offered her hand which was ignored.

'I would like to see what you've achieved, Miss Martin. I don't see much improvement here for your two hours. Look at the dust on the banisters. My daughter won't pay for this standard of work.'

Just then there came a shriek from the kitchen and Mrs Day came in shouting in excitement. 'Mammy! You should see the kitchen! And the sitting room looks as though everything is brand new!'

Zena left them to their opposing views and cycled home. Mrs Day would be all right, but she hoped there wouldn't be much contact with her mother. Mrs Francis would be a difficult person to please. When Trish Francis asked her to do a few hours for her, she politely declined.

Nelda Grey, the third of her clients, worked in a gift shop which was a part of Ilex House, a large property, the house and gardens of which were open to the public. Nelda had two children and was divorced. When they had met in a café to discuss her needs, Nelda insisted on delaying her starting for a day or so, as she insisted that she had to tidy up a bit before she allowed Zena in!

She was a charming young woman and was grateful for everything Zena achieved in the hours she spent sorting out the cheerful but chaotic household. The new way of earning a wage was, so far, very enjoyable and, apart from the disapproving and suspicious Trish Francis, she could see no reason to try anything else for a while – unless she made up her mind to move to London to join Jake.

Greg made another attempt to persuade Rose to meet his family. 'It's likely you know them, at least by sight,' he coaxed. 'Living in Cold Brook Vale no one is a complete stranger. Come to the hospital and meet them *en masse*, get it over in one visit.'

He talked persuasively but she didn't appear to be listening, playing with the clasp of her handbag, opening and snapping it shut, time and again. Then to his surprise and delight, she agreed.

The usual rule applied regarding visitors to a bed and they went in as Lottie was about to leave. Then, with the nurse out of sight, Lottie darted back and at once held Ronald's hand and they grinned like conspirators.

After some hesitant small talk, the nurse came and Lottie reluctantly went out. Ronald was laughing, a small sound in his weakened body, and said. 'Always one to bend the rules, is Kay.'

Rose reacted sharply. 'Kay? Who's Kay?'

'My nickname for my wife,' Ronald explained breathlessly.

To their alarm, Rose ran from the ward, pushed her way through the few people waiting for a turn to visit a patient and, with tears flowing, hurried across the carpark and on to the street. She made no decision about where she was going, she just had to put as much distance as possible between herself and Greg. At midnight she was again sitting in the park. Anger glistened in her eyes and showed in the tightly clenched jaw. She opened her handbag and took out a photograph of Greg which she tore into many pieces and threw into a waste bin, then set off to a place she need no longer call home. She had made a decision, made easier by the visit to Greg's family.

In London, Jake left the office and threaded his way through the drab area of London where abandoned buildings stood gaunt and dark, with broken windows like eyes watching his progress with disapproval. Cars stood in corners and the street lights showed their battered and rusty cannibalized frames. Sad reminders of someone's once proud possessions. When he reached the street where he lived, he walked to the shabby house at the far end in which he rented a room. Very cheap and, with only a short bus ride to get to the office, very convenient. That was all that it had in its favour and Jake would have been horrified if Zena saw the place he temporarily called home.

It suited him until Zena joined him, then they could find somewhere decent to live. Until she came, economy was the priority. He didn't want to waste money on comfort. His room was clean despite the state of the property. Cleanliness was always possible, wherever you lived. Eating was easy with plenty of cafés and snack bars to satisfy his hunger. He pushed at the door which scraped along the uneven tiled floor and, pushing aside piles of neglected post, stopped to look at the filthy, rubbish-strewn hall and wished Zena would make up her mind and join him. It wasn't pleasant living like this. Money was the only persuasion.

He went into his room on the second floor, knocking on the door next to his own to check that Vera, his elderly neighbour, was all right, then, in his own room, he unwrapped the pies he had bought and began to eat. He had just finished when there was a knock at the door. He was startled. No one knew where he lived and he hadn't had a visitor since he'd moved in. Post went to the office and any other contacts were via Zena in Cold Brook Vale.

To his alarm he recognized his visitor and, for a brief moment, wanted to slam the door. 'Greg? What are you doing here? How did you find me?'

'Can I come in?' Greg asked, stepping into the room.

Jake closed the door and was about to apologize but instead said, 'Does Zena know where I'm living?'

'She believes you share a flat with a friend. I came to London with some friends. I went to the office to see you and as I reached the door and saw the office was closed, I saw you and followed to surprise you. I'm no great detective, I was just lucky.' He looked around the sparsely furnished but surprisingly clean room and asked, 'What are you doing here? What happened to the decent flat you were sharing?'

'That was only for as long as it took to find this place. My friend takes messages for me and keeps up the pretence that I still live there when Zena phones, but I couldn't afford anything decent. I'm saving for when Zena comes to join me.'

'And you expect her to live here?'

'No! Of course not! We'll get married, a quiet affair mind, as most of the money will be for a place to live, somewhere much better than this. This is all I can afford at the moment, I want to go on saving, see, and I don't mind. It's only until she comes. It isn't too bad, I manage quite well, really. I wish I could get home more often though, for a bath as well as seeing your darling sister,' he said with a rueful smile, 'but that too is down to expense. When extra work is offered at weekends I grab it as it means more money in the pot and less time spent in this miserable place.'

'I phoned the house and told Mam I was going to see you, so what shall I tell them?'

'Tell them lies. I don't want Zena to know about this.' He gestured with his arms and shuddered theatrically. 'She'd be horrified.'

'She'd be shocked, but she would want—'

'She would want me to move and live somewhere more comfortable. Can't you see that with the high cost of living in London, I need to have some money to begin our life together? Living here, feeding on take-away food is all I can do to give me any chance of putting aside some money each month.'

'Can I take you out for a meal? At least let me do that.'

'Half an hour ago I'd have been pleased, Greg, but I've just filled up on hot pies from the chip shop. But thanks, and I *am* pleased to see you. With the unpleasant smells emanating from other rooms and the occasional unexplained noises and the general air of gloominess, I spend a lot of time here wishing I was somewhere else. Call again, will you?'

'Come on, Jake, at least I can buy you a drink.'

They walked to a public house some distance from the house and Jake at once asked about Greg's life. 'There's a girlfriend somewhere, isn't there? But you haven't brought her to meet the family.'

'You ask me to lie for you? All right, I want to listen, but don't repeat anything *I* tell *you*.'

'Agreed.'

They sipped their drinks and Greg began to tell Jake about Rose and her reticence to meet the family. 'It sounds ridiculous to say we're secretly engaged but she's agreed to marry me – sort of agreed – but she's still unhappy about being introduced to Zena and our parents. I got her as far as the hospital to meet them but she panicked and ran away. And this is also very odd; when I went to where she lived, a house to which I've taken her many times but have never been invited in, they hadn't heard of her. I've given her plenty of chances to explain and, well, she won't.' Jake waited silently for him to continue.

'This should have been a happy time, Jake, telling people and accepting their congratulations and the inevitable teasing, but Rose's attitude is making me feel guilty, but of what don't know. Instead of joy and excitement it's become a dark corner affair. I don't even feel able to tell the people I work with and there's certainly no air of excitement within the family. While Rose remains a stranger to them how can they be otherwise?'

Jake was careful not to offer advice, he simply said that if it were him and loving Zena as he did, he would wait and hope she would soon feel confident enough to tell him what was troubling her.

Two days after his visit to Jake, Greg was preparing to leave at five a.m. for the early works bus, when he saw a note had been pushed through the letterbox. He read and re-read it. It said simply: '*I can't see you again. I'm sorry.*' It was signed *Rose*. No love, no kisses. He frowned. What on earth had happened for her to react like this? Jake was right, he would have to wait until she explained. Was she ashamed of him? Or perhaps her own parents weren't very sociable? Or criminals? Or dangerous? Or drunkards? Frowning at his foolish thoughts he decided to be there at 5.30 when the shop closed and insist on an explanation. Then he concentrated on finishing his breakfast and preparing for his journey.

Toward the end of his shift the route took him past the shoe shop where Rose worked and he glanced in as he passed and saw a notice in the window stating that there was a vacancy for an assistant. He wondered which of the other two assistants had left and when he called there later, was shocked to be told that it was Rose who had left.

When Zena called on Nelda to do an extra two hours, Nelda was at home. All of the rooms were untidy but surprisingly, even on this winter morning, the garden was immaculate. The greenhouse was clean with seed boxes piled up ready for the spring. Nelda was clearly a woman who loved her garden and to whom housework came a poor second.

'Can you come twice a week for a few more weeks, Zena? It will give us a chance to get things under control.' She said 'us' but Zena guessed it would be down to her. That was fine. If these people could cope they wouldn't need me, she reasoned. As with Janey Day, she worked extra time at first, intending to stay with her paid hours once the work became easier. Nelda making it official meant she would be paid for the extra time she had been giving. More money in the savings for her and Jake's wedding, just as soon as he tired of London.

There were two living rooms in Nelda's house, but the 'living' took place in the breakfast room adjoining the kitchen. The other rooms were filled with the necessities for the craft work with which Nelda earned her living. Cupboards and shelves overflowed with material: wool, card, ribbons and hundreds of beads. A shelf in the kitchen had been taken over with small pieces of wood, buckets of fir cones and dried flowers. She knew it was risky tidying up a work room such as this one as, although everything was such an apparent muddle, she guessed Nelda would find everything she needed with ease. But her first plan was to rescue the kitchen from the over-flow which threatened to cover the table, soon to force the family to eat in the yard!

Gathering the different materials into one place was easier than she expected. Soon a cupboard contained all the hanks and balls of wool, including a place specifically for odd scraps. A chest of drawers held felt pieces and ribbons. Various materials were neatly packed away in boxes on shelves and everything was labelled. Zena wasn't naive enough to imagine it would look the same on her next visit but hoped that Nelda would agree that it was worth at least allowing the kitchen to be kept free.

Nelda was delighted and offered her extra money, which she refused. A plan was vaguely worked out for future visits and Zena was smiling happily as she cycled back to her parents' home, via a visit to Aunty Mabs to report on her new and interesting job.

She and Nelda met socially on occasions and on several days the children came with her to Llyn Hir for lunch and a walk through the lanes. Once, although it was cold, a weak sun shone in a hazy sky and Zena took them to the farm. Sam had invited them to meet his sheep and chickens and Digby the working sheep dog, of which Sam was so proud. Sam's father Neville came with them on the tour of the farm and took them to the large old farmhouse for glasses of milk. When the men went back to work Zena walked them through the wood toward the large old house. 'The haunted house we used to call it,' she told Nelda. Bobbie asked what 'haunted' meant. 'It means old, and neglected, with no one to love it,' Zena explained.

'Poor house', said Georgie. 'Can we go and see it one day?'

'When summer comes,' her mother promised.

On his late shifts, Greg had several times seen the bulkily dressed woman in the large hat whom he still thought might be Aunty Mabs, and twice in the early hours of the morning she was seen getting onto the early workers' bus. She had never used the bus which he was driving and he wondered curiously whether her regular questions about his hours and routes had something to do with it. A pattern began to reveal itself and one night when he guessed when and where she would appear, he waited near the bus stop and followed her when she dismounted. She led him to a café that was closed with curtains across its windows, but she unlocked the door and went inside.

He didn't know what to do; if he went in and it wasn't Aunty Mabs he would look foolish and if it was her then she was sure to be angry as she obviously didn't want these visits known.

As he watched, two men went in, both wearing suits, but there was an air of neglect about them, the overcoats were shabby and either too large or with sleeves so short they were layered with jacket and then the shirt. A third man had the smell of mothballs emanating from his clothes. A fourth man, small, slim and with lively friendly eyes stepped out from the café door and asked, 'Unable to sleep, boy?' Greg muttered something and the man gestured to the café. 'You can come in, and have a cup of tea and a game of draughts or something. She doesn't mind just as long as you behave. No arguing, mind, or out you go. Come on, I'll introduce you to Frankie.'

'Frankie?'

'She's the lady who runs the place at night. There's Frankie and Mr Thomas. Between them they keep the place open for those of us who can't sleep and have nowhere where else to go.'

'You mean the homeless?'

'Oh no, not them. Just those who can't sleep, and have nowhere to go.'

Greg didn't know what to do. He needed time to think. Making his apologies to the friendly man he walked for a long time around the dark streets. Frankie? He must have been mistaken. Mabs's dead husband was Uncle Frank, but she was Mabel. So who was this Frankie who opened a night café to insomniacs and the lonely?

He passed the café twice more and on the second time he heard a shriek of laughter and loud chatter and knew that, whatever she called herself, it *was* his Aunty Mabs in there. He made his way home on his bicycle, curious but marvelling at the secret life of that remarkable old lady.

An hour later he made a decision. He'd talk to his aunt and offer to help. After all, his hours were far from regular and sleeping day or night, depending on the shift, was a way of life. As long as he slept and was completely rested before his shifts, he would certainly be able to help once or twice a week, coming off late shift or when he had a couple of days off. Yes, it might be something he would be willing to share.

Zena was far from happy; she hadn't heard from Jake for a week. He planned to come, and even made suggestions about what they would do during his visit, but every time something happened to cancel, usually something to do with his work which entailed a lot of travel. They spoke on the phone, she wrote letters to which she occasionally received scribbled, apologetic replies explaining that his boss was demanding and he rarely had a minute to call his own and reminding her that at least the savings were increasing. She didn't feel a part of his life any more and wondered whether things would ever return to how they were.

She went into the house called Llyn Hir, and wondered whether her decision to move back there with her parents had been part of the reason Jake was so reluctant to come home. It couldn't conceivably make much difference; he had always lived in lodgings and she had lived alone at the flat, but at least they had that private place where they could sit and make their plans, share their dreams. She would write and ask him, and move back to the flat as soon as she could, if it would help.

The sight of the made up bed in the back room of her parents' home overlooking the garden which had been prepared for when her father returned home from hospital was a constant and grim reminder that there was no sign of him becoming strong enough for this to be considered. His weight loss was alarming and he seemed less and less willing to eat. He slept through most of the visiting hour.

The whole family seemed to be waiting anxiously for something, but without hope of a happy outcome. She was waiting for Jake, Greg was searching for Rose who had 'disappeared' and her mother waited with less and less hope for her father's recovery.

Aunty Mabs had found a tenant for Zena's flat and putting on a brave face, Zena had packed away most of her personal things and put them into her parents' loft, and settled back with her mother and Greg. Now, she wondered how she would really feel about going back to the loneliness of her own place. Greg had been the sensible one, renting his inherited cottage and saving for his future. Her show of independence had been a mistake. She thought of her shattered wedding plans and now Greg's too. Concentrating on Greg's wedding would have helped to take her mind off her own abandoned dream but that had fizzled out in a very odd way.

*

At nine o'clock when Mabs let herself into the night café which she and Frank, had run for a few years, she set to work in an automatic routine. Drawing the curtains over the café windows she turned on the cooker and began preparing scones and a few cakes. She gathered the carrier bag she had left on the counter and unpacked a few pieces of fruit, a couple of loaves, some meat and fish paste and half a dozen eggs. By half past nine, piles of sandwiches were made and displayed on plates, covered with tea towels. The scones looked tempting cooling on the table ready to be filled and put into the glass fronted display unit. Kettles were humming and two minutes later, her first customers arrived.

Sid and George were always the first, although they always waited out of sight until the door curtain was opened. Mabs poured two teas and put them on one of the tables, where dominoes were waiting for them. After the usual greetings they settled down for their first game.

On other tables were board games like ludo and snakes and ladders. There were packs of playing cards on others and on two, chess men were lined up ready for a contest. Newspapers and magazines were piled on a shelf. Over the next hour several tables were filled, tea and coffee and food provided and paid for and the murmur of conversations and laughter added to the sounds of simmering kettles and the clacking of the pieces on the boards. She noted there were two strangers there. People would have heard of the warmth and friendliness offered by the café and the lady called Frankie. On occasions men walking home had opened the door out of curiosity. The newcomers left after drinking a cup of tea and the others settled down to enjoy the pleasant hours.

Then the peaceful scene was disturbed by raised voices and the scraping of a chair being dragged back from a table. Mabs stepped over and took Henry's arm.

'What is it, Henry? Someone upset you?'

'I lost three games of draughts! I never lose that many. *He!*' – he pointed an imperious finger towards his partner, Arthur – 'he must be cheating!'

Arthur stood up and a fight seemed imminent, but Mabs intervened and said sharply, 'Henry, come out here with me. Now, this minute, mind!' Others stood and, after a blustering protest, Henry followed Mabs into the kitchen behind the café. The others stood protectively near, little Sid closest to the kitchen door, making a fist.

'Now, you know the rules, Henry,' they heard Mabs say. 'No arguments and definitely no fighting or you won't be able to come here again.'

Every time he tried to speak, to argue his case, she stopped him. Her heart was racing, knowing he could easily turn on her. He was twice her size and half her age. 'Listen to me. You've been banned from almost every pub in the area and if you carry on like this you'll be banned from here out of consideration for the others. Now, get back out there and I'll make you a fresh cup of tea. No more arguing. Right? No more games tonight, just read the papers and talk to the others.'

He stood for a while in the doorway between the back room and the café and Mabs waited, her body shaking with anxiety. Afraid her voice would tremble she said nothing more, just waited, fingers crossed, until he slowly went back to his seat. When he had calmed down she said, 'When Mr Thomas comes and I can have a break, you can try again to teach me how to play. Although I'll never be as good as you lot.'

The clientele of the night café – called by a few who knew of its existence as the sad café – had a variety of problems. Henry was one of the most serious worries, with his violent temper. Among the rest were those with alcohol problems, insomniacs, the lonely, several living isolated from others through lack of social skills, or with no family or anyone to care about them, and occasionally a very few who were homeless.

The homeless sometimes came to investigate what was on offer but rarely returned. They usually concentrated on finding a place where they could sleep at night, and visiting the café would have meant losing their favoured spot: they found it difficult to find a safe and peaceful place to sleep during the day. There were a few ex-soldiers who had been unable to return to their previous lives; a few were ex-prisoners unable to settle and with nowhere to go during sleepless nights.

Some found the refuge and became regulars for a while until a change of luck, or a growing confidence, led them away to better things; but a small core had been coming for years, including little Sid, George, Arthur and Henry, who Mabs knew was a dangerous man.

Ever since Mabs had retired from work and had been given permission for the night café, she and her husband Frank had spent four nights a week there, sometimes more. When Frank had died and left all the money he had so recently won, she had bought the place and, while it continued to serve as a normal café during the day, the place was hers for the night hours. Social Services were on hand when there was a chance of progress with one of the customers and Richard, a retired teacher, opened on her days of rest. Richard Thomas was himself an insomniac and had come first as a customer, but was now a valued assistant.

People who had learned of the sad café, or who had once been glad of all it offered, sometimes left parcels of food or even clothing there, but the clothes were taken to other organizations to distribute. Her job was giving the lonely and sleepless a few hours of warmth, companionship and food.

It was seven o'clock when she left to catch the first bus home, tired, but as always content with the way her hours had been spent. Now her team of cleaners would come and the place would be thoroughly cleansed for a clientele not that dissimilar to the night café. Lonely people who were grateful for a place where they were able to stretch a cup of tea to last an hour or more.

As she made her way home for a few hours' sleep, she thought again about the money she had been left. It was a responsibility she could happily have done without; blaming the windfall for Frank's death would never change. Deciding what to do with it was a constant concern. She looked on the years she had left as a chance to observe loved ones and friends to decide who would benefit from a gift of money. So far she had been unable to decide on the most needful recipient.

The family had been her first thought, but both Zena and Greg owned a property left to them by their mother's parents and too much too soon was not necessarily a good thing. Zena's Jake needed to take the responsibility of making his way in the world. Too easy and Jake would relax and enjoy not having to worry. Decent enough lad, she mused, but too concerned with pleasing others.

She had heard only last year that he'd given away his valuable watch to a lady widowed during the war who was saving to buy her seriously ill son a wheelchair. She had sold it but the boy had received his chair from a hospital charity. When Mabs told him, Jake had shrugged and said, 'Well, I can't expect to win them all. Better to try though, don't you think?'

Greg and Rose – if they ever made the wedding day – would have a good start. There was the cottage on which Greg had been earning rent since he'd inherited it and he had a good bank balance with which to begin married life. He loved his job, the same job her darling husband Frank had done and having extra money might persuade him to do something different and less enjoyable. He had plans for the future and a large sum of money would maybe change things in a way that was not for the better.

She was curious about the reason for Rose's reluctance to talk about her family. She had moved here from a town the other side of Cardiff and Mabs's spy system didn't reach that far. Her unwillingness to talk to Greg was not a good start to a lifetime commitment but she said nothing. Rose would have a change of heart once she was more confident and Greg was being loving and loyal by not pressing her. She was sure to come home soon and explain what had frightened her.

She didn't know how far Rose had run.

Stepping away from the immediate family there were many good causes and although many were tempting, she was human enough not to want to give to a large invisible organization; which would mean placing a fortune in the hands of someone she would never see, and over which she would have no control. She wanted to give the money to a person whose face she knew, someone she could imagine accepting and benefitting from an unexpected windfall.

Chapter Three

GREG WENT TWICE to the shoe shop where Rose had worked to ask for a forwarding address for her, but they pleaded ignorance. He went to the library pretending she had a book belonging to him and he needed to get in touch, just in case she had talked about her plans to one of the friendly staff. No one could help. The post office had received no forwarding address and the local postman said that anyway, Rose Conelly rarely had anything by post. He even asked at the doctor's surgery and the dentist but there was disapproval at the idea that they would pass on such privileged information.

Rose was renting a small room in south London. She was still afraid to find a legitimate job by which Greg might find her through the references given by the manager of the shoe shop in Cold Brook Vale. Instead she did odd jobs whenever an opportunity occurred. She found work helping to clear a garden for the new tenants of a neglected house, and was offered more of the same. She washed milk bottles and refilled them when an assistant at the local dairy was ill. A baker gave her work for a few mornings and she was paid with bread and left over cakes. She dug an allotment for an elderly man and earned five shillings and some vegetables, which she sold for a shilling as she had nowhere to cook them.

Taking a chance on being seen, she set off one morning back to Cold Brook Vale to collect a few things she had left behind. As the train was leaving Paddington station, a few passengers were walking along the corridor looking for a seat. One of them was Jake. She turned her head away but too late. The door slid open and he came in to the compartment and sat beside her.

'Rose Conelly? Weren't you supposed to be marrying Greg Martin? What happened, why did you run off without an explanation? Frantic he is.'

'I couldn't. So the best thing was for me to move away. He'll have forgotten me by now. We weren't really engaged, whatever he told you. Please, Jake, don't tell him you've seen me.'

'I promise, but tell me, what are you doing? Where do you live?'

Reluctant at first she succumbed to the temptation of talking to someone. She and Jake were unlikely to see each other ever again. They compared details and discovered they were living not far from each other. 'But not for much longer,' Rose told him. 'Greg will have given up trying to find me by now and I can get a better place to live once I have a job.'

'Doing what?'

'I've applied for a position selling beautiful shoes and handbags in a large department store, and I think I'll get it. I've survived on casual work since I came here and I live in a room where no cooking is allowed and a bathroom shared between the other tenants. I stuck it out because I needed the security of having a few pounds saved.'

In those moments of honesty, Jake told her about his terrible accommodation. 'I'll stay in my grotty room until I can persuade Zena to join me. It's so cheap and I can put money aside for our wedding, see.'

'You should keep away from that family,' she warned, which surprised him.

'The Martins are a wonderful family. They're the only people I have in the world. I'm lucky to be part of their lives.'

'The whole family have secrets that would shock you if they were ever told, believe me. Let Zena go, Jake, find someone more deserving of you.'

He didn't argue, presuming that she and Greg had had a disagreement and he was best out of it.

Jake was coming home, Zena sang the words in her mind as she did her various cleaning jobs, a smile on her face that wouldn't go away. This time they would really talk. Perhaps this was the weekend when he'd tell her he was coming home for good, that London had been a mistake and he was returning to Cold Brook Vale where he belonged.

He arrived by train on Friday morning at eleven o'clock, and went to Llyn Hir and explained as he hugged her, that the man who had borrowed their car needed it a while longer. 'I couldn't wait, lovely girl. I had the weekend free of appointments so I took an extra day and here I am. What shall we do? Where shall we go? I feel like a prisoner let out of jail, being back home with you.'

'It's still "home", then?'

'Always will be, love, no matter where we go. Cold Brook Vale will still be home.'

She was laughing at his enthusiasm, hugging him, then holding his arm as he picked up his bags from the doorstep and went inside. 'We'll start this evening, Jake, love. This afternoon I have to work.'

'What? I've got the whole weekend off and you have to work? Oh Zena, what sort of welcome is that?'

Still laughing she explained that it was only two hours between two and four and then she was free

'I'll go to the stationers to see your mam and then to say hello to your Aunty Mabs. That will fill a couple of hours and Aunty Mabs will fill me in on all that's happened while I've been away, I'll get more news from her than your occasional letters,' he teased. She frowned but decided he was joking, knowing he was the one who rarely made contact.

It was a wonderful weekend and the hours fled as they walked and talked and made plans. London was the only black spot as Jake tried to persuade her to join him.

'I keep hoping you'll miss this place so much you'll come home,' she admitted. 'I'm happy here and with Dad ill I really need to be on hand to help.'

'Come for a weekend. I'll find us a nice hotel and show you some of the exciting places London has to offer. I'll book a theatre, and you'll enjoy looking at the amazing shops. We can visit the parks. Oh, and it'll be separate rooms tell your father.' He grinned. 'Unless...?'

She shook her head, and ignoring his last words, said, 'We can't afford it, Jake. I'm not earning much, just enough to survive. But the flat is rented and that money is going into our savings. We don't want to spend what we've struggled to save.'

He pleaded and reasoned and eventually they agreed on a weekend for him to give her a taste of London sometime soon.

With Jake's help, Rose found a better place, a more generously sized bedsit with facilities for simple cooking and he helped her to move her few belongings. It would still be strange, living so far from everything she knew but at least she was comfortable and Jake was a friend. Over the next few days she scoured secondhand shops, and furnished the room comfortably, making it her own. A pretty couch-cum-bed cover, a few ornaments, a picture. The additions made her hopeful of settling to her new life and forgetting the harshness of her parting from Greg.

She occasionally went on dates but always ended a friendship the moment there was a hint of a commitment. She knew she wasn't beautiful and when someone told her she was, it was time to run for the hills!

She was lonely but filled her time learning shorthand and typing, which she didn't enjoy, but the thought of returning to that empty room with no prospects of a knock on her door was a worse alternative, so she studied French as well, leaving just four empty evenings. She closed the curtains and locked the door as soon as she went inside. For the rest of the time she studied and dealt with cleaning. She blamed Greg, both hating him and, at the same time, grieving what she had lost. If only things had been different.

Although not expecting, or planning to, she began to go out with Jake sometimes. She felt at ease with him, no worries about a friendship changing to something more; he was going to marry Zena. Madeleine from the office where he worked, joined them one evening and the three of them went to a concert, tickets provided by Madeleine.

Jake was pleased to see the two people getting on well and they arranged other evenings together.

*

Zena was surprised when she reached home one day to see a smart, blue sports car standing at the gate. Surely not Greg's? Or, heaven forbid, not Jake's? This looked too grand and whoever it belonged to, what was it doing here? She went in calling, 'Mam? Whose car is this? Surely not Greg's? He always says he doesn't need one.'

Her mother came out and behind her was Sam. 'It's yours, Zena,' her mother said, 'but Sam had better explain.'

'Mine? But I haven't bought a car!'

'A man called Bill Harvey brought it, but as there was no one in, he left it with me. He'd borrowed it to take his children on holiday, and Jake asked him to deliver it back to you.'

'I don't understand. To go on holiday? Jake told me the man, a colleague from work, needed it for work as his had broken down.'

Sam frowned, raised his shoulders in a 'You know what Jake is like' kind of gesture.

'This Bill Harvey,' he went on, 'said that Jake is the kindest, most generous man he's ever known. He did extra deliveries in his own time for him when his children were ill and refused to take a penny in payment. He sent flowers to Madeleine the secretary when she was off with a twisted ankle and called to see her twice to see if she needed help.' Sam looked at Zena with a quizzical expression. 'A decent bloke, your Jake?' It was more than a question than a comment.

'Yes,' Zena relied, forcing a smile that quickly faded to a frown. Surely Jake hadn't bought a car just to lend it to this Bill Harvey? She wondered how much of their savings had disappeared as he concentrated on being a 'decent bloke'.

When Sam had gone, leaving the papers and keys of the car, Lottie asked what she was going to do. 'Keep it? Sell it?'

'Jake is foolish at times but he's a generous man who can't resist helping someone in trouble. It's something I have to understand and live with.' Zena frowned. 'Uncle Sam has never liked Jake, has he?'

'Sam still blames Jake for the death of his son. Jake was with Peter when he fell into the sea. He ran to get help and Sam believes he could have saved Peter if he'd stayed. No one else blamed Jake. He was only twelve and he ran for help, which was all he could do.

But nothing will persuade Sam of that. He believes Jake ran away instead of trying to save Peter.'

The car sat there while Zena waited for Jake to explain – waited for any communication from him, but none came.

Greg knew he had to give up searching for Rose. It was clear that she didn't want to be found. The only address he had was for the house which she had pretended was her home, where he had frequently left her after an evening out. Stupidly he knocked again to see if they had any idea where she might be. The tenants had no idea why she had lied. He still half hoped that the problem which had caused her to run away would be solved and she would return to him.

While he couldn't forget Rose, there was nothing more he could do and meanwhile there was the mystery of Aunty Mabs. He was still hesitant to walk into the night café and, although he had tried to offer opportunities for her to talk about it, he felt he was prying. If she wanted them to know she would tell them.

For some reason she wanted to keep her involvement in the place a private affair. Could it be a bridge club? A charity secretly raising funds? Political meetings? He didn't think Mabs would play bridge and she was even less likely to belong to a political party. He eventually learned about the night café through the friendly approach of the little man called Sid, and smiled at the possibilities he'd considered.

Having made up his mind to face her, he stepped inside one night, but instead of Mabs, a man stood behind the counter smiling a welcome. Richard, Mabs's loyal assistant, knew who Greg was and saw no reason not to explain. So he told him the story between light-heartedly settling arguments and providing teas and snacks.

It had begun with Greg's Uncle Frank who had worked as a bus driver as Greg now did. During his late night journeys he had noticed a few people, mostly men, just wandering, apparently aimlessly passing the night hours. He had stopped to speak to several and learned that, unable to sleep for various reasons, they walked around, occasionally meeting others, to stand and talk on a corner or climb the fence to sit on a bench in the park, to get through the lonely hours of darkness. Frank discussed it with Mabs, and the night café was born.

Intrigued, Greg wanted to help but was still unsure how to approach his aunt, until early one morning he saw the first bus pass the café and, moments later, saw her rushing out, locking the café door and staring after the bus in obvious dismay. He rode towards her on his bike and stopped beside her, 'Morning. Want a lift? You can have the saddle, and I'll pedal.'

'Oh Greg, I've been visiting a friend, I have. And I missed the early bus. Don't worry about me, I'll get a taxi.'

'Hop on, I can manage a little one like you.'

With much laughter, Mabs climbed onto the saddle and, with her feet sticking out and Greg standing on the pedals, struggling good humouredly up the hills, free wheeling down again, they made their way to Mabs's flat.

'A cup of tea would go down well,' Greg said, following her inside. 'You put your feet up and I'll make it. Right?' He grinned and added, 'There's tired you must be, looking after a friend, or two, or three ...'

'You know,' she said, rhetorically.

'Yes, I do. I wanted to tell you and ask if I can help, but I wasn't sure how you'd feel about me knowing.' He winked at her. 'I see all sorts of things from my bus!'

'The night café was something me and your Uncle Frank started.'

'I know.'

'When he died I just had to keep it going. It's such a help to these lonely people – so many you wouldn't believe.' She stopped and stared at him. 'You knew it was my Frank who started it?'

'None of the family has guessed. So, can I help? Shift work means I often have freedom at the right time.' Mabs promised to think about it and Greg left her to sleep and rode home content with his night.

Helping in the café would help to take his mind off Rose too, although he still had the unextinguishable hope of her appearing. He even practised what he would say to her, sometimes promising not to ask a single question, sometimes showing anger and hurt, shaming her into telling her story.

*

Zena was at the hospital when her father turned his head and asked, 'What about you and Jake? Will he be coming home, d'you think? Or will we have to say goodbye to you as you move away from us?'

'I keep hoping Jake will come home,' she admitted.

'Can't you try living in London for a while before making a decision?'

'That would be expensive, Daddy. I have to make a firm decision to go, or,' she added softly 'or to stay.'

'Expensive maybe, but cheaper than messing up your life and having to start again.' He closed his eyes and took a few wavering breaths before adding, 'Think carefully my darling girl. Happiness is something we can be too careless with sometimes.'

Zena hugged him gently, afraid of hurting him, he was so frail. 'Thank you, Daddy. I will think about what I really want, I promise you.'

Good,' he whispered, his voice almost failing.

She left the ward to allow her parents to say their affectionate goodnight and glanced back to see he was asleep, his hand still holding her mother's.

Zena did think about what she really wanted and was certain that Jake was an important part of it, but moving away from her family and the place she loved, that was not an easy decision. Sleep wouldn't come and she read until the words wouldn't leave the page. The half formed plan for a London weekend had been forgotten.

She pictured the affectionate way her parents held hands, whispered to each other. She knew their feelings for each other were genuine and all encompassing. Whatever happened to them in their lives, nothing would change that. She was affected by the surety of the love they shared and a glimmer of doubt filled her mind. Did she and Jake have a love to compare with that? She couldn't honestly say yes.

At three o'clock she crept down stairs and made a pot of tea and took the tray to her room. At six o'clock she stood outside the back door listening to the starlings in the trees a couple of fields away beginning to chatter as they roused each other to start their day.

A decision hadn't come and she didn't think it would without Jake here to discuss it. She hadn't heard from him for more than a week and, when she had telephoned the office, the secretary called Madeleine Jones had answered. She told Zena officiously that he was out of the office and why should she know where to find him?

When Zena called at Mr Roberts's one morning he wasn't at home. She wondered whether he'd had a hospital appointment and had forgotten to tell her. But to reassure herself that he wasn't in any trouble, she knocked at his neighbour's house and was told by Doris that he was indeed in hospital but because he'd had a fall.

There was a bus due that would take her to the hospital so she left her bicycle and ran to the bus stop. A few enquiries, a brief stop to buy some sweets and a newspaper and she was directed to the ward. Insisting she was someone who would help to look after him when he went home, she was allowed a brief visit. He was sitting up in bed looking older and more frail than she'd expected.

'Mr Roberts! What happened to you?'

'I was reaching up to change a light bulb, fool that I am.'

'By reach up, I hope you don't mean you were on a stool?'

'I've done it before,' he muttered, then looked up and smiled. 'A long time ago, mind.'

After the usual warnings during which he promised to be sensible but smiling and without sounding sincere, they discussed what Zena and Doris should do to help him. The doctor didn't expect him to stay in hospital very long and explained that he would be discharged in a day or so with plaster and a sling supporting a bruised shoulder and a broken arm. She decided to take advantage of his absence in hospital and clean corners and cupboards that she hadn't been able to do without disturbing him.

Risking the outraged protests of the nurse, she begged just a few moments to see her father. To her surprise this was granted. Ronald was asleep and muttering in a distressed way and although she stayed until the nurse returned, he didn't fully wake. She was upset as she left the ward.

As she was leaving she was surprised to see her next client, Janey

Day, who was on duty at the hospital information deck. She quickly explained what had happened. 'I'll be late but I'll work the usual two hours as soon as I can get there,' Zena promised. She caught the bus back to do her two hours' work for Mr Roberts then set off for the house of Mrs Day. She was more than three hours late and unfortunately, when she reached Janey's house, instead of finding the house empty, Trish Francis, Janey's mother was there. She stood silently watching as Zena propped her bicycle against the garage wall. Her arm was raised and she looked from her watch to Zena and back again. 'I hope you intend to make up your time, Miss Martin.'

'Of course, Mrs Francis. One of my clients has had an accident and I went to the hospital to see how I can help,' Zena replied politely.

'On my daughter's time!'

'Not at all.'

'I shall have to tell my daughter of your unreliability.'

'No need, she already knows.' Pushing past her, Zena set to work and ignored the disapproving woman who followed her, hoping for a chance to complain. Determined not to be browbeaten by her she completed her tasks and left precisely two hours later, smiling sweetly.

Although it was late in the day she rang her mother then went back to Mr Roberts's house to make sure everything would be comfortable for his homecoming. Polishing a cupboard door, the clasp slid down and the door opened, allowing a pile of letters to fall out. She picked them up, stacked them neatly and closed the cupboard. As the door swung back she saw a letter she had missed. There was no envelope and she was embarrassed to see that it addressed Ray Roberts in affectionate terms. The handwriting was large and the words 'Dearest' and 'Darling' were in extra large letters. Tempted to read on, she was shocked to realize it was a letter not of love but filled with anger. Ashamed of prying, she was unable to resist reading the signature. It was from someone called, Donna.

She glanced around the room as though afraid someone would see her and know of her disgraceful nosiness. She had read enough to learn that the writer had been let down by Roy Roberts. There were demands for money, with threats. The franking on the envelope was dated twenty-two years ago. It must have meant something to him if he'd kept it for all this time. She wondered what had happened to cause such anger and felt a sadness for the man who spent so much of his time alone.

She carefully put the letter among the rest and continued cleaning the room. As though to pay for her inquisitiveness, she spent longer than she planned, and set off home contented.

Cycling down the lane heading for the main road, she heard a car coming behind her. The sound increased as the driver accelerated then it skidded past her causing her to wobble and almost lose her balance. It was gone in a flash but she recognized the driver and the car: Janey's oh-so-charming mother, Trish Francis.

She was feeling angry as she cycled on towards Llynn Hir and was glad when a van stopped beside her and Uncle Sam called out offering her a lift. The bicycle was put into the van with the sheep dog, Digby, and she slipped into the front seat and sighed with relief. Then she told him about the unhappy visit to her father, and difficult Trish Francis, making that part of the story amusing, the anger swiftly gone.

'I remember her,' Sam said with a frown. 'We were at school together. She hasn't anything to be uppity about. She's feeling important since her daughter married a wealthy businessman, but that sort of success doesn't rub off on the rest of the family, does it? It can't change who they are, much as she'd like to think so.'

Zena was glad she had refused to work for the woman. 'Her daughter Janey is very pleasant.'

'She takes after her dad, luckily for her!'

Back at Llyn Hir, Sam retrieved her bike from the van, and she thanked him and waved as he drove away. Since her father had been in hospital, Sam called more often to see how he could help. When Lottie's car was out of action for a few days, he arranged his days to be able to take her to the hospital and often gave Greg and Zena lifts to save them waiting for buses, or struggling with a bicycle when the weather was unkind.

Zena was worried that Lottie was becoming dependent on the

kindly farmer, and once her father was home, guessed that Sam would also miss his involvement with the Martin family. Then the reminder came with a jolt that her father's recovery was less and less certain. So perhaps they would be glad of Uncle Sam's help for a long time.

Worried about her father, when she reached home she tried to telephone Jake but Madeleine Jones again told her she had no idea where he could be. Madeleine then lowered the phone very slightly, making sure Zena could hear, and said sarcastically that she wasn't a lonely hearts club for pathetic women clinging to a man who obviously no longer cared. When the phone disconnected, Madeleine looked at her notebook, and marked the call as a wrong number. That was another contact which she had no intention of passing on to Jake.

Zena heard every word, as Madeleine had intended, and was shocked. Did she sound so pathetic having to admit time and again that she had no idea how to get in touch with Jake? She ignored the spiteful comment about Jake no longer caring. She reached for pad and paper and wrote to him, marked the envelope private and confidential and addressed to the office. At least that would get through. The person dealing with the post would put that aside until he saw Jake.

Angry with Jake, and herself, she wrote a short, impatient note asking him to get in touch and give her some way of contacting him apart from the office in case of an emergency. It seemed that only something serious would persuade him to talk to her. Trembling with annoyance at Madeleine's attitude, she went out and posted it.

The company for whom Jake worked had their offices in a large building that was home to three other companies. All the mail went to a front office where it was sorted into the various piles by an elderly 'post boy'. It was then delivered to the relevant office. Madeleine had always given the tedious task of sorting it between the members of staff to a junior typist, but since she began taking an interest in Jake and his stupid girlfriend, she did it herself. Zena's latest letter was opened, read and discarded.

Mabs couldn't decide what she should do about Greg. Now he knew, the secret of her night café would soon be out. Like a game of Chinese whispers, the story would be passed from ear to ear, distorting and changing as it was repeated. Soon it would be general, and probably inaccurate, knowledge. If she accepted Greg's help he might try to keep the secret as he had promised, but one day he would be unable to resist sharing it and that would be the end of the valuable oasis of warmth and friendliness for those who needed it. The secret was shared sooner than expected.

When Zena called for lunch on the following Friday, she hesitatingly said, 'Aunty Mabs, Greg told me about your night café and I think it's a wonderful thing you are doing. I promise neither Greg nor I will say nothing.'

With a sigh, Mabs said, 'Tell no one, except, just one?'

'You mean Jake? No, I won't tell Jake. He isn't the most reliable one to hold a secret. Much as I love him, I know him well enough to understand that. He's so friendly, wants to be everyone's friend and he'd be boasting about your wonderful generosity within hours! Keeping a secret like that would be impossible for him. So, no, I won't even tell Mam or Dad. That's a firm promise. If Greg helps you, and he really wants to, you can trust us.'

It was time to take a chance so when she next saw Greg, she told him she would be glad of his help on the occasions when he was free. Greg had no shifts for two days and he started that night.

He arrived at the same time as Mabs and stood watching as she went to the back room where the food was prepared, to fill plates, fill the heater and turn it on for hot water. The tables were washed then she distributed boxes of games and playing cards. Better not to try and help too soon, he decided, he'd only be in the way or get things wrong.

The regulars came as soon as the lights showed in the café and the door opened to reveal Sid and George followed by Henry and Arthur and two hesitant strangers. They greeted Mabs and nodded politely towards Greg. 'You used to be a bus driver, didn't you?' George asked.

'No, you must have seen my twin,' Greg replied. George nodded.

Better not to say more. Frankie's night café wasn't the place to ask questions.

More men arrived and Greg was soon pouring tea and coffee and handing out cakes, taking the coins and joining in the casual chatter in a joking manner that entertained the regulars.

Henry was very quiet and he stared at Greg, his eyes darting away when Greg saw him staring. Towards the end of the night Greg took a cup of tea and sat beside him. 'Fancy a game of draughts, mate?'

'No. Chess is my game.'

'I'm no good at chess, I can't think ahead and you have to work out several moves, don't you? You must be a lot cleverer than me.'

'What d'you mean by that? Because I come to a place like this, I must be stupid?'

'Not at all, I was saying that *I'm* not clever enough to play chess.'

Henry tilted the table and the chess board and pieces fell to the floor. Mabs shouted a warning and Henry went out slamming the door behind him.

'Oh, heck! Will I be allowed to come again, d'you think?' Greg said with a sigh.

The customers dispersed soon after and he helped clean up before he and Mabs went to get on the first bus back to Mab's flat where he had left his bike.

'Sorry, I didn't realize how touchy he is.'

'Forget it. I don't think it's the right thing to walk around him on tiptoe; he has to learn to tolerate other people or he'll never be able to mix with people socially.'

'Do you know much about him?'

'Nothing that I want to discuss.' She smiled to take the sting out of her words but added, 'We never pry, dear. We listen, but offer no suggestions regarding family problems. We can help sometimes, mind. We can pass them on to the various organizations willing to come and talk to any of them seeking help, but only when they ask.'

'I'll be very careful, Aunty Mabs,' he promised.

He didn't stay long. Mabs needed to sleep and he too was ready for his bed.

On his next visit to the night café, he had a grudging apology from Henry. Greg smiled and challenged him to a game of draughts, which Henry stared at disparagingly then nodded, and trounced him winning three out of four games.

Greg worked with Mabs over the next few weeks and gradually the regulars and newcomers more or less ignored him, a sign that he had been accepted, according to Mabs. It helped to take his mind off finding Rose, although every day he hoped it would be the day on which she came back to him. He knew he had to let her go, but it was not knowing why. What was it that had caused her to run away? That was stopping him from moving on.

Zena was at the hospital with Lottie one evening when her mother whispered to her father, 'I think our Greg has forgotten Rose Conelly at last, dear. He's out so often in the evenings and comes in very late. That must mean a girl, don't you think?'

A chuckle emanated from the wizened man lying on the bed. 'Good on him, I say.'

'So do I, dear. Rose had too many secrets. Better she left when she did rather than go through a marriage without Greg being absolutely certain.

'Not like us.' Ronald reached for Lottie's hand. 'We never had any doubts, did we?'

'No. Not for a single moment.'

In London, late one night Jake was walking back to his room, having been to the pictures. He was carrying fish and chips and his briefcase which he used to deliver messages and occasionally collect payments. Poking a finger through the soggy newspaper he managed to pull out a few chips and chewed, tossing the hot food from side to side to ease the discomfort as his mouth burned. As he approached his doorway, a couple of figures suddenly ran towards him and for a moment he smiled a greeting but they grabbed his arm pulled the briefcase from him, threw the package of food on the ground and ran off. Angrily he ran after them, demanding his briefcase back. One of the men turned and ran back but before Jake knew what was happening, he had been punched and pushed to the ground. He fell heavily and felt a severe pain in the elbow. Then he was rolled around roughly as the man searched his pockets and gave him a couple of vicious kicks and punches before running off with loose change and his wallet.

There were several payments in there and his first confused thoughts were how he would explain to his boss how he had lost them. Several of the smaller payments had been paid in cash, none large, but together they amounted to more than fifty pounds.

Struggling up, standing still until he was sure of his balance, he wasn't sure what to do. He had no money and, after a fruitless search no keys either. He was too far away from the flat where his friend Stanley lived but remembered that Madeleine Jones, the secretary, lived much closer. Supporting his painful arm with the other, he walked through the streets, shocked and aching where he had been punched and kicked. He felt blood trickling down his face and wiped it off with a sleeve. Heading for Madeleine, he wondered whether he should go first to the hospital but decided that all he needed was a bit of sympathy then the police.

A few bruises and a cut on his face was all he'd suffered and they would soon mend. He arm ached badly though and he stopped and removed his jacket, and fixed a sling with the sleeves. He leant on a wall for a few minutes then walked on.

Madeleine greeted him at first with delight and then concern. After a cup of hot, sweet tea she went with him to the hospital and from there he reported the assault to the police.

'I'd better let Zena know what happened,' he said, as Madeleine led him back to her flat in the early morning. 'Would you mind if I give her your address?'

'Best not to worry her,' she said conveniently ignoring his question. 'Let's wait until you're better. She can't do anything and would only worry unnecessarily. You can stay with me until you've recovered.'

She settled him to sleep on her couch with extra cushions to support his arm and a blanket over him. As he relaxed into sleep she watched him. What a stupid man he was, lying to his fiancée, a young woman who was even more pathetic than he. She smiled. At least she could have a bit of fun, interfering and clouding the waters even more than he was doing already. She loved getting involved and messing up so called happy couples. Her childhood had taught her little, except that men were unreliable and women were fools. Playing with these firmly held beliefs, was a game which she enjoyed.

Mabs was at the hospital one afternoon and she was alarmed when Ronald seemed to be unaware of her being there and was talking in a very confused manner. He was obviously distressed about something but his voice was low, the words unclear. He was convinced he was talking to someone called Billy Dove. Mabs called the nurse who administered to him behind curtains, then said that he was calmer but sleeping, and perhaps it would be better to come back later.

'My brother is very ill, isn't he,' she said to the nurse.

'Yes, Mrs Bishop, but we never give up hope.'

'What shall I tell his wife?'

'That's for you to decide,' the nurse said kindly.

Mabs went to the house near the lake and tried to tell Lottie something of what Ronald had been saying. 'He was very upset, muttering something about how he needed to get everything put right before he ran out of time. He was asking someone called Billy Dove to "get on with it", and "get everything sorted". Never heard of Billy Dove, have you?'

Back at the hospital watching over a restless Ronald, they mulled over the words for a long time but came up with nothing to explain them. He called several times for Billy to come and get things finished, but none of it made any sense. They stayed in the hospital until four o'clock in the hope of being told of an improvement but then, advised to go home, they left, still hearing Ronald talking to Billy in a croaking voice unlike his own.

Rose returned to Cold Brook Vale and dealt with the business she had come back for, in a short time. She was tempted to walk around the area before leaving, just one more look at the places which had begun to feel like home. She had made sure no one would recognize her, by wearing a hat, some glasses that made the world a bit hazy and a long, unattractive coat. On an impulse she spent the vouchers she had called to collect then, as shops began to close and the small town emptied of people, she wandered through streets and lanes she had walked with Greg and dreamed that stupid dream of. 'What if …' surely the most stupid words in the English language. Nothing would change. Greg's evil family had destroyed her life completely, her last chance of finding happiness.

It was dark and getting cold and, on the way back to the station with an hour to kill, she saw the café and decided to have a hot drink and something to eat. As she approached the door she peeped inside and was alarmed to see Greg and Mabs behind the counter pouring tea from a large teapot and laughing at something that was being said. What on earth were they doing there? She hurried away, and didn't feel safe until she had turned several corners.

How easily she could have walked in to face them! She wished she had forgotten the money she was owed and stayed away. She looked around her, fixing scenes and memories firmly into her mind, knowing she must never again come back.

The reason for her return to the town was the Twenty Club that staff at the shop had arranged. Twenty people paid a pound each week and, each week, one of the participants would have a twenty pound, one shilling voucher to spend at one of the local department stores. A draw was made to decide the order of distribution. Rose, having continued to send the weekly payments, had the voucher that week and she had to come back to spend it. She had dreamed of using it to buy things for her wedding. So foolish to have dreamed of the impossible, and having to face heartbreak.

If only she had been brave enough to tell Greg her story, but she knew now that would have led to even more painful heartbreak once the final dreadful truth had been disclosed. He would never understand. In her saddest moments she imagined the horrified expression on his face as she said the awful words.

Spending the money had not been enjoyable. She had imagined buying something beautiful for the cottage Greg owned. Instead, with little real interest, she picked up a random selection of clothes. Then she changed her mind and put them all back on the rails. Instead she bought towels, sheets, pillow cases, adding to the value of the voucher to buy good quality items. Even if she couldn't live with Greg, she would have a home of her own one day, so why not concentrate on that? Defiantly she added a teapot and some pretty cups and saucers to her packages, struggling as she walked to the station with parcels in her arms and carrier bags dangling from her hands. The porter had looked after them while she wandered until it was time for her train.

After collecting them and giving the porter a tip, she stood on the platform looking down the track. She would find an empty carriage and spend the journey day-dreaming of Greg and what might have been. She felt utterly miserable. This was the final goodbye to what should have been a wonderful future.

Greg saw her when he was on his way to the bus garage to find a hot meal in the canteen and begin his shift. He followed her to the station, where she was standing surrounded by her shopping. He bought a platform ticket and walked to where she stood, all alone, facing away from him. He didn't speak until he was behind her.

'Rose? Where have you been? When are you coming back to me?'

She turned, white-faced. It was as though she had conjured him up from her desperate misery.

'Greg! Please don't ask me. I have to get back to London. I can't come back to you.'

'Why?'

'I just can't.'

'At least tell me why. What did I do to make you leave so suddenly? Did I make demands about our families meeting before you were ready? Tell me and we can put it right.' Then he picked up one of the parcels and stared at her. 'Bedding? China? You've found someone else? Why couldn't you tell me?'

'Greg. I'm sorry.'

The train came, he helped load her shopping and she got on without another word. 'Tell me, why?' he shouted, as the train began to puff importantly, belching steam and smoke, sounding its whistle and making juddering movements as it made its slow escape. 'You owe me that at least!' He stood as the train moved away faster and faster, staring after it until the last puff of smoke had faded from the sky.

Christmas passed in a confusion of half planned and carelessly executed arrangements. The presents were unwrapped and handed out with little ceremony, the crackers lay unused in their boxes and the food a confusion of hurried meals as and when they could be managed. The whole time was punctuated with visits to the hospital and long anxious discussions about Ronald's worsening illness. Jake wasn't there. He had phoned to say he had fallen and hurt his leg and would come once he felt able to manage the journey.

As spring magically turned the trees into a miracle of bird song, fresh new, slowly unfurling green leaves, and the glories of the first flowers, changing every day and becoming more and more beautiful, Ronald Martin died. Mabs was with him as he slowly relaxed into the unmistakable peace of the last farewell. He had been talking softly but Mabs understood little of what he had said. She called the doctor, then went to the phone to let Lottie know.

'He was rambling on about property and investments, but I couldn't follow what he was trying to say,' she told her sister-in-law. 'It was as though he was talking not to me, but someone else, someone he could see but I couldn't. There were names he mentioned before, Billy Dove, among others. He's made a will, I understood that.'

Lottie was surprised. 'A will? I don't think so, Mabs, dear. Everything was in joint ownership – not that there is very much. Just the house and some savings for our old age. I'd have known if Ronald had made one and I'd have been involved in the decisions.'

'It's with Davies, Davies and Philips. Or so he said.'

'How odd. It's all so simple. There wasn't any need for a formal will.'

Family and friends gathered once the procedures were underway. They talked about the times when life had been carefree, of the childhood years, and of how everything had suddenly changed when Ronald had become ill. They ate snacks, drank tea and Lottie made a list of the people they needed to tell.

Zena phoned Jake's office and the place where he was supposedly living, but couldn't contact him. I'll write to the office. They're sure to know where he is. If he's on his travels the office has to be the quickest way of getting the news to him, she decided. Aware of his real address, Greg wrote too, but not being certain of the house number and aware of the multi-occupancy of the houses in that drab area, his letter was returned to him a few days later.

In the office, Madeleine Jones read Zena's letter regarding the death of her father and threw it away. She bought some of Jake's favourite food and went home to where Madeleine had persuaded him to stay. She prepared their meal and said casually, 'Zena hasn't written for a while. Losing interest now you're so far away, I expect. Absence makes the heart grow fonder? That's a lot of nonsense.'

'It's true of me! Zena is busy, that's all. When I persuade her to join me we'll be fine.'

'Do you think so?'

Jake didn't sleep well that night. What was he doing there? He should have gone home to recuperate after the attack, with Zena and her family – his family. With no relatives, Zena, Ronald, Lottie, Greg and Aunty Mabs were the only family he had – or needed. Going find Madeleine after the attack had been a mistake, and being persuaded to stay had been a worse one. But how could he have faced going back to that dreadful place when he had the offer of a few more days in the comfort of Madeleine's flat and her caring attention? He lay on Madeleine's couch, wide awake, planning how he would explain his stupidity to Zena.

Greg was upset after seeing Rose again and the evidence that she had found someone else repeated and repeated in his head. With little hope, he decided to try one more time to find her. He needed to know why, then he'd be able to let it rest. The fact that she was in London was no help but if he could find out which area he might have a chance. He went first to the railway station and spoke to the ticket inspector, whom he knew slightly. He had been on duty when Rose left and remembered Greg shouting after her. 'I don't know her but remember her working in the shoe shop.'

It had been a quiet time when Rose had caught the train back to London and Greg learned that her ticket was for Paddington. 'No use whatsoever!' he muttered in dismay. She could be going anywhere. He thought he might ask Jake to help in the search. After all, he probably didn't have much to do in his spare time and he might enjoy the company. Yes. Next time he had a few days off he would go to see Jake. He'd be letting Mabs down but she would understand.

He knew from his sister that Jake was not very good at letter writing so he decided to just go straight to Jake's office. He wondered whether to invite Zena to go with him. It would be a nice surprise for Jake, and Zena would be so glad to spend some time with him.

Jake had fully recovered from his injuries. There was just the inconvenience of a plaster on his arm. He hadn't gone back to work and was still staying at Madeleine's flat, being spoilt and, he had to admit, enjoying it. She was very attentive, aware of what he needed before he knew himself. He wrote to Zena, telling her what had happened and promised to come home now his injuries had faded and no longer looked frightening. He gave it to Madeleine to post and she tore it up and put it in the first waste bin she passed. It wasn't until Zena telephoned the office at a time when Madeleine was out that she learned about the attack.

'Zena,' Greg called as he walked through the door. 'I'm going to London for a couple of days, would you like to come? It's unlikely, but Jake might be able to help me find Rose.'

'You've spoken to him? You know about his injuries? Why didn't you tell me? It's no wonder I haven't heard from him, he was afraid of worrying me. Although he should have written when I told him Dad had died.'

'What injuries?'

'He was attacked. Money and his briefcase were stolen. He was beaten up and has a broken arm.'

'Will you come then? Aunty Mabs will stay with Mam.'

'Let's get the funeral over first. Jake's sure to be back for that.

Then we'll arrange a few days with him. It's what we had once planned.'

They discussed this for a while and decided to go during the week following their father's funeral, when Greg had three days off and Zena would have time to rearrange her days.

Every day Zena delayed setting off to her cleaning jobs to wait for the post hoping for a letter from Jake. 'Perhaps he can't get to a phone,' she said to her mother.

'Or maybe he doesn't like funerals.' Lottie suggested. 'We had a neighbour once who refused to attend a funeral, ever.'

'That doesn't explain the lack of a letter or a phone call. If he can't get to a phone box, surely there's someone who'd ring for him?'

'He'll be there, dear. Jake may be absentminded but he wouldn't miss supporting us on that terrible day.'

The funeral was a surprisingly quiet affair. Ronald had been ill for some time, in and out of hospital, and had lost contact with men he had worked with, and most of the local people with whom he had previously enjoyed socializing. Only twenty people went back to the house where Zena and Aunty Mabs had prepared food. There was no sign of Jake. Greg found Zena standing outside the back door alone, and, seeing she was upset, he put an arm around her. 'Don't be sad, Dad wasn't having much of a life, was he?'

She turned a tearful face towards him. 'If another person asks why Jake isn't here I'll scream.'

'Don't worry, next week we'll find out.'

'I know I'm always making excuses for him but maybe he didn't get the letters I wrote?'

'You finding excuses for Jake, me going to London in the foolish hope of finding Rose – who clearly doesn't want to be found – a right pair, aren't we?'

With Sam helping, Greg moved the bed they had prepared for their father's convalescence back upstairs and put the house back to normal. Ronald's clothes and personal belongings were away in his wardrobe; that was something their mother had to deal with. 'I hate this,' Zena said tearfully. 'It's as though we're brushing Dad out of our lives.'

A week later, leaving Lottie in the care of Mabs, they set off.

They went straight to Jake's office. 'Then, if he isn't there we can try the address of the flat he shares with his friend,' Zena decided.

Greg shook his head. 'Sorry, Sis but that's a secret I really have kept from you,' he admitted. He told her about his previous visit and the sad place where Jake lived.

'I'm beginning to realize that I don't know Jake at all,' she said in angry disbelief, 'and I was planning to commit myself to him for the rest of my life.'

'I thought I knew Rose.'

They went by underground to central London. Rose took a deep breath as they walked towards the office. It was closed. 'Take me to the place where he lives,' she said. 'I want this sorted. Is this really where he works? Or is *everything* a pack of lies?'

'On the day I met him, he was coming out of this place and he carried a brief case and waved as he left, calling "good bye" and "see you tomorrow", I'm sure he was working here then. But what's happened since I don't know.'

'Perhaps we should go home and forget about Rose and Jake.'

Greg took her to the mean street where he had previously met Jake and they knocked at the door of the room and waited. There was no response until a nearby door opened and a man told them that the occupant of the room hadn't been seen for several days. 'It's like that here,' he explained lugubriously. 'People come and they go and we never see them again.' Greg thanked the man and led Zena away.

'Now what?' Zena said with a sigh.

'We'll go to the hotel and try again tomorrow.'

When they went again to Jake's office, they gave their names to a receptionist who knocked on a door and called Miss Jones. There was no response. She opened the door saw the office was empty and shrugged. 'She isn't here. I'm sorry but I don't know where she is or how long she'll be.'

Crouched behind a filing cabinet Madeleine waited, then called the receptionist and told her never to admit those people, whispering that they were looking for her over a romance she'd had to end. Hiding a smile of amused disbelief, the receptionist promised.

Having nowhere else to continue their searches, they went to the theatre on their last evening. 'Better than sitting in the hotel moping,' Greg said. 'This has all been a waste of time.'

'Not completely. It's helped me realize there's no point in searching for someone who doesn't want to be found.' She turned to her brother. 'We should both give up.'

When they got back to Llyn Hir, to Zena's disbelief the door opened before Greg could find his key and Jake burst out and hugged her. 'Darling! My lovely girl! I had no idea you'd lost your father. Why didn't you tell me?'

'Where have you been? We've tried everywhere to find you. I've phoned the office and spoken to that Madeleine woman and written to the flat you're supposed to be sharing and to the office, marking the letter private. We've been to London and no one seems to know where you've been.'

All the time she was scolding him he was staring at her and smiling. 'Oh, Zena. My lovely girl. How I've missed you.' With his arms around her making her aware for the first time of the plaster on his forearm, they walked into the house.

'Have you really been to London? Why didn't you tell me you were coming? We'd have had a wonderful time.'

'I think Miss Madeleine Jones has been careless with messages and post, don't you?'

'No, it must be some mix up in the post room.'

'They handle phone calls as well, do they?' she said sarcastically.

He knew he ought to tell her exactly what had happened and where he had been staying – she had obviously not received his letters, but he said nothing. Madeleine must have held back the letter, not wanting to worry Zena, kindly believing it better to wait until he was recovered. He explained that the shabby room was so he could put more money aside for their wedding, and about failing to mention the attack, presuming that was where she had addressed her letter. He said nothing about how Madeleine had looked after him. That wouldn't have impressed her at all. There were times, he decided, when lying was simple common sense,

81

On Lottie's behalf, Mabs called to talk to the solicitor who had drawn up Ronald's will. 'Can you come to the house when all the family are there?' she asked.

'If you wish, but there don't appear to be any difficulties. It's quite straightforward, Mrs Bishop.'

The solicitor called at Llyn Hir on the day following Zena's and Greg's return from London. Jake was present for the reading. The solicitor had described it as straightforward, but he told Lottie in private that things had come to light which changed everything. 'There has obviously been a change in Mr Ronald Martin's circumstances and a new will should have been fully discussed. This is the only one we have, unless you have something about which I haven't been informed.'

'Just read it, please.'

'Very well.' He coughed nervously. 'To begin, I have to tell you this house had been re-mortgaged. I have no information regarding why this was necessary, the money is nowhere to be found. The debt on it was more than the money in your joint bank accounts will clear.'

'That cannot be right! We have shares and investments that would easily clear the full cost of this house twice over.'

'The stocks and investments are there no longer, I'm afraid.'

'But—we were saving for the children's future and our retirement. What's happened?'

'If I can continue, please, Mrs Martin?' Zena noticed the man's hands were shaking as he went on. 'The money in the joint bank account to be distributed as my wife sees fit between herself and our children. For Lottie there is the jewellery I have bought her. A hundred pounds is left to Mabs in appreciation of her sisterly love and affection.'

Aware that Lottie had known nothing of the contents, although Ronald had assured him she was in complete agreement, the solicitor muttered about arranging probate and keeping in touch and left, leaving the family silent in shock and disbelief.

When they had recovered sufficiently to speak, both Greg and Zena offered the money they had been left, to their mother to help pay off the mortgage.

Although she actually had enough money to clear the debt completely, and with more to spare, Mabs offered her only the one hundred pounds she had been left and asked, 'Why did he do this to you, Lottie?' When Lottie shook her head, Mabs insisted, 'Come on, this is a terrible indication of the state of your marriage, you must know why!'

Lottie went to her room and Mabs glared out through the window, and said finally. 'Give me a lift home, will you, Jake? I want to be on my own to try and make sense of this.' Then she turned and glared at the brother and sister. 'You must know what was wrong, living in the same house as them, you *must* know! Tell me. Please.' Zena and Greg shook their heads, completely confused by the last words of their father.

Long after Mabs had gone and Zena and Greg were asleep. Lottie picked up the phone. 'He knew,' she sobbed. 'Ronald knew and he said nothing. He just planned this awful way of telling me he knew.'

Chapter Four

OVER THE FOLLOWING days, life went on at Llyn Hir as though everything had returned to normal but there was still an atmosphere of unease. Lottie refused to discuss the unexpected shock of Ronald's will any further, but the mystery of his unkindness to his wife was on everyone's mind. Mabs too refused to comment. She ignored Lottie when they met. To Greg and Zena, she insisted that their mother knew the reason for their father's actions and, until she was told, she wouldn't speak to Lottie again. She was very strained in her communication with them too, but when Greg turned up as usual to help in the night café she treated him as always, with a hug and a 'Thank you, lovely boy'.

It made it difficult for them all, being unable to share their grief. Trying to avoid remarks on happy moments from the past that included their father, usually also included Mabs, who had been such a close part of their lives and avoiding her name was a constant worry.

Zena went home one day about two weeks after the funeral to find all her father's clothes tied up in a bundle. They were going to the place where tramps called to find replacements when their clothes and shoes were worn. Other items were included, that would be sold to provide food for them. His personal possessions were placed in a box from which friends could take anything they wanted. Books were left there and some records, which Lottie offered to Mabs.

'Thank you but no, I don't need anything to remind me of my brother. Unless you find a diary!' she said sharply. 'I know you must have hurt him badly and I want you to tell me how.'

'Ronald was my husband. And what went on within our marriage is my business and no one else's.'

'He was my brother, and I need to know why he acted so badly. His family was his life; you and the children were his greatest pride and delight, so what went wrong? What did you do to him?'

'If you don't want any of his books I'll take them to the hospital,' Lottie replied, ignoring the question. 'Some of the patients are glad of a book to read.'

Dismissed, Mabs left.

The house was cheered by visits from Nelda and her two lively girls. Their laughter and their endless questions brought the place to life after weeks of anxiety and worry. When she knew they were coming, Lottie busied herself cooking, making all the things children loved, cakes and biscuits, as well as sausage rolls with which Bobbie enthusiastically helped. The large garden and the fields beyond were perfect for adventurous play, with even Georgie managing to climb to where the tree-house still stood. Greg promised to get it strengthened so they could have tea there next time.

They walked in the woods and even down the rocky path to the edge of the lake, although the girls were warned never to go there without an adult. The company of the children did more that anything else to help Lottie. Zena knew this and invited them again for the following weekend.

Greg and Uncle Sam fixed the tree house ready for them with smiles of satisfaction. It had been Sam's father Neville, who had made it originally and he came to inspect their work and nodded approval. It was the saddest time and the happiest, Zena thought. Such a pity her father hadn't been there to enjoy it.

Jake was back in London but since the misunderstandings, he promised to come home every other week and he telephoned fairly regularly. With frequent communication between them and getting back to the daily minutiae there was always plenty to say and they returned to their former closeness.

Madeleine was unrepentant about her failure to let Zena know about his presence in her flat, insisting she hadn't wanted to worry his little countrygirl. Happily, Jake took the simplest way out and believed she had acted out of kindness and nothing more.

Rose hadn't been to see them since she had called and found Jake lying on Madeleine's couch. She was embarrassed, and also sad, presuming that his presence there was more than Madeleine helping a sick friend to recover. As she imagined them becoming close, she was reminded of her empty life and the loss of Greg. Sadness turned to bitterness at the thought of how the Martin family had ruined everything. Bitterness was easier to cope with than sadness. She missed the company of Jake and Madeleine but they probably didn't want her intruding.

Jake was at the shop watching the people coming out of the staff entrance and waved when he saw her. 'Madeleine has tickets for a show,' he said taking her arm and tucking it in to his own. 'You'll come, won't you? Meet you early and go for a meal first. Celebrate my mended arm. We'll be here when the store closes on Saturday. All right?' Other plans were made over the next few days and it was with relief that she returned to their casual friendship.

His arm injury still prevented him driving but did not stop Jake working. He delivered messages by bus and sometimes on foot, and collected payments. He became expert at collecting long overdue amounts, smiling with perseverance and developing a knack of embarrassing people and persuading them to pay up. He told them he only received wages on what he collected, and thanked them with great humility when they succumbed to his deceit. The plaster on his arm helped. He'd be sorry to lose it.

When something especially good happened, he celebrated by inviting Madeleine and Rose for a meal or to the theatre. He intended to tell Zena every time they went out together, to prevent more misunderstandings, but each time he changed his mind and decided not to. It was innocent and telling her might make it sound more important that it was, so he said nothing. After all it was connected with his work, keeping the secretary sweet was part of the job, she was an important cog in the wheels of his increasing success. When changes were made in the running of the firm, he was informed immediately and before anyone else, so he knew exactly what was happening. She was also good at covering when he was inadvertently late for an appointment.

There was the time a lady was almost knocked down by a car so he called for a taxi to take her home, after buying her a cup of tea in a nearby café. Then there were the hours he wasted helping a youngster to hunt for his missing dog, which they found sitting outside a café, where they then sat and drank tea to recover from all the effort.

Madeleine kept a diary of their entertainments and saved their theatre programmes writing on them the date and who had taken her, although it was she who usually paid.

Zena increased the time she spent with Mr Roberts without charging him. She liked him and was pleased to help. She had learned that he had three sons who rarely visited. Dick and William lived in Newport and Jack, the youngest, lived just a few miles away in Bridgend. She was curious to know why the three sons so rarely contacted their father and hoped it wasn't a quarrel. Quite likely it was just the usual lack of need as they grew to adulthood with lives of their own and, now involved with their own families, had allowed things to gradually drift.

She learned from Doris that it was his birthday soon. Perhaps she would find out then. He was sure to receive cards from them, wasn't he? She crossed her fingers with a silent wish.

She continued to take a few cakes when she went to clean. She enjoyed cooking and living with her mother who dealt with the catering for the three of them, she had little reason to do so. Mr Roberts happily accepted her gifts, muttering about paying her until she smilingly threatened to bring no more if he mentioned the subject again. He thought of a thank-you gift. She was engaged wasn't she? She wouldn't refuse a gift for her bottom drawer.

He banged on the wall one day soon after she'd gone and shouted, 'Doris! Do-o-ori-i-s.' His neighbour came in and he asked her to choose a suitable gift for his young cleaning lady who was so kind. 'Engaged she is, so something for the wedding, d'you think?'

'If it's that Jake Williams she's marrying it's a pot of patience is what she'll need,' was Doris's reply, 'and you can't buy that!'

'What's wrong with him?

'Feckless, irresponsible. Everyone's best friend. But as a husband, perish the thought! He thinks charm is all he needs to make his way in the world.'

'She's making a mistake?'

'Jake is harmless enough, mind, but he loves helping people and although that isn't a bad thing, old cynic that I am, I think it's the praise he needs rather than the joy of helping. Zena will always come second, believe me.'

'So, flowers then?'

'Perfect! I'll find a really pretty bunch.'

Greg began to enjoy brief visits to London, but always spent some of the time scouring the shops, foolishly hoping for a clues to where Rose was working. Several times he thought he saw her and hurried over only to find it was a stranger.

Once he did see her but at first he didn't recognize her and when he did he was so surprised he didn't approach her. She had cut her hair and had bleached it to a startling blonde. Her clothes were smart and there was such a look of confidence about her that for a moment he couldn't believe what he had seen, but this time he wasn't mistaken. He followed her, trying to decide what he would say but she jumped a bus, standing on the platform at the back of the double-decker as passengers slowly moved in and found seats. She didn't look back. He stood, staring after the bus and saw her still on the platform, holding onto the post at the foot of the stairs. Then she turned and climbed to the top deck, and he walked away.

He had noted the number of the bus and the time but wasn't sure whether he would come again. A completely new style of dress, a more impressive job and an air of confidence he had never before seen, perhaps meant a new man in her life. Unbelievably, Rose had become a stranger.

He bought a book to read on the train but although he turned pages, he didn't take anything in. Between his eyes and the print, Rose's face with its changed image interrupted his concentration.

Rose had surprised herself by discovering a skill for selling. Learning to use make-up and fashionable dress helped her confidence, and selling is as much confidence as knowing your stock and enjoying what you do. She loved her new job having quickly realized she had a flair for it. She was able to assess a price range with which a customer was comfortable and by not offering anything at prices too high or too low she helped them to relax and enjoy selecting their gifts.

She enjoyed the social side of London with Madeleine and Jake, thankfully treating Jake as nothing more than a friend; she didn't want any more traumas in her life. She had invited him to her room once, when they had needed to shelter from the rain, but both had been uneasy. Greg had appeared without warning and if he did so again when they were together it would be embarrassing to explain.

Frank and Mabs's first customer for their night café had been little Sid. He had turned up one day while the café was still only a daytime business and one day when it closed he had been upset and told Mabs he had nowhere to go.

'What about your family?' she asked, and he explained that they had taken over the house where he and his wife had lived for thirty years.

'I know it sounds impossible but it happened. Once my wife died, my daughter-in-law and son pushed me out of my room, insisting my large room was wasted on one small person and they put the children in there. Then I was moved again. What I have now is what was a store room next to the kitchen. The kitchen, I am reminded, is strictly out of bounds. All the furniture has been replaced, my things thrown away. When their friends visit I'm expected to disappear into my miserable room.'

Mabs and her husband Frank had listened to his story, at first with disbelief and then with anger. He was their reason for opening the café, Sid and others like him. The reasons varied but the people who found their café, all needed somewhere safe and warm with the companionship of others, to pass away the lonely hours of darkness.

Frank had invited a few of the night people he saw regularly from his bus, and Sid had gradually introduced them to other men who had similar stories. Some had no family, some had been left when their children had moved away. Henry had lost his family when they could no longer cope with his constant fighting, drinking and the resulting court appearances.

Mabs and Frank began to stay open later than usual and allow the men to enjoy the warmth and friendliness of an increasing group of lonely people. They usually closed after midnight. When Frank died, and Mabs found the nights long and sleepless, she'd extended the hours until early morning. Since then her life had been fulfilled. Her busy routine was nights at the café, the mornings sleeping. Then Richard Thomas came to help.

Richard was another insomniac and, once he found the night café, he became a regular. He was a retired ex-teacher. After the untimely death of his wife, he'd been spending his night hours unsuccessfully courting sleep, eventually giving up to wander the streets, where he gradually got to know others and was introduced to Frankie's night café. He became a volunteer after a few months and now Mabs – known as Frankie – worked four nights and Richard Thomas dealt with the rest, with Greg coming whenever he could.

Greg sometimes called as a customer when he had a long wait between journeys. He didn't tell other drivers and conductors though. They weren't the kind of people Mabs wanted to attract and their presence would have discouraged the people she did want. He drank his tea and ate a cake, helped when there was need and time, before going back to his bus for the next journey.

Sid, being the first of Mabs's night time customers so long ago, considered himself to be the most important and he began to check newcomers before inviting them in. He knew Mabs wouldn't have anyone who smelled of drink and if there was a sign of an argument it was he who quickly jumped up and opened the door for them to leave. All, that is, except when the quarrel included Henry. They were all a little afraid of Henry. Sid being less than five feet tall was the bravest but also the fastest on his feet if he didn't think he could cope.

When a newcomer came in late one night, Sid stepped forward. 'Hi, mate, I'm Sid, what's your name?'

'What's it to you?' the man asked. Sid shrugged and nodded to Greg, who came over and took the man's order for tea and a sandwich.

'I don't like the look of him,' Sid whispered to Greg. 'That's a prison haircut or I'm the Christmas fairy. And he's got angry eyes.'

'Don't worry, Sid. I'll watch him,' Greg promised.

The man didn't stay long but he came back the next night and for several after.

'His name is Arthur Johns,' Sid had learned, 'and he's been in prison for cheating money out of someone.'

'How do you know that?'

'Just a few innocent questions, and a couple of guesses.'

Mabs frowned at him. 'No more questions, Sid. We don't want to stop him coming.'

'But I don't like him,' Sid confided. 'I hope he moves on.'

'Me too,' another muttered. 'He's got greedy eyes.'

Mabs laughed. 'First angry eyes, and now greedy eyes! Have you two been reading books again?' she joked.

The following night Arthur didn't appear. In the local paper a few days later there was a report of a man called Arthur William Johns, who was in court on a charge of breaking and entering. Sid was jubilant. 'Didn't I tell you he was a bad 'n?'

'Sure it was *our* Arthur, are you?' Mabs asked.

'I could see straight away that he was a bad 'n.'

Mabs sighed. In a place like the night café, they were certain to attract a few unsavoury people. Best to forget about them, and carry on.

Lottie had refused to take money from Greg or Zena to help with the burden of the mortgage. It had to be cleared, she was determined on that, but the large debt was alarming and it seemed impossible. She smiled then, remembering a plaque on her mother's wall, saying 'The difficult we do at once, the impossible takes a little longer.' It might take a little longer, but it would be done, she promised herself.

She had been working until Ronald had become so ill, so decided to ask for her job back. She had been working in the stationers and called after another visit from Mabs who had reminded her she had to face up to the difficulties in which Ronald had left her. She owed hundreds of pounds and had very little in the bank. The first thing she had done was sell the car and that money had gone straight to building society.

She constantly wondered what Ronald had needed the money for, and how he had spent it, but there was no clue to be found in the papers he had left. All she knew was that the money had gone. Whatever his reason it was her task to deal with it. She was determined to leave the house for her children to inherit rather than leave them with a debt.

The mortgage had been in arrears and she had practically emptied her own bank account and used it to cover the overdue payments and for two months ahead. That gave her a breathing space. The first thing she must do was to get a job, and fortunately the girl they had taken on in her place was leaving. It seemed that luck was with her so far. It was with relief that she took home her first week's wage and parcelled it out in to the various books and tins for weekly payments and shopping and the frighteningly large mortgage. She decided to try and keep two months ahead in case there was a time she couldn't pay and with just a small amount in her purse, she began her second week with a growing confidence, but still with a fear in the back of her mind that living so precariously meant she could fall into even more serious debt if her luck didn't hold.

Both Greg and Zena insisted on increasing their contribution to the household expenses and Lottie accepted gratefully. Sam Edwards offered her a lift to work several mornings but this she refused, knowing how inconvenient it would be for him even though he'd have coped willingly. 'I have to prove to myself I can manage on my own,' she explained after thanking him. 'It's important to me.'

'Then at least tell your Zena I'll take her shopping when I get what Dad and I need, will you?'

'Thanks, Sam, but we get most of it delivered.'

He nodded and smiled. 'Any time you want help I'm there for you. All of you. Right?'

'Right.'

Zena had come to an understanding with Nelda. The place was

in a muddle every time she went there and at first she was afraid she had been too interfering by sorting out the dozens of wools and cottons and materials with which Nelda made her items to sell at the gift shop at Ilex House. But Nelda had been pleased with the result of Zena's streamlining, her visits made it easier to find what she needed and, ordering supplies had become much simpler as she could see at a glance when she was running low. Zena had improved the stock reordering system by means of a simple notepad and had gradually sorted out the muddles and brought order to the storage. She checked regularly and left notes for Nelda to remind her when items were running low.

Bobbie and Georgie had bedrooms as chaotic as their mother's workroom but she didn't make the same determined effort to tidy up after them. She moved everything and cleaned, but then put everything back where she had found it. She smiled, remembering how she had hated having her room tidied when she'd set it out exactly as she wanted it. Several times she stayed with the children when Nelda had a large order to fill and usually found some new game for them to enjoy.

To her amusement, Bobbie began leaving notes for her. 'Don't touch the table, we've set it for a teddy bears' picnic,' was one. And 'Will you tell Mammy that we are out of Marmite.'

Greg couldn't forget Rose even though she had so completely moved away from him. He needed to talk to her just once more. There had to be a reason. Once he understood, he'd be able to let go, start dating again. There was a new girl at the bus garage called Susie Crane. She was pretty and had an appealing cheerfulness that attracted him. From the little he'd learned, she seemed open and relaxed about her family, a definite improvement.

If only he could escape from this obsession with Rose – but it wasn't that simple. He had to know *why*. Those brief moments at the railway station and the glimpse of her running and jumping onto the bus, swinging aboard, hanging onto the pole before climbing the stairs was not enough. Before he invited Susie Crane out on a date, he decided to go to London for one last time.

'Zena,' he called as he went into the house. 'Fancy a day in

London? I have someone to meet and you could see Jake and we could go for a meal before coming home. Better still,' he added, as the thought entered his head. 'Let's book a theatre and stay an extra day!'

'Great! What days are you free? I'll ring Jake and see if he's in town, shall I?'

Arrangements made, they set off early. Zena enjoyed watching the scenery they passed; the fields were larger, there were fewer birch trees, but as at home, everywhere leaves were beginning to clothes the branches for the summer glory to come.

Jake was at the station to meet them. Zena and Jake left to wander around the crowded shops and Greg went to brave the large imposing store to ask about Rose Conelly.

For Zena it was a wonderful day. She and Jake bought gifts for the family and for each other, hiding them so the purchases were a surprise for later. 'You deserve the best,' he said, laughing, as she pushed him away from the window of an expensive jewellers.

'Nothing expensive,' Zena warned, 'we're saving to get married, remember.'

'You deserve only the best,' he said.

Jewellery was also involved in Greg's day but the day wasn't as happy. He stepped into the store and found himself in the fashion department and hurried through, head down feeling very self-conscious and uneasy. Then he relaxed, aware of the large number of men standing around waiting for wives and girlfriends, and nodded to a few as though sharing their bemusement at the behaviour of their women. He stopped to look around at the glittering counters and the glamorous assistants until he saw Rose. She was smilingly attending to a young lady at a jewellery counter. He stopped to watch her for a while before going up and asking to see some necklaces.

'Greg! What are you doing here?'

'I want to buy a necklace – for my mother. What do you recommend, Miss Conelly?' he added, ostentatiously reading the name on her label.

'Go away!'

'Rhinestone necklaces are pretty. They pick up the light and sparkle, don't they? Show me some of those, Miss ... Conelly,' he said, again pretending to read her name from her badge.

'They're very expensive, sir.'

He stared at her, shuffling his feet as though impatient. Rose saw the floor walker approaching and hurriedly took a tray from below the glass counter.

'Meet me after work or I'll come back tomorrow and make a fuss,' he whispered. 'Now, give me a rhinestone brooch; I think my mother would prefer a brooch. D'you agree?'

'All right. I finish today at four. Meet me at the main door.'

'You will be there?'

'I promise.' The transaction on the brooch completed he walked away to wait until she was free. He didn't really trust her but she knew that if he came tomorrow and asked about her there was a good chance she would be embarrassed, so he hoped she realized he meant it and would be there.

He wasn't under the illusion that she would be going home with him; she had so determinedly cut him off he couldn't imaginee being able to trust her again. He just had to know why she had run away. The story about someone else didn't ring true. She had changed from the moment she had been introduced to his parents. Something had been said at that meeting which made her leave him. But what could it have been? There were no secrets in the family: then he remembered about the missing money and the shock of his father's will and wondered. But how could anything his father had done be connected with Rose Conelly?

At 4.15, when he was just beginning to give up, she appeared.

With a nervous smile she guided him to a small café in a side road and ordered coffee for them both. Greg changed his to tea. Had she forgotten his preference already? He added sandwiches and a couple of cakes to the order and they sat in silence for it to arrive.

'Just tell me why you ran away,' he asked. 'That's all I want to know.' She didn't reply and he added, 'If you've found some one else, I can live with that. Just tell me and I'll go.'

'I'm not ready to marry. That's all, Greg. I was happy as your friend but I don't want anything more.'

'Tell me the truth.' His voice was low and harsh.

'That *is* the truth.'

'All right, I'll call into the shop tomorrow.'

'Please, Greg.'

'Tell me the truth and I'll leave you alone.' He looked at her and was alarmed to see tears forming and fear filling her eyes.

'There are things about me that you don't know. I can't marry. Not anyone. But especially you. Please, go away. I don't want to change jobs again, but I will if you don't promise to leave me alone.'

'Where were you living when you pretended to live in the house where I left you every night?'

'A single room, a place I didn't want you to see.'

'Why didn't you trust me? You must know I'd never hurt you and your secrets will stay with me forever. Just tell me. I can help you to sort them out.'

She excused herself, went to the ladies room and didn't come back. He waited for half an hour then joined Zena and Jake at the theatre. They all went home the following day, Zena chatting happily and Greg insisting he'd had a wonderful day with Rose.

'What d'you think of surprising Mam with a birthday party?' Greg suggested, as they left the station. 'Christmas was such a disaster and inviting a few friends to celebrate her birthday and the end of rationing at last might cheer her up. Specially if we can persuade Aunty Mabs to come.' Both events might have gone unnoticed at Llyn Hir, the lack of excitement, the lethargy that had held the family since the death of Ronald and the shock of his will, seemed to have deadened every emotion.

Zena agreed and promised to try and persuade Mabs to share the planning. She had no success. Mabs was firmly convinced that their mother was responsible for the loss of the money.

Life for the Martins seemed to exist of a succession of days without plans for the months ahead. 'It's as though we are stuck in a time warp,' Zena said to her brother.

'Let's do something completely different for Mam's birthday then,' he suggested. 'More low key. She'd hate a big celebration, it would have the opposite effect than the one we were hoping for.

We could go on a picnic, or have sausages and chips instead of a roast.'

All suggestions of a celebration received the same response from Lottie. She shrugged and said, 'Please yourselves.'

Mabs was unhelpful and made it clear that she would not be involved with the birthday arrangements.

'Aunty Mabs, you can't carry on like this. I can't believe Mam did anything so terrible that Dad could treat her so badly. You saw them over the months he was in hospital, holding hands, talking with affection and love. How can you believe she did something to deserve this? It might have been a misunderstanding or someone repeating untrue gossip, but whatever she did or didn't do, you need each other. You're both grieving for Dad.'

'Change the subject, there's a love. I can't think about it.'

Zena and Greg went ahead with the plan but the day was not a success. Even the weather had been against them with a cold wind blowing and rain drifting past the windows and they were glad to light the fire and enjoy its warmth. After they had eaten the roast meal and Sam and Neville – the only guests – had gone back to the farm, Zena looked at her mother who was staring into the coals wearing that sad and weary expression that seemed never to leave her. Opposite her on the other side of the flickering fire sat Greg, almost a mirror image of her misery. She felt the same. It was as though a shroud of gloom covered them all.

The radio hummed in the background and conversation failed to rouse Lottie out of her misery. At eight o'clock, Greg looked at Zena and gave a shrug. 'I think I'll go to see Aunty Mabs. Coming, Zena? Mam?'

Lottie said she was going to bed, Zena snuggled on the couch with a blanket and prepared to stay.

In London, Rose had changed her job and her accommodation. She didn't mention it either to Madeleine or Jake; she just moved and hoped they wouldn't find her. She had to keep right away from everyone she knew. Knowing Greg could appear at any time had unnerved her. The move wasn't an improvement. She had found a vacancy in a quality shoe shop – but nothing like any she had worked in before. This one was spacious but with fewer items on display. Each of the many types of footwear and various makes had their own department. The assistants were aloof, unfriendly and the customers were much the same and this suited her perfectly. The money was less but she felt safer in the anonymity of the store. She had moved to a different flat but not far, and was aware she was only a few streets away from Jake.

She grieved for Greg and the life he offered but knew she could never change her mind. Although it was ruining her life, she had to hold the secret safe. If she told him her story, everyone would soon know.

Jake saw her one day as he walked back to his flat but although he recognized her he didn't call out. He watched as she disappeared into a large house that had been converted into bedsits and flats. From what he'd heard from Zena and Greg, she was running away in the hope of never being found, so best to pretend he hadn't seen her.

He told Madeleine about the girl, wishing he could do something to cheer her. 'She has some secret which she believed will stop her marrying, according to Zena. What that secret can be I have no idea, but it must be something truly awful for her to give up on marriage to Greg.'

'She'll probably spend Christmas all on her own, in a bedsit where it's possible there are no facilities even to make a slice of toast,' Madeleine said sadly. 'What a pity you're committed to spending those special days with Zena and her family. They have each other and poor Rose has no one.'

'She won't join us, so it's no use asking. She refuses to see Greg.'

'If you didn't have to go to Cold Brook Vale, I could invite her to spend the days with us, you, me and Rose.' She smiled and coaxed, 'And I cook a very good dinner.'

'You're so thoughtful, Madeleine. If only—'

'If only we could think of an excuse to make it possible. What a wonderful surprise it would be for poor Rose. Isn't there any chance, Jake?'

They set off together to find her, Jake guiding them to the

building he had seen Rose enter. They were smiling in anticipation of Rose's delight when they told her of their plans for her.

Jake came home occasionally and Greg took the new conductress Susie Crane out a few times but at Llyn Hir, nothing changed. The three occupants spoke to each other less and less. There seemed nothing to say that didn't remind them of the lethargy and disappointment in their lives.

Summer passed and autumn brought its beauty as well as the warning that winter was on its way, with leaves falling, dahlias in the garden bringing splashes of colour which Lottie failed to notice. Fireworks, Halloween and early signs of Christmas began to appear.

There weren't the usual signs of preparation. No puddings made, or cake planned. The shelves that were usually filled with assorted pickles lay empty. Lottie had no interest in anything.

With determination, Zena began making plans. Jake would be home and Greg had hopes of inviting Susie to visit. She was so bright and cheerful, surely she would succeed in reaching out to Lottie and making her come alive again?

Zena was surprised to receive a letter from Jake telling her he might not be home as planned. He said that with appointments in France and Belgium, he didn't know when he'd be home, but would let her know. She gave a wail of disappointment, then telephoned the office. Madeleine answered and explained that Jake was out of the office adding nothing more. Zena then wrote to him at the office, telling him that if he wasn't there for Christmas Eve, he needn't come at all. She marked the envelope 'personal and private'. Madeleine read the letter, smiled and threw it in the bin.

Madeleine also tore up two Christmas cards: one from each of her parents. She didn't even want such reminders in the flat to ruin Christmas by their false words.

It was at Christmas that she had found her mother with a man they called Uncle Jeremy. She had come home early from a friend's house where she had been sent to stay the night, they were in bed and Madeleine, a twelve year old, had screamed, her mother had screamed and Uncle Jeremy hurriedly dressed and left.

Ignoring promises she had made to her mother in exchange for a new bicycle, she had told her father the moment he came home.

Her father had left immediately, her mother soon afterwards, and neither had invited her to go with them. Ironically, it was Uncle Jeremy's wife who had taken her in, paid for her education and looked after her until she was old enough to manage on her own. Men are unreliable and women are fools, had been her attitude ever since.

Mabs did not want to share the family Christmas and she lied. She used the untruth that her dearest friend had died for that year's reason for declining.

She decided she would stay in her flat. Or, she mused with a smile, perhaps she would open the café for a few hours. She would cook a dinner for those of her regulars who hadn't been invited to any family gathering. When she casually mentioned the possibility, she was surprised just how many there were. 'Not a word to Greg, mind,' she warned them. 'I don't want him to come. His place is at home with his family.'

There were just one or two buses on Christmas morning to take workmen for their early shifts and, with such a strange uneasy mood in the house and an absence of any cheer, Greg happily volunteered.

Driving back to the depot to collect his bike and go home, he passed the café and was surprised to glimpse activity behind the drawn curtains. He went to the door and walked in. Aunty Mabs was carrying a huge platter of turkey slices into the kitchen and on the counter were piles of vegetables. Without a word he took the platter from her and carried it through, then began cutting up the vegetables ready for cooking.

'Sorry, Greg. I hoped you wouldn't find out. I didn't want to involve you, but I liked the idea. When I asked, casual-like, if anyone was interested I was amazed at how many people would be on their own, so I decided to open up.'

'I'll go home to have dinner with the others but then I'll come back,' he promised.

'I'm cooking for five o'clock, so there's no rush. Most of them sleep during the day as you know.'

'What a peculiar Christmas this is. Rose has vanished and will be all alone in a strange place. Jake hasn't arrived as promised and, as he was given an ultimatum by Zena, it seems that now he never will. Mam is on the edge of tears and you are missing us and ruining your own Christmas as well as everyone else's. Come back with me and we can eat whatever Mam has prepared and still be in plenty of time to cook for your old boys. We'll get a taxi if we can, or Uncle Sam will bring us down in his van.'

'I can't, Greg, love. Not until your Mam tells me what happened between her and your father. He was my brother-in-law and I need to know what she did.'

'Why Mam?' he dared to ask. 'Couldn't it have been something Dad did? Perhaps he took a chance on a risky investment. He'd remortgaged the house yet died leaving large debts. Where did the money go? Some sort of gamble could be a more believable explanation, couldn't it?' Mabs didn't reply and he said nothing more. He just helped her finish the preparations and set the tables, then walked her home.

Christmas lunch was a tense affair with any light-hearted humour painfully forced, and he was glad to make an excuse of visiting friends and go back to the café.

When the diners were gathered and were wearing silly hats provided by Mabs, Arthur walked in, the man whom they all thought had been sent to prison for burglary. Little Sid ran to stand in front of Mabs. 'Sorry, mate, but this is a private party.'

'It's all right, Sid, he's welcome.' Mabs pointed to the empty chair at Sid's table and grudgingly, Sid moved aside for him to sit.

Greg set a place for him and found one final cracker. 'It was as if you'd known he'd come,' he said to Mabs, who shrugged and said nothing.

'We heard you was in prison,' Sid whispered to the newcomer.

'Yes, but I came out yesterday. I served my sentence all but a couple of days and I'm never going back.'

'That's what they all say,' George muttered.

Arthur glanced to where Mabs was slicing more meat. 'She made up my mind for me. Talked she did, while I was in prison, and what she said convinced me to stay on the straight and narrow. You can believe it or not, but that was the last time I go to prison.'

It was the most he had ever said and Sid and George stared in disbelief. 'Our Frankie visited you in prison?'

'Never!' Sid gasped.

'And not a word, right? She doesn't want people to know.'

The visit from Mabs had released something in Arthur's mind and he talked and laughed during those three hours, and took his turn at reading the silly jokes from the crackers just as the others did. Mabs whispered to Sid, 'What sort of eyes has he today, Sid?'

'It's very strange, Frankie, they're just blue. An ordinary blue!'

George shivered. 'I still think he's dangerous,' he insisted.

Greg played cards with George and Sid and hesitantly Arthur agreed to join in. He was the first to leave and he thanked them all for their welcome and repeated his promise of going straight.

Greg thought later that serving dinner to eight men, listening to their reminiscences and pulling crackers and laughing at the silly jokes, had been the happiest part of the day.

'Don't worry,' Mabs said, hugging him after the guests had gone. 'Next year will be as Christmas should be, a special time that binds families together, just like always.'

Greg smiled and silently hoped for a miracle.

On the day after Boxing Day Jake arrived in his car, loaded with gifts. Several had foreign labels and he explained that he had been shopping in strange towns, and how the language had confused him and he laughingly told them they would find a few unintended purchases among them. Then he looked at Zena and Greg and was startled at the cold expressions on their faces.

'What's happened?' he asked. 'Is everything all right?'

'Where were you yesterday and the day before?' Zena asked.

'I told you. I wrote and told you I was held up and couldn't get back. Travel wasn't easy and I had to stay until late last night.' He went to hug her but she stepped back and Greg put an arm around her shoulders protectively. 'Zena, lovely girl, what's the matter? I got off the boat, caught a train to London, rushed to the office and collected the car and came straight here. Why are you angry with me?'

'I phoned the office and you weren't there. That secretary didn't know where you were, but said she'd tell you to ring me if you got in touch. Then I wrote. Don't tell me you didn't get the letter, I just won't believe you.'

'How could I get a letter? I was in France.'

'Were you?'

'What about showing us your passport, Jake?' Greg asked, and Jake looked at Zena, his expression one of outrage. 'I certainly won't! I'm hurt if you don't believe me. I don't have to prove what *I'm* saying. *You* shouldn't doubt me.'

Greg began to close the door but Zena stood back to let Jake step inside. In silence Greg helped him to bring in his case and parcels from the car.

In an uneasy truce Lottie made a meal for Jake and they talked spasmodically about the past days, Jake insisting he had been stuck in train stations and queues as he tried to get home, the others exaggerating the wonderful time he had missed. Presents were exchanged and it was clear that no one was excited by them, except Jake who exaggeratedly praised them and remarked on the clever choices.

When Jake and Zena went for a walk in the dark, crisp night, Greg went into the dining room where Jake had dumped his cases, searched through them and found his passport. Jake hadn't been out of the country for more than two years, when France had been his destination. He put it back where he had found it, in a wallet hidden in a pile of clothing. He couldn't decide what to do. Should he tell his sister that Jake had been lying? Or speak to Jake himself? He was still undecided when Jake came back with Zena, who went straight to her room. Jake gathered his things and drove to his usual lodgings with hardly a word.

Greg knocked on his sister's door but didn't tell her what he had found. Still undecided, hoping that Jake would tell her and explain these latest lies, he said Jake was not a man to trust her life to, and left it at that. She just nodded and he closed her door, standing there for a few moments still undecided, then went to bed.

Lottie had been even more subdued over the past few days. She had cooked the food and eaten it but with hardly a word spoken. Conversations drifted around her but there was no sign that she heard what was said. She was lost in a world the others couldn't penetrate and after a while they didn't try, just talked and hugged her, bought her flowers and her favourite chocolates and tried to please her, but mainly, left her to work her way through her distress.

They guessed she had been thinking of previous Christmases and grieving for the loss of their father, but Lottie had put aside grief and was trying to think how he could have secretly taken risks and lost their money.

She couldn't talk to Zena or Greg about it, afraid she would show her hurt in anger and would say things about their father they shouldn't hear. She wouldn't offer a word of criticism until she found out what had happened. To spoil their memories of a loving, caring father and husband then find out later that what he had done was something perfectly understandable, would be a terrible mistake. But what reason could there be? She had always felt secure in Ronald's love. There had been no secrets between them.

Since his death there had been many nights without sleep as she tried to think of an acceptable explanation but found none. She had to find out what had happened. But would the truth be a comfort? Or a terrible shock?

Zena went about the routine tasks at the end of the day and wondered where Jake had gone. Back to London and that secretary whom, she suspected, had been less than diligent at passing on messages and letters?

Or had he found a room here in Cold Brook Vale with his ex-landlady? It was almost ten o'clock but she suddenly decided to try and find him. Whatever his reason for not coming home she had to at least listen to his explanation. She took her cycle and rode to where he had once lived but there was no sign of the car and, when she knocked, there was no reply.

On a whim she went to her flat, from which the tenants had gone. She needed to check that the place was clean and ready for new tenants arriving in two weeks. There was a light in the kitchen and she just knew it was Jake. Taking out her key she opened the door and walked in. Jake was sitting at the table, a jar of honey and a few cracker biscuits on a plate in front of him. 'Sorry, love, but I thought you wouldn't mind. My landlady didn't have a room, see, she needed more notice, and I couldn't face sleeping in the car.'

'Where have you been, Jake?'

'London. I was in London giving a lonely, unhappy young girl a good Christmas.'

'Madeleine Jones?'

'No, er, yes, sort of.'

Zena began to walk to the door. 'Stay tonight but tomorrow I want your key.'

'All right, I'll tell you the truth.'

'Or another lie?'

'It was Rose Conelly. She wouldn't explain why she left Greg, she just told me she can never marry. She is living in a sordid little room with no cooking facilities.' He gave an exaggerated description of a place very different from the one he'd seen. 'She's friendless and very unhappy. Madeleine found out and, well, we couldn't bear to think of her alone and without even a proper meal at Christmas time, so we invited her to Madeleine's flat and gave her the kind of day most people have.'

'So you let me down because of Rose being unhappy? Jake, we're supposed to be getting married. How can I marry someone so thoughtless and unkind?'

'You had your brother and your mother and Aunty Mabs, friends calling in. You had a home, the warmth of a loving family, good food and gifts. Rose had nothing.'

'You spent the day with Madeleine and Rose and then lied to me. I'd have thought better of you if you hadn't lied. We could have done something for Rose, together.'

'I daren't tell you, lovely girl.'

'You *daren't* tell me? This gets better and better!'

'If I'd told you and you refused, I wouldn't have been able to help her, see?' He looked at her anxiously. 'I love you, Zena, you know I do, I want you to be my wife. I want to be a part of your family. But it was Christmas and Rose had no one.'

Zena felt an irresistible urge to laugh. Seeing the smile twitching her lips Jake leapt up and hugged her. 'I knew you'd understand.'

'Like I understood when you bought a car we didn't need because a friend hadn't a car to go on holiday? And when you gave my bicycle away because a nurse in the village needed it for work?'

'I can't help it, my lovely girl.'

'Will it always be like this, Jake? You putting every lame duck you meet before me?'

'Sometimes people take advantage of me, but that's a chance I take. I shouldn't involve you, I know that, but if someone's in trouble I can't help myself. While I'm being honest, I'll admit that I'm unlikely to change.'

'Is there anything between you and this Madeleine Jones?'

'Good heavens, no! Terrifying she is! She only suggested this day for Rose because she too was on her own. To be honest, I know she wouldn't have cancelled any arrangements of her own to give Rose a good time.'

'I think she was pleasing you, not Rose Conelly.'

Jake ignored the remark and went on, 'If I'd told you about Rose, I wouldn't have needed to persuade *you* to help her, would I?'

'Perhaps not, but I wouldn't have ruined your Christmas to please someone else. I suspect your impulses are for yourself and never for me. Not ever for me. There are so many instances of you being praised for your generosity, but you were giving away things taken from someone else – including me. That isn't even honest, is it?'

'Come on, lovely girl, you didn't really mind about my giving away your old bike, did you?'

'You're evading an answer, Jake. Isn't it the truth that you just love to be loved? That you're happiest when people praise you and tell others how wonderful you are?'

'We can share this thing. There are so many ways to make people feel happy and I know you'll understand when we do it together. I won't do anything again before we discuss it.'

'No more secrets?'

'None, I promise.'

An hour later, by which time Greg and Lottie were beginning to worry about her, Zena and Jake arrived home. Both were smiling. With very little explanation, Jake was given supper, a blanket and the couch.

Zena didn't sleep easily. She was considering how she would cope with a husband who attracted lost sheep and became their saviour. She became drowsy at last and saw Rose's face, and the many people he had helped in his life plus others – strangers – in a montage of what life with Jake would be. Then the dream became nonsense and she saw Jake in a field; laughing, surrounded by sheep laughing with him and beckoning her into his world. She awoke with an uneasy feeling that she would not be able to cope.

Chapter Five

GREG AND ZENA were having breakfast the day following Jake's departure when Zena told him what had been discussed between herself and Jake, excusing his behaviour with laughter. Greg reluctantly told his sister that there were more explanations to come.

'Zena, he's been lying to you. I know it was wrong of me to search through his things but I was suspicious and looked at his passport. He doesn't work on the Continent. He hasn't been out of the country since he and I went to France with the boys from the pub. Remember?'

'You must be mistaken! He brought gifts from other countries, didn't he? He works as an agent selling protective clothing, selling on the Continent, buying from factories in Belgium. Even Jake couldn't have made all that up!'

'Sorry, Sis, but unless he has two passports there's no mistake.'

She turned away and stared out of the window. 'Come on, Greg! There has to be an explanation. I'll talk to him again.'

'Walk away, Sis. There's no future with a man who lies so easily.'

'I'll talk to him,' she replied more sharply.

Greg muttered, 'Sorry,' and left the room.

Her outrage was bravado. She knew, deep within her, without waiting for an explanation, that what Greg had told her was true. He had seen Jake's passport and the evidence it had shown couldn't be denied. But she couldn't understand why Jake would lie. Why would he pretend to have such a high-powered job? She had seen the letter from Jake's friend recommending that he apply, that couldn't have been a forgery, but that wasn't evidence he had been successful.

She didn't know what to do. There didn't seem any point in writing to Jake at the place where he lived, those letters always disappeared without reaching him. Nor at the office where her letters were opened by the officious Madeleine Jones, and phoning was never successful, either. Glad of the excuse to delay facing Jake with these new lies, she decided she would have to wait for his next visit.

Work was a good way to ease away her humiliation and hurt. Scrubbing kitchen floors was something she didn't need to do but she needed the physical effort. Working so fast she found extra corners in need of her attention at every house she visited. Janey Day called one day and asked her to go back to twice weekly visits as she was finding it difficult to manage. In the hope that Trish wouldn't be there, plus the decision that she would deal with her if she were, Zena agreed. When she couldn't find physical work she helped her mother at the stationers, giving Lottie time to shop or just have a rest. She was exhausted when she went to bed but was disturbed by unpleasant dreams.

Nelda was usually out when she went to clean, but her friend was there when she arrived one morning and between them they sorted out a few cupboards and Zena scrubbed them out and covered the shelves with paper replacing the contents in clearly defined sections again. Nelda was delighted , while wondering why they didn't stay that way. Zena avoided telling her!

'Now,' Nelda said, when they had finished a third storage cupboard, 'you are going to sit down and I'll make us tea. Then,' she said, waving a scolding finger, 'then you are going to tell me what's wrong.'

'I don't know what you mean,' Zena protested.

'Boyfriend trouble I suppose?'

'Well, things aren't as they should be between Jake and me. That's all. It'll work out.' Zena was reluctant to say more but, pushing a slice of cake and a cup of tea in front of her, Nelda sat, chin on hands, and waited in silence. Minutes passed.

'It's nothing, probably just a misunderstanding,' Zena said finally.

'I married Dave knowing he wasn't the man for me and it took seven years for me to face up to it. Zena, dear, don't marry unless you're sure. Better walk away now rather than have the complications of a marriage to pull apart. It isn't a pleasant experience and in my case, we hurt the children too.'

'I can't. It would be giving up my future and perhaps never finding someone as much as I love Jake.'

'That's nonsense! And definitely the wrong reason for not walking away, and you know it.'

'It's just that he's so kind. He always gets involved when he hears of someone in trouble. I have to accept that or, as you and Greg advise, I have to walk away.'

Nelda listened in silence as she told her some of the help Jake had given to others, including Christmas, which he had spent with Madeleine and Rose. 'It's always genuine kindness; he can't refuse to give something he has if there's another with greater need of it.' When she had finished, Nelda hugged her and said briskly, 'You're right, you have to accept the way he is if you love him, but think of the years ahead, and be aware that you will *always* come second. *Always.* You *and* your children. Second to strangers, to lame ducks and anyone with a good line in scrounging. Face it, Zena, and ask yourself it you can cope with that. You and any children you might have. Could you cope? I'm sure I couldn't.'

'I have to talk to him again, make him understand that we have to decide these things together.' She smiled. 'D'you know what excuse he gives for not telling me first? Because if I say no, he would have to forget it, and not asking means I don't have the chance to disagree and he can do what he wants.'

'But that's the same as lying! And this do-gooding is nothing more than vanity, surely you can see that?'

Zena disagreed. Jake had no ulterior motive. He didn't help people for his own aggrandisement, to impress or be admired. Ignoring the words she said, 'If I continue to consider myself engaged to him, the next year will be a testing time.'

Talking it over with someone who was not involved helped Zena to think about the situation more calmly. Jake hadn't told her, afraid she would say no and that would have been final. That might be childish, but it was somehow endearing. The motives for his lies were always a desire to do something for someone else. She shut her mind to the passport and the fresh list of lies about his job and the foreign travel; they were less easy to explain.

She wanted to write down her frustrations in an angry letter but forced herself to wait for his explanation. She knew she was being foolish, but it wasn't easy to walk away from a love she had felt for so long. All her plans for the future, all the dreams of a happy life were bound up with him. How could she walk away? He wasn't really a deceitful man, just a very kind and generous one. How could she criticize him for that? But, a small voice warned, how could she believe his deceit was something trivial, best ignored?

There were new tenants coming into her flat, which was now empty and that gave her the chance to clean and paint a couple of walls before they moved in. She used that as an excuse to write to Jake, hoping that mentioning such an innocuous subject might mean he actually received it. She was almost certain that her letters were opened by Madeleine Jones and felt irritated that she couldn't contact him apart from the office. She made no reference to the untruths about his job, revealed by Greg finding his passport, and said nothing about their ruined Christmas.

In the office, Madeleine opened it, read it and threw it away. 'Sorry, Jake, I threw it away by mistake. Something about a new tenant, there was nothing more. The flat she owns will be empty until a week from Saturday.'

'Love and kisses included?' he asked with a smile.

'Not that I noticed. It was very brief.'

Lottie had been cautiously talking to all Ronald's friends, hoping for an explanation of how he had lost so much of their money. She felt sick every time she thought of being left only a house on which there was a large mortgage. They had both worked to buy it, so where had the money gone? She had tried to persuade her sister-in-law, always a close and loving friend until now, to discuss it but she rarely came to the house and when she did it was only to talk to Zena or Greg; Lottie she ignored.

It was toward the end of January when she decided to make

an appointment with the solicitor to see if he knew anything that would help her get to the bottom of the mystery. During her lunch hour she went to the office with fingers crossed.

Mr Phillips was an elderly man, stick thin and with long, white hair. His suit was well tailored but loose, as though it had been made for a man several stones heavier, but his smile was welcoming, crinkling the skin around his bright blue eyes. He sent for coffee and invited her to sit near the open fire that burned brightly in the highly polished grate in the old-fashioned office.

'I am trying to shed light on the will of my husband, Ronald Martin,' she began.

Mr Phillips patted a file on his desk, and said, 'Since your phone call, I have been reading through my dealings with your husband, Mrs Martin. How can I help?'

'I can't understand where our money went. We had no mortgage on the property, the house was ours and had been for several years. We had savings in several places. The bank of course, and the building society, and I believe my husband had shares in other businesses. Not an enormous amount but it was for our retirement, for holidays and a few luxuries.'

Mr Phillips turned pages and forms over in the file then handed her a sheet of paper. 'These were the last dealings I had with your husband, Mrs Martin. Three years ago he withdrew all his money and put it into the bank and from there he took out a large cheque. I know nothing of what happened to it. We weren't asked to act for him in whatever arrangements he made.'

She asked question after question and the solicitor answered as fully as he was able, offering suggestions about where enquiries might begin and offering to deal with them, but Lottie shook her head. 'Later, perhaps. Firstly I'll discuss it with my husband's sister. Perhaps she knows what happened, although she seems to believe the reason was revenge for something I did.'

'Forgive me asking, but had there been a problem, Mrs Martin?'

'As far as I know, we were completely happy. I can't think of anything that worried him. The loss of the money must lie with him. It must have been something terribly urgent. We all saw that he was anxious during those last days, but by then he was confused and nothing he said made any sense. All that money and all that time – why couldn't he tell me?'

'Unable? Or unwilling? Not wanting to worry you perhaps? He might have been involved with something which he hoped to deal with himself, sorting it before you knew of the problem. Maybe unaware that he was seriously ill and was running out of time.'

'Yes, he was very distressed, particularly during those last few days, muttering about time, and when he was delirious he talked about someone called Billy Dove. I know no one of that name.'

'Perhaps it was someone from a very long time ago? Sometimes, with age or illness, memories from years ago become clearer than the present time, I understand.'

Lottie went straight to see Mabs as soon as she finished work. When Mabs opened the door she pushed it wide open and marched in before Mabs could refuse to let her enter.

The notes she had made at the solicitor's office were on a page of a notebook and she thrust it at Mabs. 'Read this!'

After an initial protest, Mabs read it and stared at Lottie in disbelief. 'What happened? Why did Ronald take all his money out of his account?'

'*Our* account,' Lottie corrected quietly.

'Why did he do that? Where is it?'

'I was hoping you'd tell me.'

Mabs's first thought was of the money she had in the bank and whether the best way of using it was to help Lottie to clear Ronald's debts. But the real need was to find out what had happened to make her well-organized and sensible brother lose all their money.

'It wasn't something you'd done? Hurt him in some way?' By way of reply, Lottie glared at her angrily. 'Lottie, I really thought he had left it somewhere else because you'd let him down. I'm sorry. I really am.' She hugged her tearful sister-in-law. Then she calmed down and said firmly, 'Our first step is the police. It's such a large amount, we need to contact the police and get this investigated,' she said firmly. 'This sounds so unlike Ronald there must be criminality involved. Lottie, I'm so very sorry for thinking you were the reason for Ronnie's actions.'

'Why did you blame me? Your accusations were the worst of all.

I loved Ronald, and no one else.'

'It did seem to be a vengeful act and for a while I thought that you and Sam at the farm were—'

'Nonsense! He's a family friend, more Ronald's than mine.'

Although the revelation that the money had gone without leaving a trace had been a shock, Lottie slept well for the first time since the reading of Ronald's will.

Together, Lottie and Mabs talked to the police who listened carefully, made copious notes and agreed to start making enquiries. One question was whether anyone close, a relative or a friend, had begun to spend more than usual. Both women shook their heads. As they were leaving, Lottie gave a brief smile. 'Sam Edwards has ordered two new barns and a tractor, but I don't think he'd convince Ronald to part with so much money.'

They talked around the mystery for a long time but no solution occurred to either of them. Mabs went back to her flat to search through any papers she had relating to her brother and Lottie went home to sit and stare into space, wondering why, after all their years together, Ronald hadn't trusted her with whatever had caused his uncharacteristic action. Neither found a hint of a solution.

Aware of the Sunday being Roy Roberts's birthday, Zena planned a surprise, with Doris and her son Kevin helping. At four o'clock she knocked on the door with Nelda and the children carrying plates of food and a large birthday cake. Doris saw them coming and quickly joined them with more food, followed by Kevin with a few brightly wrapped parcels. She knocked on the door and announced an instant party, introducing Nelda and the children as they piled their gifts on the table. As he began talking to the little girls, she looked around for cards but there was none. So his sons didn't recognise their father's birthday. She was glad they had come.

Food was displayed and Doris busied herself making tea. Kevin produced a bottle of beer and the party atmosphere took off in moments. Soon Roy was reminiscing about time gone by including his time in the Navy. Bobbie asked if he's fought with Admiral Nelson and was disappointed to be told he was too young. 'He looks very old to me,' Georgie whispered to Zena.

It was as he and Doris talked about the present day that Zena listened intently, surprised that they knew Rose Conelly. She learned very little, just that her childhood had not been a happy one but decided to ask him more next time she called. When she asked about Billy Dove, Roy shook his head.

'Billy who? Oh, Billy Dove. He must be dead, I haven't heard anything about him for years.'

'You called him "Birdie", ' Doris coaxed but he shook his head.

'Years since I heard about Birdie.'

Another disappointment.

'Where are the rest of your birthday cards, Mr Roberts?' Nelda asked.

'Still in the cupboard, Popeye?' Kevin pointed to the sideboard.

Roy shrugged. 'Might as well put them with the others I suppose.' Nelda opened the drawer and took out three envelopes, opened and revealing cards. Then she noticed the date on the franking mark and saw they were more than twenty years old. Without a comment she stood them on the top of the sideboard with the rest.

Roy spent more time playing with the girls, who daringly called him Popeye to his amusement. Between games he talked about the people he remembered from school including Billy Dove. With so many people around she decided to wait until her next visit before asking about him. It might be a way to get to the heart of the mystery of her father's money.

Zena walked into Nelda's house a week later to the sound children arguing. Their young voices rose higher and higher until they were shrieking and things were being thrown around. She ran to see what was happening and opened the kitchen door just in time to see Georgie and Bobbie, who were standing on the table pushing each other, fall onto the floor one each side of the table. She reached Georgie first and, as the child stood up scowling, she thought there was no serious damage and ran to see to Bobbie, who wasn't moving, although her eyes were open.

'Bobbie! Bobbie, talk to me, where are you hurt?' Bobbie jumped up and, aiming a final punch at her sister ran, giggling, from the room.

'You little minx.' Zena smiled ruefully at Georgie. 'Where's your mammy?' It was Sunday and she had agreed to help Nelda clear a bedroom ready for the decorators.

'I don't know, she just went out and left us,' Bobbie called sorrowfully.

'Nelda?' Zena called. The back door opened and Nelda came in demanding to know what all the noise was about.

'They were fighting,' she was told. 'On the kitchen table, would you believe! They both fell off but they don't seem to have been badly hurt, but you'd better check them.'

Georgie had a scraped arm and a bruise was already showing below her elbow. Her unrepentant sister insisted she was making a fuss about nothing. 'As usual!'

Zena left them to their mother and went to start clearing the bedroom. She heard Bobbie say, 'It's lucky Daddy didn't come and find that you'd left us alone, wasn't it, Mammy?'

'You can stop that nonsense,' Nelda said. 'Daddy thinks you are old enough to be left for a few minutes without fighting, but isn't he wrong about that?' Then Bobbie began to cry, insisting she needed a bandage. 'It's more than a bruise, Mammy, it's a scrape,' she shouted dramatically. 'I need a bandage.'

Zena called, 'I have a small first-aid box in my bicycle basket. Go and fetch it, Bobbie, and I'll bandage it to make sure it's kept clean.' Still sobbing, Bobbie watched as a bandage was applied and then went to show her sister what she had done to her.

Zena realized how difficult it must be for Nelda, coping with a busy job and caring for two lively children, while warding off criticism from an absent father. This led her to thoughts of Jake. What would her life be like with Jake, a man who kept things from her, a more deceitful version of lying – if that made sense? Always likely to give her possessions to others when he decided theirs was the greater need.

A marriage must always be uncertain. No one can really know another well enough to guarantee a perfect life: to understand how that other person would cope with unexpected changes like the birth of a child, or the sudden loss of money like her parents. She had once thought she knew Jake, but lying about his job and the successful business travel he was boasting about, how great were the risks she would be taking if she married him? Nelda might be better off on her own rather than with an unreliable man. Her father had lied to her mother by not telling her about the loss of money, yet she thought his reasons were different from those of Jake. He must have hoped to solve his difficulties before her mother found out. With Jake, what else but vanity? How long would she go on deluding herself?

She stopped dragging a small desk away from the wall and frowned. Vanity was something she determinedly denied as a reason for Jake's generosity. Did accepting it make what he does better, or worse? Was it an excuse, something he couldn't help? An obsession over which he had no control? With her mind full of these concerns she worked fast and efficiently and in less than three hours the room was empty, washed, and the floor scrubbed.

As a thank you, besides paying her, Nelda invited her to go with her to the pictures at the weekend. 'My lovely parents are having the girls from after school on Friday until Sunday, when I go there for lunch before bringing them home. We could go on Saturday. Abbot and Costello are on. They're always a good laugh.'

'Just what I need,' she said, happily agreeing.

In London one Sunday, Jake was having lunch with Rose and Madeleine. Knowing he had to face Zena with the truth about his menial job, he was feeling low. Rose suggested he went to the Labour Exchange to look for something better. 'You need a place where you can work your way up,' she said. 'A man needs to be able to keep a family. It's different with me: I don't want promotion. I'm happy being just a small cog in the wheel of things. If I were offered something better I'd refuse. I haven't the ambition for a successful career, earning lots of money, telling others what to do.'

Jake was too self-centred at that time to discuss this. 'I am going to marry Zena and I promised to give her everything she needs and most of what she wants,' he said. 'I need money and I need it fast.'

'Zena owns her flat, doesn't she?' Rose reminded him. 'And

the rumour is that Aunty Mabs has a lot of money which will be shared by Zena and Greg one day.'

'Where did you hear that?' Jake asked. 'Aunty Mabs has tried to keep that a secret.'

'There's a man called Roy Roberts who rarely goes out but seems to know all that's going on. Your Zena helps with his cleaning, and does his shopping sometimes. I overheard him once telling someone that the money Frank Bishop won hasn't been mentioned since his death but it must still be there. I didn't know Mabel Bishop then and I only remembered it recently.'

'What a pity she's fit and well,' Madeleine said jokingly. 'Perhaps one of her lonely old men-of-the-night will bump her off, eh?'

'I hope not!' Jake was horrified. 'What are you talking about? What old men? She's a dear old thing and I'd hate anything awful to happen to her. Besides it's I who— What old men?'

'The sad café, which she opens during the night, to give food and comfort to some of the lonely old men who can't sleep.'

'But I've never heard of this place, why didn't Zena tell me about it?'

That made Madeleine laugh, 'You aren't the only one to keep secrets, are you, Jake?'

Rose told them about how she almost walked in, seeing Mabs and Greg just in time. 'Mabs and her husband started it and after he died, she carried on, helped by a retired teacher called Richard Thomas, apparently. I found all this out from one of the regulars. Mrs Bishop calls herself Frankie.'

'Secrets everywhere! You've never explained, Rose, but can you tell us, now we're friends, why you left Greg Martin?'

'Sorry, that isn't something I want to discuss. It's over and that's all you need to know.'

'I can't believe Mabs Bishop is running a café for down and outs,' Jake muttered.

'Not down and outs,' Rose explained, 'and not people who are homeless. They're just people who can't sleep. She helps them fill the long hours of darkness.'

'There must still be some money for Greg and your Zena when she dies,' Madeleine whispered softly. 'You need it more than a few men who must certainly scrounge from her.'

'Zena having more money won't help me at all.'

'Then this Aunty needs persuading to give it to you instead of Zena.' Madeleine laughed and the others joined in. 'Just a dream, dear,' she said, touching Jake's hand affectionately. Rose looked on and frowned. Light-hearted it might have been but the conversation had made her resentful. Marriage to Greg would have been wonderful once she had been able to face him with the truth of her ugly beginnings, but that dream had been irrevocably shattered by his evil family.

Jake was looking thoughtful. 'I'll look for a job and then, next weekend, I'll go home and tell Zena everything. I'll have to thumb a lift, as I can't afford the fare or the petrol.' He stood to leave, reached for Madeleine's coat to help her put it on. They were the only people in the restaurant and the rest of the tables had been cleared and reset for afternoon tea, with plates, cups and saucers set out.

Madeleine touched his arm, stopped him moving towards the door. 'Don't leave the firm, Jake. I'll have a word with the boss, see if I can persuade him to give you something better than being a dogsbody. Leave it to me. I'm sure you'd do well if you were given a chance in the sales department; charm, looks and the good line in sales patter. And' – she smiled, and raised an eyebrow – an expertise in lying to cover mistakes, you'd be an asset to the company.'

Jake smiled ruefully. 'All right, I'll give it a bit longer. I'll still go home this weekend. It's time I told her the truth.'

'That will be easier if you have the offer of a better job. Another week could make all the difference. I'll talk to the boss tomorrow,' Madeleine promised. Then she went on, 'I'd love to have a weekend away, and I've never been to Wales. I haven't even seen the sea,' she lied. 'Is your home near the sea?'

'The beach is only a twenty minute walk away.' On one of his impulsive decisions, he said, 'Why don't you come? Didn't you say the flat was empty until a week next Saturday?'

'You mean I can stay there?'

'Why not? No one is using it. You too, Rose. Maybe you could talk to Greg?' She shook her head and he said, 'All right, we'll hide

119

you. Come on, it'll be fun, but—'

'It's all right, Jake, we'll pay for the petrol, won't we, Rose?'

In the night café, Greg worked with Mabs as smoothly as always, both sharing the tasks and the time spent talking to the lonely men. He could see that Mabs was wrapped up in her thoughts, but, with so many people around, he didn't risk asking her if there was a problem. He knew she was still grieving for Frank and this mystery about her brother Ronald was an added anxiety. It wasn't until the last customer had gone and they were washing up and cleaning the tables that he said, 'Aunty Mabs, the solicitor and the police are making enquiries about the missing money and maybe they'll soon have news for us. You and Mam have done all you can, so try to be patient and let it go. Leave it to the police. Worrying won't help and we don't want you to make yourself ill.'

'I can't help thinking that somewhere in my mind I have the solution. Your father had a partner with whom he put some money aside for investments, playing the stockmarket. They talked to your Uncle Frank about it and he made them agree that whatever happened, they wouldn't go beyond their initial outlay, but sometimes the promise of great wealth can turn even the most cautious of heads. Perhaps something went wrong and they had to pay out a lot of money.'

'Why did you think Mam had done something awful that made Dad leave her nothing?'

'I'm sorry, Greg, but I foolishly thought that your mother and Sam Edwards at the farm were getting fond of each other and your father was hurt and needed revenge.'

'Not a chance. Mam was happy with Dad, and he would never have been vengeful if she *had* strayed. He was such a gentle man, wasn't he?'

Mabs frowned. 'I hadn't remembered them playing the stockmarket, until today.'

'What was his partner's name?'

'That's what's been keeping my mind occupied. I can't remember.'

'Can that be the explanation? Perhaps the money is still there but we can't find out because we don't know his partner's name, if there was one.'

'There had to have been a partner, your father wouldn't have ventured into such a risky game on his own.'

The following day she went to see Roy Roberts. They had been at school together and although they had seen little of each other over recent years they greeted each other like friends.

They talked about people they had once known and gradually, Mabs brought the subject around to Ronald. 'It's taken a long time to sort through his papers. Most of it has been dealt with now but there are a few things we can't clear up. I wondered if you can help.'

'I haven't seen much of Ronald recently. As old age creeps upon you, your world shrinks. Fewer people, fewer activities, more memories heavily distorted with a rosy glow of fantasy. But ask away, you never know.'

Mabs smiled in agreement. 'We're trying to find a partner, someone who dealt with investments.'

'Money gone astray, has it?'

'No, no, nothing like that,' she protested at once. 'It's just a few things we don't understand. Can you think of anyone he might have worked with? I know he liked a bit of a flutter on the horses and perhaps a few other things.'

'Ronald tried to follow the stock market. Fat chance of someone like him making money there. You have to be a master at mathematics, don't you?'

'Probably. Anyway, let me know if you think of anything that might help. I think Lottie needs to get everything sorted so she can set her mind on the future.'

'Right then, Mabel. I'll get thinking. And next time you come remember to bring me some grapes. I've got a broken arm you know.'

Mabs laughed as she left, then the smile faded. She had a suspicion that Roy Roberts knew more than he had chosen to tell. She'd buy him the biggest bunch of grapes she could find if he could give her even the smallest clue to finding the lost money.

Jake, Madeleine and a nervous Rose arrived at Zena's flat on

Friday evening after an uneventful journey. Jake moved a flower pot, chuckled and picked up the key. Zena had taken back his key but hadn't moved the spare from its hiding place. They dropped their suitcases then went straight out to find food. They didn't want to eat inside, afraid of leaving signs of their being there. A short trip in the car took them to a smart restaurant a few miles away and Madeleine insisted on paying. They returned and went straight to their beds, Jake on the couch with spare blankets, the girls using sleeping bags on top of the bedding, but under the eiderdown for warmth.

The following morning they went out early and Jake led them by a devious route to the beach, where, on that cold day the sea looked uninviting, yet the two girls felt warmed by the inexplicable hint of excitement that summer would bring.

They spent the day driving around the area, taking in picturesque villages and small bays each bringing delighted cries from Madeleine who took many photographs and declared she had never seen anything more beautiful. They sat on a cold, rocky beach wrapped in blankets borrowed from the flat and ate chips, and drank from a shared bottle of lemonade and, like children, declared it a feast.

Sunday began early, all woken sooner than expected by thoughts of the day just gone and another to come. 'I feel like a child mitching from school,' Rose said with a laugh.

'Did you do that often?' Jake asked her.

'More often than I should! I used to write notes explaining that *my daughter* had a sore throat or head lice – they never argued about my being absent for that!' Sitting in the neat living room and making plans for their final morning, they talked for a while of their school days, Madeleine said the least, aware that the subject of her private education was best avoided.

Packing the few things they had brought and tidying away all evidence of their visit, Madeleine went back inside to check that they had left nothing behind, pausing for a moment in the bathroom. Jake put the key back in its hiding place and they set off to explore nearby beauty spots then find a pleasant place for lunch. As they drove, too fast, around the corner from where Jake had parked his car, he almost knocked Greg off his bicycle.

'Damn!' Jake muttered, 'I forgot the odd hours that he works. Sorry, ladies, but you're about to hear a long list of lies.'

Greg stared in disbelief as he recognized first Jake then Rose. 'What are you two doing here?'

Rose turned to Jake and waited for his explanation.

'Look, Greg, mate, I can explain this but not now, we haven't got time, right? I'll ring you at your mother's house tonight, ten o'clock, OK?' Without giving the startled Greg a chance to speak, he put his foot down and drove away. 'Now, ladies,' he said cheerfully, 'we have all day to think of a good story. Who's first?' Madeleine began to laugh, Jake joined in, but Rose was unable to force more than a weak smile, shaken by suddenly seeing Greg

The telephone rang persistently in Lottie's house between 10 and 10.30 but no one answered. Greg sat with Zena and they let it ring. She had gone to the flat to check that everything was clean, ready for the new tenants, and pick up the post and make sure the milk had been cancelled. She had seen at once that the place had been used, and finding a tin of Jake's brand of toothpowder, guessed he had been there. A pair of stockings hanging in the bathroom shocked her. There was little doubt about who he had brought with him. Greg had told her what he had seen as there seemed nothing to gain by covering for Jake.

The phone went on ringing spasmodically for another hour but neither of them made a move to answer it.

It had been very late when Jake and the two girls arrived back at Madeleine's flat and she insisted they both stayed with her. 'You both need a good night's sleep and your places will be cold and there won't be anything to eat. You'll be comfortable here. There are plenty of tins in the cupboard and the bread will still be eatable if we toast it.' Both were too tired to argue. Jake guessed that Zena had been told what Greg had seen and he decided he had to own up to the visit. If he told her it was because Madeleine had never seen the sea and Rose needed a little holiday, she would understand. He would promise her there would be no more lies.

Zena didn't try to telephone the office and neither did she write.

She simply didn't know what to say. She had a letter from Jake on Tuesday morning explaining that he hadn't the money to come home as he'd so desperately wanted to, and Madeleine offered to pay for petrol if she could come too. Rose came as well as she rarely went anywhere and Madeleine thought she would enjoy it. Zena showed the letter to Greg, who shrugged. 'Madeleine and Rose coming, using your flat, meant he couldn't see you, which defeated the object, didn't it?'

'There's a P.S.'

Greg turned the page and read, 'The reason I couldn't say no, was that Madeleine had never seen the sea.' He laughed. 'He never misses a trick, does he!'

When she went to clean at Mr Roberts's house, Zena was not her usual, chatty self but when asked if there was a problem, she insisted that everything was fine, perfect, just lovely.

She finished her chores and made a cup of coffee for them both and unwrapped a couple of cakes she had brought. Mr Roberts was outside, talking to his neighbour, Doris. She was about to call him in, insisting it was too cold for him to be standing out there, when she heard her name and, unable to resist, she listened.

'Sorry for the girl, I am,' Doris was saying. 'If she only half believes the fanciful dreams of Jake Williams she's got nothing but trouble ahead of her. He thinks he's a sort of all year round Father Christmas, taking from wherever he can to give favours to people who think he's a cross between a saint and a fool. She's the fool if she can't see that it's vanity and nothing else. Just vanity.'

She felt that now familiar ache of disappointment. Vanity, the word she could no longer deny. Vanity, wanting to be admired and flattered, giving things that half the time didn't belong to him, soaking up the praise.

'It's sad, I know,' Mr Roberts replied, 'and she's such a lovely girl, but she wouldn't thank us for pointing out the man's a fool. She'll have to work it out for herself. The rumour that her mother has been left almost penniless is certainly true and that's enough for them to deal with, but the gossips will have a wonderful time if Zena doesn't wake up to the fact that Jake is living in a fantasy world. He'll spend her money faster than she earns it.'

Zena went back into the kitchen and called, calmly. 'Coffee's here, Mr Roberts, I have to go now. See you next time.' She couldn't ride her bicycle. Her legs wobbled and seemed incapable of holding her upright as she walked down the drive and onto the road. Leaving the vehicle against a hedge she slipped through a gap and sat on the icy grass of a field and stared into space. She was soon shivering with the cold as well as the humiliation of what she had heard. However kindly the words were spoken, people were laughing at her.

A tractor was approaching and she heard it stop, then someone opening the gate. She forced herself to stand, and, still shivering went to recover her bicycle.

'That you, Zena?' a voice called. Uncle Sam was standing just inside the gate. He approached her with a frown. 'Are you all right?'

'I'm just feeling a bit sick. Perhaps I'm getting a cold. I'll be all right when I get home in the warm.'

'I'm just delivering some food for the horse. Wait for me and I'll drive you home. Ten minutes at the most. Go and sit in the tractor, it's a bit warmer than sitting under a hedge. What were you thinking of?'

With the cycle on the trailer he took her home, went in and coaxed the fire into a blaze, made tea and found her a blanket. 'Make sure you eat something hot, and ring the farm if you need anything and Dad or I will come.'

A new brain is what I need, she thought, after thanking him.

'Jake isn't the only one to be guilty of vanity,' she admitted to Nelda later in the day. 'That's largely the reason I can't walk away, admit to my friends and family that I was wrong. It's failure to end all my long dreamed of plans, to be no longer one of a couple.'

'So despite knowing you're behaving like an idiot, you're going to listen to Jake and try to understand him, and make him see how he's letting you down? Will this take two minutes or will you need three? Come on, you need more respect for yourself than this.'

'He might accept that together we could do a lot to help others, but as a partnership, not pulling in different directions.'

Nelda raised an arm imitating a gun aimed overhead. 'Bang! I just shot a pig!'

Zena immediately felt more relaxed, having made a decision even though she knew it was not the sensible one, and she smiled at Nelda and thanked her for listening.

'It isn't me who needs to listen, silly girl, it's you!'

The following evening Nelda knocked at the door of Llyn Hir and walked in, the girls could be heard calling from the car. 'Zena, you didn't say Jake was home at the weekend. I wouldn't have asked you to work on Sunday if I'd known. Why didn't you tell me?'

'Because I didn't know,' Zena admitted with a wry smile. 'He brought Rose Conelly and that secretary and used my flat to give them a weekend break. He didn't tell me because then I couldn't say no. They needed a break and Madeleine had never seen the sea! How stupid am I?'

'Very!' Nelda said succinctly.

'I do understand, in a way.'

'Then you really are stupid! He's laughing at you, arranging secret surprises for strangers and treating you like a big bad bully who would ruin his kindnesses.'

'It isn't like that. Not really.'

'No?' She took Zena by the arm. 'Come back to the house with us, I'll feed my zoo animals and we can sit and talk. Or, you talk and I'll listen.'

While the children ate cakes and bickered in whispers, Zena tried to explain to her friend about Jake's desire to spread happiness, about his inability to keep something when there was someone who needed it more. Nelda did what she had promised and sat silently listening.

When the words of persuasion dried up, Nelda looked at her, head on one side questioningly, waiting for her friend to break the silence. Eventually she admitted defeat and asked, 'How did that sound to you, Zena, if it had been someone else talking? Convincing? Or a load of rubbish? Or a pathetic attempt to hang on to something that should have been discarded ages ago?'

'I'm stupid.'

'No you are not. Just loyal and trusting, and in love with a man who doesn't deserve your love. Jake Williams is more a fiasco than a fiancé. Another cup of tea?' she asked without changing her tone.

Zena burst into merry laughter. 'First I overheard Doris telling Mr Roberts that she was sorry for me, being involved with Jake Williams. I was convinced she was right and I should tell Jake goodbye. Then, on the way home, I talked myself out of it again and rehearsed a discussion in my mind. I would make Jake understand that he can't presume I feel the same as he does, that he owes me loyalty, I have to come first with him, as he does with me.' She glared at Nelda in mock anger. 'Now you've thrown everything into the air again, thoughts and decisions floating about like seeds on a dandelion clock.'

'Jake might always put you second, but at least you could try putting yourself first. That way decisions might come easier. Marrying "till death us do part", it's a very, very long time if you have any doubts.'

For Zena it was another sleepless night, her thoughts were spinning between one decision and another. At four o'clock she wrapped herself in her dressing gown and a blanket and revived the fire. Then she went to stand outside, listening to the night sounds. A swishing of the branches of the trees, different sounds from different species like a gentle symphony. An occasional call of an owl, the bark of a fox, all was familiar, soothing, comforting. The stars were clear in the chill cloudless dawn and she looked up, wishing she could name them.

As she sat there, other sounds began to disturb the peaceful scene: a car in the distance; the milkman rattling his bottles and churns. On Sam's farm, a rooster welcomed the new day. Relieved that her attempts at sleep could be abandoned, she went inside, lit the fire and sat in its warmth with a comforting cup of cocoa, and the inevitable toast in front of the desultory fire, more in hope then expectation. She tried to avoid thinking of nothing but the happy moments she had just spent in such simple pleasure.

Light from the porch showed the glitter of frost on the branches of trees and shrubs, and on the dead neglected flowers from the last summer. The grass on the lawn was an uneven carpet of white with blue shadows. The winter chill was cleansing and she felt refreshed.

These were moments she wouldn't be able to share with Jake.

His reaction to finding her outside watching the magical dawn of a new day would be the discomfort of the cold and the need to get back in and close the door. But those things were trivial, there were so many things they would share, although at that moment, she couldn't think of one.

The bread was curling near the coals but showing no sign of browning to a tempting snack but, as though the smell of the food had disturbed them, first her brother then her mother came down to join her. The early hour, the darkness, the cold and the welcoming fire, made them all feel like children enjoying a secret midnight feast They talked and laughed, memories of childhood enhancing the joyful mood. Today she would hold on to these peaceful, trouble-free moments and not think about Jake or his dishonesty. Problems could wait for another day.

Chapter Six

In London, Rose met Jake from time to time, usually with Madeleine, but sometimes on his own. Jake still lived in the shabby room in the poor area of London and Rose joined Madeleine in trying to persuade him to move.

'I don't feel secure enough in the job to risk having to pay more rent,' he insisted. 'If I get a promotion then, yes, I'll look for somewhere in more salubrious surroundings.' He looked questioningly at Madeleine. 'Is there any chance?'

'I asked Jerry as promised, Jake, and he said he would consider it. Since then he hasn't mentioned it, but don't give up. I think he really is doing just that, thinking about it. I know one of the salesmen is intending to give notice this month, so I planted the seed of the idea at just the right time.'

Jake muttered his thanks. He wanted a better job, of course he did; a chance of earning more money, of saving the money he needed for the wedding and the bed and breakfast business he and Zena had planned – but he was also disappointed. Leaving the firm would have been an excuse to return to Cold Brook Vale and Zena; a chance to start again and reaffirm their relationship. He had made new friends, and Madeleine and Rose filled many happy hours but he was lonely for Zena and her family in Llyn Hir, a family he'd known all his life. Losing a job would mean he could go home and that was what he wanted, wasn't it? Or was he still enchanted with the London life and wished Zena would join him? He stopped worrying. His fate lay with the boss's decision, not with his own, didn't it?

A few days later, Jeremy Fielding sent for him. He tidied himself as well as he could, straightened his collar and tie, combed his thick blond hair, rubbed his shoes with his sleeve and hurried to the office.

He wasn't invited to sit and he stood while Jeremy Fielding thumbed through a sheaf of papers, trying to hide his nervousness, telling himself it didn't matter whether or not he was offered a better job, that either way it would make his decision for him, go home or stay in London, it would be for the best. He watched the man's face, trying to judge from his expression what his immediate future would be.

Jeremy finally looked up and gave a friendly smile. 'Jake, I've been looking at your record for the short time you have been with us and the management has considered giving you a try as a sales representative. How d'you feel about that?'

'That's wonderful, sir. I like people and I'd love to meet customers and help them with their choices. Selling is something I've always felt I would excel at given a chance.'

'You will start by accompanying one of our experienced men, then you'll have an area of your own to cover. A circle around London, taking in the home counties. Then, if you do well, we'll send you further afield.'

'Thank you, sir. I won't let you down.'

'You do have a car? And a passport?'

'Yes, sir. A passport? That sounds very exciting.'

'It is, but it all depends on how well you do during the first few months.'

As he closed the office door, Madeleine was standing there and he raised two thumbs in a silent signal to show his success. They went into her office and hugged. He kissed her cheek then, slightly embarrassed, he moved from her and sat on a chair. 'How can I thank you? Madeleine, you have been – and are – a wonderful friend. I am so fortunate that coming to this place, so different from everything I'd known, that I found you. Thank you, for helping, and being a friend and – oh, come here!' He stood up from the chair and hugged her and kissed her cheek again. This time it was Madeleine who moved away, to stand behind her desk. Jake didn't apologize.

'Shall we meet Rose tonight and celebrate?' she asked.

'Yes, I need to mark this day and how better than with my two best friends?' It was more than an hour before he thought of telling Zena.

Mabs was very glad of Greg's help in the night café as, for some reason, the numbers of customers suddenly increased. It had been open for several years and rarely attracted more than eight people, but it was as though news had spread and others came to see if it was a place to spend a few of the lonely hours.

She and Frank had never asked the customers not to talk about the place but she knew they rarely did. They wanted it to be their secret and didn't want it to be so busy that the character of their night time haven would change.

Three strangers came one night and introduced themselves to very reluctant regulars. Will, Albert and Ted all lived in a small village about three miles away and they told Mabs they had heard of it from a man called Henry. Sid whispered to her that they must have met in prison. 'Clean hands, and typical haircuts,' he said mysteriously. 'Ex-prisoners they are, can't mistake 'em.'

The men behaved without causing problems; they seemed to know instinctively that questions would be frowned on and they sat and read the papers and played the various games, Albert making Henry growl menacingly by winning against him at draughts and then chess. He stood and seemed about to accuse them of cheating but a glance from Mabs and he sat down again.

They left just before the café closed. One of them came to the counter and offered a hand, a neat, clean hand she noticed with a smile. 'Thank you, Missus, we appreciate you letting us stay. Your welcome makes us all feel more hopeful of a better future. Ex-cons we are, if you haven't guessed, but now we're going straight.' All three touched their foreheads in a salute and they left, calling good-night to the others.

The rest shuffled out soon after, calling, 'Goodnight Frankie, Greg, see you tomorrow.'

The three newcomers stood for a while on the corner of the street, discussing in soft tones the people they had met. Sid hid

131

in the doorway and stared at them. He was always suspicious of any newcomer and in his opinion, three arriving at the same time certainly needed watching. He waited until the men moved off and in the chill dawn followed them.

He didn't notice one of them leave but suddenly there were only two. Then a voice behind him, very close to his ear said,' Following us, are you? Why is that then? Frankie's little watch dog, are you?'

The others moved back and Sid felt afraid. Then the three men laughed and walked away. Sid didn't try to follow, he scuttled around the corner and ran back home.

Zena hadn't heard from Jake for two weeks. The enthusiastic keeping in touch hadn't lasted very long and the phone calls and letters gradually faded and two weeks ago had stopped altogether. She still wrote but with so little contact there seemed little to say. Doubting that there was any chance of him reading her words, but others doing so, she said nothing of any importance. There was news about the family and a few comments on her job. She told him about Nelda and her little girls; he didn't know them but the chatter filled a page. She thought of the wives whose husbands had been away for years during the war and felt a surprising sympathy for the few who had gone astray, looking for love and comfort, while the letters from their men became more and more like those from a stranger.

She rarely saw Janey when she went to clean the house but her mother was often there, watching and checking on everything. Then there were the notes. Almost every time there was a list of things Janey needed her to do. Frequently these were things she normally did anyway, the implication being her failure to do the jobs properly. She suspected that the notes were written, not by Janey, but by her mother.

One day she met Janey and asked why she was so dissatisfied with what she achieved in two hours. 'To be frank, it takes me more than half an hour to sort the kitchen, before I start on the rest,' she explained politely.

'The kitchen? But I clear up before I leave every morning. It's the one place I do try to keep clean.'

Politeness forgotten, Zena asked, 'What about the spilt flour the other morning? The dishes left in the sink for me to wash? And the saucepans and the frying pan on the table, leaving pools of grease? And a week ago, there was spilt milk and broken milk bottles on the door step. I had to make sure that was cleared away in case the children hurt themselves. It all takes time.'

Janey stared at her. 'I left none of those things. I wouldn't. I value your help too much.'

'Someone did.'

'But who? The cats, d'you think?'

'A cat is one way of describing the culprit,' Zena muttered. 'Your mother doesn't like me, does she?' she asked pointedly.

'I hope you aren't suggesting that my mother would do this? Of course it wasn't Mammy, these are the actions of a child.'

'They don't seem like the actions of a child to me.' She paused, but Janey said nothing. 'Well, I'll leave it for you to fathom but I'm giving notice. I'll come for another week to give you a chance to find someone else, then I'm leaving.'

She cycled home filled with a sense of relief. She had other people asking for her services and it would be easy to fill the hours she had been giving to Janey; and they would be pleased with what she did, not critical. With Janey – or her mother – she would never be able to do enough. She always did more than clients expected and Trish was the only one to complain. What a relief to say goodbye to Janey and her miserable mother.

It was raining and a cold wind was blowing but, as she rode, her head uncovered and hands cold in soaking wet gloves, she sang at the top of her voice, 'O-o-o-o-h, it ain't gonner rain no more no more, it ain't gonner rain no more—'

Once home, warm and dry, she sat to write to Jake again, intending to tell him she had ticked Janey off her list of clients, but after writing her address and the date, she put it aside. What was the point in writing to him? He was no longer interested. Perhaps she ought to tick Jake off her list as well?

She had the feeling deep inside her that that was she ought to do. Their romance was over. He had made a life for himself in London and he hadn't even mentioned her joining him in his brief letters.

But that dreaded emptiness opened out before her again. Marriage was what every woman wanted, husband, children and a home to build to keep them safe and secure. There was stupid pride too. She would find it hard to tell people she was no longer engaged to marry Jake. Living at home with her mother while her youth slipped by was a dreary prospect. If only she had a career, something to fill her life. That was a way to compensate for marriage, a home and children, but she wondered if that would ever be enough.

She lay awake for hours after going to bed, tossing and turning, trying to visualize a future without the dream of marriage she had held for so long. All her childhood she had played games that prepared her for home making. In that dream there had only been Jake. At five o'clock she went down, pushed sticks in to the coals to revive the fire and made a cup of tea.

She was hardly the age to give up on life. Hanging on to a man who no longer loved her, afraid of there being nothing to replace what they had once had, was pathetic. She simply had to re-think what she wanted for her future, a future without Jake. It was time to make up her mind to forget Jake, tell him goodbye and face a future without him, or, that small voice whispered, or, she had to see him and find out if there was still something there, some faint shadow of their love that could be revived as she had revived the fire. Then she looked at the grate and saw that apart from a few thin columns of smoke the fire was out.

Dawn broke in a hazy silver mist and she wrapped up warmly and walked down the steep, twisting path to the lake. Beside the clear water had always been a place to sit and think. The boat in which they had regularly played imaginary journeys on the calm water, and had picnicked in favourite places on the shore, was still there. The timbers looked sound but pale, bleached by several summers. The rope which her father had attached to the raft he had made with the help of Uncle Sam, was gone and the raft was tilted to one side, the floats, made of metal barrels rusted; one was obviously leaking.

Despite the dereliction, this was a place holding nothing but happy memories. She smiled, listening to the sound of birdsong and the rustling of the wind in the grasses, Uncle Sam's tractor in the distance, probably taking churns of the morning's milk to the platform built at the edge of the road for collection. On the first warm Sunday she decided she would invite Nelda to bring the children and have a picnic there. Could Uncle Sam repair the raft, she wondered? It would be a safe introduction to the water for the girls. Sam, Neville and Greg dealt with it at once. Once mended, the raft was firmly attached to a new double rope, to each side of the lake, creating a pulley to move it across the lake.

Lottie had repeatedly searched all the papers in Ronald's desk and had found nothing that would explain the loss of their money. She had given the shed a cursory search too but had found nothing apart from the usual receipts from household bills. Mabs agreed to help her go through everything one more time in case at the end of one of her searches tiredness had caused her concentration to fail and she had missed something of importance.

The shed was more of an office really, lined with board and with a shelf that acted as a desk, and a swivel chair. The garden tools and the various tins and bottles of weed-killer and plant food, bamboo canes and balls of string were in another building that had once been a chicken coop. The shelves of the fairly new shed were lined with boxes, some containing paid bills relating to work done on the house. Some were filled with business letters together with carbon copies of the replies.

Lottie and Mabs both read these before putting them back in the relevant boxes. There was nothing to raise a curious eyebrow. Many of the papers went back to the time they had bought the house soon after they were married.

Lottie sighed. 'This is hopeless, Mabs. If Ronald had any secrets he hid them well.'

Mabs didn't answer and Lottie turned to see that Mabs was under the shelf that had served as a desk. 'Pass me a torch,' Mabs demanded, and when she shone a light into a space close to the wall, she paused for a moment then gave a gasp. 'Lottie, I think I've found something.'

She backed out, still holding the torch and with her hand full of small pieces of torn paper. She handed these to her sister-in-law.

'One of the pieces is initialled RUM. Ronald Unwyn Martin.'

Lottie took the screwed-up pieces of paper and spread them out. 'He used to joke about his initials, didn't he? Convinced he should have been a sailor or a drunkard.'

Together they sat and examined the scraps of paper. 'It looks like a bank statement of some kind.' Lottie whispered, as though they were intruding on someone else's privacy.

'Yes,' Mabs replied, also whispering, 'But unfortunately, there's no clue to which bank it is.'

'There aren't that many. It's bound to be a local one. We'll have to ask in them all.'

Without looking at her, Mabs asked, 'Lottie, are you sure you want to know?'

'What d'you mean? Of course I want to know why he left me in debt.'

'There's nothing you've done to make Ronald give the money away?'

With an impatient sigh, Lottie whispered, 'Mabs, we'll go together, you and I. If there are secrets to learn, then you will find out the moment that I do. Is that enough for you? Does that stop you mistrusting me?'

'Sorry.'

They tried without success to join some of the pieces but all they had were unconnected pieces of what must have been several pages. A few had what was obviously part-columns of money set out ready for totalling; pounds, shillings and pence, in one instance it appeared to be several hundred pounds. Ronald's handwriting appeared on two pieces, illegible words, and his signature, written across a postage stamp which was obviously a receipt for a payment.

'What can we do?' Mabs asked, still whispering.

'We can take this to the solicitor and ask him to investigate, or to the police. Or we can ask questions ourselves and hope to find out what happened.'

'I think we should do nothing for a few days, just wait to see if something else turns up to add to what we know.'

'We don't know much, do we?' Lottie said sadly.

'Maybe more than we did an hour ago.'

Roy Roberts set off for the bus stop with Doris's son, Kevin. 'Why don't you let Mam do your shopping, stubborn old devil that you are?' Kevin pleaded. 'She could have your delivery same day as ours, she works in town and could easily bring up bits and pieces when you need them.'

'I'd rather do my own, Kevin. I don't want the neighbourhood knowing what I have for dinner,' he joked.

'Going into town is dangerous for someone as decrepit as you, Popeye.'

Roy Roberts laughed. 'What shift are you on today?'

'Six this evening till two. I hate that shift. I can't go out in case I'm not back in time and I sleep late the following day and waste the morning.'

'It messes up your love life, no doubt.'

'I manage,' Kevin said with a chuckle. 'I do miss Rose Conelly though. She was good company and as long as I kept off the serious things, like courting and engagement, she was happy.'

'I thought she was serious about Greg Martin?'

'So did he!'

'She's in London, keeping company with Jake Williams, so I hear.'

'Considering how rarely you go out, you hear a lot, Popeye.'

The bus arrived and Kevin helped Roy Roberts to board.

Roy was relieved that Kevin hadn't insisted on coming with him, he needed privacy to visit his solicitor.

The appointment was for eleven o'clock and he made his way slowly to the offices and, to his dismay, Mabs saw him going in. She called to him.

'What d'you want a solicitor for, Roy Roberts? Been a naughty boy, have we?' she teased.

'I'm changing my will and leaving everything to you,' he replied, 'and if you don't mind your own business you'll lose the lot.'

Mabs waved and walked on. She was briefly curious but soon forgot seeing him.

Roy didn't want to discuss a will. He handed Mr Philips a file containing papers referring to some shares he owned. It was time to sell them. Time was passing and old age might prevent him doing what had to be done if he waited for too long. It took less than an hour to deal with his requests.

Buses were difficult for him so he took a taxi and went to Mabs's flat and sat on the outside and waited for her. She waved as she came around the corner and he stood stiffly to greet her. 'How about a cup of tea?' he asked.

She patted a paper bag in her basket. 'I must have known you were coming, Roy Roberts, I bought two custard slices.'

'How far have you got with the mystery of the missing money?' he asked, when they sat with tea and cakes before them.

'It's none of your business.'

'I've known Ronald since we were children. I'm curious to know how someone as mean and careful as Ronald could be so careless. Poor Lottie, she must be devastated.'

'What d'you mean, mean? And what d'you mean careless? Ronald would never be careless with money. And he wasn't mean! No, too generous more like.'

'Gambling maybe? Gambling can get a hold of you.'

'Not my brother! Someone cheated him out of it.'

Roy shrugged, decided not to say more. 'Are there any biscuits to go with a second cup of tea, Mabs?' She nodded thoughtfully then went to the kitchen to bring the biscuit tin with its design of wild flowers, and opened it. They finished eating and drinking in silence, smiling at each other occasionally.

'Thanks, Mabsy,' he said, as he was leaving. 'I'll bring the biscuits next time.'

'Was there any special reason for the visit, Roy?'

'Not really, just a catch up with a friend.'

Lottie looked at the bank statement that she had just received and gave a deep sigh. The debt had hardly changed. It was going to take a long time before it was paid. She put the statement in the file where she kept the outgoings and set off for work.

She was grateful to have the job. Selling office equipment wasn't a very exciting way to spend her days and when things were quiet she was utterly bored, but at least it was giving her a chance of eventually clearing her debt. She avoided working out how many years it would take at her present rate of pay.

She opened up and looked through the orders. Only three, they wouldn't take long and then she would sit and wait for a customer either calling in or phoning their requirements. She wished she had learned to knit. At least there would have been something to do while she sat waiting.

At lunchtime as she was closing the door, her boss Mr Lucas arrived and he gestured for her to go back inside. 'Mrs Martin – er – Lottie. I have something to tell you and you aren't going to like it.'

'Is there a problem? How can I help?' she asked with a smile.

'To come straight to the point, the business is closing. I'm very sorry.'

The smile on Lottie's face slowly faltered. 'You don't mean I'll lose my job? But I depend on it and if it means extra hours or adding something to my duties, I'll agree willingly, you know that.'

'Sorry, but there's nothing you can do. The business has been failing for some time and now it hardly makes enough for your wages.'

'I'll distribute some letters advertising the services we offer. There must be customers out there? Every firm needs something of what we supply. We can build it up again.'

He shook his head. 'I'm too old to fight my way back. I think the failure is due mainly due to my lack of enthusiasm. I haven't been calling on customers as I should; collecting monies, obtaining orders and making courtesy visits to customers when their orders are smaller than usual.'

Lottie was staring at him, no longer hearing the words, her mind racing with the implications, in shock and disbelief.

Seeing the distant expression on her face he coughed to make sure she was listening before saying, 'I am going to retire. So, at the end of the month I will pay you all I owe including holidays and a little extra, and the shop will close.'

Lottie muttered all the polite expressions of sympathy and assured him she would be 'just fine' then stood in the silent shop for a long time, trying to think of what she should do. Then there were moments of anger towards Ronald. How could he have let them down so badly? The simple answer was to sell the house and use the little remaining money to rent a small place, just large enough for herself and Zena and Greg. But that wouldn't work, they would still need a house the size of the one they had. The outgoings would be practically the same, too. But what else could she do?

Belatedly closing for lunch, Lottie didn't go home. She went to see Mabs. Mabs listened then gave a hoot of laughter. 'Cheer up, Lottie, you've reached rock bottom! With this on top of everything else there's only way to go and that's up! Now then, get yourself another job. That's the first thing.'

'You make it sound so easy,' Lottie said tearfully.

Zena was planning a change, but not one forced on her as Lottie's had been. Instead of looking for clients to fill the mornings she had worked for Janey Day, she decided to give notice to some of the others. She would continue to work for Mr Roberts and Nelda and look for another way of earning money for the rest of the time. She cycled home, her mind buzzing with possibilities. It was an exciting time; the world was hers from which she could choose a new beginning. The only possibility she did not consider was Jake, and London.

Sam called at Llyn Hir that evening with some butter made on the farm. Lottie was grateful but Sam could see at once that something was wrong. Quite at home in the house he had known for many years, he went into the kitchen, put the butter in the cold store and made a pot of tea. He set a tray, added the biscuit barrel and sat facing her. 'Now, tell me what happened today to upset you?'

'I've lost my job.'

'Why?'

'The business is failing and the shop is closing at the end of the month.'

'Has it been sold?'

'No, the stationery business is just closing down. Oh, Sam, what can I do? There's the debt Ronald left me with, which even with the wages I earned would have taken for ever to clear. Without a job I have no alternative, I'll have to sell the house.'

'What went wrong with the business, trouble with deliveries? I doubt if there were errors, not with you running the place, Kay.'

'Kay?' She laughed. 'You're the only one to call me that, now Ronald has gone.'

'So what went wrong?'

'I think Mr Lucas let things slide a little. Customers would ring me up and ask why he hadn't called as promised. Orders didn't reach the shop for me to deal with deliveries. Only small errors but there were too many. It's pointless to wonder why. It's happened and I'm out of a job.'

'If the business were yours, what changes would you make to get it on its feet again?'

'I would concentrate on advertising to bring more customers. And I would make sure every customer had the best of attention so they would use us again and, most importantly, recommend us to others. Word of mouth is still the best way to make a business grow. I would also increase the items we stock, make more use of the unused space we have. I would leave piles of orders and invoices cluttering the desk, even if they're out of date. It increases confidence to see the place busy.'

'Why don't you buy the business?'

'Oh yes. I'll magic the money out of the air, like rabbits from a conjurer's hat, shall I?'

'If you really want something, a way will be found. Just don't dismiss the idea before considering it. Right?' She stared at him and he began to laugh. 'Honestly, Kay, you're looking at me as though I'd made an improper suggestion!'

Lottie talked to Mabs later that day. 'Come and have tea with us on Sunday, I've got corned beef pasties and there're some scones with fresh farm butter to spread on them,' she coaxed.

'And there's something you want to tell me?' Mabs asked, tilting her head to one side questioningly. 'Come on, I can't wait until tomorrow. Have you discovered anything about Ronald?'

'No, it was something Sam said. I told him the shop was closing and I was losing my job and he suggested that I buy the business. It's impossible, of course, but if I hadn't been left with this debt,

141

maybe I'd have tried.'

'Talk to Zena why don't you? She hasn't a job either, so maybe you can work something out between you.'

'Where does the money come from? No, it's a lovely dream but that's all.'

'Talk to Zena!'

Rose was aware that Jake was including her more and more in his life and she began to feel the usual anxiety about a friend becoming too close. Without telling Jake or Madeleine she applied for a position in a very smart shoe shop. With her increased confidence and better clothes sense, she was given the position which came with a generous increase in salary. Talking to the other sales girls before she took up the post, and explaining that she was looking for accommodation, she was offered a share in a house with three other people, one of whom was a young man. It was west of London but with good routes into the city. Only then did she tell Madeleine of her new arrangements, but, promising to keep in touch, she avoided giving her the new address. She walked away knowing that once more she was without a friend.

It would always be like this, she thought sadly as she unpacked her small suitcase and boxes, and spread her few dismal belongings around the room to make a pretence of it being her home.

Jake was angry at her disappearance without a word. They had befriended her, coaxed her out to places she might not have seen on her own and she was treating them like the enemy! He told Madeleine he wouldn't try to find her.

'I have no interest in her problems – which, on her past behaviour, were probably invented, anyway. We've tried to help her: there's no justification for her to leave without a word.'

Madeleine smiled. Putting them in a room together might be fun.

Rose lay on her bed, listening to the other house-mates laughing and talking, knowing she was utterly alone. To feel the temptations of a love affair and have to walk away was becoming more difficult.

Although it was not for Jake she grieved, it was still Greg. If only she had had a normal childhood, how simple life would have been.

Exploring the area was fun, finding shops and concert halls, exhibitions, theatres and cinemas, and a small, friendly café where she ate most evenings. But she was aware again of the lack of someone to share her pleasures. Going to the pictures and not having a friend to discuss it with on the way home gave her that familiar hollow feeling. After a month she went to see Madeleine.

When she knocked on the door, Madeleine came out and hugged her, squealing with delight. 'Come in! Why haven't you been in touch? I insist on you giving me your new address.'

Rose hesitated. 'Before I do, will you promise not to tell Jake you've seen me?'

Madeleine pushed her into the living room. 'It's too late, dear. Jake, look who's here!'

Before she could protest, Jake leapt out of the armchair and hugged her, kissed her cheek and demanded to know where she had been. 'We've missed you, haven't we, Madeleine?'

'I – er – I've been busy settling in,' she said, flustered by the disappointment of seeing him.

Madeleine went to make tea and Jake patted the seat beside him. 'Come on, then. Where are you working, another shoe shop?'

'Yes, it's another shoe shop.' She hesitated, unwilling to tell him more.

'We went to the flat several times but no one knew where you'd gone. A letter was there for you and Madeleine opened it in case it was important. It was from Greg, telling you he missed you and would like you to get in touch.'

'There was a P S, it said "no strings",' added Madeleine coming in with a tray of tea and cakes.

'Greg and I – that was a long time ago. It's definitely over, best he forgets me.'

'No one could forget you, Rosie. I don't want you to go away again without telling us. Promise? We won't tell Greg where to find you, if that's what you wish.'

Rose relaxed and, trusting him to keep his word, began to amuse them with stories about the people in the shared house and

143

some of the customers she served in the smart shoe shop where she now worked.

They arranged to meet for the pictures later that week and Rose left them, content that the friendships were safe from any problems and she was no longer alone. Jake and Madeleine behaved like close friends; arms in arm, heads together She was reassured by their closeness. Jake was not seriously interested in her.

Jake phoned Llyn Hir one evening and Greg answered. He told Jake he had no idea where Zena had gone. 'She goes out a lot more than she used to,' he explained. 'And I'm glad she does. There's no point in her sitting here night after night waiting for a letter or a phone call from you!'

'I'm thinking of coming down next weekend.'

'A visit from you? Never! That's something she's given up expecting. What are you *doing* in London? A grotty room in a grotty street and a job that's far less glamorous than the one you lied to her about.' He didn't hide his anger and Jake was silent for a moment.

'The truth is—' As his excuses were about to begin, Greg put down the phone.

'*He* called this evening,' he told Zena when she got back from a visit to Nelda. 'Probably hoping to get me on his side, but I didn't listen.'

'I'm glad I was out,' Zena admitted. 'We need to talk face to face to end it properly.'

'He said he's thinking of coming down next weekend. How d'you feel about that?'

'Tempted to run away! But it's time this was sorted, so I'd better stay.'

'He only said he was *thinking* of coming, not a definite plan.'

'I suppose it depends whether Madeleine or Rose have something better to offer!'

'Tell him goodbye, Sis. You're worth better.'

Jake went home the following weekend and although he breezed in as he normally did, as though he had been away a few hours, instead of not having contacted Zena in weeks, he was shocked when Zena didn't return his smile.

'What's up, love? Don't tell me there's more bad news. Aunty Mabs is all right, isn't she?'

'We're all fine, Jake, and well used to managing without you in our lives.'

'What d'you mean? Out of your life? I never want to be out of your life. This family is all I want in the whole world.'

'Sorry Jake, but I want you to go back to London and not come here again.'

'I can't do that! We're engaged, we're getting married just as soon as I have enough money and a better job. And' – he went on as she was about to interrupt – 'it's good news, love. I've been promoted and I really am on the sales team now.'

'It's too late. It's over and I am going to start a new life, without wondering where you are, who you're with and when you will come home, or write, or even use the telephone.'

'Come out with me, we'll go for a meal and talk about it.'

'No Jake. I want you to go. Now.'

She walked to the door, opened it and stood there until he left. He was still talking, trying to convince her she was wrong, that he loved her and just wasn't any good at writing letters. She closed the door while he was still talking and ran to her room. She wouldn't cry. She wouldn't.

Her mother came soon after Jake had gone and called up to her. 'Zena, are you there? I've got something to tell you. I need your advice, dear.'

Zena went downstairs a wide smile stretching her mouth but not reaching her eyes. 'Mam, Jake was here and I've told him we're finished. I don't want to see him again, and – and ...' Then she cried.

It was some time and several cups of tea later before Lottie talked to her about Sam's suggestion. 'Of course I can't take on the business, much as I'd love to. There would be extra debt and I'm frantic enough about the one I already have. Adding to it would be the makings of disaster. But it was a wonderful dream for a while. I've been sitting in Mabs's flat working out how I would increase the business and I could see a successful future, but it's no use. There isn't the remotest chance of me finding the money.'

'How much would you need?'

Lottie stared up at the ceiling as if she were mapping her costings on its blank surface. 'I'd have to buy the stock and pay for the business to be transferred, and then there would be the monthly rent.' She gave an irritable shrug. 'I can't do it and I don't know why I am even thinking about it. There is a very slight hope, if I can accept it: Aunty Mabs has offered to join me as a silent partner. Is that possible, do think?'

'I have a better idea.' Zena's face became animated, grief for the end of her plans with Jake momentarily eased. 'What if I came as an *active* partner? I have the savings for a wedding that isn't going to happen, and rent from the flat every month, we can use that and cope until the business starts giving us a wage.'

'No, dear, I can't accept your money. You and Jake – you've dreamed of marrying him for so long, it might not be over – and I'd hate for you to do something you'd regret.'

'Mam, it really is over. It wasn't a dream, it was a nightmare and I'm free of it. I've been an idiot, putting up with his lies and, really, he abandoned me, didn't he? How many times do I have to forgive him for his dishonesty, and for always putting me last? I've been crazy to accept how he's behaved—getting a job and moving to London without discussing it and continually lying ever since.'

'I can't take your money, but I'm so thrilled that you're offering it. Keep it until you know what you want to do.'

'Ten minutes ago I had no idea where my life was going, but now I do' She was laughing in her excitement. 'I've worked in an office since I left school so I understand running an office. I've always thought the shop didn't stock enough of the day-to-day requirements of local needs. Also, I have good typing and short-hand skills. We could advertise my services for letters, applications for jobs, instruction leaflets, work for schools and colleges, and many other things. And what if we contact a printer and make a financial arrangement to benefit us both? We could do programmes for local events, all sorts of things.'

Lottie began to laugh. 'Zena, you are wonderful. I don't think we could possibly fail.'

'We'll do it?'

'Yes, my darling girl, let's do it!' She went to the telephone and spoke to Mr Lucas for a long time, then turned to her daughter, thumbs up. 'Mr Lucas has agreed to rent us the property!' Putting down the phone she said, 'Firstly we need to make an appointment with the solicitor. Then we'll go and tell Mabs.'

Greg was surprised, then very pleased at the decision involving both his mother and sister and offered to help. The three of them went to look over the property they were about to rent, all excitedly suggesting ideas for rearranging the shelves and making lists of ideas, including people to inform, and new lines to stock. They all went to bed early, completely exhausted.

Jake called the next day but there was no one at home. He sat on the cold-frame where cucumbers were grown during the summer, pulling out weeds, and practising what he would say when Zena returned. As darkness fell he gave up and went to his lodgings.

Zena, Greg, Lottie and Mabs were in a rather expensive restaurant celebrating the promise of an exciting, new life.

The next morning, before leaving for London, Jake called again, but although their voices could be heard talking and laughing, and he was convinced they knew he was there, no one answered his knock. He hung around until realizing he was likely to miss his train. Out of pique, he took Greg's bicycle and got there with seconds to spare. He left the cycle outside the ticket office.

Chapter Seven

ZENA AND NELDA planned a visit to the lake with the children. They were taking a picnic and staying for at least a few hours. It had been one of those deceptive periods; warm, sunny, the sky an unbelievable bright blue; Autumn's final attempt to hold back the start of winter.

It wasn't far from Llyn Hir taking the twisting path down the hill from the house and with two of them carrying what they needed it wouldn't be difficult. Sam had agreed to them lighting a fire and had promised to deliver some kindling and logs to make that easier.

On the day before the outing Zena was working for Roy Roberts and he seemed very against their spending time at the lake.

'Stay away from that place,' he warned. 'It's got a bad reputation. Evil things happen there. Far better that you stay in the fields. Or even the wood, that would be better than the lake.'

'A bad reputation? I've never heard of anything terrible happening there.' She smiled, remembering. 'The lake was a large part of our lives when we were children. Greg and I used to wait at the shallow area we called the beach to watch for Mam coming home with the shopping. Mam and Dad often rowed across instead of going by road, and every Christmas, that was the way our Christmas tree arrived, with us leaping about in excitement on the bank as soon as the boat left the other side.'

Roy wasn't convinced. 'Dark, dirty old place.'

'Oh, Mr Roberts. It's beautiful. The water is clean and fresh. We all swam there, Mam and Dad too. Did you know it's fed by the stream passing through Uncle Sam's farm? There's a slow trickle

148

into the lake which goes out on the other side, and that's why the lake is always the same depth.'

'Stay away from there. You can't imagine what lies beneath the surface.'

'If the stream fails we'll find out. The lake would quickly dry out.'

Zena was startled by the shocked reaction to her words. Roy staggered away from her and sat in his chair, staring at her. 'That couldn't happen!'

'Uncle Sam says the stream has never failed, but one day it might.'

Roy didn't say any more, but he was subdued and a film of sweat covered his face as he said goodbye and he didn't go to the door as he usually did, to wave her off.

She wondered if he'd had a frightening experience there: where there was water there was always a possibility of danger. She soon forgot about his anxiety and made plans for the games they would play on their picnic.

The biggest changes to Bobbie and Georgie through their adventures in the woods and around the lake were their confidence and increasing knowledge, and their clothes. They had soon found there was more fun to be had with less glamorous dresses and shoes, and wore wellingtons, trousers and easily washed jackets.

Beside preparing a fire ready for them to light in a carefully chosen place surrounded by gravel and far away from any foliage, Sam had left crisps and boiled eggs and a few small potatoes to cook in the ashes. These were always happy occasions and it wasn't until they were gathering their belongings ready to leave that day, Zena thought again of Roy's dislike of the place.

'What happens to the fish that die in there?' Georgie wondered. Her sister answered before her mother could give a thoughtful answer.

'They get eaten up by bigger fish!' which started Georgie crying. A not uncommon end to an exciting and tiring day. Zena thought about things dying and sinking down to the bottom and thought perhaps that had been what Roy had meant when he talked about the awful stuff beneath the surface.

Taking over the office supplies business was easier than either Lottie or Zena had expected. The place was rented to them by Mr Lucas. Having allowed the business to shrink, there was little stock and very reduced good will involved. The shop closed for one week only and during that week, Zena and Lottie concentrated on contacting previous customers and finding new ones. They also visited a local printer to arrange for them to print posters and cards and menus for orders they undertook to supply, explaining to everyone about the change of ownership. Greg went around the town delivering them and Susie Crane willingly helped.

Susie, a twenty-two year old with a happy outlook on life, made friends with everyone she met. She walked with a bouncing rhythm, her long dark hair flopping and sliding out its loose bunch at her neck, which Greg likened to Aunty Mabs's in its refusal to behave. Susie had begun her first day on her own without supervision, on Greg's bus and they at once felt comfortable with each other, there had been no attempt at flirting and the casual, easy friendship was a pleasant experience for Greg, used as he had been to Rose and her complicated problems and forbidden subjects.

With Sam helping with the decoration of the shop and making extra shelves, the place was ready for business redolent with the smell of new paint and shining windows, inviting customers to call.

On the Sunday before the reopening Zena and Lottie fell in to bed exhausted, but on Monday morning they awoke early and in great excitement. Long before the opening time of nine o'clock, they were in the newly arranged premises, trying not to look anxious while they waited for the phone to ring and for their first customers to call.

They tidied things that didn't need tidying, wrote lists of things to do, looking up with a prepared smile every time someone approached the door.

Fortunately, beside the publicity organized by Zena, Greg and Susie, Mabs had talked with several business people and by ten o'clock they were busy. At one o'clock they were laughing with excitement as they closed the door for lunch.

'It won't always be like this,' Lottie warned. 'Many of our

customers were just there out of curiosity.' Surprisingly, she was wrong.

Many local people remarked on the relief of having the service available once more and news spread about Zena's ability to type efficiently and fast. She was so busy during the first few weeks and determined not to keep people waiting, she often stayed after the shop closed to complete orders. To her surprise, Jake passed the window one evening and he waved and walked past. Although that was what she wanted, it was still upsetting for him to walk past without at least saying hello. Then he was back. He'd bought fish and chips and knocked on the door smiling and offering the steaming package.

It had been a shock to see him, and she became aware of how little she had thought of him during the last few days. Her emotions went from joy at the sight of his smiling, familiar face, to embarrassment, to anger and back to regret. She opened the door and said at once. 'Thank you, Jake, but I have to finish these letters. I've promised them for tomorrow morning.'

He waved away her protest. 'I won't interrupt your work. It's just that I saw you there and guessed you'd be hungry. But,' he added, staring at her with hope shining in his eyes, 'if you want to meet, I'm staying at the usual lodgings until Sunday evening.' As she shook her head, he added, 'Just an hour? This job I have, I'd love to tell you about it. I really am a salesman now and I'm good at it.' She shook her head and he went on, 'Come on, love, we're friends, aren't we? You've been a part of my life since we were six years old, so how can we pretend to be strangers?'

'I'm glad about the job.' She looked pointedly at the door and, putting the package on the desk, he blew a kiss and left.

She watched as he walked down the street and disappeared into the local public house, then she packed up and went home. It would mean starting very early in the morning but his visit had unsettled her and she couldn't finish her work. She collected the fish and chips with a smile; she would warm them in the oven. Their smell reminded her that she hadn't eaten since lunchtime.

Zena and Lottie worked long hours and the business grew. By July, to Lottie's relief, an encouraging amount of the debt had been paid and for Zena, it was as though she had found her niche in life. Jake hadn't called again and although she occasionally thought of him and wondered how he was, they were passing thoughts. It was as though Jake was someone she had once known – a very long time ago.

The office supplies shop filled her life, although she still called on Roy Roberts and on Nelda to help with their cleaning. Nelda was more a friend and she enjoyed helping to keep order in the chaotic household, and sometimes looking after the two girls. In a way, Roy Roberts was a friend too. She was pleased to call on him and help keep his house clean and tidy and usually stayed to share gossip about the neighbourhood both present and past. He had said nothing more about the lake.

It was from Mr Roberts that she heard news of Rose.

'She's still in London? But why does she keep running away? What has Greg done to make her behave so oddly? She can't be frightened of him. He would never do anything to hurt her.'

'It isn't Greg, not really. It's anyone who gets too close. A sad childhood that she won't admit to. It took away any confidence she might have developed. Maybe she's afraid of becoming dependent on a man, convinced no one could really love her. Or maybe she doesn't like the thought of being married, being so close to someone.' He coughed to hide his embarrassment, 'You know, getting close. Loving someone and – you know – all that?'

'She'll have to trust someone one day. Loving someone, then having to run away will make a very lonely life.'

Rose was enjoying her new position in the large shoe store, with several franchises within it selling only the very best quality. She still met Madeleine to go to the theatre or for a meal, and from Madeleine she heard of Jake's progress. Jake also heard of hers. Inevitably, with Madeleine enjoying herself, involved in the lives of others, they met. Madeleine had invited them both for a meal and neither knew the other would be there. She watched with amusement as they faced each other and showed their unease.

'Come on, you two,' she said with a peal of laughter. 'Just sit and enjoy the meal I've prepared and stop looking like two cats squaring up for a fight.' She left them to it and went into the small kitchen, from where she could hear the hesitant conversation begin, with 'How are you?' 'I'm fine how are you?' When she walked in with the casserole and vegetables on a tray, they were deep in conversation, laughing as they caught up with each other's life.

Jake told them both about Zena's new career, boasting about her as though he was in regular contact and was told every new development. In fact, he learned all he knew of her activities from the lady where he stayed on his visits home and although he had been home a few times since he had seen Zena at the shop and had bought her fish and chips, he hadn't tried to see her.

He spread out the little he knew, giving the impression that he was regularly informed. Perhaps that's why I'm such a successful salesman, he mused. Telling lies and expanding what I know to give the impression of knowing a lot more. Lying makes me good at the job, but lies were how I lost Zena and my future as part of the Martin family.

Thinking about her and the bleak future he faced without her, he announced one Friday when he went to Madeleine's office to hand in his sales forms and order details for the week, that he was going home to try one more time to talk to Zena. 'I've tried to forget her but I can't. I'm going to Cold Brook Vale to persuade her to try again to get back to how we were; happy, in love and planning our life together. I'll start looking for a job nearer home. I'll ask my landlady to send some newspapers and I'll start applying for jobs.

'Oh, Jake! What a shame,' Madeleine said, pouting in disappointment. 'I've bought three tickets for that play you wanted to see. Good seats too. Now I'll have to find someone else to come with Rose and me, and that is never as enjoyable as sharing the evening with friends you know well.'

'Sorry. I'd have told you sooner but I've only just made up my mind.'

'Does it have to be this weekend? If you haven't arranged anything ...' she coaxed.

'I don't suppose a week will make any difference. I'll write to my landlady and arrange to go next week. Thanks for booking for us. You'll tell Rose, will you? I don't know her newest address. When will that girl settle down, d'you think?'

'When she faces her demons I suppose.'

'There's something she can't risk others finding out, but I can't imagine what secret she has that's so terrible, can you? I can't see her as a villain.' He laughed. 'Rosie the ex-convict? That's crazy.'

'She's a frightened goose. It must be something from her childhood, although what it can be that makes her fear marriage I cannot imagine.'

'I try to reassure her that she's safe with me; she knows I only want to be her friend. I want to marry Zena: there will never be anyone else.'

Madeleine raised a quizzical eyebrow. 'You're sure of that, are you, Jake?'

A few days later, Madeleine answered a knock at her door and was surprised to see Greg there. 'Greg? What are you doing in London?'

'I'm with a coach party booked to do a sight-seeing tour and a theatre. Is Rose here by any chance?'

'No, of course she isn't. She doesn't live here!'

'I don't suppose you have her address?'

'I do,' she replied pompously, 'but I've promised not to give it to anyone.'

'Why? What does she think I'm going to do? I only want her to explain why she left.'

She went to the small desk and took out a piece of paper. 'Rose needs me as a trusted friend, so not a word about how you found it. Promise?'

'I'll think of some story to explain how I found her. After this I won't bother her again. I just want to know. I accept it's over between us, in fact, I've been seeing someone else, someone uncomplicated and happy. Tell her that if I don't manage to see her, will you?'

She gave him the piece of paper. 'She won't be in tonight, at least not until nine o'clock.'

'Thanks, Madeleine.' He left, clutching the piece of paper and at once began to plan his opening words.

*

154

On their way to meet Madeleine at the theatre, Rose was talking to Jake about Greg. Jake tried several ways to persuade her to explain why she was avoiding Greg, but she refused. Thinking of him, of what she had lost, was producing more anger than sorrow. Thinking of Lottie's success angered her more. She had never been punished for what she did. Everything worked out well for that evil woman called Kay!

They strolled through the busy streets, where people were filling the pavements with chatter and laughter. Heady perfumes were vying with the fumes from the buses, cars and taxis, and the smells from the restaurants already preparing for the evening rush. Gone were the formal office clothes and the casual dress of shoppers and mothers with children: the extravagant dresses, the smart evening suits as well as the loud, confident voices were indications that these were people bent on a lively few hours of fun. Fuming with resentment, Rose noticed nothing.

Rose and Jake stood in the foyer and Jake said, 'I want to marry Zena: there will never be anyone else. It's partly the dream of belonging to a family, to really belong,'

'What do you mean? You must have a family of your own.'

'I didn't know my parents.' He was alarmed at Rose's reaction to the casually said words. She turned and stared at him, her face losing its colour.

'You're an orphan? You were abandoned?'

'Not really. I knew who my parents were, but they left me and went to live in South Africa. My father had dreams of digging for gold. But the last I heard of him he was working in a factory earning a pittance and my mother had left him.' He looked at her; she was obviously distressed by his words. He hesitated, then, with an arm on her shoulders, asked softly, 'Is that what's worrying you? Are you an adopted child?'

'Of course not!' she snapped. 'Don't be ridiculous, I'm Rosemary Conelly and I lived with my parents.'

Jake wasn't convinced, but he changed the subject, bought a programme and coaxed her to look at the portraits of famous actors and actresses displayed on the walls. She looked but she seemed too distressed to take in the faces in their ornate frames or his words as he talked about them. She seemed relieved when Madeleine appeared and she at once began discussing some of the customers she had served that day.

Jake didn't become involved in the play, his mind was at the house called Llyn Hir, and Zena. He left as soon as he politely could, after finding a taxi and seeing Rose and Madeleine on their way. He wrote to his landlady when he reached home asking for the local paper listing job vacancies and went out to post it. Impatient now he had made up his mind, he tried to guess how soon he might expect a reply.

'Why don't you stay the night, Rose?' Madeleine offered, as the taxi approached her flat. 'Quickly, make up your mind before the taxi changes direction.' Rose agreed thankfully. The house where she now lived was noisy, with tenants coming in at all hours of the night, and the sound of footsteps, clattering on the stairs covered with noisy linoleum, was a nightmare. It was even worse when a late-night reveller tried to be quiet. Slow, hesitant footsteps were always accompanied by stifled giggles and cries as someone stumbled. A quiet sleep in Madeleine's flat was too good to refuse.

A bed was made up and Madeleine thought of Greg sitting on Rose's doorstep waiting for her. She smiled as she wondered how long he would wait.

Jake's landlady responded quickly to Jake's request for copies of the local paper and by good fortune it was the post boy himself who gave them to him as he passed through the busy room. He sat down at once to apply for jobs. He had four ready to post, when Madeleine offered to type them for him. 'They look much more impressive when they are professionally typed,' she told him.

At the end of the day she handed him carbon copies of the letters and assured him the top copies were already on their way. She smiled as she glanced at the waste bin where she had hidden the letters after tearing them up.

Greg went home after sitting until very late on the step of the address Madeleine had given him. He assumed she had returned and, seeing him there had gone away or entered by a back entrance. Either way it was clear that she didn't want to see him. He had to get a train; the coach with his friends on board had long gone.

When he stepped off the train, on which he had slept for three hours, he was wide awake. Glancing at his watch, he knew that the night café would still be open. Putting on a determined smile he opened the door to see Mabs beginning to pack up. Cups and plates were piled ready for washing up, the food cabinet was almost empty, and he went straight away to help, waving to the few remaining customers.

'Greg? Where did you spring from?'

'I went to London with the annual outing from the social club, but I missed the coach back so I caught a train. Any chance of a cup of tea and a sandwich?'

He talked about the show he hadn't seen as she made him a plate of food. Arthur, Sid and the newcomers Will, Albert and Ted stayed on, glad of an extra few minutes of warmth. Sid was still the last to leave. Having taken on responsibility for Mabs's safety, he always stood watching until she stepped on to the early bus and waved to him. Greg saw him now, gesturing for the others to go but they grinned at him and drank their last cup of tea with irritating slowness.

'The stationers is doing well, isn't it, Greg? Your mam and Zena work hard and they're building a successful business. Who'd have believed it, eh?'

'I think they're amazing.' He lowered his voice. 'If the takings continue as they are, they'll be millionaires in a twelvemonth', he joked.

'Your mother knew the trade and Zena had the skills and the necessary experience so they couldn't fail. You've been clever, going around gathering new and old customers. Come on, shift yourselves,' Mabs called as the last cup was put away. 'It's time I was in my bed. See you soon,' she added, as they trooped out.

Zena still did her cleaning jobs, unwilling to let Nelda or Mr Roberts down. She used the money to help her through the week, refusing to take more than a token amount from the business as wages, although business was slowly increasing and their weekly bank deposits were encouraging.

One lunchtime, a burly figure approached the shop, tried the door then walked to the corner, coming to the shop again at the back of the building. The flat above the shop was occupied and the tenant used the back entrance. Lottie only bothered to lock that door at night so the door gave easily to the gloved hand. The till was opened, the money taken and the figure was about to leave when he stopped and went onto the small store room. He pulled the files from the shelves, opened them and mixed the contents with a large boot, kicking them about angrily. The contents of the kettle was spilled onto the store of envelopes and typing paper added to the mess on the floor. Then the figure hidden in hooded duffle coat and heavy boots, left.

On that Friday, a few days after Greg's visit to London, Lottie and Zena went back after lunch with Mabs, to find the shop door wide open and the till completely empty. Zena stared at her mother's shocked face for a moment then ran to the phone to call the police. The phone had been pulled from the wall and smashed. She stepped warily into the stock room, half afraid of finding someone there, then wailed her dismay.

The shelves had been emptied, everything had been pulled off and lay in a muddled heap on the floor. Worse still the paid and unpaid bills were scattered, the books being prepared each day for the accountant, lay open with the used pages torn out.

To their surprise, the police arrived before they could gather their thoughts and find a telephone.

'Someone rang but he wouldn't leave a name,' they were told. The police took statements and asked people living or working near if they had seen any one near the shop at the time it was unattended. One lady who sat at her front window above the sweet shop for much of the day remembered seeing a man standing staring into the shop.

'He leaned in and looked around but didn't go inside,' she told the sergeant. Encouraged to describe him, she said he was 'big – huge' and might have had a beard. She smiled, her eyes glittering with enjoyment, thrilled to be helping in what she described as a daylight robbery. She went on to describe his clothes, closing her eyes as though to see him better. 'Trilby hat, scruffy suit, raincoat and a bright red scarf.' She opened her eyes, a dejected expression on her face, spread her hands in disappointment at not having more to offer. The sergeant said he might have been the man who called the police. 'What a pity I dozed off and didn't see the robbery,' she sighed. The policeman sighed and looked at his notes, which he suspected were worthless, thanked her and went away.

When Greg heard, he immediately thought of Arthur, the ex-convict who had been in the café when he and Mabs had been talking about the success of the stationers. The clothing was not unusual, but they sounded like those worn by the man whom Sid had described as having greedy eyes.

Arthur didn't appear at the café for a week. Greg knew he had to tell of his suspicions although the policeman laughed. 'A burglar with a beard? Something to make him easily recognisable? And in case you missed that, he wore a bright red scarf. A stupid thief if I've ever heard of one, then.'

Their mind was eased from the distress of the robbery by the increase in business giving them little time to dwell on it. Although it was only the end of October, reps were coming in with Christmas on their minds and promises of a better choice if orders were taken early. Surprisingly they were also receiving increases in orders for dance tickets, annual dinners, bridge cards; anything a customer requested would be on order within the hour. Determined to make Christmas a time to boost their business, there were crayons, pen sets, pencils, stationery boxes to fit in school satchels and similar items as gifts for children. Trade grew and increased their hopes of an end to their debts.

The year was set to end happily for them, Greg enjoying the company of Susie Crane, although still unable to free his mind of thoughts of Rose. Zena was no longer dreaming of a magical trans-formation of Jake into someone she could rely on, and Lottie was learning to cope with life without Ronald.

*

In London, Jake knew he had to go home for Christmas. He had received no replies to his applications for interviews in his plan to return home. That was one reason to go back for Christmas. The main one was that after his stupid behaviour the previous year, he knew Zena would never forgive him for missing another – even though she hadn't invited him. He wished he hadn't been persuaded by Madeleine to forget his intended visit, but she had already bought tickets, and he couldn't disappoint her, could he?

He went shopping with Madeleine and Rose and bought expensive crackers, a watch and a necklace, besides a variety of foodstuffs they had never seen in his home town. He made sure to pack his bank book to show Zena how well his savings – their savings – were growing. He crossed his fingers and hoped she still loved him enough to care. He would soon find out if the absence had made her regret telling him goodbye.

Although he knew he was being silly, he braced himself before telling Madeleine, afraid she would find a way to stop him going. As if she would bother. Last year was all about Rose and her unhappiness. This year, Rose was settled in a job she enjoyed and shared a house with people she liked. And recently she had seemed very happy, excited, almost as though she were holding a secret that would one day be told and would amaze them. They teased her on their evenings out when he was not travelling, but she wouldn't tell them what was giving her such secret joy.

Rose was happy, Madeleine would go to friends and, free of concerns about them he would go home and persuade Zena he had changed. No lies, no giving away possessions to people whom he thought deserved them more. He would concentrate on her to the exclusion of everyone else. Nothing Madeleine could say would change his mind this time. He checked the car, worked out the best route and began to count the days, like a child waiting for Father Christmas.

Bypassing Madeleine, he went to see his boss and asked for an extra day off over the Christmas holiday. When he was asked why, he decided to be completely truthful and not spin any of the stories his busy mind so easily invented. He explained that he and his fiancée had problems and he needed to see her, spend some time with her so they could get everything sorted out. He wasn't very hopeful, this wasn't the way to talk to the man who could sack him. Why was he such a fool, he wondered gloomily, as the man sat and stared at him for a frighteningly long time?

'I believe my employees work better when they are happy,' he said finally.

For Jake it sounded like the introduction to a speech telling him he should leave, that there was no room for people who are unhappy in his empire, but the man smiled, and said he could have two extra days leaving on 22nd and to make sure he had everything happily settled when he came back on 28 December.

Giddy with excitement, believing the permission was an augury for a good outcome, he danced outside the boss's office then ran to tell Madeleine. This was going to be the best Christmas ever!

Zena and her mother were setting off for the shop when a motor bike was heard coming up the hill. A hand waved and a smiling Kevin stopped beside them.

'Hello, are you coming to see us?' Lottie asked curiously.

'No.' He grinned at Zena, and lowered his voice. 'I'm going to the h-h-h-haunted h-h-h-house. What about that then?' He referred to the abandoned house at the end of the lane passing Llyn Hir, at the edge of the wood above Sam's farm.

He explained that he had been asked to open it up for the electricians and the gas inspectors to check everything for safety as someone was going to move in. He answered a few questions but knew very little apart from his instructions to look over the place and list anything that needed fixing before the tenants arrived. As they were about to move on, he looked at Zena. 'Fancy coming for a look-see?'

'That,' she replied, 'is an irresistible invitation. Yes, please.'

She looked at Lottie, who assured her she would manage in the shop for a couple of hours. 'There are only two people coming to pick up orders, I can manage until lunchtime of you want to stay awhile.'

'I'll take you back to the shop, right?' Kevin promised.

The house looked large and gloomy in the early sunless morning and Zena remembered the creepy feeling she had felt on childhood dares, when she went with giggling friends along the drive to peer through windows.

The door opened smoothly and there was no clutter of forgotten post on the tiled floor. Kevin flicked the switches but no lights came on. He held her hand and led her firstly along a passage through a ragged, green baize door into the kitchen, which was huge.

The room had a fireplace in front of which was something that looked like a Dutch oven, something with a row of hooks which would have been placed in front of a blazing fire to cook meat. The window was large, but letting in minimal light through its dirty panes. There was a long table with a few chairs, and a sink filled with dead insects and dirt, a gas cooker and what looked like a food safe that belonged outside in a shady place.

In silence they explored the rest of the house, Kevin still holding her hand. A few rooms looked reasonably orderly but the rest had been the repository for unwanted, discarded, dust-covered items. Where there were curtains they were filled with dust that bloomed out when they were touched, and in places had lost their colour and were rotting.

Although it was cold, they sat outside to wait for the surveyors to arrive. They talked about the stories they had invented as children. Even though they hadn't known each other then, their adventures at the lake and the old house were surprisingly similar. He opened his heavy coat and wrapped her against him, an arm around her shoulders, and she snuggled against him, glad of his extra warmth.

The surveyors were there for more than an hour, measuring, and making notes before thanking them, and going on their way. They checked the rooms to make sure nothing had been disturbed, and Kevin locked the door and then they too prepared to leave.

'Someone is going to have a job getting that place habitable,' Zena said, looking back at the unloved house.

'Want the job?'

'Only if I can burn all those curtains!' She was shivering.

'Put your coat on backwards,' Kevin said, and shook his head when she laughed. She did so, and once on their way she realized it had made sense. The collar was high around her throat instead of there being the gap in the lapels, and she arrived at the shop warmer than she'd expected.

Zena was approaching Mr Roberts's house a few days later when she saw someone leaving, running fast, he turned towards her then ducked behind a hedge. Curious she pressed hard on the pedals and cycled in the same direction. As she reached the hedge where he had disappeared, she felt a pull at the bike, and was aware of someone behind her pulling on the saddle, slowing her. Then, before she could react, the bike was pushed on its side and she fell.

For a moment she lay there, and foolishly thought about the cake and pastries she had brought for Mr Roberts; they had spilled onto the ground and would be ruined. Then her leg began to hurt, then her ankle that was pressing against the chain, then her elbow started to throb. Slowly she picked herself up. Stopping to collect the wrapped gifts, even though they were probably just a package of crumbs, she left the cycle and limped in to the house, calling as she let herself in.

Doris ran out of her door at the same time and went to help Zena who was limping badly. 'What happened? I heard shouting and came out and there you are, an accident looking for somewhere to happen,' she joked, then she realized that Zena was badly hurt. 'Come on, love, let's get you inside. What happened to you, fell off your bike, did you?' She led her into the kitchen and called, 'Roy? Where are you? Come here. Young Zena fell off her bike. Where is the man,' she muttered.

'Someone pushed me off,' Zena said, tearfully. 'I didn't just fall.'

Doris helped her to a chair and she began to shiver, her arms trembling and her teeth chattering. 'Right,' Doris said. 'Roy must be out, so you'd better come in with me and we can get you a good hot cup of tea with lots of sugar.' As she began to lead her out, arm around her, talking soothingly, reassuring her, the hall door opened and Roy Roberts stood there, his eyes wide with shock, his hand that held the door handle smeared with blood.

'Roy? What the...? What on earth is happening here?'

'A burglary. That's what.'

163

'I'll get you both cleaned up and comfortable then I'm calling the police,' Doris said, as she filled the kettle and set a tray. Then she went to Roy's kitchen cupboard, took out the first aid box and began cleaning Zena's wounds, wrapping her grazed leg and arm in bandages. Then she attended to Roy, who had bruises already developing on his face. 'Tell me what happened?' she demanded, 'the police will want to know every detail, mind.'

'I don't want you to tell the police,' he said. 'I can't tell them anything. I didn't see the man, he just pushed past me and ran out.' Then with an alarmed glance at Zena, he asked. 'Did you see him?'

'No. I couldn't describe him, he pulled on the back of my bike to stop me and then pushed it and I fell. I didn't even get a glance at him.'

Roy shrugged. 'Waste of time calling the police.' Then he realized his neglect and turned to Zena. 'I'm sorry, I was so shocked I didn't think of asking you how you are.'

'Got any cake, Roy?' Doris asked. 'Carbohydrate is good for shock.'

Zena pointed to the bag she had been carrying. 'There's a cake in there but I don't know if it will be fit to eat.'

She was still trembling when, after cake and several cups of sweet tea, she told them about the break-in at the shop. 'Could it have been the same man?' she wondered. She told them the description given to the police by a neighbour and at once Roy insisted that it must have been the same man. 'It's all coming back to me. I remember now, he was burly, dressed in shabby clothes and he wore a red scarf.'

Doris praised his memory but Zena didn't believe him and wondered why he had lied. The description had been a fantasy imagined by an old lady who had enjoyed momentary importance.

After the police came, asked questions and were gone, they went out to see if the bike was fit to ride. Apart from a twisted handlebar and a brake that was stuck, it looked possible to ride after a few adjustments, but Doris looked doubtful. 'I'll call Kevin, he'll give you a lift home and you can collect the bike tomorrow when you're feeling better. He's asleep, but he won't mind me waking him. Good lad, our Kevin.'

THE END OF A JOURNEY

Zena was quiet as they waited for Kevin to appear. A strong suspicion was growing. The man who had been seen standing at the doorway of the shop at the time of the break-in could have been one of Mab's night café regulars. Several of them were exprisoners, and they could easily have overheard Greg or Aunty Mabs mentioning that the shop closed and was empty at lunchtime. She crossed her fingers and hoped she was wrong.

Riding pillion on a motor bike was something she would normally have enjoyed but afterwards she had no recollection about the ride apart from hugging Kevin as she had on the ride to the old house. Her mind had been full of all that had happened, suspicions and possible reasons for the attack on her filtering through her mind, faces and names, all abandoned. There was no one in her life who would do such a thing, except the customers in the night café about whom so little was known.

She explained the lack of memory to Kevin, when he called the next day to ask how she was, he said. 'Right, then. Next time I have a Sunday off, I'll take you for a proper ride. Clear your mind of the whole thing. Right?'

She smiled and nodded, but she didn't think it would happen. On a summer's day perhaps, but in December? Definitely not!

Nelda rang Zena to ask if she could look after the children when school finished but when she heard of the incident at Roy Roberts's house, she changed her plans and called with flowers and some chocolate. 'Poor you! What did the police say, is there any news about an arrest?'

'I don't think they stand a chance with the robbery at the shop, or finding the maniac who pulled me off my bike.' She explained to her concerned friend what had happened but couldn't talk of her suspicions that the man was one of Mabs's night café regulars. She had promised to say nothing about Mab's secret night-life and was determined to keep her word.

Days passed and the police had so little to go on that they had little hope of finding Zena's attacker. There seemed no reason for it unless it was someone having a bit of fun. 'The theft from the shop could have been done by someone wandering through the village and, seeing an opportunity, took the money and ran. The door was unlocked,' the constable her.

'Why did he make such a mess in the store room? If what you say is true then he'd have got out as fast as he could, not stop to mess up the files and papers.'

'He might have been looking for something he could sell.'

'Among statements? Receipts? Invoices?'

'We are thinking of all the angles,' the constable assured her, but Zena thought his words were hollow, convinced that he didn't believe them any more than she did. 'You've arranged for a stronger lock to be fitted?'

'Of course,' she said impatiently. 'It isn't only the money – that we can ill afford – it's the anxiety for my mother when she's here alone.'

The young constable made vague promises and a few sympathetic noises, scribbled a few notes in his book and left.

Jake was leaving the office on the 20 December before he told Madeleine that he was leaving after work in two days' time. He hadn't mentioned it before, half afraid she would find a reason to stop him. Rose wouldn't be a reason this year, she was happily settled with new friends and it was unlikely she would be spending Christmas alone.

He spent the evening ironing – a job he hated, but he wanted to look his best when he met Zena – and packing clothes and gifts for the family. Then he cleaned the room and threw away any food that was likely to smell before he returned, and lay on the bed and dreamed about a happy reunion in which all their differences would melt away. He had to persuade her to try.

The next morning he was met, not by Madeleine but Millie, a shy young typist, who told him that Madeleine had had an accident and would be in after a visit to the doctor. For one guilty moment, Jake wondered if this would cause him to change his plan. Then sympathy returned and he asked what had happened. Before she replied, the phone rang and he was told by the typist that Madeleine couldn't walk, she had strained her ankle badly and wouldn't be at work until after Christmas.

'How on earth will she manage?' Millie said. 'She lives alone and it's Christmas, with everything closed down.'

'I'm not far from her flat later today so I'll call and see what we can do,' he said. His glum expression was not for the struggles of Madeleine, but anxiety for his own arrangements. He knew that even with his future dependent on the next few days, he would be unable to walk away and leave her in trouble.

Millie called him back and handed him a letter. 'This came for you this morning,' she said. 'That's the third one this week! Aren't you lucky. I never get any letters except and Christmas and birthdays.' A glance at the envelope told him it was from Zena. He didn't open it as he needed a quiet moment to read it. Millie's words about this being the third didn't penetrate as he thanked her and pushed it into his pocket.

When he finished his calls he went first to see Rose. She was sure to help Madeleine after receiving so many kindnesses from her. Rose wasn't there. Another tenant offered to give her a message, but that wasn't reliable enough. He couldn't leave unless he knew that someone was there to help Madeleine, even if that someone was himself. A small voice inside him murmured that this was exactly the kind of situation that Zena would never understand.

He left a note and pushed it under Rose's door promising to call back later, then went to find a café to eat and pass a couple of hours. There was still no sign of Rose. He drove back to the office and pushed his day's orders and cheques through the letter box. Another visit to Rose, another note passed under the door, then, with no alternative, he went to see Madeleine.

He knocked on her door and heard her call, 'Wait, please. It will take me a minute or so to answer.' He heard shuffling foot-steps and the tapping of a walking stick until she finally opened the door. Giving a sigh of relief she hugged him. 'Jake, I knew you'd come.' Struggling with an obviously painful foot, she led him into the living room.

'Sorry it's so late, but I've been trying to find Rose to see if she can help while I'm away.'

'She's at a party tonight and she's going to Norfolk for Christmas, so she can't help me. There's only you, Jake.' She struggled to sit in an uncomfortable dining chair. 'For this evening at least,' she added sadly. 'I just don't know how I'll manage.'

'Can't you go to your parents?'

'Definitely not. But even if I chose to, they both live in France. How d'you think I'd get there?'

'There's time to arrange the journey. I can help, I'll book everything before I leave in the morning.' He tried to speak with determination but he was wavering.

'Sorry, Jake, I'm on my own; there's no one who will help. I'll have to manage, won't I? Perhaps, if you could do some shopping for me ...'

'Maybe I could leave my visit home for a day or so, but, Madeleine, I really have to go. I have to put things right between myself and Zena.'

He drove back to his sparse room which looked even less inviting now he had cleared everything ready for his departure. Angry with himself, he knew he would have to stay at least for another day or two. Thank goodness he hadn't told Zena he would be there.

Greg stepped off the London train. It was still very early but he was meeting Jake at twelve and hoped to find Rose soon after. He fingered the note in his pocket with a cutting from the newspaper attached. A death announcement. Rose's stepfather had died and, unsure about writing to the house where letters could so easily go astray, he hoped to see her, tell her and perhaps persuade her to go back with him to see her stepmother and offer sympathy.

He waited at the place he had suggested to Jake they would meet but after more than an hour had passed, he knew Jake was not coming. He was unaware that the letter he had written making the arrangement had been read, torn up and thrown in the litter bin. With a sigh of irritation, he set off to find the house where Rose lived.

This wasn't his kind of place and he felt like a visitor from another world. The voices were almost like a foreign language, the shops weren't the same and even the buses sounded different from the familiar buses at home.

He found the house, went in and knocked the door of her

room. No reply. He gave an irritated growl. This has been a waste of money and time. He had written to Jake over a week before and asked to meet him, stating a time and place and Jake hadn't bothered to turn up. Now his kind thought in letting Rose know about the death of her stepfather had gone wrong too. He stepped out into the street, tightening his scarf around his neck, pulling up his collar and tightening his trilby more firmly on his head. It was very cold. A keen wind wailed between the buildings and sent leaves and rubbish bowling along the gutters. Storm clouds were a heavy grey and seemed to be low enough to touch the roofs. He was fed up and a long way from home.

With his head bent against the wind he stumbled as he bumped into someone. He began to apologize but stopped and stared angrily at the man, who, like himself, was wrapped in extra clothes. 'Jake! I waited for over a hour, where were you? Weather put you off, did it? Couldn't be bothered to meet me?'

'Meet you? What are you talking about? Why are you here?'

'I wrote explaining about Rose's stepfather and asked you to come with me when I tell her. I gave a time and place but you didn't turn up!'

'What about Rose's stepfather? Ill, is he? I haven't had a letter from you.'

'Of course you did. I posted it days ago.'

They found a café for a late lunch and it became clear that the letter hadn't arrived. Or, Jake was beginning to suspect, it had arrived but not handed to him. He belatedly remembered Millie remarking on that morning's letter being the third that week. 'I'm sorry, Greg, but – and this isn't a made-up excuse – I think my mail is being given to the wrong person.'

Greg showed him the obituary Then they went back to the house where Rose lived and prepared to wait.

'Madeleine told me Rose is going away for Christmas but she should be home this evening. How long can you stay? '

'I can't wait to get home, to the soft, clean sea air and the peace and quiet of living in Llyn Hir but I think she would want to know, so I'll suffer the city for another couple of hours, or,' he said hopefully, 'perhaps you could tell her?'

169

'Madeleine has hurt her ankle,' Jake explained. 'I wanted to see Rose in the hope she would stay with her until she's able to walk easily.' He looked away from Greg's curious gaze. 'Truth is, I was all ready to leave for home today, but, Madeleine, well, I can't leave her in such a state. I have to get some help for her.'

'Why?'

'It's Christmas; she's hobbling about in two sticks. I can't leave her without help, can I?'

'And if you can't find any help? What then?'

'I'll still come home but I'll have to shorten my visit.' He looked at Greg's cynical face. 'All right, what would you do?'

'Oh, I'm an old-fashioned sort, I'd put my fiancée first.'

Before Jake could say anything more, Rose approached the door, stopped and called to them. 'Greg? Jake? What are you doing here?'

'Freezing to death!' Greg said. 'I have some news for you, not good news I'm afraid.'

'Tell me.'

'Let's go inside.' The room was no warmer than the street and, with hands stiff with the cold, he took out the cutting again and handed it to her. He put an arm around her shoulder but she pushed him away.

'Oh.' She thrust the cutting back at him. 'I suppose you think I should go and see Mother,' she said harshly.

'The reason that *I'm* here,' Jake said, 'is that Madeleine has hurt her ankle and she needs some help. I have to go home, but we can't leave her without some help over the holiday. Can we?'

'I'll cancel everything and stay with Madeleine,' Rose said. 'Mother will have to wait.'

'You can't do that!' Greg gasped.

Rose looked at him, 'Madeleine's friendship is more important to me than my stepmother.'

'Is there a phone box near here?' Jake asked. 'I'll ring my landlady and see if she has a spare room. What about you and Madeleine coming? You can see your mother and stay with us. It's the best solution.'

It was agreed and, two hours later, Madeleine and Greg were

in Jake's car and arrangements were made for Rose to travel down after the shops closed on Christmas Eve. When they stopped for a warming drink somewhere near Gloucester, Greg looked at Jake and demanded, 'If you hadn't been able to arrange this, you'd have stayed with Madeleine, wouldn't you?'

'I'm sorry, Greg, but it's what I do, what I am. I can't ignore someone in need of something that I have. In this case, my time. One day Zena will understand and know I love her in spite of the things I do for other people.'

'That's presuming that my sister is a fool. I think you're in for a disappointment, Jake.'

Rose didn't want to see the cold, unkind woman who insisted she called her mother. The room into which she was ushered like an uninvited visitor was cold too. Not even a bar on the electric fire offering a semblance of welcome. There were no Christmas trimmings and not a single card on display. How had she survived sixteen years living here, she wondered? She didn't stay long. She said her piece and came out in just under four minutes, calling, 'I'll see you tomorrow,' knowing that was not going to happen.

Greg was waiting and they walked to the room Jake had booked for her, and joined Madeleine who looked quite excited at the prospect of an unexpected Welsh Christmas. Greg wondered if he was the only one who noticed how frequently she walked on her damaged ankle when she thought no one was looking.

'Is your mother all right?' Jake asked and Rose glared at him.

'Of course she is. She wouldn't let a trivial thing like the death of her husband change anything!'

'Rose, you can't talk like that!'

'Oh yes I can. One day I'll tell you the truth about my *loving* stepmother; what it was really like living in that awful place. It's something I've never told a soul. But not now, so don't ask!' Her eyes were bright with unshed tears.

As they walked back to the lodgings Jake put an arm around her shoulder and this time she didn't pull away.

Chapter Eight

GREG AND ZENA were in the front garden of the house, carrying some refuse to the bin near the gate, when a car went past. They looked at each other in surprise. Apart from the big house at the end of the lane, beyond it was a neglected woodland and Uncle Sam's farmland. So where would the car be going?

'That's the third one I've seen this week,' Zena said. 'Do you think the new tenants for our haunted house are coming at last?'

'Builders to knock it down more likely. According to what you saw when you went in with Kevin, it's in a poor state.' He grinned, a boyish, mischievous grin. 'Shall we go down tonight and look around like we did when we were little?'

'Scare ourselves silly, you mean? Yes, why not.'

Wrapping themselves against the gloomy evening, and armed with two torches, they set off about nine o'clock. It was very cold and a mist had settled close to the ground. When they came to the edge of the woodland they stopped. Moisture dripped from the evergreen leaves of holly and ivy making small rhythmical tapping sounds. Other unidentifiable squeaks and scurrying sounds made them look nervously about them, their eyes trying in vain to pierce the moist darkness.

They were tempted to give up and turn back but continued on, more afraid of the teasing they would face from Lottie and Mabs if they ran home scared, than anything they could imagine confronting in the eerie darkness. In the distance there was the occasional hum of traffic, close by there was silence, broken only by the sound of their footsteps. The quiet made them whisper and tread carefully to avoid unnecessary noise. 'I feel like an interloper,'

Zena whispered, and Greg whispered back, 'We are! We passed the sign warning trespassers to go no further, minutes ago.'

The large wooden gates creaked as they pushed them open and they went slowly along the drive, listening for a sound that might represent danger. Although they knew nothing was there to harm them, their childhood memories returned to make their hearts race as though the dangers were real, reliving their childish adventures when every leaf that moved made them start in fright.

Soon they began to laugh as they pictured what they must look like, creeping along towards an empty house like the scared children they had once been. Again the eerie silence around them sobered them, stifled their laughter, as they headed for the steps leading up to the porch and the imposing front door.

Leaves had built up in the porch but there was a pattern shaped like twin fans where the doorway had been carelessly swept, presumably by the broom that stood in a corner. 'Someone's been here since I came with Kevin,' she whispered. 'Perhaps they're still inside, watching us.'

'How can you imagine that!'

'The porch, it's been swept, the leaves weren't neatly piled up like that.' She flicked the torch on briefly, the darkness greater because of it. They stood for a moment then walked down the steps and along the side of the building.

Peering through a dirt-stained window revealed nothing and they went further, towards the back of the house. No lights showed through the mist and peering through other windows revealed nothing. It was difficult to make out the path amid the overgrown weeds, but with growing confidence they turned another corner towards the back door. They stopped in shock seeing a car parked there revealed by a thin light coming through a window that looked out onto what once had been a lawn. A voice from inside, called, 'Karen? Are you there? Can you find the Bing Crosby record for me?'

Before they could turn away they heard the sound of footsteps running towards them and Greg pulled Zena against the wall. A man came lumbering past without seeing them, dressed in heavy clothes and carrying a bag over his shoulder. A large, wide-brimmed hat on his head added to the impression of a very large individual. He was enormous and, as he passed very close to them a musty smell invaded heir nose. 'A tramp by the smell of him,' Greg whispered. In the faint light from the window they saw that he was bearded. Then, a branch of a holly tree touched his head and his hat came off and revealed a head of thick, white hair. They waited until he passed them, afraid to move, until the sound of his footsteps faded then they ran, uncaring about being seen, for the gate.

They slowed their pace and relaxed as they left the house further and further behind. By the time they were back at Llyn Hir they were laughing breathlessly, as they tried to tell their mother about their adventure between giggles, exaggerating what had happened, adding to the fun.

'It was fun,' Zena admitted, 'but I wouldn't fancy going there on my own, even in the daytime.'

'I bet that old man we saw has been sleeping there and was as frightened as we were at finding it occupied.'

From the first moment he had met Susie Crane, Greg had warmed to her. She was small, barely up to his shoulder, rosy-faced, with wildly luxurious hair in a soft shining light brown, and she extended a cheerful smile for everyone she met. Greg had spoken to her on her first shift, welcomed her and promised to help with any problems she might have, although he was certain even at a first meeting that she wasn't the type to need help with anything she encountered. Behind the smile was a young woman brimming with confidence.

They had been out together a few times and, when they met in the canteen and he told her about the previous evening when he and Zena dared to go to the big house, he didn't exaggerate his nervousness! He implied that he was looking after his sister. Susie crocked an eyebrow and gave a mischievous grin. 'All right, it was creepy,' he admitted, 'but we both knew there wasn't really any danger.'

'It sounds like fun,' she said. 'Was there really someone talking, or was it a ghost? If you go again, can I come?' Her blue eyes were shining at the prospect of a ghost hunt. Greg thought that searching for ghosts with Susie would most definitely be fun.

He invited her out for a meal a few days later and he laughed as she told him some of her misconceptions about the job, and about the customers she was getting to know, and a few who thought that, as they were neighbours, they might get off without paying.

'No chance of that!' she said firmly. 'I like this job and I want to keep it.'

Greg asked what she was doing at Christmas. 'You're local, so I presume you live at home?'

'Right, and there are aunties and uncles and cousins by the dozen. Why don't you join us? Mam loves visitors and likes nothing better than a full house at Christmas.'

They made plans for a visit to Susie's family on Christmas evening, and Susie was invited to Llyn Hir for afternoon tea on Boxing Day. Greg rode home singing at the top of his voice, peddling in time to the music. He would forget about Rose; they were unlikely to meet again anyway, and enjoy the company of the light-hearted and uncomplicated Susie.

When he reached home a phone call told him that Rose was coming for the few days and he shed his happy mood like an over-sized cloak. His feelings were mixed; pleased at a chance for her to explain, and disappointed. He explained to Lottie that he might have to rearrange Susie's visit to avoid Rose and Susie arriving together. Lottie couldn't see why but she said nothing. Greg and Zena had to sort out their own problems.

On the phone to Madeleine's flat, Greg asked Jake when Rose was likely to come to see him and explained about Susie. 'Just a friendly invitation,' he assured Jake.

'Hang on, Rose is here, I'll ask her.' Rose shook her head firmly at the question of when she would visit Llyn Hir. 'I won't be calling there. Please tell Greg, will you?' Then Jake mentioned Susie, Greg's new 'friend' and she reacted even more strongly.

'Why should he change his plans? He's free to see anyone he pleases, we're finished and he knows it.'

Still holding the phone, Jake whispered, 'He's hoping you'll have a change of heart, Rose. You know how he feels about you.'

'I have no desire to marry Greg, not now, not ever. Tell him that, will you, even though he knows it already? I hope he invites this Susie and I wish him nothing but happiness. Greg and I are history! Nothing will change my mind. There, is that clear enough?'

After reporting her response, Jake replaced the phone. 'Why, Rose? For goodness sake, tell me what happened to make you dislike him so much?'

'Nothing happened and I don't dislike him. I just won't marry him.'

'Then there's someone else?'

'There is no one else, I don't want to marry him. Why doesn't he accept that?'

The night café had had extra customers during the weeks leading up to Christmas, including a tall, white-haired man in his sixties, who looked enormous until he shed several layers in the warmth of the café. His name, he told them was Percy and apart from that he told them very little. He chatted in a friendly manner but was adept at avoiding answers to direct questions. Mabs frowned at Sid more than once, who as usual was taking on the responsibility of checking any one who came.

Greg wasn't certain at first, but, as the man prepared to leave, piling on layer after layer, and found a large hat from his bundle, he recognized him as the man who ran past as he and Zena were hiding at the back of the old house.

It was Mabs's firm rule that no questions were asked, but Greg walked out with the man called Percy and said, 'My sister and I were at that old house down towards Edwards's farm a week ago. D'you know the place? We used to go there as kids and we went back trying to remember how frightening it used to be. Daft, eh?'

'It's still frightening. I spend the days there and get out of it at night. I overslept one day and it was dark when I came away, chased by a strange voice when there's no one there.'

'But we saw a car, someone must be living there.'

'That car hasn't moved in years. I sleep in it sometimes when the rain's bad. But it smells of mould and mildew and it takes days to get the smell out of my stuff.'

The man was well spoken and Greg dared to ask, 'Why do you

live like this? It's clearly not the life you're used to.'

'Oh, you can get used to anything in time and I have nothing to go back to.' He walked away to find somewhere to sleep away the daylight hours before returning to spend the night hours with Sid, Will, Albert and Ted and the others.

The atmosphere at Christmas in Llyn Hir was, according to Greg, like a speckled egg, going from light moments to dark moods, dependent on the ebb and flow of their visitors. The most irritating hours were when Madeleine came with Jake as though she had the right to be there, ensconced in the family, taking the seat closest to the fire that had once been their father's and expecting to be waited on, treated as a valued friend. There was a tension that was difficult to define; it was as though they were waiting for Madeleine to leave but were too polite to even hint at her departing. They all glanced surreptitiously at the clock, willing the hands to move faster.

When extra food treats or surprises were revealed, like extra crackers to pull, to read out stupid jokes and wear the hats, Madeleine squealed with delight and the artificial laughter was a pain to Greg's heart. 'Why doesn't Jake go and take her with him?' he muttered as he went to the kitchen to help Lottie bring in yet more food at ten o'clock. Jake stood eventually at 11.30 and it was difficult for the family not to stand as one to hand them their coats.

The happiest moments for them all, were when Susie was there. She fitted in so comfortably and was immediately at home with them all.

Rose stayed away from Llyn Hir; Zena didn't give Jake any opportunity to explain his actions and both situations created tension. Mabs and Lottie talked of Christmases in the past when, through rose-coloured spectacles, everything had been perfect. Madeleine seemed to be the happiest, self-assured, smiling, and frequently thanking Lottie for her welcome. It was only when Jake and Madeleine were at their lodgings and the family were on their own that they could relax and remark about the peculiar atmosphere, at a time that is usually so happy. They all blamed Jake.

Greg's visit to Susie's family were the best of all for him. He was enveloped in a house filled with lively, chattering relatives, whose names he didn't manage to sort out. He called everyone, darlin', or Butty and no one objected. The evenings were filled with silly party games, sing-songs around a badly played piano, and moments of calm when he and Susie talked about themselves, strengthening their friendship. The time passed quickly and he stayed late into the night on the two visits.

He walked home smiling happily, occasionally bursting into song, revelling at the sudden change in his life. It was only when he got into bed that thoughts of Rose returned to worry him. Somehow he had to achieve a definite end to the problem of Rose before he could relax and enjoy the delights of Susie Crane and her family.

His final thoughts before being claimed by sleep were of Susie and her light-hearted approach to life, free of the worries that held Rose back from relaxed comfortable, happiness.

Jake asked Rose several times when she planned to revisit her stepmother and stay long enough to offer sympathy on the death of her stepfather. She eventually promised to go that evening, one day before they were leaving to return to London.

'Shall I come with you?' Jake asked. 'Not to go in, just to walk with you?'

Rose shook her head. 'I'll be fine, it isn't as though—' She stopped and shook her head. 'I'll be fine.'

He was curious as she set off to make the call, remembering how she had lied about where she lived when Greg walked her home. She was a strange girl; hemming herself in with secrets, cutting other people out of her personal life. He walked in the same direction as Rose for a while, heading for the lodgings where Madeleine would be waiting to go with him to Llyn Hir for an evening meal, an invitation which, true to form, Rose had refused, and also true to form, Madeleine had persuaded Lottie to make.

He hadn't intended to follow her, but when they reached the main road and he had to turn left, when Rose turned right he did the same. She didn't seem in any hurry. She stopped to look in shop windows, still with their slightly battered displays of Christmas cheer, then she sat on a bench just inside the park. He almost ran into her but managed to stop and keep out of sight. She sat there for ten minutes and Jake began to get anxious about the meal Zena's family would have waiting for them. He didn't want to give Zena another reason to be disappointed in him.

Then it began to rain and he pulled the back of his raincoat up and over his head, his arms uncomfortably raised. Surely she would move now? She seemed unaware of the rain that was quietly increasing in intensity, softly murmuring against the ground. Footsteps were heard in the distance, and laughter as people ran for shelter. Then it was quiet, just the pattering of raindrops in an empty world.

He had to talk to her and hoped he could explain his presence. She was carrying an umbrella yet she sat there getting soaked, wearing only a short jacket, a skirt and a useless felt hat. As he was about to reveal his presence, she stood and slowly, oblivious of the rain that was coming down in a hissing curtain, strolled on through the park.

Unable to leave her, afraid for her, wondering what to say, how to help, he gave up on keeping dry, let his coat slide back down to his shoulders and followed. At the other side of the park she jumped on a bus and he stood watching it making its sibilant way through the flooded gutters, out into the road and disappear in the gloom of the miserable evening.

He ran then, back to the lodgings where Madeleine was curious for an explanation when she saw that he was drenched. He told her about Rose and they discussed her as they walked, this time under the shelter of an umbrella, to where another evening with the Martins awaited them.

They left early, anxious about their friend and, when she was not back at the lodgings, they hoped that she had eventually visited her stepmother. Jake couldn't settle. He kept visualizing her sitting on that lonely park bench oblivious of the rain, and at eleven o'clock he went to try and find her. Unbelievably, she was again sitting on the park bench.

He ran to her, put his arms around her and held her while she clung to him and cried. When she had calmed down, he dared to ask, 'Did you see your stepmother?' This made the tears flow again.

He put his arms around her 'Sorry, Rose, I shouldn't have asked, it isn't my business.'

'They aren't my stepparents! The Conellys never adopted me. They repeatedly reminded me that I was there on sufferance and was an ungrateful child. That I'd have been left in a home with no one to care about me if it hadn't been for their generosity. Generosity! Then, on my sixteenth birthday they told me to go. Just like that. So suddenly I thought for a moment they were joking, although they never made jokes.'

'Didn't they want to help you? See you settled? Make sure you were able to look after yourself?'

'They found me a room. A lovely room. An expensive room. But with a rent I couldn't afford, but which would have impressed their friends with the "good start" they had given me. I had to leave after a week as I couldn't pay it.'

'What did you do?'

'Luckily it was summer and I spent the night wandering and sleeping spasmodically on a bench like the one where you found me. A girl at the shop let me share with her for a week, then I found a room. A shabby room.'

'A room you couldn't bear Greg to see?' He felt her nod against his shoulder.

'Was your step— foster mother pleased that you called tonight?'

'I didn't call. I've been walking around all evening, sitting on benches, just like that first night on my own.'

Jake kissed her lightly on the cheek then coaxed her to walk on. She was shivering and they were both soaked through to the skin. They went into the lodgings where Madeleine was dozing in front of the grey melancholy remains of the fire. With minimal explanations, and revealing little of what Rose had told him, he helped Madeleine to take Rose to her room and went into his own.

When he went up to see if Rose needed a hot drink, he asked, gently, 'Is this why you won't marry Greg? Because you can't tell him? Surely there's no shame or embarrassment in your story? The way the Conellys treated you was evil. There's no shame on your side. Greg would help you to forget your unhappy childhood and you'd build a good life together. The Martins are good people and they'd welcome you, make you understand that you're wanted and loved.'

'You think the Martins would understand? The Martins? That's a sick joke!' She refused to discuss it again.

At Llyn Hir, the days had passed following the usual traditions of parcel opening, meals and snacks and, as it was the first Christmas without rationing, the fare was unusually generous, but for Lottie there was something lacking. It was two days after Boxing Day and in a couple more most shops would opening, but Lottie and Zena had decided to give themselves an extra few days. 'No one will want writing-paper and envelopes for a while, we might as well enjoy more time to ourselves.'

'It has been a strange Christmas,' Zena mused, as she read through some of the cards on display. 'You're right, Mam, there has been something lacking. It was more than Dad not being here. Something of the spirit of Christmas wasn't here. With the recovery from the awful war years, marked at last with the end of food rationing, it should have been extra special, yet something was missing.'

'Not so much lacking, as something added,' Lottie said. 'We have always had a houseful at Christmas. With Mabs here for the week, people calling, staying for drinks or a meal and your father and I loved it. But I don't like having people we don't know thrust upon us. Jake had no right to invite Madeleine then expect us to entertain her. Sorry, dear,' she added, as she glanced at her daughter. 'If it were only Jake, well, that would have been fine, wouldn't it?'

'I don't know.' Zena gave a sigh. 'When he's away I relax and I'm happy, my life is full without him, I plan without wondering whether he'll be included and sometimes I hope he will forget us and stay in London. But when I see him, I realize how much I miss him. Not so much this time,' she added harshly. 'I'm well aware that Madeleine is more important to him than me; inviting her to share our Christmas makes that clear, and it changes things. *And I don't think her ankle is as painful as she pretends!*' she added petulantly.

Lottie laughed. 'That sounds childish, but I admit I think the same.'

'Mam, let's go out. We can go and see Nelda; you like spending time with her and the two little girls, don't you?'

'But Jake and the girls might come. They aren't going back until tomorrow. And surely Rose won't go back to London without at least coming to say hello.'

'What better reason for going out? She has really hurt Greg and made it worse by refusing to explain why she behaved as she did.'

'It was very odd. She was never relaxed with us, but that day was different. She was reluctant to go and see your father in hospital that day. Perhaps Greg pushed her into going and, I don't know, she took offence, maybe? Something changed and she walked away from us all.'

Uninvited but certain of a welcome they went into Nelda's chaotic house where toys and cards and decorations were spread, higgledy piggledy all around the living rooms and the kitchen. Bobbie and Georgie began to show their presents to them but very soon the six-year-old Georgie brought her favourite books to Lottie, seeing in her the grandmother she sadly lacked. Nelda's ex-mother-in-law lived too far away for visits, and Nelda's parents lived in France.

Over cups of tea and cake, Nelda told them that Roy Roberts was ill and instead of going back home, after the couple of hours spent enjoying the lively company, they went from Nelda's to see him, loaded with cakes and biscuits and even a couple of Christmas crackers Nelda had packed, to cheer him up. His face was still bearing scars from the attack two weeks before, bruises yellow and fading, the scar of a graze across his cheek still visible.

'I hope you haven't been fighting again,' Zena admonished at once. 'Some of those bruises look new.'

'They are,' a voice called from the kitchen, and Kevin appeared waving a teapot. 'Hello, Zena. Anyone for tea? Or something more interesting? What about you, Popeye, a glass of cider?' he asked. Zena went into the kitchen to help, although she doubted whether she could drink any more tea that day.

'He's been fighting, but he won't tell me what happened,' Kevin whispered. 'I think it was his son, Dick. Tricky Dicky. He rarely comes but when he does there's a argument or worse.'

'Attacking his father? An old man?'

Kevin smiled at her, 'No, not really. Popeye provokes him, trying to make him listen to his side of the story.'

Remembering the letter she had guiltily read, Zena asked, 'Is it anything to do with someone called Donna?'

'How did you know about her?'

'I heard the name somewhere,' she lied.

'Donna was the cause of his wife leaving him and the sons have never forgiven him. Dicky has frequently demanded his father helps their mother financially but Popeye refuses, insisting that she left him, so he owes her nothing. Fond of him I am, but he didn't play fair with his family and I can sympathize with his sons.'

'But fighting with his father, that's terrible.'

'Protecting himself was all the old man was doing. Old Popeye was a boxer in his youth and can still pack a punch. He'd never hit anyone. Not Popeye; he's too afraid of hitting too hard.'

'But his face? That must have been some retaliation!'

'No, that happened when I came in to separate them. He ran into the door in a rage. He didn't raise a hand except to protect himself from his son's abuse.'

'What are you two nattering about out there?' Roy demanded. 'Where are the drinks?'

Zena felt disappointed. She thought she knew Roy Roberts, believed he was a gentle, kindly old man who was lonely for a family who neglected him. What Kevin had told her was such a shock, that she made excuses and hurried away in case her change of attitude showed on her face. What a poor judge of character she must be.

There was a note beside the door when they got back to Llyn Hir. It was from Jake and Madeleine, telling them they had called but missed them and would call tomorrow before setting off for London.

It was tempting to be out when they came but with no time given that wasn't possible. It was ten o'clock when Jake arrived and he was alone.

'Hello, my lovely girl.' He leaned towards her expecting a kiss, but she moved away to close the door. 'I want to go to the farm to ask Sam if he'll sell me a few eggs for the girls to take back to London, see. Will you come with me? He doesn't like me very much and he's more likely to say yes if you're there.'

She reached for her coat and called to her mother, 'We're going to see Sam and Neville, will you come with us? The fresh air is what we all need,'

Sam greeted them with delight but the smile faded when he saw Jake. 'Go and see Dad, he'll let you have a dozen. Mixed sizes, mind, none of your London nonsense here!' and, as Jake went off to see Neville, Sam turned and hugged Lottie and Zena.

'It's no good, I can't stand the man,' he admitted. 'It's twelve years now since he left my son to drown but it's still just like yesterday when I see that man.'

'Jake didn't leave Peter to drown, Sam, you know that. He ran to get help as he couldn't swim and there was no way to save him himself.' This had all been said many times before but Sam just shook his head. The loss of a son was a lifetime of painful memories. How could he ever forget blaming Jake?

Lottie held his arm. 'They'd spent hours on the lake with the boat and the raft as safe as anyone could be, but the sea was different. They had no idea how strong the waves were, used to the calm water of the lake. They learned how different on that day but dear Peter paid for the lesson with his life.'

Through the window they saw Jake coming back carrying a box from which straw stuck out, obviously holding the eggs. 'Look,' Sam said apologetically, 'can you come this afternoon and have tea with us? Mabs sent us some pasties and a fruitcake, Dad cooked some sausages. and we'd love to share them with you.'

As Jake knocked on the door, they opened it and, calling goodbye to Sam and waving to his father down in the yard they set off back to Llyn Hir. Jake made no comment about the lack of welcome, just chatted about the chickens and the donkey that was in the field as company for the retired horse. It was only what he'd expected.

When she knew the three friends had set off back to London.

Zena gave a sigh of relief. She had avoided a heart to heart with Jake. The days had passed and left her unscathed.

Susie met Greg before starting a shift and they sat in a café and dissected Christmas. Susie didn't mention Rose, whom she hadn't met but about whom she was achingly curious. She was also curious about Jake and Madeleine. Greg explained a little about the long standing friendship and engagement of his sister and Jake, and her recent change of heart about marrying him.

'It was a very strange Christmas, so many cross currents and uneasy moments. Without Dad being there it was bound to be different from the usual but apart from that, the mix was wrong. We were all glad that you were there, Susie. You made it bearable with your bright, happy personality.'

'Nonsense, I was an intruder and you were all being very kind to me. I was made to feel welcome mind, and I love your Aunty Mabs.'

They kissed briefly as they parted and went to begin their shifts, stopping at the doorway for a final wave.

It was a week later, having belatedly celebrated the New Year with friends, that Susie passed the night café and saw Greg going in. She began to follow him, puzzled by finding a café open at such a late hour, but at the door she stopped. Looking through a gap in the blind, she saw Aunty Mabs greeting him affectionately then handing him a pack of sliced bread and a wedge of cheese. She watched, curious about his presence there as he disappeared into what was obviously a kitchen, coming back wiping his hands on a clean white towel. He opened the bread and began making sandwiches. She was afraid of being seen and hurried towards the taxi rank on the corner, but as she did so, a small, bright-eyed man approached and said, 'It's all right to go in, miss, anyone who's lonely or can't sleep is welcome at Frankie's café.' Then he recognized the uniform only half hidden by an overcoat. 'Oh, sorry, miss. Excuse me,' he added as he pushed past and slid his small frame around the door, 'my mate is waiting for a game of draughts. Trying to teach me chess, he is. Fat chance of me learning that!' He smiled and closed the door.

Later as the place was closing, Sid told Greg and Mabs about the curious young woman. 'I thought she was looking for a bit of warmth and company like the rest of us, see, and then I saw that she was a bus conductress.'

Greg asked for a description, and Sid's response was vague but it convinced him it had been Susie when Sid said she had long hair tied back in a bundle and she smiled 'like an angel'.

'I might have to tell her about the café to stop her telling others,' Greg explained to Mabs. 'Also, I don't want there to be secrets between Susie and me.'

'It's hardly a secret any more,' Mabs said. 'Just as well too, or lonely people wouldn't get to know about it either. I didn't want it talked about too soon or it might have attracted the wrong people. Or too many for the idea to work.'

In London, the atmosphere in the office and at Madeleine's flat was subdued. Rose was depressed by Madeleine's half-joking, half-unkind description of what she called, 'The horrors of Christmas *en famille*.' She was convinced that the occasion had been ruined by her being there. She thought of the happy moments with Greg and the many, many more unhappy times throughout her life and wondered if she would ever go again to Cold Brook Vale.

Madeleine guessed that something had happened between Jake and Rose but neither could be persuaded to talk. She planned theatre visits and meals at the flat and in restaurants but the heart had gone from their friendship. It was time for things to change.

Jake increased his journeys and was making a success of his new career. He phoned to talk to Zena several times, to share his news, but she refused to come to the phone. He wrote to her but the letters were thrown away by Madeleine.

Rose was tearful at times, refusing to repeat the things she had told Jake. On other occasions she was angry and then too she offered no explanation. Madeleine was becoming bored and tried to think of a way to liven things up. They were all looking for something but unable to find it.

*

Although Zena didn't want extra clients for her cleaning list, there were a few who approached her with a request for a weekly visit. She regretfully turned them down. The shop and the typing services kept her busy and she still called on Roy Roberts and Nelda. Then a most surprising request came from someone who introduced herself as Karen Rogers, housekeeper to the tenant of the place locally known as the haunted house.

Memories of her and Greg's late night visit made her want to refuse, embarrassed by her nosiness. She remembered the voice calling for someone to find a Bing Crosby record and the man running as though in fear of his life as she and Greg had hidden in the darkness.

They had played in its grounds as children and dared each other to approach the grimy windows and look inside, before running away screaming, insisting they had seen ghosts. Zena smiled at the memories. Those memories were still strong: even the recent visit hadn't changed them.

She was tempted to make an appointment, just to go inside and see what the place was actually like, although, she told her brother, it might be a disappointment to find ordinary rooms, filled with ordinary things. It would be a pity to lose the magical memories of their childhood fears and imaginings. She thanked Mrs Rogers but declined.

A few weeks later, when the weather was bleak and snow was threatening, Karen Rogers called at the shop and asked again. 'I do what I can, but there is too much for me to manage,' she explained, 'with shopping and cooking and the laundry as well.'

Zena still looked doubtful and she added quickly, 'Don't worry about the size of the house, we only use a part of it. Most is closed off, furniture covered and all I have to do is open the windows occasionally. But if you could come to help me for as many hours as you can spare, I would be so grateful.'

'How many people live there?' Zena asked, the expression on the woman's face melting her resolve to refuse. 'Will there be cooking involved? Or shopping? If I agree to help I won't have time for more than a couple of brief weekly visits.' Aware of the size of the place, she knew that wouldn't be enough to make it liveable.

'None of those things. I want help to keep the parts in use clean and all the rest, that has dropped to the bottom of my list,' Mrs Rogers admitted.

Zena agreed to think about it. A week later the request was repeated and finally, accepting that there was time between her shifts at the shop and the irregular typing she was given, she agreed.

On her fist visit, she arranged to go very early and spend a few hours deciding what was most needed. Her journey there was very entertaining. She was cycling just a short distance from home along the narrow road which led only the house that was her destination, when she saw a small boy, dressed warmly in a heavy overcoat, that almost hid him completely, a too large, knitted hat and scarf and carrying a paperboy's delivery bag. He was standing pulling withered leaves from the hedge and didn't seem to be going anywhere. Zena stopped and asked him if he was all right.

'Yes, miss. I'll go home in a while.' She noticed he was shivering with the cold despite his layers of clothing. 'I just have to stand here for a while, just a little while, miss, then I can go home.'

Something about the way he was glancing along the lane made her suspect the reason for his hesitation. 'Do you have to deliver a newspaper to the big house?'

'Yes, miss, and I'm not going!'

She smiled. 'We used to pretend the place was haunted when I was about your age. It isn't, of course. That was just a silly game that we invented to frighten ourselves. It's just an ordinary house. Bigger than most, that's all.'

'I'm not going.'

'Then I'll take it for you, shall I?' She offered her hand for the paper but then changed her mind. 'Better than that. I'll walk with you and we'll see that there's nothing to be frightened of.'

'I'm *not* frightened, miss.'

'I am! So, shall we walk together?' She reached for his canvas bag and put it across the handlebars.

They talked as they walked and the boy told her his name was Geraint and he lived with his mam and had no dad. 'He was a soldier and he died,' he explained in a matter-of-fact tone. 'I'm delivering papers to earn money to buy Mam a birthday present, see.'

As they turned the curve in the road that would give them the first sight of the house, he went quiet and held the handlebar of the bike for reassurance. She talked to him about the trees, giving their names and describing the beauty to come when the leaves and spring blossoms appeared. His feet were dragging but he walked on until they faced the wide and impressive front door. She waited until he had pushed the papers through the letter box then knocked loudly. She held his hand tightly as he began to leave. 'Stay and meet Mrs Rogers,' she said. 'You'll like her.'

The door opened and the smiling face of Mrs Rogers appeared. She spoke firstly to the boy. 'You must be Geraint. Thank you for coming all this way with our papers. Would you like a drink of milk before going back?'

'Thanks, but I'll be late for school.' He turned and ran and was quickly out of sight.

'Knock on my door tomorrow and we'll walk together,' Zena shouted.

Mrs Rogers took Zena into the kitchen which was huge. Windows were large and should have let in plenty of light, but the glass was covered in grime and in places it was impossible to see anything beyond them. A light burned from the ceiling and from sconces on the wall near what must have once been the preparation table but which was now completely covered with pots and pans of indeterminate age.

'These should have gone for scrap ages ago,' Mrs Rogers apologized. 'I just can't find time to attend to these things.'

After discussion, Zena agreed to come each morning for a week, then settle to regular visits. It would take a week to dispose of the rubbish, and scrubbing would be her main occupation. She smiled when she thought that for a week, Geraint would have company on his uneasy walk. Between them by telephone, she and Mrs Rogers arranged for a scrap merchant to dispose of the unwanted and ancient pans and for a gardener to start tidying the entrance. A laundry service was contacted and weekly collections organized.

'I haven't coped very well, have I? I've done nothing like this before and so much of my time is taken just looking after my employer,' Karen explained.

'When will I meet him?' Zena asked, but Karen shook her head. 'No hurry,' Zena said quickly, waving hands to dismiss the idea. 'Whenever it's convenient, but if I could look at the house, at least the parts of it for which I will be responsible?'

She was shown up a wide, intricately carved staircase and doors were opened on three of the bedrooms. All were furnished with items hidden by dust sheets. There was one door she wasn't shown. 'Sorry to sound mysterious, but that room is out of bounds,' Karen told her. 'Nothing to worry about, it's just there are things that are important and not for public display.'

'Valuable?'

'Yes, sort of valuable.' A cough was heard coming from the out-of-bounds room. Zena looked at her companion but no explanation was forthcoming and they moved on, back down the stairs to the living room that was beautifully but sparsely furnished and to a small library lined with books and where a cheerful fire blazed. 'This is my sitting room,' Karen explained. She gestured with a thumb towards a partially opened door disguised as part of the shelves. 'My bedroom is in there.'

Before she left, Zena had a few more suggestions to make the house more pleasant. They arranged for a window cleaning firm to come and deal with the grime built up over years of neglect. Rubbish removal, professional cleaners followed by decorators, were needed in the kitchen, obviously the priority. The rest, Zena decided, she would gradually deal with herself.

The next morning she was pleased to see Geraint waiting for her and they walked down the lane, Zena pushing her bike loaded with his bag, and the boy showing more confidence. This time he accepted the glass of milk and ran off with slightly less haste.

By the end of that first week, the house had changed a great deal. The walls of the kitchen had been thoroughly cleaned and would soon be a cheerful buttercup yellow, the windows shone like jewels bringing more light into every room and Karen was delighted with the changes.

Geraint had changed too, his forays into the dangerous

'haunted' house had given him almost hero status at school and he even hurried ahead of Zena on Saturday. When Zena asked if he would like her to walk with him on Sunday, he said there was no need. Rather self-consciously he thanked her and added that he had some tips to add to his wages and would be able to buy his Mam something 'Real good'.

Working at the house, she was amused to learn it was called SunnyBank, which seemed more relevant now compared to a week ago. It was very tiring work and she went home after several hours of heavy cleaning, content with the way her days were filled. Greg came with her one morning to look at the trees that had been allowed to become too large for the garden and he went with Karen Rogers to talk to some professional tree surgeons about their disposal. Trees came down and the wood put in a store to dry and be used on the fire. The unwanted small branches were built into a bonfire and Geraint and two friends came with Greg and Susie to watch the fun as it burned.

'It's like seeing the house coming to life,' Zena said, and Greg agreed glumly. 'But it's lost the magic of creepy nights frightening ourselves silly.'

The third bedroom was never opened and although Zena occasionally heard movements inside, she didn't ask; Mrs Rogers didn't explain and clearly preferred she didn't admit her curiosity.

Chapter Nine

AFTER BREAKFAST ON Sunday morning, Lottie showed the latest bank statement to Greg and Zena. 'The amount I owe has gone down remarkably thanks to you, Zena and your help with the business, but there's still a very long way to go, isn't there?' she said with a sigh.

'It's always slow at first, but once it starts to come down you'll feel better about it. Why don't you take my offer of using my savings?' Greg asked. 'I have a useful amount, rent from the cottage which has needed little maintenance since Gran left it to me. With Rose gone, I can't see me needing it for a long time. Better to use it to get rid of this debt.'

Lottie shook her head. 'No, dear. This is my problem and you're helping just by being here and helping with your weekly contribution.'

'I don't imagine I'll be getting married very soon either,' Zena added. 'Isn't it strange how things have all fallen apart? Losing Dad, then Rose leaving Greg, and Jake and I ending something that we both thought would last a lifetime.'

They both pleaded for their mother to accept their help but Lottie refused. She reached for her coat and wellingtons announcing that she needed a walk. Zena and Greg sat for a while discussing the financial situation, puzzling as always about the unexplained loss of the money and the loan on the house. Hesitantly Zena asked Greg if he thought there might have been some serious quarrel between their parents to account for it. 'The suspicions raised by Aunty Mabs haven't really gone away,' she admitted.

'There has never been a sign of Mam and Dad being less

192

thanhappy. I'm sure we'd have noticed.' He grinned then. 'What if it was Dad who was the guilty one? After all, the mystery of the missing money lies with him, not Mam.'

They amused themselves for a few moments, imagining what their father might be guilty of. 'A master criminal, a thief maybe?

'Or a blackmailer who became a victim of a blackmailer?'

'Or the murderer of Mam's secret lover?' They were laughing as their ideas became more and more preposterous.

'The mystery is, even if there is some guilty secret in Mam's past, or Dad's, that doesn't explain what happened to their savings. Where did the money *go*?'

'And it wasn't Dad's to dispose of, it was *their* savings. Some came from Gran, and Mam has worked for most of her marriage. It wasn't solely Dad's money to part with.'

'But it's gone and no one knows where it is. Stashed in a bank vault, or hidden under the floorboards of some mysterious cottage on the wilds of the mountains.'

'That's a thought! What an exciting family we have.'

It was an hour when Zena was walking through the wood, gathering branches of the sticky horse chestnut branches to put in water and enjoy seeing the new leaves unfurling, that she stepped out from behind the trees above the Edwards's farm. Walking towards her she saw her mother arm in arm with Uncle Sam. Something about the way they walked, close and slow, stopping occasionally to talk, made her hesitate to call or wave a greeting. It was as she stopped at the edge of the wood and was about to disappear among the leafless branches that she glanced back and saw them kissing.

She froze with shock and immediately convinced herself that Uncle Sam and her mother were more than the friends they declared themselves to be. It was a subject she had never seriously considered; never seeing her mother in any role other than caring for herself and Greg, providing love and security, making them feel utterly safe throughout their lives. To imagine her mother as a lover was impossible, alien to the picture she held of her. It was very unsettling, unacceptable, frightening; even though she reminded herself that her mother was still a young woman and Sam had been a widower for many years.

Her heart was racing as she hurried back home, dashing straight up to her room and closing the curtains as though blotting out the scene she had witnessed. She lay on the bed and her thoughts became even more shocking as she imagined her mother in the arms of another man. That *had* to be why her father had treated her so badly, there *had* been malice in the unexplained disappearance of the money. Her previous joking with Greg had become a cruel truth. How could she face her mother, and smile and pretend everything was all right after this?

She heard her mother come in and waited until she heard her in the bathroom then ran down the stairs and out of the house. She needed to talk to someone, either Greg or Aunty Mabs. It was cold and she needed a thicker coat but grabbed the nearest, a thin waterproof, as she fled. Remembering his shift pattern, she knew Greg wouldn't be home for hours, so she went to see Aunty Mabs, cycling furiously as though chased by demons. She had to talk to someone or she would burst.

Mabs took a while to open the door and Zena was so distressed she didn't notice the sleepy look that suggested the knock on the door had awoken her aunt. Tearfully she told Mabs what she had seen, gabbling in her shock and the haste with which she released her dismay. Mabs put the kettle on, wondering as she did so why making tea was always the first reaction to a problem. Something to do with your hands, she decided, as she gave the tearful girl a cup and saucer to hold. When Zena finally calmed down, she said,

'Your mother and Sam Edwards have been close friends since they were children and I don't think there's anything more wonderful than; having a friend who's lived through your highs and lows without criticism and that's what Sam is, a good, trusted friend and nothing more.'

'But they looked so – so – happy,' Zena finished lamely.

'And you think that explains why your father, my brother, did something spiteful and uncaring? I don't believe that and neither should you. Whatever Sam and your mother feel for each other, I can never accept your father's cruelty. I thought so for just a moment and I'm still ashamed of my reaction. Something happened but it wasn't spite or revenge. Your father wasn't like

194

that. One day we might find out what happened, but until we do, we have to trust your mother and believe her when she says she never did anything to hurt your father. Now, my lovely girl, drink your tea and there're some cakes on the table, ready for the café, I can spare you one.'

'You didn't see them, or you'd think the same as me.'

'I don't need to see them to know Sam wasn't the reason your father left his money somewhere other than to his family.'

'Then did he lose it gambling?'

'Of course not, Zena, love. Your father wasn't a gambling man, certainly not with money needed by his family.'

'Stocks and shares? That's gambling isn't it?'

'Risking everything? Including the house? That's even more unbelievable than your mother having an affair with Sam Edwards! Come on, love, we'll find out what happened eventually, and in the meantime, stop tormenting yourself – and me – with nonsense.'

'When he was dying, Dad mentioned a man's name several times. Billy Dove. Do you know him?'

'I've never heard of a Billy Dove, and neither has your mother,' she said pointedly. 'No romance there either.'

They talked for a while longer but although Zena smiled and told Mabs she was reassured, the memory of the kiss between her mother and the man they had always considered an honorary uncle, remained. How could she face her mother and pretend nothing had happened?

She had planned to go to the shop before lunch to type a few letters she had promised for the morning but decided to go in early the following day instead. Yet, going home wasn't going to be easy.

When she approached the back door she heard laughter and recognized the voice of Greg's new friend, Susie, and sighed with relief. Having Susie there would give her time to calm down and accept Mab's explanation of what she had witnessed.

They were in the kitchen, her mother bending down turning roasting potatoes and Susie sharing tinned fruit and cream between four dishes. 'Oh, good. I see there's nothing for me to do,' she announced, waving at the girl who was licking the serving spoon before dropping it into the washing-up bowl.

'Sorry, Zena, you and I are down for the washing up. I've sort of invited myself for lunch. I hope you don't mind?'

'I couldn't be more pleased,' Zena replied, truthfully.

Sam called later with eggs and some sprouts and leeks. He smiled at Zena, showing her the contents of the bag. 'Leeks, your favourite.'

She nodded and looked away.

Sam went to stand behind where her mother was sitting giving the cutlery an extra shine and placed a hand on her shoulder. Lottie's hand went up to touch his. When several attempts to talk to Zena achieved no response, Sam asked quietly, 'Is something wrong? Has something happened that's worrying you?'

'It's all right. I can deal with it, Uncle Sam.'

She went up to her room unable to sit watching for more signs of affection. Aunty Mabs was wrong. Her father must have guessed, as she had. Thank goodness Susie was there to ease the painful embarrassment that she felt every time she looked at her mother. She didn't go back down until she heard him call and the door close as Sam departed.

Soon after lunch was eaten there was the sound of a motor bike approaching and a loud knock on the door announced the arrival of Kevin. 'Come on, Zena, your carriage awaits! Fancy a trip down Gower? There might even be a café open where we can have tea. Or,' he went on, not awaiting for her agreement, 'perhaps you can bring a couple of sandwiches? Hi, Mrs Martin, lovely day for a ride, eh? I'll bring her back before morning,' he said, with a wink, 'maybe.'

Almost bemused by the sudden decision that she hadn't actually made, she allowed Kevin to fasten her warmest coat around her and add a scarf and a woolly hat, and with hastily packed food tucked into her pockets, they set off with Lottie, Greg and Susie laughing as they waved them off.

Nervous at first, but reassured as Kevin didn't overdo the speed, they talked over his shoulder as she clung to him and relished the joyful sensation that was almost like flying, safe behind Kevin, warm apart from the icy cold air on her face. They stopped in the shelter of a barn and ate some of the food they had brought then went back home via a different route. She was sorry when they were back at Llyn Hir.

He went in with her, helped her to take off the heavy coat and laughed at the rosy glow of her cheeks, telling her she was beautiful, asking Susie and Lottie to agree, then asked, 'Where's the tea pot, then?'

He didn't stay long, but seemed completely at home, going out to refill the teapot when he wanted a second cup, helping himself to the cakes Lottie had made. He thanked them for their hospitality and promised they'd do it again soon and, as before, they all stood at the door and waved as he left.

'What is the name of that whirlwind?' Susie asked as they went back indoors.

'That was Kevin, he's a neighbour of Mr Roberts, who he calls Popeye.'

Susie looked at her. 'Don't expect him to ask you out.' When Zena frowned, she added with a laugh, 'He won't ask, he'll just tell you! But he's seems like a lot of fun.'

'He's kind to Roy Roberts, he and his mother help him when he needs it – and is willing to accept it.'

'I don't think many want to help him if it's the Roy Roberts I'm thinking of. He didn't treat his wife very well and his sons have had no help from him at all – at least, that's how the story goes, but maybe that's only the half of it.'

Zena didn't know enough to comment so she said nothing.

When Rose and Jake arrived at Madeleine's flat one evening, they were told to close their eyes and wait for permission to open them. Amused, they did as they were told. They opened them slowly to see, proudly installed in a corner of the room, a brand new television. The *Radio Times* was fluttered in front of them and Madeleine told them they could each choose a programme to watch. In fact they watched everything on offer and the set wasn't shut down until the programmes ended. They were all laughing with excitement at all they had seen.

They scoured the pages and marked programmes they wanted to see on other evenings and Madeleine laughed away their promises of not becoming a nuisance. 'You're my family and I'll enjoy everything more with you than being on my own,' she assured them. 'Now, what shall we watch tomorrow?'

It was after Jake had left that Rose told Madeleine that she too felt part of a family, 'for the first time in my life,' she added.

Madeleine coaxed gently and for the first time Rose opened up and told her something about her lonely, sad childhood.

'Is that why you left Greg? Unwilling to talk to him about your childhood?'

'He pestered, insisted on knowing all about me and I hated it. I lied about where I lived and he found out. I couldn't tell him the worst of it. Then something happened; something so terrible I had to get away, right away. So here I am, with you and Jake as wonderful friends and all memories of Greg and his hateful family with secrets far worse than mine, far away and soon to be forgotten.' She turned away and Madeleine could see a tear drifting down her cheek.

'Is there anything else you want to talk about? Just between you and me of course.'

'I went back and broke into the stationers shop run by Zena and her mother Lottie, sometimes called Kay.' She spat out the last word, hating the sound of it. She heard a sound and looked up and realized that Madeleine was stifling laughter, which burst from her as she leaned over and hugged the unhappy girl. 'What a surprising girl you are, Rose,' Madeleine said, helpless with laughter. 'I didn't dream you had such behaviour in you. Well done!'

'Well done? It was a terrible thing to do – wasn't it?'

'Not at all. In fact, why don't we plan something else?' Madeleine wiped her eyes and slowly calmed her laughing. 'I don't know what the Martin family did to deserve your anger, but it's obvious you need to get revenge, so let's have a think. Tell me what you did when you went into the shop.'

Guiltily at first but gradually beginning to enjoy the confession, Rose told her about the money she had taken and the mess she had made of the files. 'I spent the money on the chocolates I bought for you,' she added, which made Madeleine laugh louder than before.

Although Rose guessed it was only a bit of fun, they discussed finding out all they could so that when an opportunity occurred they could plan something to make Rose feel better about whatever she had suffered at the hands of the Martins. Their ideas went from unkind to absolutely crazy and Rose laughed as she hadn't laughed for years – if ever.

They brought the conversation around to the Martins whenever Jake was with them and casually found out a lot about the routines of the family including the night café and office supplies and the finances of both. Then Madeleine began to suggest ways of having fun and upsetting the Martins at the same time. She was intensely curious, especially about Lottie sometimes called Kay, who had upset Rose so much. Learning it was Lottie's nickname only added to the mystery, but knew she had to tread carefully and wait until Rose wanted to divulge more of her story. It was obviously more than an unhappy childhood.

Greg finished his shift at eleven and went straight to the night café. Susie was working days and they had made no arrangement to meet. He'd decided to tell her about his voluntary night work to avoid misunderstandings about his mysterious disappearances. Susie was becoming too special to risk losing because of trying to keep the café a secret. He opened the door and, as usual, the conversations ceased as all heads turned to see who the new arrival would be. He waved a greeting and set to, washing dishes then starting on a fresh batch of sandwiches.

Around 2.30 a.m. the three ex-convicts, Will, Albert and George arrived, pleased to tell them they all had a job. They worked as night cleaners in the kitchen and offices of a factory, working from 10 until 2. They were congratulated and Mabs gave them a cup of tea and a cake on the house, showing Greg crossed fingers that it might continue.

Conversations rose and fell between concentration on the games they played. Greg smiled at Mabs, both happy with the sound of people content with their regular night-time haven, an escape from the loneliness they had once known. Then at five o'clock the door opened and Susie walked in.

'Any chance of a cup of tea for a lonely girl who got the early bus instead of having a lie-in?' She winked at Mabs, then smiled at Greg. 'All right, I know I'll have to earn it! Where's the washing up?' Greg hugged her and Mabs smiled and poured the tea. He was aware of a warmth that spread and imbued his whole body with a sense of wellbeing, which he recognized as happiness.

Susie coming to the café changed things between them. They relaxed, knowing there would be no secrets to jump out and disturb them. He visited her family with the comfortable feeling he was no longer a stranger; and was sure of a welcome. She called without invitation to Llyn Hir and, when she was passing, would pop into Office Supplies for a chat with Lottie or Zena. In a very short time she became a part of the close family involved in the daily arrangements and welcomed by them all. Yet, hidden behind her natural good nature and happy smile a worry lurked, a worry that Greg was still holding a place in his heart for the secretive Rose Conelly. She decided to make a few discreet enquiries.

She helped in the café for a few hours the following night and, when the café closed and Greg was about to give her the usual kiss on the cheek, she turned her head and their lips met. Their arms around each other, they stood for a moment, each wrapped in their own thoughts, wondering where this would take them. Greg thought of Rose and saw the image of her fading, but not vanishing. It hovered in his mind, a faint, mocking image. Susie was also thinking of Rose and wondering how best to persuade Greg to let dreams of her go.

Zena continued to enjoy the two branches of her working days. She helped to clean for Roy Roberts and do some shopping for him. She also made him a cake and occasionally a few savouries. Nelda was more a friend than a client, although she still insisted on paying her for her constant and usually futile attempts to keep her home orderly. They went out once a week when Nelda had a babysitter and Nelda continued to bring the girls to visit Llyn Hir. They were promised walks through the wood when the weather allowed and they drew pictures in their books of what they imagined they would see.

Friends would have described Zena as a happy person. Her life was full, she had friends and work she enjoyed, but now Jake was no longer a part of her life she felt incomplete, as though she were constantly waiting for something. He phoned occasionally and his conversations were full of his job, the places he'd seen and the theatres and films they had attended. It was always *they*, not *I* and there was no doubt that all his social activities were with Rose and Madeleine.

In one letter he told her Madeleine had bought a television and described the wonderful programmes they watched. She found it more and more difficult to add her own news. There was less and less to tell him about the town where he had once lived. There didn't seem to be anything of interest to say about her own life. A walk through the woods with the ground hard and sparkling with frost? Greg and Sam going fishing and catching a few small cod? How dull it sounded compared with his.

In a spirit of defiance she wrote a letter, enthusiastic about the walk in the winter woodland, the squirrel she saw searching for food on a cold but sunny afternoon, the wild ducks that flew over morning and evening. She also told him about the growing friend-ship between Greg and Susie – for whom she was full of praise.

She sometimes wondered if she should have joined him London, briefly regretting her decision not to, but although life in that fasci-nating city sounded very exciting, she knew it wouldn't have been right for her. It was clear that the love she had felt for him had not been honest or strong, it had been habit, and not love at all. Best to let it go.

A reply to her letter came a few days later, just a brief note saying he envied her the walks and the sight of the wild duck, and telling her they were coming for the weekend, staying at the usual lodgings. Rose as well, so perhaps she will talk to Greg this time, he added as a postscript.

Susie started her enquiries about the Conelly family with her own family. She learned from her parents that Rose was fostered, not adopted, and although she used the name of Conelly, on her sixteenth birthday she was told to leave. She was also told that Mr and Mrs Conelly showed no affection for the girl, criticizing her to everyone for her dullness and her stupidity, and remarking constantly how grateful the girl should have been but was not. Susie felt a growing sympathy for Rose and wondered whether her miserable childhood was the reason for her fearing to show affection or accept it. Being constantly rebuffed as a baby and a child must have made it impossible to think of loving and marrying and all the stages of life that were normal.

From what she gathered by feeding the gossip – about which she refused to feel guilty – Rose was never hugged and never included in days out or the holidays that her foster parents regularly enjoyed. She had never been given a birthday party nor allowed to attend parties given by others.

Susie felt great pity for the lonely, emotionally damaged girl, but she couldn't tell Greg what she had learned. He would accuse her of listening to gossip, which was true, but besides, she couldn't risk offending him and possibly making him feel again the sympathy for Rose that she herself felt. Such a conversation might drive him to try again to persuade her to open up to him. She went to talk to Mabs.

'No apology needed for trying to find out why Rose has problems,' Mabs assured her after listening to what she had learned. 'She obviously suffered a sad and lonely childhood and her low self-worth is understandable, but isn't it odd that when love was offered she walked away?'

'Afraid of another rejection, I suppose.' Susie looked at Mabs, wondering how she would react as she went on, 'Should I tell Greg? Help him to understand why Rose walked away from him? Or is it best to let things fade away?'

'Fond of him, aren't you.' Mabs smiled. 'I for one would be very glad if thoughts of you helped memories of Rose fade away. He would never have been happy with her, we all know that. She carries a sad dark cloud with her, while you, young Susie, are filled with happiness and spread sunshine wherever you go!'

'He makes me happy.'

'Tell him if you must, and if it drives him to try to make another attempt to gain her trust, then it's better you know now.'

On Sunday morning while Zena was preparing a meal for the

family and Susie and her parents, there was a knock at the door which was immediately opened. Jake called, 'Zena, lovely girl, are you there? There's someone I'd like you to meet.' He stood at the door with a wriggling, furry brown dog in his arms.

'Jake, you can't have a dog. What are you thinking of?' She reached over and took the fussy bundle in her arms.

'I saw a van stop in the middle of Swindon. The driver put her out on the pavement and drove away. Poor love, she chased the van for a while then stopped and looked around panting with shock. I opened the car door and lifted her in.'

'But what will you do with her?'

'I took her to a vet and she's soon to have puppies, which is why she was abandoned, I suppose. Poor little thing.'

'But you can't keep her.'

'No, love. I was hoping you and Greg will look after her. She's called Betty.' The little dog gave a bark.

'Betty?' The dog barked again.

'How d'you know her name?'

'Because every time I say it she barks. Don't you, Betty?' The dog barked. He smiled at her and Zena looked from him to the dog and began to melt.

Lottie came in with a scuttle of coal, saw the dog and, as Zena had done, took her in her arms. Already smitten by the time Jake had repeated his story, there was no question about Betty being given a home.

Jake stayed for a couple of hours, walking with Zena and Lottie, with Betty trotting contentedly beside them. He asked Zena if she had thought any more about joining him in London, but, making a joke of it, she said, 'How can I? She wouldn't like living in the city, would you, Betty?' Betty barked. 'That was definitely a no!'

Over the following days, Zena and Greg took the dog for a walk to help her familiarize herself with the neighbourhood. They went down the rocky path to the lake and, to their surprise, young Geraint was there. After playing with the dog and getting them both wet, he asked Greg about the raft, this having been repaired by Sam and Neville and was floating on the calm water firmly held by the arrangement of strong new ropes. They took Geraint for a ride across the lake and back, with the dog barking all the way. Geraint was allowed to pull on the ropes helping Greg to bring it back to where they had begun and was very impressed.

'You can come whenever one of us is free to go with you, but never on your own,' Greg warned. 'If I find out you've come on your own you'll be banned.'

Geraint promised. 'Thanks, I think it's wonderful,' he said, his eyes shining with the sheer pleasure of it all. 'I won't tell my friends either,' he added. 'Just in case they think they can use it.'

Over the following weeks, Lottie took charge of walking the dog. She left Zena in the shop and took the dog on what she called Betty's sight-seeing tours. She was taken to the farm and introduced to Digby, Sam's sheepdog, who became her friend. They visited the vet and were reassured about her condition She was given toys, a bed and a blanket, and preparations were in place for the birth of the three puppies the vet promised.

Winter showed no signs of weakening its grip and Lottie spent less and less time at the shop, using the little dog as an excuse. Zena didn't mind. She still managed to clean for Roy Roberts, her friend Nelda and was gradually helping Karen to clean rooms in the house that she was still amused to learn was called SunnyBank. 'What a name for a creepy old, haunted house,' she laughed, as she told Aunty Mabs.

Chasing out spiders and other interlopers, scrubbing and polishing revealed an attractive house with well-proportioned rooms elegantly carved staircase, ornate ceilings and floors that were in perfect condition once the dirt had been removed. It was hard but satisfying work. She was content.

She was at SunnyBank working through a list of tasks left for her by Karen, who had to see the doctor. The house was filled with that clear silence that makes every sound resonate, emphasizing the hollow emptiness. She dropped a box of cutlery into the sink for cleaning and the sound went on and on, bouncing off walls and she looked around as though afraid of disturbing ghosts. It felt different knowing Karen wasn't there, even her own footsteps were an intrusion in the quiet, empty rooms and she found herself tiptoeing to and fro.

She started to make herself cup of tea and it was as she turned off the kettle, which had disturbed the silence for a while, that she heard something clatter upstairs. It must have been the wind, knocking something off a window sill. Even on chilly March mornings, Karen liked to open a window for a while. Then she heard the sound of someone muttering and a drawer opening and closing. The voice of the man was raised and she heard angry words as the man searched for something.

Was it a thief? Should she face him? Or run to a telephone box and dial 999? The voice then cried out as though in pain and without thinking she went up the wide staircase and glanced at the locked room. The muttering was coming from there. She crept forward and listened.

'Is that you, Karen?' the voice asked. 'I seem to have cut myself and I can't find the first aid box.'

'Hello?' Zena whispered in her fear. 'Mrs Rogers isn't here. Can I help?'

'Who are you?'

'I'm Zena, I help Mrs Rogers with the cleaning.'

'You'd better come in, Zena. Can you fix a bandage, d'you think?' Before she could answer, the front door opened and Karen called a greeting.

'I'm up here, Karen. I think the gentleman in this room has hurt himself,' she said. As Karen ran up the stairs, Zena hurried down and went into the kitchen, where she stood and waited for Karen to come back down. For something to do she prepared a tray with two coffee cups and biscuits, for Karen and the mysterious man upstairs. She heard footsteps coming very slowly down the polished wooden stairs and waited, half expecting to be told to leave, accused of interfering.

'You'd better make that coffee for three,' Karen said, as she walked slowly into the room. 'It's time for you to meet your employer.'

Zena turned and stared as a large, young well dressed man followed her in. She noticed that Karen was holding the man's hand leading him. He wore dark glasses and, as Karen guided him to a chair, she realized with great sadness that he was blind. Karen introduced him as 'Mr James Penberthy.'

Stupidly Zena offered her hand as she said, 'I'm Zena.' She stepped closer and found his hand and he gripped hers and shook it firmly. She chatted a little as she made coffee under Karen's instruction as to strength, then reached for her coat. With a friendly comment about the next of her clients waiting for her she went to the door. Mr Penberthy called her back. 'What did you say your name was?'

'Zena, Mr Penberthy,' she said, hurrying out of the door.

She cycled home, unaware of the icy cold that crept into her clothes and chilled her. She was impatient to tell her mother about the odd occurrence and wondered about the tragedy of the inhabitant of the out-of-bounds room, Mr James Penberthy.

For no particular reason, she wrote to tell Jake about the unexpected encounter. It was so strange, she needed to talk about it and, after discussing it with Lottie, Greg and Susie, none of whom knew anything about James Penberthy and Mabs who could add nothing either, a letter to Jake was a way of sharing the strange encounter. Although the letter was mainly about the house they'd always called the haunted house, she mentioned Susie several times, hoping Rose would stay away knowing that Greg had someone in his life whom they all liked very much.

In London, Madeleine and Rose were waiting for Jake before setting off for Cold Brook Vale and she opened the letter addressed to Jake and read it to Rose, making remarks about Greg's lack of loyalty, ignoring the fact that it was Rose who had left. While they waited for Jake they discussed in a light-hearted manner some of the ways in which they could punish the Martins, particularly Greg, for his lack of loyalty and other misdemeanours undisclosed. Rose pretended with her; it was such fun but she said nothing of the reason for her sudden hatred of the Martin family.

When they were settled into their rooms in the usual lodgings, Jake went to visit the Martins. He knelt down at once to greet Betty who was larger than he remembered. He asked for a health report and praised them for the excellent care she was receiving. Then he said hello to Zena and the others and she greeted him warmly, sharing the delight of the little dog but with no sensation of excitement. She was relieved to find that the love she had felt for so long had faded leaving behind just familiarity and friendship.

He politely asked Lottie and Zena about the business and they told him all they had achieved and what plans they were making to expand. 'Although,' Lottie admitted, 'I'm leaving more of the running of the business to Zena these days.' All his questions were polite but on subjects about which he clearly had little interest, questions such as any visitor might ask.

When Zena began to discuss the man who lived at SunnyBank, he was puzzled. He knew nothing about her strange encounter and he hadn't received any letter. 'I bet Madeleine has it, she's forgetful at times. When they come to the office she always takes them back to her flat as she knows we'll meet up sometime soon.'

They filled him in on the little Zena had learned, but he knew of no one called James Penberthy. 'Remember how we used to make up stories about the house being haunted?' he said, looking at Zena and Greg. 'Dared each other to go inside, we did, and then we'd run away yelling to frighten the ghosts. Good fun. Happy days, eh?'

They reminisced for a while then Jake said, 'I remember the house was once owned by a man called Dove. Billy Dove I believe. Nickname 'Birdie' of course! He moved away a long time ago.'

'My father mentioned him a few times,' Zena said, at once interested. 'Who was he?'

'I have no idea, he was well out of my league. We all hoped he wouldn't appear on one of our visits. We were probably more frightened of meeting him than a ghost! We stayed well into the trees when there were lights on in the house.'

Lottie looked hopefully at Greg. 'We can ask the solicitor to try and find him—'

'Why d'you want to find a previous tenant?' Jake asked.

'Oh, it's just something the present tenant might want to know.'

Jake didn't want to stay long, he knew he no longer belonged there, things had changed and now he was just a friend calling on the family, no longer anything more. He knew he was responsible and silently grieved for all he had lost. He asked about Aunty Mabs. 'I know about the night café. Isn't that dangerous for her?

207

Leaving there so early in the morning carrying money, when there are so few people about, isn't she in danger of being robbed and perhaps hurt?'

Greg explained. 'She hides it in the café each night and I take it to the bank every Friday.'

'She hides it? Where? The place is used by other people during the day, isn't it? She seems to be taking risks.'

'It isn't anywhere obvious.' Greg smiled and whispered, 'She hides it behind a skirting board in the kitchen, would you believe!'

'And,' added Lottie, 'she has a spare key in the disused drain-pipe outside the back door! Crazy I know, but twice she has forgotten her key and had to get a taxi back home to collect it.'

'I hope you aren't as casual about Office Supplies. Especially since the break in.'

'No, we're very careful about locking the door from the entrance to the flat so no one can get in from the back. It's all safe now.'

Greg added with a grim smile, 'Or it will be, once the new door is fixed. The present one could be pushed in by a seven-year-old!' They all laughed and Jake remarked how simple life was in Cold Brook Vale, compared to his part of London.

When Jake left they went out to see him off and were shocked at the deterioration in the weather. A wind had strengthened and the temperature had dropped. They shivered as they stood in the doorway to wave him off in his smart, noisy little car.

In a touch of melancholy, Zena stood with her arms wrapped around herself shivering in the cold darkness and listening until the sound of the powerful engine faded. She wondered how such certainty, the plans she and Jake had so confidently made, could vanish and leave nothing in their place.

Inside the house they could hear the wind gusting, wailing now and again as it disturbed a loose panel on the corner of the old shed. A few metal objects could be heard rolling around on the yard, the branches of the trees swayed, and creaked as they touched against each other. The radio warned of worsening weather.

The storm increased in fury and Zena found it impossible to sleep. She glanced at the clock then wrapped herself in a dressing gown, threw a blanket over her shoulders and went down. The door was unlocked and she wondered if that meant Greg was on his way to work. Then the door opened bringing a wail of wind and a scattering of debris from the garden. Leaves, small twigs and earth covered the hall floor and he came in. Together they pushed to hold the door in place against a fierce, determined wind and lock it.

'Where on earth have you been?' Zena demanded. 'You must be mad to risk going out in this.'

'Jake and the others are going back to London tomorrow and I wanted to try one more time to talk to Rose.'

'Oh, Greg. We all hope you'll choose Susie.'

'I have. But in a strange way I still need to know why she suddenly changed from a woman who was considering marrying me to someone I don't know. Susie is the one to make me happy and even in my most confident moments with Rose I had doubts about her bringing me anything but an insecure feeling of her one day leaving me.'

'Did you talk to her?'

'It was crazy to expect to. There were lights on although it was past eleven o'clock, but when I knocked the door, Madeleine answered and said Rose had nothing to say to me. If I manage to see her without that woman who's appointed herself bodyguard I might get some answers.'

'Talk to Jake, he might be able to arrange something.'

'I tried and he promised to try. I might go to London just one more time. Susie's right, I need to get this half and half involvement with Rose out of my mind.'

'Will Jake help, d'you think? He and Rose seem in thrall to the wonderful Madeleine!'

Greg shrugged. 'You're right. He's second in command in keeping her away from me.' He frowned. 'What could it have been? Everything was looking hopeful then that visit to the hospital and it was all over. We were all there and no one remembers Dad saying anything hurtful.'

'She's never said much about her childhood, which I believe was sad and lonely, so it might have been because we were all there, a close family, making her doubt her ability of breaking in to our

209

circle, afraid perhaps of always being a stranger and never really belonging.'

'What happened to cause her such low esteem? She's been away from the Conellys for years. She doesn't have friends, at least she didn't until Madeleine and Jake.'

'Roy Roberts knows something of her history, but he won't tell.'

With the wind still threatening to lift the roof, they sat and drank cocoa and ate toast and listened in wonder at the ferocity of the storm. At two o'clock Zena began to doze and they went up to try once again to sleep.

Back in London, having delayed their return until late in the day, Jake went to Madeleine's flat and helped the girls unload their luggage, then went home to his dingy room. He was earning enough to move to somewhere more comfortable but was helping by giving a few shillings each week to a woman in the room next to his, who had broken a leg and was unable to get about. He would move as soon as she was well enough to cope without help. He bought and paid for some shopping every week, plus arranging for someone to do her laundry. She promised to repay him as soon as she was well but he smiled and waved away her thanks. To give meant just that: giving meant helping without expecting repayment or reward. Lending, now that was something different.

A few days later, when the three of them were eating a meal in a local café, Jake told them about the precarious way people lived in Cold Brook. 'It's a different world,' he said. 'Imagine hiding your takings behind the skirting board! And a spare key in a drain pipe! Did you ever hear anything so daft? And Zena and Lottie are even worse. They hide their daily cash in a cocoa tin in a cupboard!'

He talked about the differences in the two places, comparing the freedom of not worrying about thieves in his home town and having to make sure everything is almost bolted to the floor in the part of London where he lived.

'Will you ever go back?' Madeleine asked.

'Leave here? I can't imagine life without you two to entertain me,' he replied. Madeleine glanced at him and saw what was a suspiciously sad expression in his blue eyes that belied his brightly spoken words. 'Things change,' she said quietly. 'That's good, isn't it?'

The little dog presented them with three puppies and they all spent hours watching their progress, proud of the way Betty cared for them. Zena realized that the arrival of Betty had changed their lives but more for her mother than the rest of them. Zena managed the shop apart from the mornings when she did her cleaning as well as dealing with the business side. Lottie just agreed to any suggestions she made on what to order, and prices to charge and gradually, Lottie spent more and more days at home with Betty and the puppies.

The vet advertised the puppies and found homes for them when they were eight weeks old. Lottie and Betty recommenced their daily walks, and visits to Sam and Neville at the farm. She dealt with the running of the house but it was Zena who did the baking every Sunday morning and Greg who dealt with the routine chores. The clearing of the garden after the storms of winter had been neglected and it was Greg and some of his friends who dealt with clearing the debris and lighting a celebratory bonfire as spring began to change the drab browns into fresh vibrant greens.

Lottie talked a lot about the walks and the farm, and Zena and Greg were surprised to learn from Neville that she had been cooking for them for weeks. It was as though she was slowly trans-ferring her loyalty from Llyn Hir to Sam and the farm.

Seeing her mother with her arms around Sam as they walked with the two dogs through the wood one evening gave Zena a sickening jolt of resentment. A mingling of half formed suspi-cions about the missing money, of disloyalty and perhaps jealousy. Turning away to avoid them she passed the house called SunnyBank and sat on the bank outside the gates until resentment gradually eased and common sense returned.

Her mother was not yet fifty and young enough to enjoy years of happiness. The thought was a revelation to her and she began to think about her mother as a person, a young woman with a future to fill. She thought of the alternative; for her mother to continue looking after them until she and Greg married and left Llyn Hir, and then settle into old age and the end of hope of anything more than a slow decline. She deserved more. 'She and Dad were happy,' she said to Greg later. 'She cared for him and did all she could to make his life a good one. Ours too. But we shouldn't expect her life to end too because Dad's did.'

They talked about it for a long time, trying to decide on the best approach then told her where their thoughts had led them. Lottie listened anxiously, a frown creasing her brow, then she smiled as they ended their rather confused comments with, 'If you and Sam are more than friends, we're completely happy about it and wish you years of happiness.' Sam came that evening and he shook their hands as though he were a stranger newly introduced. They talked as easily as they had always done and Zena knew that nothing much had changed.

'I'll run the business and gradually pay off the debts we raised to buy it and after that, there should be a reasonable income for us.'

'If only the loss of your father's money could be explained, then life would be just about perfect,' Lottie said.

'It all sounds good enough for me,' Greg said. 'Don't you think so, Betty?' The dog barked a reply.

'That definitely means "Yes"!' Sam said.

Chapter Ten

WHEN ZENA WENT to do her weekly clean for Roy Roberts there was no reply to her knock. She called Doris his neighbour and was told he was in hospital. She left her cycle at his door and caught the bus to visit him, stopping to buy fruit and some chocolate on the way

She was surprised at how frail he looked. There were bruises on his face and his eyes looked weary. 'Mr Roberts? What happened?' she asked, although Doris had told her he'd had a dizzy spell and had fallen down the garden steps.

'Those damned steps want cleaning, I slipped on some moss,' he said.

'You didn't feel giddy or anything?'

'No I didn't. I slipped,' he said firmly.

'I'll see to that as soon as I get back there,' she promised, aware of his denial. He hated even a hint of his needing extra help.

They talked for a while and she promised to do the usual cleaning plus a few extra chores. 'I can get into a few corners, with you out of my way,' she teased. He gave her a list of shopping and insisted that, 'Once I'm back home I'll manage without people fussing about the place, so don't listen to the nurses!'

She told him Jake was supposed to be coming at the weekend and that Rose would probably be with him.

'Keep your Greg away from her. She won't make him happy.'

'They've broken up and it seems to be irrevocable, although he still has no idea why she ended it.'

'Best he forgets her.'

'Why do you say that? She seems pleasant enough, although

Greg never felt really secure about their plans. He felt that something was holding her back. You must know something, Mr Roberts, or you wouldn't say Greg should forget her. Can you explain why she acted in such an odd way?'

'One day I'll talk about it, I promise. But not now.' He waved his splayed hands in front of her to close the subject and said, 'Now that Susie Crane, she's a lovely girl and I can imagine her and your Greg being very happy.'

'I agree with you there. She's so relaxed and easy to get along with. But I think his curiosity about Rose is holding them back. If he knew why she had so suddenly left.' She coaxed but clearly her curiosity wasn't going to be satisfied so she talked about her friend Nelda and the two lively children, which pleased and entertained him. She left, promising to see him on the following day, hoping to persuade him to tell what he knew about Rose that made her an unsuitable wife for Greg. He needed to get the facts so he could forget her and enjoy the bright uncomplicated happiness of Susie.

Although she knew he hadn't really slipped on the steps, she went back and scrubbed them thoroughly, her mind on what he might tell her about Rose and hoped it would be something she should share with her brother.

Roy Roberts was in hospital for three days and when he came home it was clear that he was unwell. The bruises from his fall were changing colour as they healed but he was unable to move about without getting breathless. He went as far as the garden to look at his flowers but was tired when he got back to his favourite chair. He slept a lot more than before too, and she discussed his failing health with Doris who looked in regularly and assured her he was comfortable and well fed.

When Zena cleared some plants from the edges of the path to make sure there was no danger of him tripping over them, even though he'd hardly been outside since his stay in hospital, she found a lot of abandoned food in the bin. He clearly wasn't eating as much as they believed.

She visited often and once dared to ask if she should write to his sons to tell them he'd been in hospital after a fall, in case they wanted to visit. He didn't raise his voice as she half expected, he just shook his head.

'It's too late to hope for a joyful reunion if that's what you're thinking,' he said sadly. 'If they did come, they'd immediately start on about how cruel I was to throw them and their mother out.' His eyes crinkled into a smile at that and added, 'That's another story for me to tell you one day, young Zena. I wasn't the villain, you know, and the truth makes an interesting story. But not yet. It still makes me angry and anger is so tiring.'

'Perhaps you ought to write it down for your sons to read one day. There must be two sides to the story of which your sons have been told only one.'

'You believe I'm not as wicked as some think?'

'I think you're a kind old man and your only crime is a temper that stops you from being able to state your case coherently.'

He gave her a key before she left. 'Just in case Doris or Kevin aren't about to let you in.' She tucked it in her purse and waved goodbye.

Nelda's girls were increasingly frequent visitors to Llyn Hir. The woods and the lakeside were scenes for adventures that were made safe by the company of Zena, their mother and now the dog as well. Sam invited them to the farm on occasions. He and his father showed them around the farm and children's delight and happiness spread around them all. The lake was the place where they had picnics and they looked longingly at the boat which was out of bounds, apart from when it was on the shore upside down to provide shelter when a shower threatened to spoil their fun.

It was Sam who suggested checking its condition to make sure it was safe to use. 'Then, if Nelda agrees, we could introduce them to the fun of being on the water, which isn't very deep but deep enough to be a danger. We have to make sure they understand that they must never come here on their own.'

Greg and some of his friends checked the boat which seemed perfectly sound and just needed a coat of paint. They contacted the local boatyard and they sent someone to make sure there were no hidden problems. Both of the girls were competent swimmers so they were pleased to tell the girls about the surprise that was planned.

The raft, which was still used occasionally for shopping trips, was checked regularly and was an easy way of crossing the water. If it was on the wrong side it was a simple matter to pull it across.

It was Sam who took them on their first trip around the lake accompanied by screams of delight. While Zena and Nelda watched and shouted encouragement Sam pretended to let them pull the boat back to shore.

It was the first of many visits as summer strengthened and picnics were a regular occurrence. In July, as school closed for the summer, Nelda arranged for a manager to look after her business for a month, having worked hard all winter to make sure her shelves and store cupboards were full. She took the girls to see her mother in France, and their other grandparents, then the rest of the time she was at home, dealing with the garden and taking the girls on day trips. Their favourites without doubt were the days they went to Llyn Hir. Both girls had a birthday in August and both insisted on a party at the lake.

The weather was warm and for the first time they were allowed to swim in the rather chilly water. Both Nelda and Zena went in with them and made sure the girls were between them and the little beach. A few days later they swam further with Nelda in close attendance and never far from the ropes attached to the raft reaching from shore to shore.

On what was to be their last day before school began again, confidence had grown and Georgie swam across the lake. Then to everyone's alarm she dived below the water. Zena and Lottie struck out immediately. Georgie bobbed up waving something. 'Look what I found!' she shouted, 'It's treasure!' Trying to hide their fright, they all swam back and Georgie showed them a purse made of soft, rotting leather with a rusty frame and fastener.

Bobbie tried to snatch it from her but Georgie was quick to run to her mother and insist the treasure was hers. They all watched as the leather was torn back to reveal the contents. Georgie was clearly disappointed. 'It's only a key,' she said with a pout, throwing it onto the ground. Her sister grabbed it. 'It's probably the key to some treasure,' she said and at once the girls were arguing over possession. Nelda grabbed it and handed it to Zena. 'Yours, I think.' Still arguing, the girls set off back to Llyn Hir. Zena looked curiously at the old purse and the rather large key. It looked similar in size to the one belonging to Roy Roberts. She would show him, perhaps he might know of a house with a similar lock to his own.

The weather continued warm and Zena went to SunnyBank and continued to do the basic cleaning one room at a time. It was a large property and had two staircases and six bedrooms, most of which were moderate in size. In every room she tackled, she washed floors and polished furniture and mirrors and picture frames until it was possible to imagine the elegantly designed, attractively furnished rooms being used. She didn't see James Penberthy again and Karen didn't mention him.

Then several pieces of furniture disappeared. A table from the hall, extra chairs and a cupboard that had stood close to a couch. Other pieces were moved. Where a cupboard had been placed across a window, it now stood at the back of the landing where no one passed. In two rooms rugs were taken up and put outside wrapped in sacking. The rooms didn't look bare, they were still well furnished but less cluttered. Zena guessed that the changes were to make it easier for James Penberthy to move around his home.

One morning when she went in to start work, Karen met her at the door and asked her not to stay. 'I'll pay you for your time,' she said, handing her an envelope, 'but Mr Penberthy has a visitor and doesn't want any interruptions. Can you come again two weeks from today, please, dear?'

Zena pocketed the money, which amounted to three weeks' payment wondering if she should have refused it, but the door had been quickly closed. She pushed the cycle down the drive and stood for a while before setting off to relieve her mother at the shop.

She cycled slowly along the lane edged with patches of glorious summer flowers, enjoying the quiet of the morning. Before she had gone past the first bend in the lane she heard a vehicle approaching and stopped to tuck herself into the side of the narrow lane. The engine sounded powerful and was travelling fast and, when it turned the corner, she saw that it was a car followed by a large van. She let it pass. Then, with unashamed curiosity, went back to see it arrive at the door of SunnyBank.

The driver of the car stepped out and helped James Penberthy, guiding him to the steps to the front door, where the blind man stopped, turned his head as though using memory to see his way, then pushed away the man's guiding hand and went up the steps and through the door unaided apart from a walking stick. The van was unloaded and bedroom furniture was taken into the house. Curiosity partially satisfied, Zena rode away.

She was almost at the end of the lane when both vehicles returned, no longer in a rush, and turned towards the town centre. She went into Llyn Hir and changed into something more suitable for the shop and cycled down to join her mother.

The farm van was outside the shop and she hesitated, waiting until Sam had left before going in. It was still strangely embarrassing for her to see their mother and Uncle Sam showing affection, albeit casually. She found her conversations with him stilted, uneasy and admitted to her brother that she was still half convinced that their loving relationship had begun long before their father had died and was the reason for him leaving so little to his family in his will.

Greg disagreed. 'If that were true, why would he punish us? Surely he'd have given us a mention or at least an explanation? *We* did nothing to hurt him even if Mam did – which I doubt!'

Wanting to believe him, she listened and tried to understand how a long term friendship could suddenly turn to love.

Having seen Zena waiting until Sam had left, aware of her daughter's doubts, Lottie tried to explain.

'There have been times in our lives when your father and I needed a friend and Sam was always there. We shared his sorrow when his wife died; Mavis had been my best friend since childhood. When his son Peter drowned, we grieved with him. Losing Peter was like losing one of our own.

'Before your father died there was nothing more. It's only recently that we have begun to think about sharing our lives. I hope you can understand. You and Greg will be leaving soon, finding someone to love, building families of your own. I could stay here and wait for visits, getting old and more and more lonely, *or* I can start a new life of my own with a man who respects me and cares for us all.' For an answer Zena stood up and hugged her mother.

When the shop closed, Zena went for a walk. The evenings were beginning to draw in but when there was a chance to sit beside the lake, it was there she went to calm troubled thoughts. Thoughts of her mother and Sam faded and she began to think about Jake. She felt a sudden regret for pushing him out of her life. Regret that was momentarily tinged with jealousy as she imagined him in the arms of Madeleine and then, shamed by her imaginings, she silently wished them both well.

Before she returned home her emotions had tilted and turned and she knew she had to talk to Jake, clear her mind of him, let him go. Fear of remaining alone, never having a family, staying with her mother and Sam were pushed aside. She would still have a good life, whether or not she married. It was nonsense to think differently. To persuade herself that marrying Jake was better than being alone, that was insulting to herself and to Jake. She decided to go to London and spend a day with him, say their final goodbyes. At that moment she fully understood how important it was for Greg to do the same regarding Rose. It would have to be soon; hanging onto something that was no more than a distorted memory was foolish and pathetic. It also presented a risk of Greg losing Susie.

When she opened the door, the telephone was ringing and it was Jake, telling her he would be there that weekend, but without either Rose or Madeleine. Her emotions did a somersault and she didn't know whether she felt pleasure or panic. She went to see Mabs.

She was so tense that she started talking as soon as Mabs opened the door. 'Why am I so afraid of change?' she asked. 'It seems Greg and I are both guilty of that. Greg can't let Rose go even though he is so happy with Susie. I hated the thought of Mam with Uncle Sam – or anyone else – and I've been afraid that if I let Jake go I'll never find anyone else.'

'Let me tell you my news before we get onto the psychology of love.' Zena noticed then how serious her aunt looked. 'What's happened? Are you all right?'

'The café was invaded this morning, soon after I left. They

ruined everything they could. And they found the money.'

'Oh, Aunty Mabs. I'm so sorry. Are you all right? Was there much taken? How did they get in?'

'How did they get in? – That's why I said invaded, not burgled. They used a key. Somehow they found out where I hid the spare and they also knew where to find the money. So it's someone I've trusted, isn't it?'

'That's the saddest thing of all,' Zena said. 'One of your customers, I suppose? Only Greg knows where you keep the key, he's told no one but me and Mam. There isn't anyone else.'

'You don't know him, but there's a man who's been coming since your Uncle Frank and I started the night café and he's appointed himself my guardian. Sid never leaves until I'm out of the premises and the door is locked. He watches until I'm on the bus unless Greg or Richard Thomas is there. I was late leaving this morning. To tell the truth I fell asleep and caught a later bus, and there was only a couple of hours before the day café opened. Late as it was, Sid was there until I was safely on my way. The thief must have known exactly where to look to have managed in the short time before the day staff arrived.'

'And this Sid, he wouldn't have been involved?'

'Definitely not. Neither would any of the others.'

'Some of them have been in prison—'

'No matter. I trust them all.'

'What do the police think?'

Mabs shook her head. 'The night people need this place. That's why I haven't told the police. They would question all my regulars who would feel hurt and disappointed. I can cope with this, but hurting them would make everything ten times worse.'

Zena told Greg when he came home and asked him if he had mentioned the café's primitive safety arrangements to anyone.

'No, of course not.' He frowned then added, 'Well, I talked about it to Jake, joking about the differences between our safe and secure village and his perilous part of London. But he wouldn't steal from Aunty Mabs and never break things for the fun of it. He's fond of her. You know that.'

'Of course I do, but who might he have told?'

'Come on, Sis! I know you don't like the woman but I can't imagine Madeleine coming all this way to steal a few shillings.'

'Poor Aunty Mabs. I'm going down to help clear up before the café opens. She's done most of it, making sure everything was straight for the day café, but there'll be shopping needed to replace what was ruined and broken, and some extra baking to do.'

'I'll come too and we'll make some better arrangements regarding security.'

Once the day café closed, Mabs set about cooking scones and sausage rolls, Zena and Greg cleared up the mess left by the thief – or thieves. It was Greg who found the envelope screwed up and thrown towards the rubbish bin. It was written in Zena's handwriting and addressed to Jake.

They discussed the mysterious find then Zena put it in her pocket and thought about the best way of facing Jake with it. Surely he wasn't responsible for the robbery? But how her letter to him had found its way there was something that needed a good explanation.

The following Friday Jake arrived, full of apologies, explaining that his neighbour, Vera, had a hospital appointment and he couldn't let her go on her own. 'I've been helping her with shopping and all that since her accident,' he added. He had unpacked a few belongings at the usual lodgings and had come straight to Llyn Hir.

Lottie, Greg and Zena had been sitting with a meal keeping warm expecting him to arrive at any moment. Being late was not unusual for Jake, but when an hour had passed, they ate the meal and Zena went to the pictures.

'Can I wait till Zena gets back, Mrs Martin?' he asked. 'I've come a long way and I don't want to go back again without talking to her.'

They chatted easily, questions and answers on life in the village, friends they shared, then Greg mentioned the robbery at Aunty Mabs's café.

'Is she all right? She wasn't hurt was she?' Jake looked alarmed but with concern for Mabs. Not, Greg decided, with any recognizable sign of guilt. 'One of her customers, was it? There are a few doubtful characters, aren't there?'

'No, she doesn't think it's one of the people who spend their nights there. Somehow, word got out of where she keeps her money and where the spare key is hidden.'

Jake stared from one to the other. 'No, Greg! Not me! I'd never hurt her, I'm fond of her, you know that.'

'You knew about her casual security arrangements.'

'I'd, I'd never tell anyone.' Then he paused. 'All right, I did talk about it, to Rose and Madeleine but they'd never … come all this way to steal a few pounds? It has to be one of the night people.'

'Where was Madeleine on Thursday?' Greg asked quietly.

'In London. No – she was visiting friends in Aylesbury. But it can't have been her, she was there when I went after work, we had tickets for a concert.'

'And Rose?' Lottie asked.

'She didn't want to come, she doesn't enjoy the same music as Madeleine and me.'

'For some reason we can't fathom, Rose dislikes us,' Lottie said. 'Perhaps she—'

'This is crazy,' Jake interrupted. 'Why are you looking at someone who lives in London? It has to be someone local.'

'Find out where she was, will you, Jake?'

'No, I won't!' He stood up and reached for his jacket. 'I won't stay here and listen to this nonsense. Please tell Zena I'll be leaving tomorrow at ten and I'd like to talk to her.' He left without another word.

Zena was told what had happened and at nine the following morning, before she went for her weekly visit to Roy Roberts, she called at the house where he regularly lodged and was told he was at the garage filling the car for his journey back to London.

In fact, Jake was at Llyn Hir, where Lottie told him Zena would be cleaning for Mr Roberts for the next couple of hours.

Zena waited for half an hour fingering the envelope addressed to him that had been found in the café after the robbery. Going to the pictures had been childish but the truth was she didn't know how to show him the envelope and state their suspicions. Whatever she said would come out wrong and he would refuse to explain.

222

He probably wouldn't accept that it had been found where she said it had been found. Whatever he had planned to discuss with her, it had not been important enough for him to actually find her.

Jake waited at the house, then set off for London. On the way he passed the shop, which was closed. Zena had made it emphatically clear that there was nothing she wanted to discuss.

A week later, Roy Roberts mentioned to Zena her idea of recording his version of what had happened on paper. 'I think it would be good if you will write it down as I tell it. Could you do that for me?' She thought about it and decided she would. She collected notebooks, pens, ink, blotting paper and set off to begin. Thank heavens for her shorthand skills.

It was difficult to keep him on the subject he wanted to explain. His thoughts wandered between his childhood, which was unhappy, filled with criticism and punishments, and the life he'd dreamed of giving his own boys. He was evasive when it came to facts. At one point he turned the conversation to Rose Conelly. 'That's why I understand why she behaves like she does. She suffered the same kind of misery as I did. I handled it differently, that's all.' He looked at Zena, scribbling furiously in shorthand as she tried to preserve his outpourings. 'She'll never be happy, that one. She won't forget and never tries to understand why she was treated so badly. Best to forgive even if you can't forget.'

'You wanted to record what happened before your wife left, taking the boys?' she asked hopefully.

As though unaware of her question, he said, 'Your father was a fool. He trusted people. Wouldn't look the truth in the eye.'

She eventually got him back onto the subject and he told her that his wife accused him of having an affair with her sister, Donna. 'Rubbish it was,' he said, 'and Donna told the story purely to make trouble. We were in the bedroom but that's not a sin, is it? I was helping her to turn the mattress and we fell, laughing as I tripped over the corner. Donna went all coy and refused to confirm my explanation. Some people get their satisfaction by making trouble for others. They find happy and contented characters the most entertaining when they mess things up for them. Take that girl for example. She was so twisted with jealousy, she hated seeing people happy and—'

'What girl are you talking about? Donna? Rose?' It was a few moments before she looked up and saw that he was asleep.

She went in to see Doris next door and stayed for a cup of tea, popping back twice to see if Roy had woken. 'I think I'll go home and try to write down his thoughts another day, he's obviously too tired to concentrate,' Zena said. They both went for one more look and found the poor man had been sick.

'He's still asleep,' Zena whispered.

Doris pulled her away from where she was trying to undo the buttons of his shirt to remove the foul-smelling garment. 'Leave him, love. I think we need an ambulance.

Roy was taken to hospital and the next day, when she enquired, she was told he'd had a heart attack. She visited him and dared to ask if she should contact his sons to tell them he was ill, but again, he refused. 'Their mother told her version of what happened. I'm the villain and always will be. The truth has gone for ever.'

'Will you tell me what really happened?'

'When I'm well enough to get out of here, we'll talk about it. There's maybe some of the story I can tell, but not all.'

'Are you sure I can't write to them?'

He shook his head. 'They wouldn't believe anything I told them and perhaps it's for the best, no point in trying to persuade them that their mother was the one, not me. Not after all this time.'

Zena and Greg were walking Betty through the wood and came to the gate of SunnyBank. The house appeared to be unused, rubbish had gathered around the drive and the front door, curtains were closed and it had an abandoned look. They heard footsteps then saw a heavily built man coming from the side of the house towards them struggling with a large sack.

'I know him. That's Percy, one of Aunty Mab's night people.' Greg called and the man stopped, half-turned as though about to run, then put down his burden and waved a hand. They waited at the gate as he approached.

'Hello, Greg, who is this lovely young lady?' To Zena's surprise he was beautifully spoken. 'I hope my appearance didn't alarm you, my dear.'

'This is my sister. Zena, meet Percy,' Greg said. 'What are you doing in there? It's private property.'

'I'm taking my bedding away. I've been sleeping here during the day for a few months off and on but I heard in the post office that the tenants are coming back so I thought I'd better clear out before I'm caught.'

'Why do you sleep in the day and go to the café at night?' Zena asked.

'Perhaps I will when I find a decent place but to be honest, I sleep here in the daytime because this place gives me the creeps after dark. I can't stay here at night.'

Greg laughed. 'A giant like you afraid of ghosts?'

'Of course I'm not, but it isn't a place to relax and sleep at night. Sleep comes easier in the daylight hours. Then, if you hear a noise, you can look and discover the cause. Unexplained noises hidden in darkness can keep me awake for hours.'

'I've been in every corner of the house and there's nothing creepy about it,' Zena told him, still smiling at the thought of the large man avoiding the dark hours.

'I've seen you, Miss. You're cleaning ready for the return of the tenants, aren't you?'

'Yes, but they aren't due for a few more days.'

Percy nodded agreement. 'So I understand.'

They walked with him for a while, as he explained that he didn't want another winter sleeping rough. 'I've found a room not far from the centre of the village and I intend to visit Frankie's café for a few hours each night. Until I can train myself out of the regular nightshifts,' he added with a laugh.

With just a few more days before Karen and James Penberthy returned, and with only Roy Roberts's and Nelda's cleaning to fit in, Zena booked a train for London. She would find an hotel easily enough and would find Jake and face him with the incriminating envelope.

When she turned up at the office at 5.30 on that Friday evening, she saw him coming out and he was alone. He was overjoyed to see her, hugged her and began chattering about where they would go, what they would see, and unavoidably she was caught up in the excitement.

'As a first step,' he said, 'we'll eat. There's a small café just around the corner and it stays open all evening so we can sit and talk, and I can get over the wonderful surprise of seeing you standing there, like a dreamed up apparition waiting for me.' With an arm around her, smiling happily, he led her to the café.

'What did you think of my having two weeks off with pay, from cleaning SunnyBank?' she said, and was surprised at the lack of understanding on his face. 'You did get my letter?'

He frowned, then said, 'That's generous, but why would they do that?'

'Because they'll be away for a couple of weeks and want to lock the house up.'

'Great news.'

'And what about the new customers I wrote to you about, Curtis and Sons, a large manufacturing company needing everything in the stationery line, as they were let down by their previous supplier. Isn't it wonderful?'

'Congratulations, I didn't know about that.'

'Of course you did, Jake! I wrote to tell you.'

'Sorry, love, but you didn't mention that. You must have forgotten.'

She decided then to tell him the truth even though he would realize she had been trying to trick him. 'Sorry, Jake, but the truth is, Aunty Mab's café was robbed a few days ago and we found an envelope there, one written by me and addressed to you. It had been opened, the letter was missing, and from the date, it was the one in which I told you about the unpaid weeks and the large contract.... I'm sorry!' she said, as she saw his eyes widen with shock. 'I'm truly sorry I tried to trick you, but I don't trust your friends and I had to find out if you or they were involved.'

He listened in silence as she explained in detail about the theft, and about the key and the stupid arrangement of hiding the cash behind a skirting board. 'Apart from Greg, Mam, and me, you were the only one who knew and, I'm sorry, but I thought, if you talked about it to Madeleine and—'

'Zena, I *did* tell Madeleine and Rose. We were talking about the differences between living in a safe corner like Cold Brook Vale and the part of London where I live.'

'Then it's possible that one of them was involved?'

'No.'

'Not even by telling someone else? Someone who would take advantage of the information?'

'No. They don't mix with people who would steal. Besides, who would travel so far for such a small amount of money? It has to be one of her customers.'

'She doesn't believe that. Sid, one of her regulars, has appointed himself her guardian and he never leaves until he sees her get the bus or a taxi. On that day there was very little time between her leaving and the day staff coming because she fell asleep.'

'Could it have been this Sid?'

'Definitely not.' She hesitated then asked, 'Do you know where Madeleine and Rose were on that night? Thursday of last week?'

Ignoring her question he said, 'We'll have to leave it for the police to deal with.'

'She didn't call the police.'

'So she must think it was one of her regulars.'

They argued for a while, Jake convinced it was one of the night people, and Zena unable to put aside her doubts about Rose and Madeleine.

'All right, love. I'll try to find out where Rose was on that night.' He thought for a moment then shook his head. 'No, I'm wrong. That was the night before. I didn't see either of them on that night, but I honestly don't think either of them capable of such a thing. Why would they?'

Zena went home the following day, convinced the visit had been a waste of time. She doubted whether Jake would question Rose or Madeleine and common sense told her he would be right not to try, it all seemed so pointless. Her mother was out and Greg was working so she went to see Mabs.

Mabs smiled an enthusiastic welcome. 'Come and see what your Greg has arranged,' she said grabbing a coat. 'Come on, there's a bus in five minutes.' She bustled her out and refused to discuss anything until she had examined the new arrangement. The café was still open with the day clientele and Mabs waved and went through to her kitchen. She waved an arm with a 'ta raa!' and Zena saw a new safe built into the wall. 'And that's not all,' Mabs said proudly. 'The door has a padlock and the spare key is with a friend living around the corner.'

As it was almost time for the day café to close, Zena stayed and helped Mabs prepare for the night customers. Then they went back to Mabs's flat and had a meal. Zena gave details of her brief visit to London and Mabs shook her head.

'What were you thinking of, love, going all that way? It was a few pounds, definitely not worth travelling all that way to steal. Someone must have seen me pick up the key one day and had heard about my stupid hiding place and took a chance. Stop worrying about it. It's over and won't happen again.'

'Why would a thief stop and destroy the food and break things? All that unnecessary damage. It was the same person who broke into our shop, it must be.'

'It's over,' Mabs said, 'Whoever it was has had their fun, it won't happen again.'

A week later, when Mabs was closing the door on a windy, rainy morning, she hesitated about going home. The street was dark and clouds seemed to touch the rooftops. She had missed the bus and was about to go out and look for a taxi when lightning lit up the darkness and thunder rumbled and roared overhead. She would be soaked just walking to the taxi office so she decided to sit and wait for the storm to ease. She was tired and her old coat wouldn't keep out this heavy rain. The prospect of arriving home in wet clothes didn't appeal and comfortably settled in a chair in the kitchen, she gradually fell asleep. She roused a few times and still the storm raged around her.

A glance at the clock told her there would be a bus in a little over two hours but it was better to spend the few hours in the dry rather than struggle home in this. She gathered her coat around her, found a stool for her legs and relaxed again into sleep.

The noise of the storm drifted around her but didn't disturb her sleep, but a small scratching sound did. She opened her eyes to find the place still dark and listened intently. Someone was at the shop door. For a moment she was afraid to move, then she slowly eased herself out of the chair and reached for a weapon. Her fingers touched a large tin of baked beans. At least it was something to throw.

With her heart racing she peered around the kitchen door into the shop. Someone outside was trying to turn the knob, and seemed to be pushing the door. There was nothing she could do. If he managed to force the door she would be trapped. The noise of the storm had lessened slightly and to her relief she heard footsteps walking around to the back of the building. Cautiously she opened the door and ran to the taxi office. 'Police, and fast,' she shouted as she jumped in.

The police found nothing suspicious and warned her about being there during the night hours on her own. 'I'm not usually on my own, but Robert Thomas couldn't come and Greg was working and—'

'If that happens again, you must close. Do you understand? You never know who's about these nights. What you're doing is wonderful, Mrs Martin, but your safety is more important than having to deprive lonely people of a few hours of company when you can't get help.'

She went home and started measuring the ingredients for the night's baking. 'Always best to keep busy when you've got a worry,' she muttered. She checked the flat doors twice and went to bed.

Lottie was out. Greg and Zena invited Susie to discuss the attempted break-in. They didn't want the commitment of sharing the work of the night café but Susie suggested asking the rest of the drivers and conductors to stop and check whenever they passed, make people aware of their presence.

They both thought that a good idea. 'If whoever was responsible sees several people hanging around and checking on things there's far less chance him trying again.'

'Then you think it's a man?' Zena queried. 'Not a young woman with problems?'

'That's so unlikely we can forget it. Madeleine is obviously quite wealthy, hardly the type to consider this as fun, and Rose, she's too nervous. The damage that was done, in the shop and the café, smashing things, messing the files and papers, destroying food, that's a seriously unbalanced thing to do.'

'Well I hope Madeleine and Rose continue to enjoy London and will forget all about us.' Zena was still unconvinced. She smiled at Susie then turned to the dog.

'And do you agree, Betty?' The little dog barked.

Zena continued to visit Roy, calling often to take some shopping and to make sure he was comfortable. Doris and Kevin were in and out and she felt that between them they could do all he needed to make a good recovery.

He began talking easily about the early years of his marriage and his three sons. 'It was a very happy time, but then, something so terrible happened and ...' Although he tried to explain something of what had changed everything and ended with his wife leaving and taking his sons away, he stumbled, as though trying not to say the words that were trying to reveal themselves. 'Best to keep it all locked away, it's too late.'

It was then, for some inexplicable reason, Zena remembered the purse and the key that the children had found in the lake. She took it out, and explained its appearance. 'The key's similar to your back door key, the one you lent me once and I wondered if you knew of other houses with a similar lock. Often a builder will use the same materials for other houses.' She took out the remnants of the purse from a bag and showed him the key. His face distorted with shock. Alarmed, she ran for Doris. Kevin came and he ran to call an ambulance. Later that day when she telephoned the hospital it was to be told he had died.

Zena grieved for a man she had liked and for the loss of the information he had wanted to pass on. She looked at her scrappy notes and felt she had let him down; about the shock he had shown at the sight of the key, she and Doris thought was nothing more than coincidence. The fatal heart attack would have happened anyway.

The funeral was arranged by Doris and Kevin. Roy had given them details of what he wanted. It was Zena who wrote to his sons and they arrived two days later. The youngest, Jack was the most clearly upset at the loss of a father he hadn't been allowed to know. William and Dick seemed united in their determination not to be swayed from their anger against him.

Without involving herself in their attitude, Zena read out the words she had written down, including the denial of his guilt and the little she knew about Donna's accusations. She offered them carbon copies of the pages she had typed and walked away without discussion.

Jack read most of what she had written, then followed her. 'We didn't see my father or Aunty Donna after the row. It seems a pity that something so misunderstood could have caused such misery.'

'What happened to Donna?' Zena asked.

Jack shrugged. 'She went away. Norfolk I believe. Mam refuses to talk about her, even now.'

'It isn't my business but I don't think your father deserved losing you.'

As Greg approached, Jack asked, 'Do either of you know Rose Conelly?'

'Yes,' Greg said. 'I do. She moved to London a while ago. Why?'

'My mother talked about her several times. I'm curious, that's all.'

'What do you know about her?'

'Only that Mam felt sorry for her. She used Rose to remind us of how lucky we were, you know the sort of thing, "Poor Rose would be glad of a decent coat that was brand new and not an ill-fitting hand-me-down, and there's you complaining because you don't like the colour!" I didn't know Rose, in fact I sometimes thought she was an invention to make us feel guilty,' he said with a smile. 'Dick is the oldest, he might remember her.'

Greg didn't bother to ask. He would never find the solution to Rose's problem and he might as well accept it. He took out his diary to check on shifts, Susie might be free tonight, he would call in and find out. A much wiser prospect than worrying about Rose.

Chapter Eleven

T HE SONS DIDN'T stay long and Kevin called to tell Zena that a
will had been found. The place would be sold and the proceeds
shared between the three sons. The youngest, Jack, called at Llyn
Hir to say goodbye to Zena. He knocked tentatively at the door
and was already walking away when Zena opened it and invited
him in.

'I just wanted to say thank you for being kind to my father,'
he said. Zena waited, aware he was about to add something more.
'Do you know anything of what happened when my mother took
us away? You see, I don't think Mam told us the truth about what
happened. She is holding something back and will never talk about
it, even now we're old enough to understand.'

'All I know is that Mr Roberts insisted he wasn't the guilty one,
but guilty of what I don't know as he never explained. Sorry I can't
be more help. I do know he had a bit of a temper and maybe that
was the real reason she left him.'

Jack looked away. 'No, it was Mam who had the temper. She
hit out at him sometimes. A hot temper over in moments. He was
carrying on with Mam's sister, or that's what she told people, but
Aunty Donna left soon after and she's never been in touch, so I
presume that much was true, shame must have kept her away.'

'Your father started to talk about it but he didn't get far enough
to help you. He insisted he wasn't the one in the wrong. I doubt
whether the truth will ever come out after all this time. If there
is a different story it died with your father. Best to forget it, Jack,
and accept that a marriage failed as so many others, and leave it at
that.'

Zena thought of the letter she had found written by Donna but said nothing. Dick and William had asked if she would sort through the cupboards and dispose of anything she thought was of no value and leave the rest for them to pick up later. She wondered whether any evidence of what had happened so long ago would be revealed. Dick gave her a few pounds which she accepted, and the three of them went back to their lives of which their father had never been a part.

Jake's neighbour, Vera, who had depended on him for several weeks, recovered from her injury and was well enough to go out unaided. She left a note on his door asking him to call and he went into the room that was comfortable, cosy and so much more of a home than his own. She was smiling and holding out an envelope. A man sat in the armchair and he stood up and offered his hand.

'This is my son, Mick,' Vera said, waiting as they shook hands. 'And this is for you.' She pushed the envelope towards him. 'It's all I owe for the shopping you've done over the past weeks.'

'No, Vera, there's no need for this. I did it because I wanted to. It wasn't a loan, it was a gift.'

'You're saving to marry your Zena, aren't you?' He shrugged and was about to argue, but she said, 'Then it isn't yours to give, is it, dear? It's savings for you and Zena, lucky girl that she is. You have to take what I owe for her sake. She must always come first, dear. Your time was the greatest gift. Time is harder to give than money and you gave me your precious time generously. '

Vera's son thanked him for helping his mother and went on, 'My wife and I had no idea how difficult life had become for her. We live a long way away and with the children and schools and work, well, months went by and she wrote us such cheerful letters, we let things slide.'

'Now, Jake, I have to tell you I'm leaving.' Vera put a hand on his arm. 'I'm sorry, I feel I'm letting you down leaving after your kindness, but it's best.' Mick explained that they had found a bedsit close to where he and his family lived, where he and his wife could care for her when needed.

In one of Jake's impulsive decisions he hugged her and said,

'That's perfect, Vera! I've decided to leave too and I can move away knowing you'll be comfortable and cared for.'

'Back to your Zena?'

'Of course,' he said, but he was lying. Then, in a strange revelation, something became very clear. It was time for more than a change of address.

Jake and Rose had slowly reached a better understanding after Rose had told him something of her miserable childhood. The fact that he had lost his parents and coped with being brought up by strangers, surviving without resentment, made her feel more valued, the constant reminders of being abandoned by her unfeeling mother – as described by Mrs Conelly – faded and she relaxed in his company. They still went out to restaurants and to the theatre with Madeleine, but they met for a meal sometimes, just the two of them and she would walk with him, arm in arm and even share a gentle kiss when they said goodnight.

When Jake thought of going back to Wales, the Welsh *hiraeth* – the longing to be back home – engulfed him in the moment he told Vera he was moving. The flash decision lightened his heart. The image of Zena running into his arms, all the problems caused by separation fading as they declared their love for each other, was there, waiting for him. The tensions, the misunderstandings were not real, more like stories that had happened to someone else, or had been seen in a rather foolish film. Zena and life in Cold Brook Vale were there as they had always been, waiting for him to return. Then he woke to reality and knew it was over, and had been for a long time. The revelation had been nothing more than a fantasy. Zena was no longer a part of his life and would never be again.

One evening as he and Rose were strolling back to her rooms after a visit to the cinema he put an arm round her shoulders and she snuggled closer. 'Rose, I'm very fond of you. D'you think you could feel anything stronger than friendship for me? I want you to feel safe with me. I'll never let anything hurt you.'

'What about Zena?'

'We've both struggled to keep alive something that died a long time ago. Zena and I have known each other since school, I've been a part of the Martin family for ever. It was a habit which we are both ready to break. It's already in the past. I want a future with you, Rose. I know we'll be happy. You and I had a bad start to life but we can have a wonderful future.'

'It's a bit soon to accept that you're free, but I do feel safe with you and once I can face up to the rest of my story and tell you the worst of it, I think we can be happy together.'

'That's good enough for me.' He kissed her gently and felt her respond. 'There is one thing I have to do. I have to go and tell Zena, make it clear that we'll be friends but nothing more. You understand that I have to do that?'

'No! I don't want you to see the Martins ever again. Promise me, Jake.'

'All right, we won't be friends. We'll live in London and there won't be any need for us to visit again, but I have to talk to Zena, just once. Why don't we both go? You can stay at the lodgings as before and I'll spend no more than half an hour, before coming back to you. We can both say our goodbyes to the place where we were born.'

She didn't look very pleased but gave an abrupt nod.

Both Greg and Zena had rent coming in from the properties left to them by their maternal grandmother. It was in the bank and with both of them no longer considering marriage, they decided to spend some to give their mother a treat and they decided on a television. More and more people were talking about what they had watched the previous evening. The weekly drama was a favourite and the music hall style entertainment and comedy programmes sounded like enjoyment for them all. They bought a set and arranged for it to be delivered and tuned in while their mother was at the weekly cattle market with Sam and his father.

A place was decided on and the set was placed on a wooden tea trolley with castors to make it easy to move around. The two men set it up and with one on the roof moving the aerial and the other watching the picture and shouting instructions, they were soon satisfied that the picture was as good as it would get.

When Lottie came home she stared at it, then looked at them, a smile widening on her face, then she hugged them.

'It's for you. Our gift for coping with everything like a hero,' they told her.

'It's wonderful, just what we need. Thank you, darlings.' They handed her a copy of the *Radio Times* and sat with her discussing the programmes which they would watch that evening.

'Typical!' Greg said in mock anger. 'I'm working the late shift. It'll be finished for the evening before I get home!'

Sam came a few days later and they all sat, with Mabs, Susie and Kevin who had called unexpectedly, laughing at a comedy. He took photographs of them, and when the photographs were developed he was pleased with the results.

They all looked so happy that Zena took one to send to Jake. She wasn't sure why, perhaps to show him that she wasn't grieving his absence any more. Or maybe to remind him of what he was missing? It was still hard to accept life without him; even though she knew that they would never marry, she hoped they would remain friends.

Madeleine opened Zena's letter and showed the photograph to Rose, who looked upset and then angry. 'Look at them! How can they be happy after what they did? I hate them and they shouldn't be happy. They lost the right to that a long time ago.'

'When, Rose? When did the Martins lose the right to be happy?'

'A long time ago,' Rose repeated and refused to add anything more.

Madeleine showed the note and photograph to Jake, explaining that, as usual, it had been opened in the post room. 'Rose was very angry, she insists that the Martins have no right to be happy but won't explain why.'

When Jake asked Rose why the photograph made her so angry, Rose shook her hands in front of him, waving away the question. 'One day I'll be able to talk about it, but not now.'

'That's fine by me. I won't ask again, but when you want to talk, I'll be here to listen.'

'When are you going to talk to Zena?'

'You understand my wanting to?'

'Of course. The sooner the better. I'll spend the weekend you're away looking for a flat for you, shall I?'

He hugged her and although she moved away, she paused for a moment, slightly more willing to accept the contact.

Zena still helped at SunnyBank, the house called the haunted house for so long. She often met Geraint the paper boy when she set off in the morning. He was no longer afraid to knock on the door and sometimes, Karen would be waiting for him with a cake and a glass of milk, which he willingly accepted. He waved nonchalantly at Zena and she made sure never to mention his early hesitation. She saw that he now walked past SunnyBank and took a short cut through the wood to deliver newspapers to other cottages. He was confident now, having learned the paths and animal tracks that led him by a shorter route to Sam's farm and beyond, no longer afraid.

Zena saw Mr Penberthy sometimes and, when she told him her full name, he said, 'Yes, your father, Ronald Martin was a fine man. He was a good friend when I needed one.'

'You knew my father? From the war years? Or as a child? I don't remember him mentioning you.'

'I would like you all to come for the day a week from Sunday, all of you, your Aunt Mabel too. There's something I want to tell you all. Come for morning coffee, lunch and stay for afternoon tea. Will you come?'

Zena glanced at Karen, who nodded. 'Thank you, Mr Penberthy, we'd love to.' She wondered what he would tell them about their father and couldn't decide whether or not to tell her mother that their host knew him and spoke well of him. Could they be about learn something to explain the missing money? That was unlikely. She hoped her mother wouldn't have the same thought only to suffer another disappointment.

Two days later there was a telephone call apologizing for cancelling the Sunday arrangement, 'Mr Penberthy had to go away unexpectedly, but will you still come?' Karen asked. 'Instead of a formal lunch, I can change it to a buffet, so if you like you can invite your friend with the little girls too. It will be a pity to waste the food.'

Nelda and the girls accepted without hesitation and the girls insisted that it would be an adventure. '"Adventure" is their favourite word at present,' Nelda explained.

Although it rained, they all wore suitable clothing and went for a walk first, through the trees and along the paths until they were in sight of Sam's farm. Karen took out a map when they arrived back at the house and showed them the area, explaining where Zena lived, pointing out the Edwards's farm and the paths they had walked, while Zena dried Betty.

Food vanished like magic, and what was left Karen packed for them to take home. Bobbie and Georgie were muddy, their clothes were no longer fresh and clean, their long hair was tangled and ribbons were lost, but they went home happy with their adventure and hugged Karen before they left.

Nelda took Mabs home in her car with the two excited girls. Lottie, Greg and Zena walked. They went into the house and stared in disbelief. The television was no longer there. The set, and the wooden tea trolley on which it had sat, had gone leaving a space between the sideboard and the window.

'Burglars! Greg gasped. 'Look, the wireless has gone too.' Foolishly they looked around the room as though the items would magically reappear and even looked outside the back door. It wasn't quite dark. Bewildered by the mystery they looked around a while then went back inside. Greg went further; he walked to the edge of the path that zig-zagged down the rocky route to the lake. In the dusky light he saw something was lying on the small beach. Halfway down he spotted the trolley, broken and lying some distance from the path. He looked up and guessed that it had been dropped over the edge of the steep cliff. He went on down and found the television, half in and half out of the shallow water, the screen broken and obviously ruined. What sort of a burglar takes something just to throw it away?

They called the police but it seemed more an act of spite rather than a theft. They reminded the officer of the damage to the stationers during a break-in and Mabs's café – about which they hadn't been told. But there seemed no sensible explanation. Individually they wondered who could dislike them so much they would enjoy upsetting them in this way. No one came up with a solution, although Greg did have the rather guilty, brief suspicion that Rose was angry enough even though he had no idea why she resented them so much. He didn't speak of it, it seemed so unlikely. Things like that didn't happen to people like them.

'It must have been thieves trying to steal them and getting frustrated when they couldn't get away,' he said, and for want of a better explanation, they all agreed.

Jake was in France for most of the following week, placing orders for garments and collecting samples of new lines to discuss with his boss. It was Friday of the following week when he left to go to Cold Brook Vale. He rang Llyn Hir, and Lottie told them they would all be out for the whole of Sunday. 'Coffee, lunch and afternoon tea at the house you and the others pretended was haunted,' she added with a laugh.

'Pretended! We believed it!'

He went very early on Saturday and drove straight to his usual lodgings. He unpacked the few clothes he had brought and went out to eat. He would go to Llyn Hir and if Zena wasn't there he would make arrangements to see her early the following day, then go back to London. He wanted to get back to Rose. His home was no longer this village where he had spent his childhood. London was where he wanted to be. London, with Rose and Madeleine and the job he was enjoying. A life with Zena was nothing more than a foolish dream.

It wasn't yet twelve and he was most likely to find Zena at the stationers. He went straight there. He had no qualms about her being upset. This was just tying up the odd ends of something they both knew was over. He was smiling when he opened the door and walked in. Then he frowned. 'Aunty Mabs? What are you doing here?'

'Helping out. What are *you* doing here,' she asked pointedly.

'Where's Zena?'

'Up sorting through the house where Roy Roberts lived. It's

something his sons asked her to do.'

'I'll call at Llyn Hir later.' He went out, he didn't want to dribble out explanations to Mabs. He was disappointed not to see Zena, he'd hoped to be on his way back to London before evening. He walked to the popular beach with its golden sands that attracted crowds in the summer months. Today few people wandered with dogs and children. He met no one he knew. Doors were closing and he was no longer a part of this once loved place.

He walked back and sat looking at the lake for a while, remembering the fun they'd had as children with the boat and the raft. Remembering too the day his friend Peter had drowned, not in the lake but in the sea. Staring across the calm, still water he realized that the raft was moving towards him. He waved and helped by pulling on the rope until Lottie stepped off with her shopping bags. He carried her bags up the steep rocky path and halfway up he saw the remains of the tea trolley some distance from the path. Lottie explained about the robbery. 'Sam saw someone struggling with a heavy object on the path. From the height and general build and the clothes he guessed it was a man but could add nothing further. The police don't hold out much hope of finding him.'

'Was it a robbery gone wrong? Perhaps he was going to use the raft to get away?'

'Of course! Why didn't we think of that? We presumed someone had thrown it down the path out of spite. The raft is a better explanation. We hated to think someone disliked us enough to simply ruin something we enjoyed.' They were smiling when they reached Llyn Hir. Zena opened the door to them and they went inside.

While Lottie went to the kitchen to unpack her shopping and make sandwiches, Zena and Jake looked at each other, both wondering where to begin. He had been working out ways of starting the conversation but in the end it was Zena who said,

'You're happy in London aren't you, Jake? I'm glad. You made the right decision. We had a lovely childhood, but now it's time to choose our own way forward, isn't it? Is that what you came to say?'

'We'll stay in touch, won't we?'

'Of course. I'll want to know all your news. How is Rose? Has she explained why she walked away from Greg? He's not sorry it ended; he's very happy with Susie, and we all like her very much, but he would like to know why.'

'I'm taking care of her and she's gradually opening up, but I doubt if Greg will ever be told why.'

On one of his impulses, he invited her out for lunch the following day, and was relieved when she shook her head.

'We're all invited to visit the Haunted House for the day,' she said with a smile. 'Remember how we used to frighten ourselves creeping around there? It's furnished now, the grounds are gradually being tamed and it's a pleasant home.'

'I'd forgotten. Why are you invited? Is it someone we know?'

'I helped clean the rooms when they first moved in and it's an extra thank you, I suppose. And no, it isn't anyone we know. James Penberthy, who is blind, and a woman who looks after him called Karen.'

'You're happy, are you, Zena?'

'Completely. And you?'

'I think my future is in London, with Rose.'

It was a solemn meeting yet both were smiling as Jake sat and ate a sandwich for politeness sake before driving back to collect his things. He felt utterly weary and sat in his room for more than an hour. Then, instead of driving back he stayed another night. He slept late and drove back in a leisurely manner, stopping to look at small towns on the route, eat a meal, before picking up speed and heading back to London, and Rose.

Although refreshed by a good night's sleep he was tired when he stopped the car outside Rose's flat. He wanted to go back to his miserable room and sleep, but first he needed to tell Rose that all was well, that he and Zena were happy with the situation. To his disappointment, she wasn't in. He didn't feel like going to Madeleine's, the most likely place to find her, and instead went home to his miserable room and slept.

At two o'clock the following morning there was a knock at the front door and he turned and settled back to sleep. It couldn't be for him. No one came here, and who would want him at such a time? The knocking went on and he dragged a blanket around his shoulders and went down. He opened the door prepared to complain and Rose stood there. In the light from the hallway he saw excitement clear on her face, her eyes shining, her lips parted, unable to stop smiling. He stared at her in disbelief. 'Rose? Is everything all right?'

'Perfect, everything is just perfect. Aren't you going to invite me in?

She danced about the room, laughing and half telling him something before starting to tell him something else. He was laughing with her as he asked what had happened.

'I've dealt with the Martins and next weekend I'm going again, this time to ruin any chance of their ever being happy again.' She paused to laugh. 'I've dreamed of this, Jake. Once this is done I can forget them all and be happy. That's what I'm doing, making them as miserable as they've made others with their deceit and lies.'

He tried to persuade her to explain, but although she had calmed down she wouldn't explain. 'You can come with me, see how they face up to the truth about themselves. You will come, won't you, Jake? I'll need you there.'

'I don't think you should do this. What will you gain by hurting them? They're good people.'

She flopped onto the ancient armchair and closed her eyes. 'You'll understand when I face them with the truth. I'm tired, I thumbed a lift back to London, wasn't that adventurous of me?'

'Risky! Where have you been?'

'Tell you tomorrow.' She curled up in the chair and closed her eyes.

He spoke to her but she didn't respond. He tried lifting her intending to carrying her to his bed but she flopped and refused to move. Worried, he lay back on his bed and lay there watching her, concern making a frown deepen on his brow. What had she done and what was she planning to do next? A shiver of fear chilled his body. He knew so little about her; she guarded her private thoughts like a person surrounded by enemies.

Then she opened her eyes and smiled and he opened his arms. Slowly she stood and stepped over to lie beside him. Terrified of frightening her, he held her close and felt her relax into sleep.

He was soon very uncomfortable on the narrow bed. His muscles tightened as he lay at an awkward angle but he was afraid to move. His shoulder felt as though it would never straighten again. Eventually he had to move but he would have to do so with care. From the little she had told him, he believed this was the first time she had ever been so close to another person and he didn't want to risk waking her, maybe embarrassing her. Slowly he slid further towards the middle of the narrow bed. She didn't wake, but snuggled closer.

Happier than he could remember feeling before, even with Zena, and more comfortable, he relaxed into sleep. Then she turned and was facing him, her head on his shoulder, her soft breath like a caress against his neck. He was almost afraid to breathe in case he woke her. He didn't want this night to end, but his back was soon painfully stiff again. His arm, under her pillow, was numb, his neck felt about to snap, but he dared not move, but even the discomfort couldn't keep him awake and he too, slept.

She woke at seven and sat up, while he stayed perfectly still, wondering what her reaction would be. To his surprise, she said, 'Thank you, Jake,' as though her sleeping beside him was a normal occurrence. 'I couldn't face going home to be on my own. I needed company after the excitement of last weekend and my plans for next week. You will come, won't you, Jake?'

'I'll make us some coffee,' Jake said, struggling to straighten his cramped body. 'Then we'll go out for breakfast. Then, will you tell me what all this is about?'

'I visited the Martins and ruined their television last week. Yesterday I broke windows and they didn't even notice when they got home. It was wonderful, but the best thing was that I made a momentous decision. I'm going to tell everyone their sordid secret, her dishonesty, about how she ruined my life. I'll make them face up to what they did. And when I do I want you to be there, Jake. Then you'll understand everything. We can build a life free from secrets and shame.' She smiled and her expression made Jake shiver. 'You'll know everything when I tell their disgusting secret.'

Jake insisted on going immediately. 'We can't wait until next weekend with this hanging over us,' he said. What had she done? What would she do next? He didn't know what to do. Should he tell Lottie and the others? Or plead with Rose to forget any further actions and hope it would blow over? His instinct was to run, leave Rose to find her own solutions to her problems as this was more than he could cope with.

Saying very little except insisting that they went at once to Llyn Hir and settle whatever it was she had on her mind, she just smiled serenely. As soon as she set off to her flat to change and go to work, he went to see Madeleine.

They talked over what had happened and Madeleine admitted that she knew about Rose entering the stationers and messing things up, and Mabs's café. 'I know it was wrong, but it had already happened when I learned of it and it was such unlikely behaviour for someone and timid as Rose, I stupidly thought it might be a good thing. I really didn't expect her to do anything more.'

'What do we do now?'

'Go with her and hope that we can salvage something from the mess. The police were called, you say?'

'Yes, Rose heard that they think it was a burglary gone wrong. A thief, or thieves disappointed at not finding money, damaging things in frustration.'

Jake cancelled his appointments for the next two days, pleading family illness, then went to find Rose and insisted on her coming with them.

She fought against the decision, insisting she wanted the whole family there to listen to what she had to say. They telephoned from a phone box soon after they set off and asked Lottie if she could make sure Greg and Zena were there at three. 'Mabs too,' he added but said nothing of the reason. That seemed to satisfy Rose and she relaxed and enjoyed the journey with anticipation of delights to come.

When they walked in to Llyn Hir, Sam was there. Zena stared at Rose and went out to bring in a tea tray and food. Rose refused any. She was breathless with excitement.

'Well, Rose? We're waiting for your explanation,' Lottie said with mild irritation.

'I was abandoned when I was only a week old,' she began. Lottie gave a sigh. Greg looked away. Jake said, 'As I was, remember? It happens, love.'

'I was left in a shoe box with only a thin covering to protect me. My mother was obviously hoping I would die, wouldn't you say? It was in October. A cruel month and a cruel mother.' At this Lottie frowned and glanced at Sam.

Rose faced Greg and, raising her voice, said. 'That's why I could never marry you, Greg. You see, your mother, Lottie, sometimes known as Kay, is my mother too.'

She seemed very calm now and she looked at Lottie who stared at her, her hand gripping Sam's. 'You're so wrong,' Lottie whispered.

Sam put an arm around Lottie's shoulders. 'Kay, my dear, I think it's time to tell Zena and Greg everything.'

'Kay! That's what gave you away! All my foster parents told me was that my mother was Kay something. When I heard your husband call you Kay, I knew.' There was a brief tense silence and Greg offered, 'Perhaps Mrs Conelly meant the letter K as the first letter of a name? Katherine? Kate? Karen?'

Lottie raised a hand for quiet. She reached out to her son and daughter. 'I'm sorry my darlings, I wouldn't have chosen to tell you like this but, yes, I did have a child, long before I met your father. I was barely sixteen and ignorant. But the child was cared for, adopted legally, loved and grieved over, and certainly not abandoned in a shoe box.'

'That's what the Conellys told me and I believe them. Thrown away with the rubbish! Cruelly abandoned with little hope of my being found.'

'I'm not your mother, Rose. And I'm thankful for that. You've used your beginnings as an excuse for misery and resentment and cruel lies.'

'It's the truth.' She pointed at Lottie. 'Your saintly mother deprived me of everything most take for granted. I had nothing. No love, no family, no history, nothing. She ruined my life.'

Into the stunned silence, Lottie said, 'Sorry, Rose, but the child I had, born in October 1919, was a boy.'

It was a very subdued threesome who went back to London. Rose went to her flat, refusing to stay with Madeleine; Jake went to his miserable room and Madeleine went home filled with remorse for her interference and shameful support for an unhappy and bitter girl.

They didn't meet again.

Two days later, Jake gave his notice and a month later, went back to Cold Brook Vale. He didn't contact Zena but saw her occasionally, often with Kevin, sometimes on his arm and often flying past on the motor bike. He didn't know where to go next, what to do. He knew he was good at selling and maybe there was a future for him in that field, but all he wanted for a few weeks was a simple, quiet life to mull over all that had happened.

Greg thought of the narrow escape he'd had and proposed to Susie, but the mood was wrong, he knew that and regretted not waiting. The family was in shock, emotions deadened by the revelations about Lottie and the misplaced revenge carried out against the family by Rose.

Zena knew Jake was back, staying at the usual lodgings but didn't contact him. She too wanted time to think over what had happened and Kevin, good-natured Kevin who asked nothing and simply offered a friendly arm to hold, was all she needed.

For Zena and Greg, the shock of learning about their mother having a child was slowly accepted. Rose's bitterness based on untruths was hard to understand.

Susie turned down Greg's proposal of marriage, promising to reconsider once the pain and shocks had subsided.

Life was a quiet interlude; they were all licking their wounds and making plans for pleasanter things.

Chapter Twelve

ZENA CONTINUED SORTING through the cupboards of Roy
Roberts feeling sad at his sudden death. She regretted not
having learned the facts about his disagreement with his wife.
He had hinted that the truth was not what his wife had told their
sons. It was a story that needed telling for the sake of William who
was so angry with him, and Dick and especially for young Jack
who wanted to believe his father wasn't the villain his mother had
described.

She had a sack in which to throw stuff obviously of no value,
old newspapers and torn letters, receipts years out of date, broken
records, abandoned toys. A row of boxes lined up against the wall
were for other items which needed to be considered by the sons. If
in doubt she put aside items she thought might be worth saving.
One box held papers for the sons to search through. They might
include details about the family that the boys would want to keep.
Surely even William would want to save anything relevant to his
family's history?

She picked up the disintegrating purse found in the lake and
threw it onto the pile destined for the bin, then hesitated. The key
might fit the house or the shed, a spare key might be useful. She put
it with its purse in another box silently named, the 'maybe' pile.

There were letters which she put in a separate box. There was
probably nothing of interest but that decision was not hers. She
looked around her at the assorted piles, boxes and sacks of what
had once been an orderly room and sighed. She wasn't exactly
helping, just making a mess. There was a letter written in large
letters as though written in anger, it was irresistible and she picked

it up and read:

'I can't cope with this. Please come and talk about it.'

It was signed Mimi. Sadly, she put it with the rest. Later, she asked Doris who Mimi was.

'That's that wife of his. Miriam she was christened, mind, but she didn't like it so she called herself Mimi.'

'You didn't like her?' Zena dared to ask, guessing the answer from Doris's tone.

'Had a foul temper she did, and goaded poor Roy, attacking him with fists and even a weapon sometimes, trying to make him hit her so she could blame him and get more sympathy when he threw her out.'

'He told me the story about his sister-in-law Donna was untrue.'

'I don't know what happened, but Miriam left and he refused to help her. She could have gone to the courts but she didn't, so I've always believed the fault was with her and not him.'

'What happened to Donna?'

'She left soon after and no one heard from her. There was one letter apparently, which said she was moving to Norfolk. No one saw her again.'

'Now we'll never know.'

Lottie was coming back with shopping on the raft. She knew it was silly to use the lake when it would have been easier by bus without the steep path to negotiate, but somehow it was a touch of the past that pleased her. Perhaps she was aware of the changes to come and felt a nostalgia for the happy times when the children were small and life offered nothing but a future holding continued contentment.

In those happy days, a promise of a picnic or a boat trip around and back again, or a visit to Sam's farm for a ride on the gentle old horse, was enough to make Zena and Greg forget anything that ailed them. Life had been so simple and now, with the family likely to break up and the house sold, she was touched with a melancholy, despite the excitement of marriage to Sam and a new life as a farmer's wife.

She stopped the raft in the middle of the lake and sat for a while in the silence and the peace of the tranquil lake, so close to a busy road yet hidden away like a magical world far from normal life. She thought about the confusions of Zena's breakup with Jake and the embarrassment of Rose's resentful outburst.

At least Rose's error had made her face up to telling Zena, Greg and Mabs about the baby she had given birth to so shamefully and who was still frequently in her thoughts. She regretted not telling them sooner. As so often in the past, she sat on the gently moving raft and daydreamed about how life would have been for her if she had refused to part with him. But it had been impossible She had been sixteen, and completely obedient to her parents' decisions, following the arrangements made for her without a murmur of argument, hiding her fears behind a frightened face.

Her arms still ached, needing that small baby to fill them, even after Zena and Greg. She wondered where he was, what sort of life he'd had. She had been told nothing except he had been given to a loving family. She had to believe that.

There had been so much upheaval since Ronald died, she mused. But Greg was happier for the loss of poor, bitterly angry Rose. She suffered from her abandonment which had been followed by living with the unkind, uncaring Conellys and it shocked her to imagine her own lost child suffering in the same way. She knew that wasn't so; he had been legally adopted by a family who wanted him. Rose had suffered from the unkind people who had fostered her, reminding her constantly of her unfeeling mother discarding her like unwanted rubbish – a story that was unlikely to be true, invented by the Conellys to torment a helpless child.

Greg had been terribly hurt by Rose, but he had found happiness with someone new. Susie Crane would make him a good life partner; she wasn't the type to let anything worry her. She would speak out and get things sorted; deal with what life offered and smile as she coped with its challenges.

But what of Zena? Lottie stared into the depth of the deepest part of the water, the sun shining and revealing small fish darting about and she could even see right into the depths, at the stones and waving fronds of weed on the bottom. Zena and Jake were no longer the happy couple planning to marry and she didn't think

Kevin was the one to make her daughter happy either.

As she stared through the still, clear water, lit by bright sun, she became aware of something unusual amid the stones. A long shape, maybe a discarded sack of garden rubbish, although it was unusual these days to find abandoned rubbish as the path from the village was overgrown and difficult to navigate, especially with what looked like a filled sack. Curious, she lay down on the raft and stared, but the movement of the raft caused ripples and the scene disappeared. Perhaps she would tell Sam in case it was something that would harm the wild life.

Later, Sam went to investigate with a hook intending to drag the bundle to the edge. He leaned over to help pull the object onto the raft and a length of clothing slipped out and wrapped itself around his arm and he recoiled with shock. Could it be a body? He pulled back to the shore and asked Greg to call the police, then he told Lottie and Zena to go inside and make tea. He refused to discuss what he might have found.

He and Greg went back for another look. They knew they should leave it until the police arrived but somehow they felt guilty at leaving it there. If it were a body, it had lain there for years, yet to walk away and leave now seemed wrong.

Foolishly in that cold water, Greg stripped off his outer clothes and went in. He struggled to push away some large stones that were holding it in place. Sam dived in with him, having stripped off jacket and trousers, and slowly they brought the rotting sack close enough to the shore to examine it. Several layers of material fell as they moved it and they went in twice more until everything was on the small beach. The contents appeared to be women's clothes. They ran up to Llyn Hir, teeth chattering like castanets and Lottie ran a bath and found some clothes belonging to Greg that might fit Sam, scolding them for the idiots they were.

The two policemen complained at their not waiting for the professionals, and nervously went to look at the bundle of clothes. After examining it they agreed it seemed likely to have been discarded as unwanted. 'Maybe thrown away by a widower, clearing his wife's possessions,' the constable suggested. 'There's nothing of value.' Police divers went down but found nothing else on the lake bottom, apart from one shoe, which they added to the contents of the rotting sack.

The police promised to arrange for its removal, but Sam offered to deal with it, not wanting the path from the village to be opened by many people passing through, encouraging people to come and visit the place. He valued the privacy of the lake and felt protective of its varied and fascinating denizens.

The sack was rotten, as were most of the contents, but as they unfolded some of the garments they found, folded inside a dress, several pieces of jewellery. These were put on one side although obviously of little value, being rusted and broken.

By the following day the path from the village was no longer overgrown. Everyone wanted to visit the scene where a mysterious bundle had been found and what Sam had dreaded happened; the path was opened by people gaining access by pushing through the undergrowth, cutting back branches and tearing up plants as they made their way to the lake, which looked as serene and innocent as usual. Groups would pause on the bank to stare and chatter for a while. Wild rumours abounded, many convinced it had been a body. Some insisted it was a tramp, called Felix, who hadn't been seen for years; another believed it to be an airman – a victim of a war time crash– but soon the novelty faded, as newspapers reported the find as nothing but a sack filled with old, rotting clothes. Fewer and fewer people came and in a week, the path was left to recover.

Zena remembered the purse with the key which, she had learned, would open Roy Roberts's door. She remembered the man's distress when she had shown him the purse and was convinced the clothes had belonged to his wife and had been discarded after she had left.

She took the police to Roy's empty house and showed them the tattered remnants of the purse and the key. They looked at the piled up contents of Roy's cupboards and drawers, gave them a cursory examination then left, satisfied that the find had been the result of a widower's way of disposing of his dead wife's things, weighted down by stones and now with nothing to tell its story. Rumours began, although it was impossible from where, and they even reached Geraint, the paper boy – who declared Roy Roberts's house and the lake to be a better places for ghosts than the house called SunnyBank.

When Zena next went to clean there, she met Geraint who lamented the fact that that his paper round didn't include deliveries to Roy Roberts or Doris. 'That's a real haunted house, I'll bet,' he said cheerfully. Zena wanted to remind him, with disapproval, that Roy Roberts had died, that it wasn't a joke, but she refrained. He would learn about the sad side of life soon enough.

Karen was there but Mr Penberthy was still away. Karen seemed worried but didn't reveal the reason for his continuing absence. They worked together on the last of the once abandoned rooms and Zena was delighted to be invited to go with Karen to an auction house to bid for the last few items needed to complete the furnishing. Within weeks the large house was completely furnished and new curtains hung at every window.

A few weeks after Roy's funeral, his son Jack came to see Zena, wanting to talk about his father. 'If there's anything you want to ask me about him, I'll tell you as much as I know,' she promised.

'Was he violent?'

'I would say no. You did know he had been a boxer when he was young? Kevin told me he was strong and had a punch that won him quite a few fights. But as well as learning to fight, he had learned to control his anger. He told Kevin he would never dare to hit anyone, with such a powerful punch, he was afraid he might hit harder than intended.'

'I feel so bitter about my mother,' Jack said. 'She cheated me out of a life knowing my father.'

'Your father wanted it that way. He wasn't the villain but decided to take the blame. He knew that your mother would look after you better than he could.'

'She told us he refused to help us. Why was he angry with us?'

'Perhaps she didn't tell you the truth,' she said softly. 'Doris told me he sent money regularly to all three of you, until you were eighteen.'

'I don't understand.'

'I doubt we ever will. But he loved you, and wished his life had been different, that much I do know.'

*

Sam and Greg fished in the lake but returned the fish unharmed. The water looked so tranquil but Sam knew it would still have a tinge of horror after those few minutes when he thought the sack contained a body. Until seasons changed and brought fresh new life to the creatures living there, that thought had ruined his pleasure of the lake. By the time winter had passed, the path to the village would be over grown once again and the lake would settle back into it previous peaceful mood. He persuaded Lottie to continue using the raft, and Nelda's girls still enjoyed trips on the boat. They didn't know about those first dreadful moments when he touched the rotting sack and a dress wrapped itself around his wrist, a memory that still gave him bad dreams.

Since Ronald's death, Zena and Greg had tried repeatedly to find Billy Dove, the man their father had mentioned and who had been known to Roy Roberts. 'Why didn't we ask Dad to tell us more about him when we had the chance?' Zena moaned one morning as they were cycling down to the village.

'That's the thing about life, Sis, there's always plenty of time, until it runs out without warning.'

'That's very philosophical for this time of the morning, Greg!'

'There are so many secrets waiting for the right moment to be told and left until it's too late. It's making me think more seriously about everything. Rose's hatred making her do all that damage believing our mother was also hers. Your Roy Roberts taking the blame for a vicious wife for the sake of his sons, who hated him because of his wife's lies.'

'The biggest secret is Mam's first born. How d'you really feel about us having a half brother? I've pretended to be all right about it, but I'm frustrated not knowing who he is, where he is.'

'Those questions are running through my head too but we'll never have answers. Adoption is always private, not even the mother is told where he lives or the name he was given.'

'He would be about thirty-four years old.'

'I hope he has a good life.'

As they reached the end of the lane, a car sounded its horn and stopped. The driver's window was lowered and Jake leaned out. 'I've got a job!' he shouted.

Greg waved and rode on but Zena dismounted and went over. 'Well done. What are you doing?'

'Selling!' He smiled widely. 'D'you know, Zena, love, when I came back home, I was full of regret for going to London and messing everything up between us, but it was an education. I learned so much, confidence in my own abilities mostly. Mainly that I'm a good salesman, I really am! I also learned a few lessons on life and living – and honesty. Will you meet me tonight so I can go all philosophical on you?'

'Not you as well,' she said with a laugh. 'Greg has been talking about the "deep mysteries of life" and now you!'

Jake had found a job with a firm selling kitchenware and excelled at it. His experience in London had given him the confidence needed to persuade people to buy more than originally intended. The timing was perfect. With a final easing of goods for sale after years of austerity, wives were throwing away well-used and battered saucepans that until recently couldn't be replaced. In kitchen-ware, new styles came on the market and although there were still some restrictions on availability, Jake, with his newly discovered confidence, which he translated as 'downright cheek', was a great success.

Refrigerators suitable for small kitchens were available at a price possible for the average housewife when bought by weekly payments and Jake took on the new luxury to add to what he was already offering. He explained all this to Zena over a meal in a local restaurant, and she marvelled at the way his life had changed.

'Why did you leave London?' she asked. 'Surely there are better opportunities in a big city filled with people with lots of money, than around here, small towns and small wages?'

'I enjoyed it, love, there's no doubt about that, but after a while, the success lacked excitement. I felt anonymous, invisible, a stranger among strangers. A small fish in a large pool isn't for me. I'm happier as a very small fish in a very small pool, if you see what I mean.'

'But you were successful, and you had made friends.'

'You'll laugh at this, but forget all my stories about the exciting life I led. My neighbour, Vera, was almost eighty years old and apart from the office and Rose, she was my only friend.' He looked at her, a serious expression clouding his eyes and reached over and held her hand. 'I did her shopping for a few weeks when she had fallen and broken her leg. When she was able to get about again, her son arrived, having been told nothing about the accident until then.

'She handed me a piece of paper on which she had written down everything I had spent, together with the full amount of what I'd spent, even though I'd told her I didn't want it, that it was a gift not a loan. D'you know what she said?'

Zena shook her head, expecting another of his stories about giving to people who needed it, proof that although he had changed in many ways, his attitude to others remained the same.

'She asked about you, then said I had no right to give money that was not mine to give. If we were saving to get married, half of the money was yours and I should respect that. She also said that my real gift to her, a treasured gift, was my time.' He looked embarrassed as he added, 'I didn't tell her we were no longer planning to marry, see. I couldn't accept that it was over between us. I still can't.'

'I don't think a few words from an elderly, temporary neighbour is going to change the habits of a lifetime, Jake.'

'But they have. You'll see, if you'll agree to try again. I'll still want us to help where necessary but with time, not money and only as a couple, both of us, together making the decisions, not me.' He smiled ruefully, 'And, most critical of all, without publicity. I was obsessed with being everyone's friend. I've been such a fool.'

Zena would soon have no reason to go to Roy Roberts's house. The cupboards and drawers were emptied, their contents sorted into lots for the sons to look through. There was only the shed – a task she didn't relish at all, imagining spiders watching her from the dark corners. It was no longer a pleasure to prop her cycle against the gate and walk in smiling as he stood to greet her.

She missed him. The loss of Roy and all that followed had tainted more than the waters of the lake. She concentrated on building up the office supplies business, with Jake surprising her by sending her several new, important customers. The shed remained a vision at the back of her mind, like SunnyBank had been for young Geraint the paper boy, she thought with a smile. She would have to deal with it, but found reasons to delay.

She still cleaned for Nelda, and the children continued to visit Llyn Hir for adventures in the wood and fields. She also visited SunnyBank but James Penberthy was absent for several more weeks. Karen and she worked on the house, Karen taking her when she was free, to auctions to buy small items of furniture and rugs and a few pictures, changing the place from a once unloved building to a welcoming home, bringing the house to life.

There wasn't much to do, but she started working on the garden during the hours for which Karen paid her, bringing bulbs and border plants and setting them in a neatly dug bed near the entrance. She vaguely wondered why so much time and money was being spent making the place attractive when the owner would be unable to see it, so bought several plants known for their perfume: lavenders, roses, sweet williams, to give him pleasure when spring came.

The day came when she was told that William, Dick and Jack, Roy's sons, were coming to inspect the house and arrange for its sale. Today she could delay no longer, she had to tackle the shed.

Kevin came to help and he removed most of the contents, stacking garden tools and a wheelbarrow and endless boxes of various powders and liquids promising wonderful yields for plants and death to pests. They would fill the bin once again.

There was a large chest of drawers in a corner and nervously, she pulled open the drawers, expecting to see movements as insects were disturbed for the first time for many months. She stumbled back when she pulled open the first one, it was empty and she had expected a struggle. Kevin opened the rest and surprisingly all but one drawer contained nothing. The final one contained a tin, sealed with tape. 'Should I open this?' she wondered, looking at Kevin to help her decide. 'It isn't rusted, in fact it looks new. It can't have been here very long.'

He shrugged and then nodded. 'You've been asked to sort out the rubbish from the rest. It probably contains seeds he was planning to use. Best that you check.' He grinned. 'Besides, I'm curious.'

They struggled with the tape and, when the tin was opened, found it contained only a single brown envelope. On the front of it was written, 'Miss Zena Martin', in block letters followed by her address. In smaller letters was added, 'personal',

'I'll take this and open it in front of his sons,' she decided. Reluctantly, Kevin agreed.

It was easy to dispose of the garden tools. A rag and bone man, one of several who walked the streets asking for unwanted metal instead of calling out the age old cry, took it all a few days later. The following weekend, the sons were coming to take away the rest and a 'for sale' notice would appear. Zena arranged to meet them at the house and she would then open the letter.

To her disappointment, only William came. When he had examined the various collections, she took out the letter. 'It's addressed to me, but I wanted to open it while you are here in case there is something you need to be told. I hoped Dick and Jack would be with you.'

William sat on an armchair and waited while she opened and read the letter silently.

'Well?' he asked irritably. She began to read the letter aloud.

'"Sorry I couldn't tell you all this, Zena, but I found it too distressing. It's a story of a ruined life and I'd like at least one person to know the truth."'

William gestured for her to read on.

'"I was never the violent one," it continued. 'Miriam was the one with the uncontrollable temper. Here are some of the dates on which I was treated in hospital—"'

William stood up and tried to snatch the letter from her. 'Lies!' he shouted. Throw it away, it's more of his lies, trying to blame my mother for his thuggery!'

She put the letter behind her back and he began to push her against the wall, reaching to take it from her. Breathless with fright, she said, 'You've inherited some of your mother's less attractive traits then, haven't you!'

'Give it to me. It's lies, you haven't the right to read it.'

Struggling to stop him taking the letter, she raised her voice, 'William! Get off me; it's mine, addressed to me!'

Kevin appeared at the door and she gave a sob of relief as he hit out at William and pulled him away. While Kevin held him tightly in a painful shoulder hold, with a shaking voice Zena read the rest of the letter.

'"Here are some of the dates on which I was treated in hospital, you'll find the causes to be: accidents in the garden, a fall down the stairs, accident on my bike, an injury at work. I was always good at making up excuses.

"She attacked her sister Donna, accused us of having an affair, and I took the blame because I knew the boys needed her. They were so young and I didn't think I could give them a good life. I sent money every month until they were eighteen and ended it with a lump sum. She had never shown any sign of hitting them, and she promised she had never felt the slightest urge to do so. I took a chance I suppose, but believe me, I kept a close eye on things in case they were in any danger. The doctor was aware of my worry and each time I contacted him he told me he had seen no sign of her harming them, that they were happy and in good health."'

The letter ended with assurances of his love for them and his wishes for them to enjoy a happy life. There were a few sentences about Zena and Kevin and Doris with thanks for their friendship and he had signed it Dad/Roy/Popeye – which Kevin explained.

Zena kept the letter. William was still refusing to be convinced and she feared he would destroy it. 'I'll take it to the solicitor who will make sure Dick and Jack will read it,' she said, as she and Kevin left.

It was a puzzle solved and Zena's thoughts soon went back to the biggest puzzle in her family's life. Why had her father deprived their mother of money that had rightfully been hers? If only she could find Billy Dove, perhaps that would eventually be solved too. She spoke of her concerns to Jake, aware of how much she had missed him being there when something was worrying her.

Could she risk relaxing into trusting him again, letting her life slip back into the certainty she had once known, that they would spend the rest of their life together? Although she knew that love for him was only just below the surface, she had serious doubts. His sojourn in London had been a life-changing time for her as well as Jake. But talking to him about the missing money and the elusive Billy Dove, that was different. She needed someone to talk to and Jake was the best person for that. He had known her family all his life, so who could be better?

With his growing list of customers he promised to ask about Billy Dove whenever an opportunity arose and although he did as he promised, there was no hint of the whereabouts of the man. Besides his customers, he asked in various pubs and one or two people remembered the name but no one knew where he had gone after leaving the village.

On a sunny day when the trees was showing their late autumn colours and the lake looked serene, Nelda came with the children who were dressed in wellingtons and mackintoshes and wearing brightly coloured knitted hats, ready for some fun. They walked to the lake but then asked to go into the wood and perhaps call at the farm, and although Georgie doubted whether she could walk there and back again, they set off. Betty went with them, and she walked and ran around following the two girls, much to their delight. As usual, they asked their mother if they could have a dog of their own and the answer always the same, 'Not until you're older'.

They gathered a few fir cones which Nelda promised to make into owls for them and selected sticks which they 'really, really need to take home,' tucking their treasures into pockets and under their arms. Nelda and Zena smiled, knowing that they would soon tire of carrying them.

Instead of going to the farm they stopped at SunnyBank when they saw Karen brushing the porch. She offered tea and cakes and they went inside, the neat porch quickly cluttered with abandoned, muddy footwear. A game of hide and seek in the huge house delighted them and, when they turned for home, they were happy at the way their day had turned out. 'I love playing hide and seek,'

Georgie said, 'We'll go and see Uncle Sam next time.'

When they got back to Llyn Hir, there was a stranger sitting on a seat outside the front door. He stood up and offered a hand. 'Hello, which of you two ladies is Zena? I believe you're looking for me. I'm Billy Dove.'

They all stared in disbelief. They had begun to think the name was an invention out of Ronald's confused mind.

He was quite elderly but smartly dressed. His white shirt had been carefully ironed, his shoes polished to a mirror shine. His white hair and neat beard added a distinguished look to the handsome face. Bright blue eyes crinkled as he stood to greet them. He turned and reached for a stick leaning against the seat. 'I try to pretend I don't need this,' he said with a smile. 'Such vanity at my age!'

Zena stared for a moments before taking the man's offered hand. 'Mr Dove? We would like to ask— I'm sorry, please come in.' They all went inside, and Zena offered him a seat near the fire. 'I think you might be able to help us with a mystery.'

'I'll make tea,' Nelda said, disappearing into the kitchen.

'The trouble is, I'll like to talk to you with my mother and brother here, is there any chance you could stay a while?'

'I'm staying until tomorrow, will that be a help?'

'Tomorrow! I don't think I can wait that long! Mam and Greg will be here in about half an hour, if you could spare the time?'

'Your father?'

'No longer with us, I'm sad to say.'

'I see. I helped him some years ago and I wonder if that is what you need help with now. But I'll do what you ask and wait for the rest of your family.'

Bobbie and Georgie helped to carry in plates filled with cakes and biscuits, Betty following hoping some would be dropped. Then they asked if they could go outside.

When Lottie and Greg returned, the girls were nowhere to be seen. Instead of listening to Billy Dove's answers to questions for which they had waited so long to ask, they ran out calling their names. There was no reply.

Grabbing coat and torches, they hurried out, Lottie pausing

only to phone Sam. Greg went to the lake. Nelda ran down the lane with Lottie, calling their names and the name of the dog, fear in their hearts.

Lottie went through the woods towards the farm, Zena and Nelda went into the garden of SunnyBank. Nelda banged on the door and shouted at the top of her voice. Karen opened the door nervously, wondering who it could be. In shrieking voices, Zena called, 'Bobbie! Georgie! Betty! Where are you?' Nelda explained that the girls were missing and Karen shook her head. 'They haven't been here since you all left.'

'Will you help us search the barns, please?' Zena urged. 'It's almost dark and they'll be so frightened.' They continued to call their names and that of the dog but no responses broke the silence.

'What worries me,' Zena confided to Karen in a whisper, 'is that the dog hasn't barked. She always barks when we call her name. Always.'

The barns were searched and there was no sign of the children. Tearfully, Nelda asked Karen to call the police.

Georgie was trying not to cry. Bobbie was walking confidently along a narrow rarely used path and talking as though she knew the way, but in fact nothing looked familiar. The trees seemed bent down as though to restrict their way and were becoming thicker, catching on their clothes, pulling their hair free from the bobble hats they wore.

There was a wider path leading from the one they were on and Bobbie said, brightly, 'Here it is, this will take us straight back to Mummy.' Saying the word 'Mummy' made her panic. 'Where is Mummy?' she wailed, all confidence gone. 'Why hasn't she found us?' She began to cry and Georgie stretched up and put her arms around her and patted her back and said, 'There, there, darling. It'll soon be all right,' just like their mummy did when they were upset.

'Why don't we ask Betty to help?' Georgie suggested. They both talked to the little dog explaining that they needed her to take them home. Calling her name, making her bark each time cheered them slightly, gave them hope of being found. They listened and what they heard frightened them and they clung to Betty and begged her to be quiet.

There were sounds of someone approaching, and lights flashed across the trees distorting them, making strange shapes and moving patterns that made the wood an alien place, filled, so Bobbie believed, full of bad people.

'We have to be quiet, ' Bobbie warned her sister. 'The wood is full of bad people who want to hurt us.'

'Mummy will come and chase them away, won't she?' Georgie whispered. They knelt down behind a tree, hugging the dog when they saw shafts of lights waving through the branches. They were coming closer, then they heard something coming through the undergrowth behind them. They screamed in fright, screams turning to sobs until Digby the farm dog ran up to them in great excitement. He was closely followed by Sam, hidden at first by the light of his powerful torch.

It wasn't until he spoke that they began to be reassured. Then there were other lights and other voices and there was Zena and soon after and with everyone shouting in excitement and the girls howling with relief, Mummy was there. And everything was all right.

As so often, Nelda's first reaction was tearful relief, a close second, again as so often, was to scold and threaten with what would happen if they behaved so badly again. She carried Georgie, Greg carried Bobbie and they made their tearful way back to SunnyBank. Karen reached for the phone to tell the police, then Sam's father, they were found and were unharmed.

'I can't understand why Betty didn't bark,' Zena said, as they sat feasting on hot toast and cocoa.

'We kept her quiet with these,' Bobbie said, showing a handful of biscuit crumbs from her pocket.

'Don't ever do that again,' Zena warned. 'If you ever wander off again, we can always find you with Betty's help.'

It took a while to get the girls ready to leave, with the girls recovering from their fright and beginning to enjoy telling their story to the patient Mr Dove. Finally they were gone and Lottie turned to the man for whom they had searched for so long, hoping so desperately to learn something about Ronald's money.

'When my husband died,' Lottie explained, 'there was no money in the bank and he'd taken out a mortgage on this house. He said I should talk to a man called Billy Dove, but he didn't tell me why, or who he was. The missing money was a shock. There was no explanation and I was left to try and clear the debts or sell the house – our home. Can you shed any light on what happened?'

'I was a policeman for many years and, when I retired, I worked as a private detective.' He frowned and fidgeted in his chair. 'I'm a bit troubled about this, Mrs Martin. You see I don't know how much of ... of your story ... you've told your children.'

'It can't have been anything to do with the child I had before I married Ronald.'

'So they do know. That's a relief. Yes, it was exactly that. Ronald knew, you see and he employed me to try and find out what had happened to the child, just to make sure he was safe and happily settled with his adopted family.'

'Ronald knew?'

'A very caring man, your husband. It's difficult to find an adopted child, the rules are very strict, but with perseverance and a lot of luck, I did find him. From time to time I checked on his progress and Ronald was content that his life was a good one.'

'He knew. All this time he knew and said nothing. He just watched over him.' Lottie was tearful and Zena hugged her. In silence they waited for the rest of the story.

'Your son had a business, but he made an error, expanding too fast, and he was at risk of losing everything. He needed money for a few months, to tide him over the shortfall that would be cleared once two of his properties were sold. The interim was a dangerous time and to help him, Ronald arranged to lend him the money, believing absolutely that the money would be back in his bank in three months.'

'But it wasn't.'

'It would have been, but unfortunately, your son was involved in an accident and was in hospital for a long time. He left the running of his businesses to his manager who knew nothing about the loan. If he had it would have been settled at once. It wasn't until quite recently that he found out that the loan hadn't been repaid. He employed someone like myself to find Ronald, but the man failed to find him. Just a few months ago, they contacted me.

'I will go to see him tomorrow and everything will be sorted. Of that I am sure. Like Ronald, your son is an honourable man, Mrs Martin.'

'Will I be allowed to meet him?' Lottie asked. 'Please don't ask if you have any doubts. It's enough to know he's had a good life and is an "*honourable man*". And I wouldn't wish to upset his parents – the people who brought him up.'

'If I think it's advisable, I will ask how he feels about meeting you.'

They were all very subdued after a taxi had driven Billy Dove back to his hotel. Thoughts whirled, curiosity about the lost brother making pictures in their minds. Sadness and joy jumbled in equal quantities as they envisaged meeting this stranger and welcoming him into the family. That they would actually meet was doubtful, they all knew that, but they dreamed about it anyway.

Greg went to help at Mabs's night café and Lottie went with him. While Greg set the tables and prepared food, Lottie told Mabs all they had learned. Mabs hadn't known about the baby until the outburst from Rose and was sad, having no children of her own. She imagined the years they would have enjoyed watching the child grow but she hid her sadness from Lottie and instead praised the people who had adopted him. 'You couldn't have wished for anything more from the sound of it,' she said encouragingly. 'He was a part of a loving family and, according to all you've learned, he had a very good start in life.'

'The saddest thing is that Ronald knew. We could have talked about him and mourned together. I could have admitted the guilt I still feel at parting with him. Instead I've hidden my secret and all these years he must have been waiting for me to tell him.'

'We are all careless with happiness. I've been bitter about losing my Frank, blaming the money he won for his death. His clothes are still in the wardrobe, but d'you know what? Today I'll take them out and, if they aren't ruined by moths, I'll offer them to Percy, him who was sleeping in SunnyBank. I think they'll fit and it might turn things around for him if he smartens himself up a bit.'

'That's a wonderful idea, Mabs. It's time for all of us to change direction.'

'And something else, while we're talking sense for a change. All these months since my Frank died, I've been trying to think who should have Frank's money after I'm gone. Now I've decided.'

Lottie waited, watching Mabs's smiling face with its bright eyes and its frame of untidy hair, sharing her smile.

'I'm giving it to me! I'm going to buy a small cottage with a garden, I've always wanted a garden. There, what d'you think of that then? I'm inheriting from me!'

'Wonderful! And I hope you spend it all. The best of everything is what you deserve.'

'I might buy you a wedding present, mind.'

They laughed and hugged each other like the friends they had always been.

Zena decided not to add to the list of people she cleaned for now Roy Roberts no longer needed twice weekly visits. She had enjoyed the short career as 'a lady who does' and Nelda and her daughters had been a wonderful addition to her life. Roy had been a friend too, and she was sad at his death. But remembering some of the other people she had met, like Janey Day with her delusions of grandeur and her truly awful mother, Trish, she thought she would concentrate on building the office supplies business instead. Jake often found her a new customer and he took an interest in the stock she held, sometimes suggesting new lines.

But she would keep the two cleaning jobs that were left: Karen at SunnyBank still needed her, and she would continue doing her best to prevent Nelda from disappearing under an increasing pile of her crafts material.

She was on her way to Sunnyside when a car approached, coming from Sunnyside. She pulled in close to the hedge and, as the car went slowly past, a man on the back seat waved. Mr Penberthy? He wouldn't have been able to recognize her. Perhaps the driver told him there was a cyclist and he was just being polite, she decided.

She went in and walked through the hall and down to the kitchen. Karen was sitting at the table and opposite her was Billy Dove.

'We've been having a very interesting talk,' Karen said. 'It isn't my story to tell, but if you'll wait until James comes down, Billy has something to tell him that will interest you as well.'

'I don't want to intrude. I'll get on with the bedrooms, shall I? Bedrooms, then the bathrooms and, if you're still talking, I'll go home and finish another day. All right?'

Karen just smiled and offered Billy more coffee. Zena declined and went upstairs. If he wasn't so old, I'd say she was smitten, she thought with a chuckle.

She had finished the first bedroom when she heard the sound of a car, and voices as someone entered the house. She went into the bathroom and started removing the towels to replace them when Karen called. They probably want more coffee, she decided and went to the kitchen, calling, 'Coffee for three?'

'No, Zena, we need you here, please. Coffee can wait.'

Puzzled, Zena went into the comfortable lounge and sat on a chair near the window, then stared in surprise when she saw her mother there and her brother, Greg. Both were smiling. 'Why are you here?' she asked, then remembering her manners, she said 'Good morning,' to Mr Penberthy, who asked, 'Can you move away from the window, please, Zena. The light affects my eyes.'

She moved to sit near the door and he thanked her. 'I can now see a little,' he told her and she showed her surprise and delight by jumping up, congratulating him and shaking his hand. 'What wonderful news! I'm so pleased!'

'I have more good news, thanks to Billy.'

She turned to look at Billy Dove and frowned. 'You haven't found out more of our mystery, have you?'

He reached out and touched Lottie's arm. 'My dear, I have found your son. Are you ready to learn about him?'

Lottie's arm began to shake 'Yes,' she said staring at Billy.

Billy pointed to James. 'James Penberthy is your son. Born on 7 October thirty-four years ago.'

Both Zena and Greg thought their mother would faint and stood to support her but the moment of shock passed and she stared at James as though trying to see in him the tiny baby she had loved and lost all those years ago.

'James? You were called James? It was what I requested but I was told the adoptive parents make their own decision.'

'They were kind, loving people and would certainly have done what you had asked.'

She couldn't think of a single question to ask apart from, 'Have you had a happy life?' which sounded banal, foolish.

James smiled, 'I couldn't have asked for better.' He turned to Zena and Greg. 'The only time I was in serious trouble and they couldn't help, it was your father who came to my rescue. A good and generous man.'

'D'you mean he was *your* father?'

'No!' the protest came from Lottie and James in chorus.

Billy spoke for the first time. 'He had asked me to find your son, Lottie and when I did he watched over him and when he found out he was at risk of losing his business and his parents losing their home, he lent James the money he needed. It was a bridging loan, as I said. Unfortunately James was involved in an accident, and he was in hospital for several weeks. It was then he lost his sight. The loan from your father helped his business to survive, but there was a delay in the money from the property transactions. When he eventually managed to get back to dealing with things, he was shocked to find the loan hadn't been repaid. He searched desperately but couldn't find the address to return it.

'Since then there have been several more visits to hospital for operations and all the time he was searching for me to enable him to return the money to your father.

'Messages from Roy Roberts reached me eventually and when I knew James was recovered and looking for me I came, and – the rest you can guess.' He pointed to the table. 'There's a cheque there which will cover the loan and the interest it has accrued.'

'It has been in a separate account, you see, waiting for you to be found,' James explained. 'My parents will be pleased to meet you when the shock of all this has faded a little,' he added. 'If you would like that?'

'We would like that very much,' Lottie whispered.

They were silent for a moment, then they all started talking at once. Karen made coffee, then opened a bottle of wine instead and the meeting, so full of unexpected delight, became the very best kind of party. When they eventually left, James rather formally hugged them all, then Lottie kissed his cheek and there were kisses all round including Karen, and there were tears when the three left to return to Llyn Hir.

The first thing Lottie did was to go to see Mabs. She was sleeping but soon forgot catching up on her night's activities as Lottie shared the unbelievable news.

'Come this afternoon and meet him,' Lottie invited. 'My son, your nephew. It's like a dream, but one from which I don't want to wake!' It was as an afterthought that she told Mabs about the return of the missing money and that was another story that brought tears. 'Ronald knew about my shameful past, the beautiful son I'd had to give away and he said nothing. But he watched over him in a lovely, caring way. And helped him when he needed a large sum of money, still without telling me he knew.'

'A wonderful man, like my Frank,' Mabs said sadly. 'How they would both have loved being a part of this special day.'

The family were gathered for lunch few weeks later at Llyn Hir, where Lottie and Zena had prepared a large meal. Sam was there with his father, Neville, Jake and Susie had been invited and James and Karen too. There weren't enough chairs but no one minded. Garden furniture was brought in and somehow people found a place to sit and eat.

The meal went cold. With so much to say, there was no urgency to satisfy hunger, but it was eaten anyway. Photograph albums were produced by James and Lottie and it was five o'clock before anyone thought of leaving.

Mabs said thoughtfully, 'We've all been on a long journey. Greg went looking for answers to Rose's anger, and his homecoming was finding Susie. Zena has been searching for someone and realized that she didn't need to look, Jake was here all the time – he just needed to grow up! Jake went to London looking for a miracle but discovered that Cold Brook Vale is the place for miracles. Lottie went searching for the reason for Ronald's missing money and found something more precious, a gift of a new member of the family, our James. I've been on a sort of journey too, trying to hold tight to my Frank, but I've accepted that although he's gone, he will always be a part of me and I'm ready to move on.'

Greg patted Betty. 'Even Betty' – he waited for her to bark – 'even she has been on a journey. We don't know where it started but she found her way to us, thanks to Jake, and we're so glad to have her.'

'That's it! This is the end of a journey for all of us,' Zena said, reaching for Jake's hand.

1	2	3	4	5	6	7	8	9	10
11	12	13	14	15	16	17	18	19	20
21	22	23	24	25	26	27	28	29	30
31	32	33	34	35	36	37	38	39	40
41	42	43	44	45	46	47	48	49	50
51	52	53	54	55	56	57	58	59	60
61	62	63	64	65	66	67	68	69	70
71	72	73	74	75	76	77	78	79	80
81	82	83	84	85	86	87	88	89	90
91	92	93	94	95	96	97	98	99	100
101	102	103	104	105	106	107	108	109	110
111	112	113	114	115	116	117	118	119	120
121	122	123	124	125	126	127	128	129	130
131	132	133	134	135	136	137	138	139	140
141	142	143	144	145	146	147	148	149	150
151	152	153	154	155	156	157	158	159	160
161	162	163	164	165	166	167	168	169	170
171	172	173	174	175	176	177	178	179	180
181	182	183	184	185	186	187	188	189	190
191	192	193	194	195	196	197	198	199	200
201	202	203	204	205	206	207	208	209	210
211	212	213	214	215	216	217	218	219	220
221	222	223	224	225	226	227	228	229	230
231	232	233	234	235	236	237	238	239	240
241	242	243	244	245	246	247	248	249	250
251	252	253	254	255	256	257	258	259	260
261	262	263	264	265	266	267	268	269	270
271	272	273	274	275	276	277	278	279	280
281	282	283	284	285	286	287	288	289	290
291	292	293	294	295	296	297	298	299	300
301	302	303	304	305	306	307	308	309	310
311	312	313	314	315	316	317	318	319	320
321	322	323	324	325	326	327	328	329	330
331	332	333	334	335	336	337	338	339	340
341	342	343	344	345	346	347	348	349	350
351	352	353	354	355	356	357	358	359	360
361	362	363	364	365	366	367	368	369	370
371	372	373	374	375	376	377	378	379	380
381	382	383	384	385	386	387	388	389	390
391	392	393	394	395	396	397	398	399	400